Romantic Suspense

Danger. Passion. Drama.

Her Sister's Murder
Tara Taylor Quinn

Cameron Mountain Refuge
Beth Cornelison

MILLS & BOON

HER SISTER'S MURDER
© 2024 by TTQ Books LLC
Philippine Copyright 2024
Australian Copyright 2024
New Zealand Copyright 2024

First Published 2024
First Australian Paperback Edition 2024
ISBN 978 1 038 92172 7

CAMERON MOUNTAIN REFUGE
© 2024 by Beth Cornelison
Philippine Copyright 2024
Australian Copyright 2024
New Zealand Copyright 2024

First Published 2024
First Australian Paperback Edition 2024
ISBN 978 1 038 92172 7

MIX
Paper | Supporting
responsible forestry
FSC® C001695

Published by
Harlequin Mills & Boon
An imprint of Harlequin Enterprises (Australia) Pty Limited
(ABN 47 001 180 918), a subsidiary of HarperCollins
Publishers Australia Pty Limited
(ABN 36 009 913 517)
Level 19, 201 Elizabeth Street
SYDNEY NSW 2000 AUSTRALIA

Cover art used by arrangement with Harlequin Books S.A.. All rights reserved.

Printed and bound in Australia by McPherson's Printing Group

Her Sister's Murder
Tara Taylor Quinn

MILLS & BOON

Dear Reader,

This is a book of my heart in several ways. It's set in a state in which I only lived full-time for two years as a little kid, but that has been a second home to me my entire life. But more, it tells the story of young love that wasn't trusted, got lost and then found again. My true-life story in those few words. It's also the story of fortitude. Of refusing to give up even when life seems to be prepared to deny you forever. A lot of us have been there at one time or another.

It's a suspenseful, twisting and turning mystery that kept me on the edge of my seat, some days literally, as I was writing. I didn't know how it was going to end until it did. The best kind of book to read or write!

But most of all, it's the story of love. True love. In its various forms. This book depicts everything I believe in. The love that is real and strong enough to endure. To win out over evil. To bring us a happiness that far surpasses any other joy we could possibly feel. Love isn't just in the moment, or temporary. It endures. Even if we lose it. If we let it, it will find us again.

I hope love finds you over and over.

Tara Taylor Quinn

DEDICATION

For J—the twin of my heart. Our days in the hills, and all the years after, sustain me, still. Love doesn't die.

Chapter 1

Gravel crunched above him in the darkness. Freezing in place, all senses on alert, Blade Carmichael went into defend-and-protect mode. Listening. His eyes were the only things moving as he took in the rim of the eight-foot-deep half-acre hole in which he stood.

Being trapped in a pit, inspecting footers, wasn't something he'd choose to do without daylight, or without others around. But with darkness falling, and his company expanding so quickly, he hadn't been able to get to every site with the sun still shining down on him and with his crew still present.

The sound came again, weight on gravel. It wasn't the rolling sound of a vehicle. Didn't have the normal rhythm of footsteps, either. Was something being pushed by someone on foot? Or dragged?

Whatever was up there, it didn't belong. He'd locked the temporary gate behind him, as he always did when he drove on-site. The plowed and flattened land was clearly marked with keep-out and no-trespassing signs.

There had been a series of weird things happening lately. He'd been pretty sure someone was following him but had no proof—just a blue sedan. Sometimes it was parked down the street from his house with no one inside that he could see. And then he'd seen it outside a restaurant where he'd been eating. Across from his office, twice. And once when he'd been driving, a few lanes over and a couple of vehicles back.

But then, he tended to err on the paranoid side of watching his back. Spending seventeen years wrongly accused did that to a guy.

He hadn't noticed the car as he'd driven to the site, but that didn't mean it hadn't been there somewhere.

His truck was up top in full view.

Someone knew he was down in the pit.

No one was authorized to be on any of his sites after dark. No one. Ever. A rule that, if broken, cost an employee their job. Or garnered a call to police and a trespassing charge.

Turning off the light strapped to his head, he backed up slowly to the footers he'd come down to inspect, careful to keep his own boot crunch at a minimum. Once there, he leaned back, pressing himself into the dirt wall of the pit. Jeans and his button-down shirt and tie didn't offer much protection. All alone and thinking he was just going to be doing a few quick measurements, he'd left his hard hat on the front seat of the truck.

He hadn't felt real fear for his life in a long time, not since he'd mastered both target shooting and martial arts. His heart pounded, and he didn't welcome the sensation of snakes slithering in his gut. He reached slowly for the Glock 9 mm holstered to his belt, legally allowed in Michigan if it was visible, and by his concealed-carry permit if it wasn't. He'd never used the pistol, other than to shoot targets.

He'd never killed anything.

But the world thought he had. Even though he'd never been formally charged, and had a completely clean record.

More gravel turning. Crunching. Getting closer. Was someone coming to get revenge? The paranoia that he'd been fighting fairly successfully in recent years suddenly surfaced with a vengeance. There was nothing on the lot to steal.

Nothing there at all but dirt, some rebar cemented into footer framing and him.

The sound was definitely scraping. Or dragging.

Dirt?

Was someone moving a large mass of dirt?

To bury him in his own pit?

Horror clawed at him. After so many years full of dread, were the death threats he'd received finally becoming reality?

No, he had to get a hold of himself. He was a grown man running a successful business in a town where his past wasn't an issue.

The investigation had been thorough seventeen years before and as soon as he'd been released from custody, he'd immediately, and legally, dropped the McFadden from his name. Leaving Blade Carmichael McFadden behind, he'd hoped.

The only evidence against him had been circumstantial—strengthened by the fact that there were no other viable suspects. But even though the DA had decided not to press charges, public opinion had been swayed against him.

But not in Rocky Springs. Not in the small Michigan town where he'd made a good name for himself.

Was someone from the past on his lot? Had they come to make him pay? Knowing he had nowhere to run? To hide?

Struggling against the unhealthy thoughts, he tried to focus on the sounds above him.

The scraping sounds were coming closer. He was a standing duck.

What if someone local had heard about his past?

The only way out, the stepladder he'd brought down with him, was all the way on the other side of the pit.

And climbing up would do nothing except make him an easy target.

No matter what was going on, someone was on his lot, illegally, in the dark.

Gun in his hand, safety off, he listened and watched the rim, waiting for the first sign of whoever was up there to show itself. His only chance was to stay alert and get a shot off first.

A feat he should be able to accomplish. He'd been on high alert since he was seventeen years old.

Maybe getting to the ladder was the best bet. He could climb slowly. Crouch down. Get a look at his would-be assailant before they got to him.

Blade was already acting before he'd finished the thought. Moving softly, sliding quickly along the dirt floor, he kept himself crouched and balanced as he leaned into the wall of dirt his crew had dug.

The sound was closer. Almost directly above his head. He wasn't going to get to the ladder in time. He stopped moving and pressed himself into the dirt with all of his strength. Gun in both hands, barrel pointing upward, he slid his head backward an inch, then two, attempting to see without being seen.

Throat dry, tight, he couldn't swallow. But mixed in with the fear, surprising him, was a bit of relief. No more dreading that this day would come...

But it still might not have come. He had to stay calm. Focused. Deal with the moment, not the past.

He hadn't killed that sixteen-year-old girl. But he hadn't hung around to make sure she made it back to camp safely, either. Not that he'd invited her to the party, or even that she'd have left with him if he'd asked. She'd been having too much fun hanging out with the others. But he'd been a senior camp counselor. She'd only been a junior...he shouldn't have left while there was still a junior there...

He shouldn't have been there at all. None of them should have been.

The dirt against his back reverberated slightly. From weight on the ground directly above him. Had to be right at the rim of the pit. He couldn't see a thing but dirt and sky. No moon. No stars. And no assailant visible to him.

But someone who knew he was in that pit was right above him. Illegally there.

Bracing for a load of dirt or a bullet that would bring searing pain, he kept his eye trained above, arms and hands set to use his pistol at the first sign of movement.

Tense, ready, he waited.

The one thing he had going for him, a man thought to have murdered a sixteen-year-old girl when he'd been just seventeen himself, was that he'd never, ever physically hurt anyone.

Before he had time for another thought, rocks and clods of fresh dirt started to tumble around him, hitting his head, his shoulders. Some were big enough to bruise him and obstruct his vision. He couldn't see anyone up above. But he couldn't just stand there and die. He'd learned long ago he had to bear his own load. Cocking back his pistol, he pointed the barrel to the sky, and pulled the trigger, not to kill, but to warn, to scare and then, if necessary, to defend.

Before the bullet had even reverberated through the air, a body landed on the dirt at his feet.

* * *

Former FBI agent turned private detective Morgan Davis had dread in her gut as she entered Rocky Springs just after sunrise. She'd gotten the call in the very wee morning hours and had been instantly up, showered, dressed in black pants, a white cropped blouse and black flats, and was out the door, making the two-hour drive from Detroit in record time.

Maddie, I've got him...

The internal words started before she realized their intent. No. She wasn't going back there. Not to the time. Or the false hope.

She wasn't a sixteen-year-old youth camp counselor anymore. She'd lost her youth the night she'd lost her identical twin sister. Murdered by someone she'd thought was one of her closest friends, the only guy she'd ever had a serious crush on. The only one who'd ever shown any interest in someone as straitlaced and serious as she was. The only guy who'd asked her to be exclusive with him.

Maddie had been the vivacious one. The honey that drew everyone to them. And kept their attention when they arrived. Morgan had the same perfectly aligned features, striking blue eyes, blond hair and slim, long-legged build, but she'd rarely been noticed. And, introvert that she was, she'd been perfectly content to sit in her sister's shadow, watching out for the both of them, planning their futures.

Until that last summer at camp. Maddie hadn't wanted to be there. They'd heard the school counselor talk about a need for counselors at the summer youth camp, alighting Morgan with interest. Interest she'd known her twin wouldn't share, just as Maddie hadn't been paying attention during assembly that morning. During the rest of the mandatory meeting, while her sister kept exchanging looks with a boy across the aisle, Morgan worked it all out. They'd spend their first summer apart. Maddie going to cheer camp and Morgan being a counselor at the youth camp they'd attended for years. It would be good for them...they could text every morning and every night...and have so much to tell each other at summer's end.

As it had turned out, their overly strict, older parents had jumped on the guidance counselor's call for help. The twins had started counselor training that very afternoon...

And that had been the end of life as they knew it.

Following the prompt from her dark blue SUV's navigation system, Morgan turned and then turned again. She'd never been to Rocky Springs. The beach town hadn't had any crimes calling for FBI presence when she'd been with the Bureau.

And Sierra's Web, the nationally renowned firm of experts she'd joined the year before, hadn't sent her there, either.

She wasn't there on official business. Yet.

She was there because a non-FBI law enforcement acquaintance had fulfilled a promise.

Blade Carmichael's name had shown up in a crime scene report that made it over the unofficial BOLO wire across the state. Word of mouth traveled fast when a guy showed up dead in a ditch at the feet of a suspected killer. Morgan's acquaintance knew she'd want the information.

According to the report that had been read to her so early that morning, Carmichael had been in a new-build basement dig. The body had landed at his feet from up above. He'd heard footsteps. One set. And then nothing. The form had been unmoving, lying with a leg bent underneath it and both arms splayed out. He'd immediately dialed 911, then ran to a ladder and climbed to the rim of the pit. He saw no blood, no sign of anything, except for a strip of dirt that looked like some kind of heavy box or blanket had been dragged across it, cutting a path on the newly cleared land.

He'd made a quick perusal of the site and headed back down to the body.

Male, based on the dark pants, he'd told the operator on the line, and light-colored dress shirt. Short hair, mostly dark. Gray tinges, perhaps from the moon's reflection? The guy was face down. Carmichael couldn't get a feel for age.

He had checked for a pulse and said something about flesh not yet cold to the touch of his fingers.

The lack of pulse was evident, though. He'd been touching a dead man. No bleeding profusely from a killer's bullet. Not bleeding visibly at all, and not pooling from beneath him, either.

The suspect—she couldn't not think of Blade that way—hadn't been arrested when law enforcement arrived. There hadn't been sufficient evidence against him to warrant doing so. But Morgan knew better. Blade Carmichael was someone whose alias—Blade Carmichael McFadden—might not show up in official police records. But it was definitely at the top of the suspect list in her personal memory.

He'd grown up in another beach town—South Haven. Another town she'd never visited. One he'd vacated abruptly when it had become known that he was a murderer and his father's business had tanked. The family, just him and his parents, had moved to Grand Rapids, and then, upon his high school graduation, to Florida. He'd returned to his home state to attend the University of Michigan, graduated with a degree in business management and settled in the burgeoning, if still small, beach town of Rocky Springs.

Why he'd gone to all the trouble to change his name and then return to his home state, she didn't know. Except that, even as a teenager, he'd loved the state. The Great Lakes.

The vast outdoors. The seasons. Those were the kinds of conversations he'd had with Morgan years ago.

While Maddie had talked constantly about getting out and seeing the world, wanting to move to California or New York, Morgan had loved Michigan, too. The natural beauty of forests and streams, bound by the Great Lakes and a lot of wide-open country.

It felt right to think about something good as she prepared to enter hell.

Her phone rang. Slowing, she saw Jas's ID on her dash screen, pulled to the shoulder and picked up.

"Hey," she greeted her ex–FBI team member and close friend. Because she knew if she didn't pick up, Jasmine would go into full agent mode.

"I heard about the murder, Morg. Tell me you aren't headed to Rocky Springs."

Glancing at the Carmichael Construction sign on a stick stuck in the ground just ahead, she figured, since she'd reached her destination, she wasn't headed anywhere. "I'm not."

"You're there already, aren't you?"

She wasn't going to lie. Silence was the only other option.

"It's not good for you." FBI Special Agent Jasmine Flaherty knew, more than most, that Morgan was somewhat obsessed with getting her sister's killer behind bars. Legally. Rightfully. Forever and ever, world without end.

It was partially why she'd left the Bureau.

"The dead man is Shane Wilmington. He was another counselor that summer. One who had been at the party, too." An unsanctioned gathering, just down the beach from camp property, reached through a hole in a very old and never very strong wire fence.

She idled at the curb as she explained herself. She trusted her friend with her life—and needed Jas to know she could trust Morgan, too. She wasn't just there because *the name* had unofficially popped up in a new murder investigation. But when the dead body had turned out to be someone else from that night...

What investigator worth her salt wouldn't at least get herself to town and see what she could find out?

"Be careful."

"I will." Morgan's words were confirmation of how she lived every minute of every day.

"And call me. The second you know anything. And when you're headed home."

With a grim face, she agreed to do so and hung up. When she got to the gate, she showed her Sierra's Web private detective credentials to a uniformed guard, and pulled forward onto the lot legally occupied by the man who'd killed her sister.

She wanted to be all brave and strong. Unflappable. She wanted to be the woman who'd earned her reputation as one of the best agents the Michigan Bureau had ever seen. Instead, when she took in the newly plowed ground—the vehicles, some with bubbles, some not, the crime scene tape around a big hole in the ground with a crane hovering just off to the right of it—she started to shake.

Heart pounding, she took a deep breath. Pushed away her need to cry.

The crane was there to remove the body, she knew. The rest of the folks—forensics, crime scene investigators, detectives and officers, she determined by vests and vehicle markings—might wonder why a private detective was on scene.

If the guy guarding the lot had actually read her badge,

recognized it and told anyone who she was, she'd tell them why she was there. Unofficially. Because they might have a serial killer on their hands. One who committed murder seventeen years apart.

As it was, no one seemed to notice as, her Glock at her hip and creds in her back pocket, she made her way toward the scene of the murder.

Chapter 2

Morgan took half a dozen steps and stopped. Carmichael was at the scene. She hadn't expected that. Not nine hours after the crime had been called in.

She started toward the less populated end of the pit. The crane was there, without an operator inside it from what she could see. Closer yet were a couple of crime scene techies wearing gloves, bagging things she couldn't make out. The body was already in the morgue, undergoing an autopsy to determine cause of death.

The body. How jaded she'd become.

She hadn't known Shane well. Hadn't liked him all that much. He'd encouraged Maddie's wild side, rather than helping her rein it in, encouraged her to bad-mouth her parents, agreeing with her regarding their over-the-top strictness.

From what Morgan had heard, Shane had been the one who'd instigated the parties that had gone on after hours that summer…

He'd been a kid then.

And a successful real estate broker on the day he died. A husband and father. A churchgoing man.

She'd been hoping to chat with the lead detective. To find out what they knew so far in terms of the current crime, and to float the Blade-Carmichael-as-a-serial-killer idea.

She hadn't planned on Carmichael's presence. He'd been questioned hours before. She'd been hoping he'd be in jail, on suspicion charges with a forty-eight-hour hold, if nothing else. Not standing in conversation with a couple of suited men.

Did that mean he was getting off again? That he'd managed to commit the perfect crime a second time?

Over her dead body.

Would he know her if he saw her?

Her hair was still blond. Still long. Up in a bun. She still had the long legs, and not a lot of girth on her. But she was at least twice as strong as she'd been back then.

And not the least bit introverted if it came to getting the answers she sought.

When she looked in the mirror, she didn't see any resemblance to the young girl she'd been before Carmichael had murdered her sister. It was the eyes. They used to mirror a soul that was alive. And a life filled with hopes.

Now they just reflected the truths she saw.

And heard.

"He said he shot the bullet straight up from here," one of the CSIs said, shoving a long piece of tube in the dirt, pointing upward. The other calculated an angle for the downward trajectory and they both moved to where the bullet should have landed. She wondered if they already had the shell casing.

Shane's body had been found with a bullet through the side of his head. Entered and exited. But the deadly shot hadn't happened at the construction site. He'd already been dead before he'd been dumped. Blade Carmichael claimed he'd only shot his gun once, from the pit, to defend himself from whatever was above him, but the entire story was too contrived. How would someone else have gotten on-site if the gate was locked? And how had he gotten away without being seen? It wasn't like someone could have just walked on-site dragging a body and then disappeared into thin air. Chances were, Carmichael had already killed the man—probably with a different weapon—then turned over his registered weapon with the one bullet missing. That would explain any gunshot residue that could be found on him—shooting that bullet in the air.

It would also make it look like he'd been in the pit before the arrival of the body—needing to defend himself. An alibi, of sorts.

Along with the late-night inspection, due to a job starting early and thus giving him an overpacked schedule necessitating the after-hours incident.

It was all so clean.

Too clean.

Calling in the body had been a bold move.

Across the way, Blade pulled over a guy in jeans and a T-shirt who'd been headed her way. Had a quick word with him. And then turned back to his other conversation. He'd glanced at her. Gave no indication whether he knew who she was.

She didn't have any idea what friends he currently had. How far up the chain they went. As far or further than his father's friends in the past? Maybe not high enough to save a man's local business, but enough to keep charges from being filed against his seventeen-year-old son.

Just looking at the grown-up version of that seventeen-year-old blew up a host of emotions inside her, and it took her a second to get her bearings back. The shape of his face, rounded head with angular chin, the dark hair that was shorter than she remembered, but still bearing that distinctive wave at the back…those legs. They all found answers within her. Recognition of something she'd once thought to be as hot as it got.

He'd been the only guy she'd known who she hadn't been able to walk away from and forget. *Still was.* But for vastly different reasons. He'd been the first really close friend that her sister didn't share. And the real blow had been that she'd thought he shared her feelings. That they'd been destined to meet. To spend the rest of their lives together.

Right up until he'd sneaked off and partied with her identical twin—and then, in a rage, had killed her.

Probably because while Maddie was a flirt, always up for escapades, and loads of fun...she had very distinct lines she didn't cross. Having sex at sixteen had been one of them. Mostly because their parents had set such strict guidelines for their freedom to come and go and Maddie hadn't wanted to risk losing their trust, or the few benefits they'd had.

And, she'd once told Morgan, because when she entered into that kind of relationship, she wanted to be old enough to live with the guy if she wanted to do so. Not have to do it in the back of a car and go home to bed.

The only saving grace from that night was that Maddie hadn't been sexually violated. She'd fought her attacker. He'd panicked, thinking someone was going to hear them, and had killed her without getting what he was presumed to have been after. And Maddie—the biggest flirt in their school—had gone to heaven a virgin.

The jean-clad man was upon her. She noticed his red bushy beard more than his eyes as he gave her a nod.

She nodded back at him and took a few steps to the side as he climbed up into the crane.

Two similarly clad guys were inside the pit with a CSI, digging in the dirt. Probably looking for the casing of the bullet Carmichael claimed to have shot. They'd have waited until dawn to begin searching for it.

Uniforms had given her good information in the past and said things a detective might not be as willing to share. As soon as the two officers aboveground finished their conversation, she'd head over to them. As she took a step in that direction, two things happened at once. The crane's engine started up and Carmichael turned fully around.

He was looking straight at her. She stared back. Daring him across the thirty-foot distance. To challenge her. To try to convince her that he had nothing to do with Shane's body in his pit.

He started her way. Moving slowly at first, and then more quickly. As he neared her, he called out. Then hollered and broke into an all-out run. Straight at her!

In front of everyone...

When she realized that he wasn't going to stop, Morgan stepped aside, backed up quickly to avoid him, only to have the maniac dive right for her.

His body slammed into hers with enough power to rob her of air and she landed with a bruising force, his body shielding hers from the freshly plowed ground.

A horrible clanging accompanied their fall. And something slammed against the ground just beside them. Hard enough, heavy enough to give nearby earth a jolt.

Heart pumping, Morgan pushed herself away from Blade Carmichael, reaching for her Glock, but didn't get it pulled as she saw all the law enforcement personnel running. Every single person on-site—like a tornado—hurtling toward them.

She sat up. Apart from him.

"Are you okay?" Blade's voice carried what sounded like real concern. And a lack of recognition?

Breathing hard, she couldn't look him in the eye. Didn't want to look at him at all. Or have his touch on her skin, warm and cushioning as it had been. "Fine," she said, staring at the crane's boom, which had just crashed to the ground.

It would have crushed her if Blade hadn't moved so quickly to get her out of the way.

She could have been killed.

Almost *had* been killed.

Blade Carmichael had just saved her life.

And just prior to that Blade had called over the crane operator, given him some kind of instruction, upon seeing her standing there. After which the operator had gone directly to the crane. Put the near-fatal accident in motion.

Had he given the order to kill her? Changed his mind?

Had he intentionally set circumstances in motion to allow him to risk his life to save hers? To divert attention away from him as a murderer?

The theory was a bit much—and yet, a completely believable explanation for what had just taken place.

Even so, as the detectives and officers reached her, all eyes wide, all wanting reassurance that she was okay, Morgan kept her most rancid thoughts to herself.

He'd body slammed a law enforcement official.

Blade stepped aside, giving way to the detectives and officers clamoring to the woman's side, as she showed her credentials.

And then, mouth open, he recognized her.

And understood why she was there.

He'd body slammed Morgan Davis. *The* Morgan Davis.

The cacophony of rising sun, dirt, a crane boom implanted in the ground, his operator climbing down to stand beside him, voices clamoring, fell away. Nothing in his world made sense, and all Blade could hear were the words of a devastated sixteen-year-old Morgan Davis.

Murderer! Get away from me! You killed her! You killed her!

He'd fallen in love with her that summer. Had been certain she'd been falling for him, too. Had gone over to comfort her...

He could still feel the strength of those fists slamming against his chest until the leader of the female camp counselors pulled her away. And the nurse took hold of her. Leading her off.

It was the last time he'd ever seen her...

"Morgan?" He said the word aloud. He hadn't meant to be heard—it just escaped.

He was shocked to see her, and yet...her presence made perfect sense, too.

Shane's death...his body being dumped at Blade's construction site...the tie to youth camp, to Madison Davis's death...

She glanced over at him, almost as though she'd heard him call her name. Their gazes locked. He wasn't going to be the first to look away. He'd done nothing wrong.

Her gaze held the expected hatred. A determination she hadn't had at sixteen.

And something more.

Something indefinable. Deep. Painful.

It was that something that had him not only looking away, but turning his back, too. An officer took charge of him then, asking questions as they walked over to the downed boom together. His operator, Lonnie, joined them. Gave a full account of his actions since he'd first approached the crane that morning. Blade answered questions about inspections. About assembly and disassembly procedures for all six of the cranes owned and operated by Carmichael Construction.

And he kept ex–FBI agent turned private detective Morgan Davis in his sight, at least peripherally, at all times. He hadn't known she'd left the agency to team up with some private firm that had one of the detectives on-site falling all over her.

Her being there couldn't be good. But he shouldn't be surprised, either. He'd known she'd gone into crime solving. Had heard from a friend of his dad's with the South Haven police that she'd joined the FBI. Easy to figure out why. He got all that.

Just hadn't expected her to turn up so early. To have gotten word in the middle of the night and made it to Rocky Springs by dawn.

And now she'd almost died on his construction site, too. Because of a malfunction with one of his cranes. Right after he'd spoken with the operator.

The only thing that made sense about that was if someone was framing him.

But who? And had Morgan just been targeted personally because she'd been at camp, too? Or had the crane incident just been meant to make him look bad? A shoddy contractor with unsafe equipment?

If Morgan was being targeted, who'd known she was going to be there?

All things he had to find out.

Adrenaline filled him. Could it be that his chance had finally arrived? Was he actually going to be able to find the real killer?

Though he'd been questioned a good part of the night, he hadn't been charged with anything.

He figured that the detectives were still looking at him. He'd cooperated fully. Had granted them access to his home, his computer, his business and personal accounts. They'd know soon enough that he worked most of his waking hours. He ate out a lot. Fished when he could. And worked more.

He'd been told not to leave the state.

Like he had anywhere else he'd want to go.

Certainly not to his parents in Florida. Not with this hanging over him. He hoped to God it was done and gone before they ever got wind of it. He wouldn't take them through that hell a second time.

What if, once again, the police didn't find enough evidence? Whoever had killed Madison Davis had managed to get away with murder once. Blade couldn't take the chance that he'd be able to do it a second time.

He couldn't count on the police.

There was only one person he could think of who would be good enough, determined enough, to get to the whole truth.

No matter the danger. Or the cost.

One person who needed the truth as desperately as he did.

A person who—if he'd understood correctly when she'd shown her credentials—was for hire.

The woman who was certain that he'd killed her twin sister.

Chapter 3

Shaken up from the crane incident, Morgan was more determined than ever to insinuate herself into Shane Wilmington's murder case.

But she knew that she couldn't officially do so, not unless she could convince whoever was in charge of the case to hire Sierra's Web. If Blade Carmichael was a serial killer—and she was convinced of that—the FBI could take jurisdiction. Which would make it Jasmine's case. She gave her friend a fifty-fifty chance of even letting Morgan get close to the case, let alone paying a hefty sum to hire her to work it.

She'd offer to work free of charge. Hell, she'd pay the Sierra's Web fee herself. She just had to find someone with the authority to bring her on.

No way she could get this close and not be able to finally find justice for her sister.

Since nearly being smashed by a crane had drawn attention to her presence on-site, as soon as Carmichael was led off by an officer, Morgan went straight to the man who appeared to be in charge. She introduced herself with her credentials out to Detective Chad Larson, a tall man with a mustache from the Rocky Springs Police Department. She met the only other detective in the department, too.

Ramon Gonzalez, who was shorter and stockier but also had a mustache.

"I have an interest in what happened here due to a different case I'm working. I'd sure appreciate any professional courtesy you can give me, any details you can share."

Gonzalez looked her over and glanced at Larson, who said, "We've taken molds of footprints, but don't expect to get anything from them. With all the construction boots worn on the site yesterday, it's pretty well impossible to differentiate, or even get full sets of prints. Carmichael's were all around the bottom of the pit and part of the rim, but they would be, either way. He's already admitted to being on-site, inspecting the footers inside the pit, when the supposed body dump happened. The curious part is the area where the body would have had to go over. There were no footprints, but we found a path of tamped down earth, like a piece of cardboard or heavy plastic bearing a heavy weight had been dragged." The man sounded focused, sincere, but she found it a bit too clean, again.

She was supposed to believe that local law enforcement actually thought that someone had done the body dump and then, what, dragged the cardboard backward as the person ran from the scene, covering his footprints as he went, as Carmichael claimed? The man had said he'd heard footsteps…

And the crane incident? No one had known that she'd be at the site. And no one could have predicted that she'd walk where she had.

But she'd seen Carmichael look in her direction as he'd spoken to his operator. The man had moved immediately to the crane…

And Carmichael had saved her life in front of a gathering of law enforcement.

"It's too coincidental that that boom fell right after a dead body was removed from the pit," she said aloud to the two men.

"Blade's convinced he's being set up," Chad Larson said, and Ramon nodded. Her heart sank as she caught the nuance in that statement.

"He's convinced? As in, you believe he really believes that?" Because if they did, they'd also have to believe that Carmichael knew he hadn't done it. They'd have to believe he hadn't. "Or you think he's using that theory as a cover-up?"

Larson's brows drew together. "It's too early to answer to that," he responded, as though realizing that he was talking to an unknown private detective—albeit ex-FBI who was working for a highly respected firm of experts—and not one of his officers.

His dismissive tone left her completely dissatisfied. She'd wanted to hope that the Rocky Springs Police Department was going to succeed where others had failed. That these guys were going to catch on to Blade Carmichael McFadden, and finally bring him to justice.

With her adrenaline already pumping, dread quickly flooded her, as she saw the past repeating itself. The guy had a way of convincing people that he was, above all else, a good person.

Blade Carmichael's forthright manner, his seeming honesty and unassuming self-confidence had sucked her in, too. Convincing her to open her heart to him even though she'd made a vow to herself that she wouldn't get swept up by a boy during hormonal high school years, like Maddie had, almost monthly, to an inevitable sea of tears every time.

She had to talk to the guy. She wasn't an impressionable

sixteen-year-old kid anymore. Nor did she still instinctively trust that people were good until they proved otherwise. Instead, she'd developed a sense for reading people. One that had served the Bureau, and many clients, well.

"Do you mind if I speak with Mr. Carmichael?" she asked both men. She had to get her own feel for Carmichael's testimony. It was the only way to find the lies.

They shook their heads simultaneously, telling her she was free to speak with anyone she liked, giving her a green light that catapulted her inner drive into full gear.

She was walking toward him with definite purpose.

Blade had just finished with the officers. He'd been told to be available to the detectives as needed and was free to go about his day.

He chose to wait for Morgan. The woman exuded power and he'd be a fool to give her any further cause to tighten the noose around his neck until he suffocated.

He liked her hair in a bun. It drew attention to the striking shape of her face. And those unforgettable blue eyes.

The look with which she speared him wasn't at all promising. And still, in spite of the obvious antagonism, he considered her approach a good sign. Once upon a time, she'd shared her soul with him. He'd known her better, on a deeper level, than he'd known anyone else. Before or since. Had followed her stellar career with the Bureau, too, as best he could with a retired South Haven contact as his source of information.

She hated him. But he knew she'd be fair. That she'd fight to find the truth. Expecting him to be punished to the full extent of the law—yes. But if she found the truth, she'd know he wasn't guilty.

And then he could be done with her. Be done with the

pain of her betrayal. He'd needed her that awful morning. Had counted on her being the one person who'd know he hadn't done the horrible things they were claiming...

"Mr. Carmichael," she called out to him while he was still a few feet away. "May I speak with you?"

He waited silently, an answer of sorts, until she reached him. And then said, simply, "Morgan." He'd never been one for subterfuge. They weren't strangers.

"I'd like a few minutes of your time," she said, not calling him out on his familiar choice of address. Allowing it? Or simply ignoring it?

"As a person from the past who's as concerned as I am about the body that showed up here last night? Or as a detective?"

"I'm both."

Not much of an answer. He needed her proffered conversation to go well. Had been given the opportunity to win her expert help and wasn't sure how to go about succeeding. He could feel her defenses as almost physical pricks to his skin.

"I'm guessing you think I murdered Shane," he said, the words making him slightly sick, and yet, relieving him of pressure, too. He had to get it out to get rid of it.

"As a professional investigator, I see you as a prime suspect."

Okay, then. He'd wanted it out there.

"And personally?" He knew as soon as the words were out of his mouth, they were the wrong ones. On every level.

Just...standing there with her...it was the first chance he'd had to actually have a conversation with her since the morning her sister's body had been found and she'd screamed at him to get away from her.

He'd spoken to her in his mind so many times over the years.

Prior to that godawful morning, their last conversation had been him asking her to be exclusive with him, and her immediately agreeing.

She hadn't issued a comeback to his reference to their past. Acknowledging that they had a personal history. And for the first time since the body had landed in his pit the night before, Blade experienced a dread-free second or two. It quickly vanished. But it had been there.

"I apologize for the question," he said. "It was out of line."

He knew what she thought, personally. She'd screamed it at him loud and clear that last morning. *Murderer! Get away from me...*

But maybe...just maybe...he had a chance to change her mind?

The thought came out of nowhere. He pushed it aside. What she thought of him ceased mattering seventeen years before. But if changing her mind meant he was finally exonerated, maybe he should try.

"I'm fine to speak with you," he said. "But if you wouldn't mind, I'd like to go home and shower first. We could meet in say...forty-five minutes...at the Ellery Café on Blossom Street. It's right on the beach and I'll call ahead and get us an outside table."

Sounded like he was making a date. "That'll give us privacy, and yet we'll be in a very public place where you'd feel safer."

She straightened. "I was a special agent with the FBI, Blade. And am now officially considered an expert in detective work with a nationally renowned firm. I've taken down serial killers and terrorists. I'm not the least bit afraid of you."

He believed her.

Acknowledged her point with an accepting nod. For a second there, he thought he saw a momentary glistening soften her gaze. It was followed so immediately by a return of stone-cold determination that he wasn't positive he'd seen it but rather, had transposed a moment from the past onto a very disturbing present.

He noted the weakness in himself so it didn't happen again. The young man she'd known back then no longer existed.

And the man he'd become didn't need her softening. He needed the determination that brimmed her eyes like shards of steel as she stared him down.

"Can you give me forty-five minutes?" he asked again. He wanted her off the crime scene. Away from detectives. Away from any other Carmichael Construction mishaps that could already be in motion, ready to hang him.

He needed to be able to talk to her, just Blade Carmichael and Morgan Davis. Not as the kids they'd been, but as the honest and hardworking adults they'd become.

Her not quite bitter nod of acquiescence wasn't a good sign.

But it was a reprieve, and he was willing to take what he could get.

Morgan hung around the crime scene after Blade left, looking at the details through her own investigative lens. Letting questions come as they always did when she gave herself to a case, and looking for answers, too. She spoke to the uniformed officers. Most of them knew Blade. They could hardly believe he'd murder someone.

But they weren't ruling out the possibility, which she found encouraging.

And then she left. She typed the café address into her vehicle's mapping system, and, looking in her rearview mirror as she always did, settled back for the ten-minute drive.

Pulling to a halt at a four-way stop, she noticed that a police car had pulled up behind her. It was still there as she turned and turned again. Small towns only had so many ways to get from point A to point B and she was headed to the most popular strip in Rocky Springs. Another car, black and luxurious-looking, a Lincoln or Cadillac she guessed, pulled behind the police car after the second turn. And then the cop turned off.

She hadn't been able to make out which of the officers she'd spoken to had followed her off the lot—he or she didn't get close enough—but she was glad to know that they were prevalent about town. Maybe even watching out for her.

Nine minutes later, she pulled into the café parking lot, her gaze drawn toward the beach and the expansive blue lake beyond. Movement at her side drew a quick glance.

The black car was in the café parking lot. But when she glanced over it suddenly sped up and left. It happened so fast she couldn't make out any of the driver's identifying features. Wasn't even sure if the person behind the wheel had been male or female. She'd seen white skin topped by dark hair. But her own skin was crawling. She was sure it was just her senses on overload, but she made a quick call to Jas, just in case. She told her friend that she'd felt like she'd been followed from the site and described the black car as best she could.

They lived dangerous lives. And had learned not to ignore gut feelings. Yeah, they turned out to be nothing sometimes, but the one time they weren't "nothing" they were thankful they'd listened.

Blade was pulling in just as she ended her call. As she watched him jump down out of his truck…all male and a summer love grown up…she wanted to phone her friend back to report in on another danger that could befall her. And most definitely did not make that call.

That girl she'd been in the past had died right along with her twin. No way she was going to give her any chance at life. Or allow a murderer one second's chance in hell of resurrecting her.

True to his word, Blade had a table waiting for them outside on a patio with enough space between tables to give them privacy. She wasn't hungry, though she should be, so ordered oatmeal and toast with her coffee. Blade had the same. She'd agreed to talk to him for one reason only, to get what information she could. And if he thought he was going to con her…

Neither pretended pleasantries as their waitress left them alone at the table for the first time.

"I need to find the killer," he said, his steaming cup of coffee untouched. "The police couldn't do it seventeen years ago, and I can't let my whole life rest on them being able to do it now. I need your help, Morgie."

She stiffened her back. "Don't you dare call me that."

"I'm sorry." He looked her in the eye as he issued the apology. Didn't try to excuse or even explain his lapse.

"I know what you think of me," he said, continuing to hold her gaze. "I also know I didn't kill your sister back then. And I didn't kill Shane last night. It's pretty clear that the two have to be connected. No way Shane's body ends up in my pit, while I'm there alone, by accident. Or coincidence."

"Especially considering that he lives in Grand Rapids," she allowed. Purely as a fact pertinent to the situation. She told herself not to get sucked into Blade's seeming sincerity.

He'd managed to lure her at sixteen. She'd talked to him about feelings, soul-deep yearnings, other things that she hadn't even shared with her sister.

Not again.

"You've got a vested interest," he continued. "Obviously, you haven't been able to let the past go, either, or you wouldn't have driven through the night to get here."

"If you think you're going to distract me from proving that you killed Shane, you're wrong."

He didn't falter, didn't even blink. He leaned in closer. "I'm telling you, I want the truth as badly as you do."

"I can't just waltz onto a case. I have no jurisdiction or right to even be here. The fact that I was allowed at the scene, and that the detectives chose to speak to me, was professional courtesy. Period."

"But you've been looking for proof ever since your sister was killed, haven't you? It's pretty clear you've put word out or you wouldn't have known to be here less than twelve hours after I called in the body."

He'd always been the smartest guy at camp. Which had partially been what had drawn her to him. That and his maturity.

"You wouldn't be here if you didn't intend to do your own sleuthing. All I'm asking is that you let me help," he said. "Let's do this together. It's clear whoever killed Shane is out to hang me. My life will be an open book to you. Look everywhere. Interrogate me until we're numb. Just find something…"

Was he for real? Or just really good at manipulating people to get what he wanted?

Which would be…absolution from a second murder?

If he'd killed Shane, the best chance she had at finding out why, how and where would be through the open door into his life he'd just offered her.

But more than that…he'd given her what she couldn't invent for herself. The in to officially be a part of the case. "It'll cost you," she told him.

He didn't even blink. "How much you want? Name the price."

Okay, things were moving too fast. He was playing right into what she wanted and needed. Giving her a way in.

He was playing *her*.

She shook her head, but held his gaze, gaining strength as she did so. "It's not my price," she told him. And, reaching for her creds, pulled a card out of the thin leather pouch that held them. "You want me on this case, call Sierra's Web and hire me. You'll need to sign permission forms that allow me access to every piece of evidence, every communication involved with your case. It'll be like I'm your lawyer, only I'm going to shadow every move you make."

She was only taking him on if she could do so officially. With the firm's teams of experts right there with her.

No way was Blade Carmichael going to pull any wool over her eyes a second time. He might be playing her, for reasons of his own. But with her right there, with the firm there, following up on everything she heard, every email, every piece of forensic evidence she brought them, Blade would be the one who'd be played.

Right to the finish line.

At some point, if she was monitoring him, he'd say something, let some little detail slip, that would allow her to prove that he killed Maddie. Because no one, not a living soul on earth, knew her sister's case as well as she did.

When Blade stood, pushing his chair back, and walked away, she cursed herself for being too straightforward, pushing him too hard. Maddie had been the one of them blessed with the art of finesse. It was a gift Morgan could have used to get the man to give her exactly what she most needed.

An in to the case.

She stayed at the table long enough for their food to be delivered, and to let the waitress know she needed to settle the bill. Hadn't even received the check yet when Blade was suddenly back.

"Done," he said, just as her phone rang.

He was eating oatmeal when she hung up from Glen Rivers Thomas, the Sierra's Web forensic partner to whose team she was assigned.

Blade had given the firm an open account, with the caveat that Morgan be the lead on his case. Not just on his case but running it.

If he thought he was going to pull the wool over her eyes with his faith in her then he was setting himself up for a major disappointment.

Pushing her untouched breakfast aside, she leaned forward. "Rest assured, that when I find the proof, whoever killed my sister is going down. Forever." She stared at him with an intensity that had cowed lifetime criminals. "He will not see another day outside of prison walls. There won't be an attorney good enough to get him off." Like the high-priced guy his daddy had hired to keep Blade from ever being officially charged seventeen years before.

"From your lips to God's ears."

Wow. Invoking higher-ups. His statement didn't impress her. But the way Blade held her gaze, his own eyes steady, unblinking...

Either he really believed she'd find him innocent, or he was the most arrogant, self-confident, unconscionable man she'd ever met.

Too bad he didn't know she'd lost her ability to be moved by smooth talk the night Maddie was killed. The night her heart had died, too.

And if he'd managed to amass friends in Rocky Springs, people who'd fallen for him as hard as Morgan had, he could have had someone in a black vehicle follow her from the crime scene. Maybe to make sure she kept her word to meet him at the diner, or to see who she spoke to between leaving the crime scene and keeping their breakfast plans.

And there was the cop who'd pulled out right after her. Did Blade have the town's police force in his pocket, too?

Perhaps he thought the surest way to make certain that any unturned stone she might turn up would be magically destroyed before charges could be filed was to follow her.

Was that why Blade was hiring her, to stay one step ahead of prosecution?

"Tell me about the crane. How does it suddenly just fail at a crime scene?"

He started, sitting straight up in his seat, as she got to work.

Interesting.

He hadn't been sure she'd agree to help him. In spite of how convincing he'd been.

Without pushing for confirmation that she was agreeing to take his case, he started explaining about bolts and pins, assembly and disassembly of booms. Talked about statistical chances of a boom falling, and the most common causes. And ended with, "There's no way that crane failed by accident. Inspection and safety measures at Carmichael Construction are overkill, and everyone knows that a single infraction will get you fired. Period. Someone had to have tampered with the crane." His voice filled with intensity as he continued. "That particular crane was scheduled to be at that site starting today. Any number of people had access to that knowledge. Equipment schedules are posted. No way someone could have aimed that accident at you, but the boom failing—that was no accident."

There was one way it could have been aimed at her. If Blade had instructed his machine operator to make it happen.

He had access to equipment schedules. And clearly knew how to manipulate a boom failure. He'd pulled his operator aside, while looking at her, and given some direction.

Her gut lurched. Part of her, that young woman she'd thought completely dead, wanted, just for a second there, for her to believe he didn't do it.

She didn't trust those kinds of feelings. Most particularly not with Blade Carmichael. She trusted facts. So she regurgitated the ones that had been covered so many times in the past, and in her mind over the years.

"You went to the party. You told me you weren't going, but you did." She'd jumped back a decade and a half. Didn't feel the least bit sorry for the abrupt change in her interrogation.

If she sounded like an accusatory girlfriend with hurt feelings, so be it. She didn't give a damn.

His shoulders dropped, his chin falling to his chest. She grabbed her purse, ready to leave before the bill finally made it to the table. Let him pay for it.

"I was senior camp counselor." His voice stopped her. "Shane was making some off-color jokes about being with identical twins. I didn't trust him. Not knowing that Maddie was going to be there."

"And yet, according to your testimony, you left early. Left her there."

"Because he had. I stayed until he left."

"But you told police you thought he was the killer."

"They asked who I thought could have done it—among the kids at camp."

There was more. So much more. Maddie's class ring found in the pocket of Blade's jeans in his cabin the next morning. The little ribbon cross Morgan had made for him that day in craft class, and that she'd slipped into his shirt pocket herself, clutched in her dead sister's palm...

He'd have answers for them all, she was sure. Had read the reports, and knew those answers weren't the truth.

But she'd get there. She'd hear him admit every step he took that night. In time.

Maybe not right away.

Probably not before she opened up every crevice in his life to find out why and how Shane Wilmington's dead body had ended up in a Carmichael Construction pit.

But she'd get there.

And when she did, he'd have to look her in the eye and... What?

What could he possibly say or do that would ever, could ever, melt the ice she'd been encased in since her sister's horrible death?

Chapter 4

Blade wasn't going to look for any aspects of Morgan's character that could be remainders from the past. Even if her twin's murder hadn't completely changed her, he *knew* it had made him into a person that did not, in any way, resemble the young man he'd been.

The twinge of optimism that coursed through him as he paid the breakfast bill and walked back to his truck—the flood of relief—was only because he now had an expert detective on his case.

The fact that the expert was Morgan Davis was merely a consequence of her having become that expert after Maddie's death.

And that, his gut knew, was no coincidence. Morgan had wanted to be a novelist. A purveyor of stories filled with hope and happy endings. Not a hard-nosed, physically honed pursuer of bad guys.

Before she'd left the restaurant, he'd called his attorney to release his entire client folder to Sierra's Web, a copy of which would be on Morgan's computer within minutes. She was checking in to a local hotel on the beach—her choice—and ultimately at his expense, as the cost would be added to his bill with Sierra's Web. He'd agreed to cover all costs of the investigation.

One of the partners from Sierra's Web would also be contacting local police, asking for access to case files, and would be putting in requests for all police reports from seventeen years ago, too.

Morgan had asked for the rest of the morning and afternoon to peruse the information and consult with her Sierra's Web teams, before speaking to him again.

Almost as though she'd known he'd been up all night and desperately needed some rest before heading full tilt into battle.

They'd be meeting late that afternoon, at the Carmichael Construction office, just off Main Street in Rocky Springs. She'd made it very clear she intended to dig into every aspect of his existence, including his laundry basket, if she determined the need.

And what she said she needed was nonnegotiable. He gave access or she walked.

Every mandate she'd laid down had been followed by a long pause, as though she'd expected him to put up resistance, or at least question her motives. Maybe she'd been waiting to see at which point he'd balk—giving her a clue where to start her search for evidence.

Truth was, he'd give her complete access to every thought he'd ever had, every memory, and the gunk from every drain he'd ever had access to. If it could help her figure out what seventeen years hadn't revealed to him, his high-paid attorneys or the highly qualified law enforcement personnel who'd worked Madison Davis's murder case, he'd give her everything.

He had nothing to hide.

Except perhaps the dirty underwear in his laundry basket. Leaving the clothes he took off in a pile at the top of the basket—she could analyze the hell out of them and he hoped the Sierra's Web forensics team did just that—he cleaned the skivvies out of the basket. He put the handful of items in the washer, and started the small load.

Call him weird, paranoid or just plain comical—he didn't want Morgan Davis thumbing through his various shades and designs of dirty gray and blue briefs.

Let her see them in his drawer, fresh from the dryer, on top of the pile of the others he'd tossed there after laundering them. She'd find them if she did as she'd said she was going to do and went through every drawer, cupboard and hiding place in his space.

He'd been through that particular humiliation before. Having his entire bunk area and trunk searched at camp. And then his bedroom at home. Followed by the rest of the house when nothing turned up in his private places.

Nothing turning up to incriminate him was a great thing. He fully understood that. But trying to prove something with nothing—that was not so good.

Showering with the washer going hadn't been his best decision, so Blade's rinse-off was quick, and then he tidied up his house a bit while he waited to get the clothes in the dryer before he could drop into his chair for a nap. It wasn't like the two-thousand-square-foot ranch home on the opposite end of the beach from town was a mess. But he ran his hands over the countertops, just to make certain there wasn't something sticky there.

And ran the vacuum and a quick wet mop over the floors where appropriate for the same reason.

The dust…it was just going to have to do its best to look good. No way he was taking up that challenge. His once-a-month house cleaning service wouldn't know what to do if he didn't leave the mysterious, floating lint bunnies for them.

Underwear in the dryer, he'd just pushed back in his re-cliner when his phone buzzed a text. Thinking that it was a foreman from one of his many jobs—or the client/owner of the property that was now a crime scene—he picked his phone up off the table beside him.

And froze as he read.

Not enough that you killed one sister, you're going to in-volve the other one in your schemes, too?

He hadn't recognized the number. Shouldn't have opened the text.

And didn't know who to call.

Was he wrong to have hired Morgan?

Should he quickly fire her and make certain that noth-ing about his life touched hers, again?

No. His mind gave him the immediate answer. No, be-cause, just as he'd told her, she'd come to town on a few minutes' notice as soon as she'd heard that there was suspi-cious activity that could involve her sister's cold case. She'd be there whether he'd hired Sierra's Web or not.

For all he knew, she'd sent the text from some other phone, just to test him. It wasn't like she trusted him, any more than he trusted her to have his back.

Their path wasn't one of soulmates, or even friends. They were two people looking for the same answer. And the need for that absolute truth was what bound them.

Period.

Once he'd reasoned his way out of the hell of dread, Blade forwarded the entire message, including the sender details, to Morgan.

Following her mandate to keep her fully in his loop. He'd do it as long as it served his quest to find a killer.

He'd once thought he'd be spending his whole life telling Morgan all his secrets.

Funny how promises made forever could be so quickly broken.

With the opportunity of her lifetime falling into her lap, Morgan needed her stuff. The laptop computer designated to strictly digital information pertaining to Madison's case. Copies of all reports, lists, investigations she could get her hands on. Case photos. Search links, websites on topics from evidence hiding in dirt, to teenage hormonal behavior. Camp attendee lists. Snapshots of their lives since. And, of course, Blade Carmichael's life history, as far as she could get without a warrant. Then there were her physical case files. A lot of them were copies of hard copies of the digital information.

There was also the scrapbook of photos of her and Madison growing up. It kept her going when she started to lose hope. And the box she still kept that held the mementos of Blade Carmichael from that summer. Not for nostalgia's sake—God no. She needed them to help her cognitive skills pertaining to the case. Reminding her of things he'd said, places on campgrounds they'd visited together…small details that could point to solving the murder when put together with a new piece of evidence.

She had no idea why she'd saved the box at sixteen. Hadn't realized she had, until she'd moved out of her parents' home after college and found the small box in a bigger one filled with her things. And with all her newfound criminal investigation knowledge simmering in her brain, she'd figured she'd possibly found a gold mine.

Morgan was halfway to Detroit when her phone buzzed a text and her automated system read it aloud for her. Signaling an abrupt exit, she took the ramp just ahead of her, and pulled to a stop in the gas station at the end of it. Read the text. And then, sending it to the Sierra's Web team, she called Hudson Warner, the IT expert partner, and asked him to ping towers, as well as the number. She needed to know if there was imminent danger to herself, to Blade or to anyone else.

While she waited to hear from the Sierra's Web home office in Phoenix, she texted Blade, telling him the team was on the text and asking him not to respond. To which he replied with a thumbs-up emoji.

And she had to wonder…had he texted himself? Burner phones were a dime a dozen. Could be purchased at most grocery stores and a lot of gas stations. It wouldn't have been difficult for him to grab one on the way home from breakfast. To further suck her in.

Or prove to her that he was going to keep her in the loop.

He was likely playing her, she reminded herself. Making her pay for turning her back on him the morning after the murder. Granted, she'd been harsh. But she'd been sixteen and had just been told her identical twin had been brutally murdered. And that Blade was suspected of the murder.

They'd questioned her about her relationship with him. Had asked her to try to remember everything he'd said to her the night before…

The inquisition had happened before her parents had arrived. She'd been terrified. And so consumed by grief she'd been unable to process most of what was coming at her.

They'd shown her the cross she'd given Blade the day before, the one she'd made on a whim, showing younger kids what they might do during the craft hour she'd been monitoring. She hadn't known until later that it had been found on her sister's body. But she'd known that the cross had been of huge significance in the midst of the horror of that morning.

Her car's audio system blared with a ringtone. Glen's number popped up on the dash screen.

"Burner phone. From a tower just south of Rocky Springs." The man delivered the news she'd expected, and, thanking him, Morgan got back on the road.

Noting that a tan car that she'd seen behind her for a while before she'd left the freeway was back, a minute or two after she'd reentered traffic.

She hadn't seen anyone get off at the exit. There most definitely hadn't been a tan car at the gas station.

Shaking off the sense of doom, Morgan took a deep breath, and with it, took control of her mind, too.

In her condo, she made quick work of gathering up her things. Some extra burner phones, her main laptop. And, of course, clothes and toiletries. She could buy new, charge them to the case, but why?

She wasn't out to hurt Blade Carmichael. She was out to prove that he killed her twin sister, and then to make certain that he spent the rest of his life in prison.

If she could prove he'd killed Shane, she'd have a great start.

Searching Carmichael Construction's client list would be first on Morgan's to-do list once she made it back to her hotel.

She'd been given several hours between breakfast and meeting up with Blade again, but four of them were being spent driving back and forth to Detroit. She wasn't going to be able to have as much prep work done as she'd have liked. But she knew the case.

Shane was suddenly dead at Blade's feet after seventeen years without new evidence pointing to the murder suspect as a killer. Shane had also been at camp with them, and at the party the night Maddie died. And Blade had specifically pointed the finger at Shane when Blade had been questioned by the police. She had the official report.

Had looked at it again, just before she'd torn out of her condo that morning.

There had to be more between the two men than either of them had ever let on. Shane knowing something from the past…a constant threat to Blade, with Blade having something to hold over Shane, too, she guessed, as nothing else made sense.

An illicit affair at camp that had some criminal or life-changing implications? Something worse?

Considering the young man she'd known, the suspicion was plausible. Shane's egotistical way with the girls at camp, the way he'd left broken hearts and laughed about them, could easily point to the guy having pushed other boundaries too far. And been caught by senior counselor Blade, who'd made it his business to watch over him.

If Shane had told Blade that he didn't care if his secret was told, or had come clean to his wife or police or whoever he hadn't wanted knowing whatever Blade had on him, then the next logical step would have been for Shane to blackmail Blade with the murder information. Or, more likely, go to the police.

That would mean Blade would have to kill Shane to shut him up.

It all made sense. Good, investigative sense, as far as theories went. A starting place for digging deeper.

Energized, with adrenaline flowing more freely than it had in years, Morgan drove the miles back to Rocky Springs with an eagerness to get to work.

She couldn't stop watching her back, though. That was

something else that had become an integral part of her that long-ago summer. The police had questioned her extensively, and she'd figured out that they'd needed to know if someone had perhaps murdered her identical twin sister by accident. Maybe their target was really Morgan.

Unless the murder was solved, that question would always be in the back of her mind. She'd never spoken the possibility aloud. Never even told her parents. Or heard them speak of it.

But there it was, lurking, as she checked her rearview mirror and noticed a camel-colored sedan, nondescript, like a dozen others on the highway with them, a few vehicles behind her. Again.

The entire way to Detroit, she'd had the feeling that someone was following her.

Like the car that morning.

And now, the same tan car?

It made no sense. Her rational brain shook off the sense of doom. Even if someone *was* following her, the idea that there'd be two different someones, or that a person would take the trouble to change vehicles during the task…it didn't point to sound thought processes.

What did kind of gel, though, was the idea that seeing Blade again had just slammed a part of her back into the past—which meant residual paranoia could resurface. She needed to stay on top of that fear, beat it before it got her.

Her years of criminal study, physical workouts, target shooting and working for the FBI had helped her overcome it in the past.

It wasn't far-fetched to think that small portions of that fear still lurked inside her. Enough to jump forward given the right circumstances.

Her job was to make certain she didn't give it a playing field.

And still, she watched. Noted that as she turned from one highway to another the same tan car, or one identical to it, with the exact same hood ornament, followed her off the exit. And was over one lane and four vehicles behind her again.

Pulling out her phone, she opened the camera. Needing to get a photo of the car just for her own peace of mind. She'd look it up later to reassure herself that her instincts had been in overdrive in the moment. Because another person related to her sister's murder had just been killed.

She couldn't make out the license plate. Even when she slowed, the car didn't catch up to her. Which only fed those little mean spears of paranoia.

With her phone to her ear, as though she was making a call, she flipped it out flat a couple of times, got what shots she could. And spent the next few miles attempting to put the matter to rest in her mind.

She was somewhat successful, until she turned off at Rocky Springs. The car didn't follow her. But driving through town, she was certain she saw the black car again.

A team being paid to make note of all her comings and goings? Taking money in exchange for keeping her in sight at all times?

Blade Carmichael was a rich man. He'd had an inheritance from grandparents. And had built a solid, very successful construction company from the ground up. He'd never married. Had no kids.

A guy like that could afford half a dozen teams of people willing to follow a single woman around her life. Reporting back everywhere she went.

In case she stumbled onto something he didn't want her to find? A burial ground of evidence?

Or talked to someone he didn't want her meeting with?

At the moment, it was the most likely explanation. Why would anyone else care where she went, or who she talked to?

Unless, maybe someone she'd helped put away who'd recently been released from jail?

She considered the thought's validity for all of two seconds before mentally adding a task to her Sierra's Web tech expert's to-do list. She would need a search of all her cases and cross-referenced with people recently released from prison.

She'd been planning to send the request upon completion of her first day's work in her hotel room, before going to meet Blade.

A request that flew out of her mind as her phone rang, just as she pulled into her hotel parking lot. It was Glen Rivers Thomas, the Sierra's Web partner who'd hired her.

"Rocky Springs police has agreed to allow us official access to the case," the man reported as soon as she'd answered. Glen was the strong silent type if ever she'd met one. "And we've got our first head-scratcher," the man continued without allowing her time to express her relief. Or gratitude. "Cause of death," Glen said. "Shane Wilmington was shot, but his official cause of death is a broken neck."

Her gasp came out of nowhere, filled her car. Thankful that she'd already parked, Morgan said, "Someone broke his neck, then shot him?"

"You'd think, but no. Shane was shot first, but it was a through and through…"

Damn. No bullet. Blade Carmichael was the luckiest son of…

"He died from some kind of heavy pressure against his neck. Someone standing on it, maybe. Or applying a whole lot of weight to something pressed against it."

"Rage," she said, uttering the first thing that came to mind.

While the thud of her own lead weight hit her gut. She'd figured Shane's death had been the result of a truce gone bad. A seventeen-year secret about to be exposed.

Something like that didn't happen humanely.

It came from a potful, years full, even, of panic-induced rage.

She might not have the bullet to tie Blade's gun to the murder, but her suspicions about him had just amped up off the scale.

And why in the hell was she shaking, feeling any disappointment at all, while bursting with the first taste of victory she'd had in years?

Chapter 5

Blade was seated behind his desk, his own set of case files—and private investigations conducted on his behalf over the years—spread before him, as Morgan walked in late that afternoon. The company receptionist out front had been told to send her back as soon as she arrived. And the young man, Duane, a college student, had buzzed Blade to let him know she was on her way down the hall.

He'd been pacing when Duane's communication had come through, and stood from his armed leather desk chair as she rapped lightly, and let herself in. The king welcoming a business associate to his lair. Or so he needed her to think. It was immature, he knew.

He had no reason to impress Morgan Davis with his success. She was the woman who'd once professed she was his soulmate and within hours had had no belief in him at all.

More accurately, maybe, he was reminding himself that he was no longer that young man whose entire life had irrevocably tumbled in the space of a blink. He'd closed his eyes to sleep, in love and with his future stretching gloriously before him and had been awoken by uniformed men with guns pointed at him, while another slapped handcuffs on his wrists.

That moment had shaped every single one that had come after.

"You've already got all the official reports." He started right in, standing there with his large desk covered in files organized in the order in which he planned to deliver them to her. Picking up the first stack, he handed them over. "These are private investigations I've had done quietly over the years. Unfortunately, none of them turned up anything I could take to the police."

Brow raised, Morgan gave his face a quick glance, and then she reached for the files, her focus clearly on them.

He gave her kudos for that.

And wasn't surprised when she sat down, seemingly immersed, judging by the long pauses for reading and page turning, in the file he'd purposely placed on top.

His seventeen-year dossier of Shane Wilmington. Starting with everything he'd collected over the internet during all that time, followed by private investigator reports.

She didn't comment. Didn't even look up. Eventually, he sat. Watching her.

Assessing.

Not only her reaction to the information in front of her, but her entire demeanor. Straight shoulders, tight chin. Defensive posture.

For a split second, as a shard of remembered fear shot through him, he second-guessed his decision to hire her firm. But he quickly shut down the unwanted drama. It was a skill he'd learned far too young. Trouble had a way of finding him. There was no point in borrowing more.

The antidote to that worry was positive action. Movements, thoughts that steered him away from the darkness, and into the light. Doing everything he could, no matter how long it took, to prove his innocence. Rather than dwell on the fallout from living under a cloud of false accusation.

A new cloud.

Fear shot stronger that time.

And, with his elbows on the arms of his chair, he steepled his fingers, concentrating on the woman seated on the other side of his desk, poring over information.

Looking for that one elusive little piece that could hang Blade, probably. Except that he knew for a fact it wasn't there.

He had not killed Madison Davis.

That was his positive reinforcement. No one would ever find definitive evidence to press charges against him because he hadn't done it.

There'd been no DNA samples taken from the body. Maddie had died a virgin. And nothing conclusive, in terms of fingerprint evidence, taken from her clothes or skin.

Shane Wilmington had been seen making out with her, behind a cluster of trees, at the party. Blade had been the one to break them up, and to warn Shane that he had to leave immediately.

He'd suggested Maddie do the same, but she'd been waiting on a couple of the other female counselors. Girls she'd walked over with. He'd tried to convince all three of them to vacate the area, to allow him to walk them back, but when one of the guys pulled out an outdoor camping projector and a movie, he'd known he'd been fighting a losing cause.

The movie, a popular teen horror flick he'd seen and found…boring…hadn't drawn him nearly as much as his bunk and thoughts of his newly established exclusive status with Morgan Davis. The only reason he'd attended the party at all was to keep an eye on Shane. And with the other counselor back in the boy's camp, with a firm warning that

Blade was going to report him if Shane got anywhere near Madison Davis after hours again that summer—Blade had turned in.

"This dossier on Shane…" Morgan's voice yanked Blade out of the darkness he'd been attempting to avoid. "Who else knows you have it?"

He shrugged. "My lawyer knows I've kept tabs over the years. The PIs I've hired know about their involvement. There's never been anything turned up to report…" He repeated what he'd said earlier.

Morgan glanced up at him, frowning. Studied him for a few seconds and said, "Your lawyer, was he at the scene earlier this morning?"

Lower lip pursed, Blade shook his head. Shrugged, and said, "I had nothing to hide. I was in a ditch when a body dropped over the edge at my feet. I dialed 911 immediately. And stayed put."

She nodded, still watching him. "Might have been good to have him there, just the same."

He disagreed. Calling his lawyer would have made him look guilty. "There was nothing I could say to incriminate myself," he explained, telling her the truth that he lived by. He never even drove over the speed limit.

"You do realize that this…obsession…you've had with Shane all these years…looks bad for you, in light of what happened last night."

Her use of the word *obsession*, the pause…a deliberate move to disarm him? Or had she had difficulty getting the word out? The stone face she showed him gave nothing away.

There was no opportunity at all to read her as he'd been able to do in the past.

He looked her straight in the eye. Steel to steel. "I did

not kill your sister," he said, conviction in every word. "Shane is the only other viable suspect. I don't want to go to my grave a suspect. So I keep my intentions an active part of my life."

He was not obsessed. He was determined. There was a huge difference. "I make trimonthly checks of his social media. And hire a detective once a year," he told her. "And part of that is a conscience thing, so I can sleep at night."

That caught her attention. She turned her head slightly but was still focused on him. "Explain that."

"If the man murdered your sister at sixteen, you think he stopped there? That he'd never lose his temper, or raise a fist to someone, again?"

As she held up the opened file with both hands, Morgan's immediate response was, "It would appear that he's lived a stellar life."

He got that. A privileged, much-loved guy who took deliberate actions to ensure that his reputation shone bright enough that people didn't see a double life, lived in darkness for a decade and a half.

He nodded toward the file she'd laid back on top of the others on her lap. "You see anything in there that would lead to the man ending up dead in my pit?"

She nodded, the movement seeming, maybe, like a sense of concession.

Something got Shane Wilmington killed. And Blade knew for an absolute fact that he didn't murder the man.

"He wasn't just killed." Morgan's words got Blade's complete attention. "He was shot, but the cause of death was a neck broken by deliberate pressure. Like a shoe on his neck." Her gaze couldn't have been more pointed. She was looking for any sign he might give her to indicate some prior knowledge of the fact. Or some satisfaction taken from reliving it.

Knowing anything, and everything, he did, could and would be construed to fit preconceived notions, Blade remained still. Schooling his thoughts, his features, as he'd learned to do his last year of high school.

"Overkill," he finally said, when it became clear that she wasn't moving on without some kind of response.

"You know anyone who had any reason to be that angry with him?" Morgan asked, still pinning him as though her gaze was a microscope with a camera chip embedded inside.

"Besides me, you mean?" he shot right back, without a blink. "If you were to consider believing that I'm not guilty of Madison's murder, then it's conceivable that I'd feel a good bit of rage toward whoever did do it and framed me." He didn't sleep at night by pretending things weren't there. He slept by acknowledging every aspect of everything that happened, so he'd be prepared if and when someone came at him with bogus theories.

He might not be able to exonerate himself yet, but he could do everything in his power to ensure that he wasn't knocked completely off his axis a second time.

"Of course, if you're going with that theory, then we'll at least be on the same page in terms of finding someone who is not me who killed your sister." The words weren't kind. He didn't hesitate at all, or glance away, even for a second, as he uttered them.

"Sierra's Web was given access to Shane's financials," she said then, surprising him. Had he just won a round? Or was she just done with the conversation?

When his brain processed the ramification of what she'd just given him, he sat forward. "And?" A man's financial life revealed everything. And it had been the one aspect of Shane Wilmington's business that he'd never been able to access.

Morgan's headshake depleted his surge of energy. "There's nothing anywhere in his life, not his accounts, his phone records or tax filings that show any discrepancies, or even hints at possible secrets lurking anywhere in the underbelly."

Had that been a note of disappointment he'd heard in her voice?

"By all accounts, building a profile from what we have— and your information really just confirms it—my sister's death was a life-changing experience for Shane. His entire life, his relationships, his family life, even going back to his college days, he was different from the second he returned home from camp. He started attending church regularly. Became studious, where before he was lucky to skate by as an average student. He even started up an antibullying program his last year in high school, and it's grown to multistate proportions. And every year, he traveled to meet with new student bodies around the country, talking about why bullying hurts everyone."

By the time Morgan had finished, Blade felt as though she'd been cramming her thoughts down his throat. Not from her delivery. There'd been nothing but professionalism in her tone and expression. He couldn't really say what was hitting him so wrong.

Until…it occurred to him. The woman was sitting there singing the praises of the only real suspect in her sister's murder—and still pointing her accusatory finger straight at Blade's heart.

Who'd have thought her lack of belief in him, her lack of support, could still rankle so much? Even with seventeen years' distance between them.

Those years, they'd changed all of them. Him included. Meeting her gaze calmly, Blade offered, "Getting away with murder could do that to a guy. Scare him straight. If it was an accidental thing. He didn't mean to do it. He's not psychopathic…"

He let his words trail away, as his thoughts took off silently, and spun in another direction.

If Shane *had* killed Madison, then it did stand to reason that to someone who loved Madison dearly, who'd lost even more than Blade had that night in the woods, there could be a rage-filled need to see Shane pay.

It was human nature to need to find justice. Especially after an act had taken away life as you knew it.

Shane and Blade—victims of justice? The one killed, the other framed for murder. A second time.

Morgan still couldn't seem to let go of Blade's culpability in whatever happened that night. Her dislike of him had emanated off her like hot coals at the crime scene that morning.

Because he'd attended a party to watch over Shane. To protect Madison and the other girls from the egotistical womanizer.

Based on all research and investigations, no one had any reason to kill Shane Wilmington.

Except Morgan Davis, if she'd figured out Shane had murdered her twin.

Morgan's mind flew across the criminal landscape in front of her. Her sister's murder. Shane Wilmington being caught making out with her that night.

Maddie's obsession with Shane.

Maddie's class ring, which she'd been going to give to Shane, being found in Blade's pocket the next morning.

Neither Shane nor Blade having alibis for the time of the murder—within an hour after the unsanctioned party broke up.

The little ribbon cross Morgan had made and given to Blade before curfew that night—a sign of their exclusivity commitment—clutched in Maddie's hand when she was found early that next morning.

And seventeen years later, Shane Wilmington found dead at Blade's feet.

She stared at the man, sitting behind his impressive desk in a business he'd grown from the ground up—and clearly still worked with his own two hands, alongside the more than a hundred people he employed.

If Shane had been blackmailing him, threatening to expose some proof that would put Blade away for Maddie's murder, then why would Blade have killed the man on his own job site? Or dumped him there, and then called the cops?

With all his equipment, and job sites, the man could have easily dug a hole deep enough to make Shane disappear forever.

Unless he somehow thought he could point to the man for Maddie's murder without Shane having a chance to rebut, hoping to clear suspicion from himself...

She gave her head a mental shake. No way he'd do that by planting Shane's body at his own feet, making it appear as though he'd just killed the man. He would at least make it look like someone else had been at the job site. Or plant some proof of Maddie's murder on the body.

Blade had a good life. Had built a new world for himself, in a lovely town, living in Michigan, on the beach, just as he'd always wanted. Why would he mess that up by bringing up the past that haunted him?

As much as her mind needed to believe that he was her sister's killer—needed to believe that she knew who'd killed her sister and her only quest was the proof to put him away—Morgan's gut wasn't completely buying into the story.

Because her mind couldn't seem to back it up with irrefutable fact. Not even in theory.

Blade killing Shane—okay, if he'd killed Maddie, that could be pretty easily argued. The blackmail theory was a solid one.

But implicating himself in the murder?

Unless he'd done so just to throw everyone off track.

Calling the police…hiring her as soon as she'd shown up in town…

He'd walked away from one murder without charges being filed.

Was that his signature? Committing crimes and insinuating himself so fully into the scene from the very beginning, while knowing that investigators would never find proof to convict him?

If she could just outsmart him…find that one little detail he'd missed…something he'd failed to cover up. A signature he was unaware of that he'd repeated at both crimes.

She had to watch his seventeen-year-old interviews with police again. Compare them to that morning's reports.

All she needed was one small, elusive thing to wrap everything up nice and clean and move on. Try to find a good life for herself. One that included her career, of course, but maybe every waking hour didn't need to be spent investigating crime.

She'd been staring Blade down. He'd been staring right back. Getting them nowhere.

"If not you, then who?" She blurted the question that

she'd been trying to push away for hours. Aside from her, Blade Carmichael had spent more time than anyone else investigating her sister's murder. And paying for it, too. She had to know what conclusions he'd drawn. What he told himself that let him sleep at night.

For curiosity's sake if nothing else.

The tension in his face fell away, leaving a bleakness there that shocked her. The expression lasted only a second or two. She could easily pretend she hadn't seen it.

Except that Morgan didn't pretend anything anymore.

Truth and provable facts, and the search for them, were the only things she allowed to occupy space and time in her mind.

Blade hadn't answered. She raised her brows.

"Shane," he said then, meeting her gaze full-on. And then shrugged again. "He's the only person who makes any sense at all."

Other than Blade, of course. But she agreed with him, that if it wasn't him, Shane had to be it. Maddie wouldn't have gone into the woods with anyone else.

And the camp was a secure facility. Surrounded by walls that Maddie had once told their parents resembled a prison. Security cameras had been at every entrance, and triple-checked. After becoming an agent, Morgan had spent hours viewing every minute of every one of those tapes to no avail. Not a single unauthorized vehicle had entered or exited that night, and the approved vehicles that had, had been through forensics, with the drivers all having alibis. No one had walked in. Every camper, every faculty member and staff person had been checked out.

"So why, seventeen years later, is someone getting rid of him and trying to frame you for the murder? Why would someone need to take out both of you?"

His gaze sharpened to points, and then softened. His jaw clenched. A vein in his neck popped out.

"What?" she asked him, heart pounding.

"You said last night's murder was a crime of passion."

"Of rage, yes," she agreed.

"I can only think of one person who'd have reason to carry that much anger inside, who'd maybe given up on the system doing its job. Seventeen years have passed, and the case is no closer to being solved…the culprits are no closer to being brought to justice."

The way he was looking at her…not with meanness, but a definite chill…hit her.

"Someone who's so fed up she quit her job and went into private practice."

She knew exactly what he was thinking. What he was about to say.

Lifting the pile of folders on her lap to her chest, Morgan held on to them, stood and, with one fluid movement, turned to the door.

She'd reached the opening, had turned the handle to complete her escape when, from behind her, she heard Blade's voice.

"Now you know how it feels."

Chapter 6

Morgan was still shaking, inside and out, when she reached her car.

Blade's words reverberated around her as she drove to the hotel, and they were still with her as she let herself into her second-floor beach-view room.

She'd left the curtains open, could see the great Lake Michigan flowing in waves toward the sand and away again.

Michigan's waters had always had the power to soothe her. It was something she and Blade had had in common—communion with their state's natural gifts. A desire to live in Michigan for the rest of their lives.

Now you know how it feels.

It wasn't just that he'd said the words.

Or even that his intent could have been to get her goat.

But he'd concocted a theory in which a law enforcement official might find merit. Leaving her to suspect that he hadn't just been drawing some kind of parallel conclusion to prove a point. He'd been giving her his honest thoughts.

Blade knew she hadn't killed her sister.

But he thought she'd murdered Shane Wilmington? Was that why he'd hired Sierra's Web? To catch her in her own *web*?

Horror washed through her. Again and again.

For herself.

And slowly, as an hour passed into two and she tried to find calm in the sun setting over the water, for him.

Now you know how it feels.

In all the years since Madison's death, she'd never once considered how Blade had felt that morning, when he'd come to her, a look of disbelief and fright filling his face, and she'd screamed at him to get away from her.

She'd thought he'd been going to try to convince her to be his alibi or something. Or something. She had no idea what she'd thought. Only that he represented an end of life.

An end of innocence. Of love.

But looking back, as a mature adult, one who'd seen all the bad the world had to show her, who'd sat with many families grieving for missing or murdered loved ones, having to pour salt in their wounds with the questions that would lead her to their truths, to the justice they'd needed…

That look on Blade's face, if she was remembering it correctly…why hadn't she ever seen it in her mind's eye before?

Had she ever looked?

Allowed herself to let him in that far?

Had his sudden advent into her life, the new shocking lead in Maddie's case, opened places in her mind that had been closed since she'd been told her sister was dead?

Blade had been frightened out of his wits. Looking to her for something. Help? Comfort? Even just the belief that he couldn't have done such a thing?

Now you know how it feels.

She wanted his words to be snarky. An attack. Getting back at her.

They hadn't sounded that way.

Nor did they feel that way.

Did he really believe she could have killed Shane Wilmington?

Pacing her room, she looked to the water, to the few people left enjoying the beach so late in the day, and found... nothing but cold chills. The kind you got when you were sick.

His theory had been pretty well-thought-through. To the point of suggesting that she'd left the FBI due to a frustration with the system.

There'd been truth in that statement. A lot of it. Not geared toward Maddie's case, specifically, but in her inability to go where the wind took her on investigations due to the Bureau's red tape and policies. She'd become an investigator so that she could bring answers, some peace, and hopefully the ability to move on, to families who'd lost loved ones. Or who had loved ones who disappeared. Or were the victims of other crimes that were waiting to be solved.

She'd worked a case with Sierra's Web the previous year. Part of a baby-kidnapping ring. Some of the babies who had been stolen and sold had been shipped to Michigan. Seeing what Sierra's Web had been able to do, which the Bureau hadn't had the means to do...had been a life-changer for her.

In a good way.

And she could see how that life choice, made so recently before Shane Wilmington ended up dead at Blade Carmichael's feet, pointed to the possibility that she'd ceased being a federal agent because she'd needed freedom to get justice for herself. Vigilante style.

What she couldn't see was how to walk away from the case. She didn't know who'd murdered her sister. She thought she knew. Had very real suspicion. But she didn't *know*.

And she didn't even have a good suspicion about who'd

killed Shane Wilmington. She couldn't rule out Blade, not with her head, anyway, but she had questions.

Too many of them.

All without answers.

Plopping down to a love seat on the far wall of her room, Morgan ordered her mind to collect itself. To make a plan and execute it.

She needed to be on Blade's payroll.

And whether he suspected her of Shane's murder or not, he needed her, too.

If for no other reason than because the two of them lived under the shadow of the same nightmare. Neither of them would ever be free to live any kind of normal life until they found the answers they'd both been apparently seeking, separately, for a decade and a half.

Those files that Blade had given her that afternoon... why, if the man had committed the crime, was he still spending so much money to find the proof?

Hiring Sierra's Web that day made sense. He had a fresh murder at his doorstep, pretty much literally. But for the past seventeen years?

Why had he kept such thorough tabs on Shane Wilmington?

And then found him dead at his feet?

She could come up with logical theories for each question, separately. But not one that fit both occurrences.

Maybe Shane had been blackmailing him somehow, like she'd thought, threatening to go to the police with some kind of proof that Blade was guilty in Maddie's murder. And maybe Blade had really been bold enough to kill the man, and then make it look like he was being framed.

But why do that?

Why not just bury the guy? Make him disappear forever?

Unless he knew someone, or something, could tie him to Wilmington?

Now you know how it feels.

Dizzy with the rapidity of her mental circles, Morgan thought about ordering dinner from room service. She glanced around for the menu and was distracted by the pile of files she'd carried in with her. Stacked on the desk. Next to the box of them she'd brought from home, which was on the dresser.

She needed answers.

And, oddly enough, not just the name of a murderer. Or two.

Pulling her phone out of her pocket, she tapped the number she'd put on speed dial, as she always did when she took on a new client for Sierra's Web.

"Yeah." Blade sounded tired. Just that. Bone-deep tired.

"Have you eaten?" Not a business question. But a practical one. She had to eat if her mental acuity was going to return in full force.

"No."

"Can we meet for dinner? We can discuss theories we've come up with over the years." It was the only place that made sense to start.

Brainstorming with colleagues. Even when everyone shared a theory, there were always small differences in perspectives that shone light on small details that oftentimes led to larger truths.

"Considering the text I received after we dined in public today, I don't think that's a great idea. But I could pick up something. Bring it there."

To her small hotel room? He'd overshadow the place.

"How about I come to you?"

"I'd rather be the one out driving at night."

It was a bit late for him to get all macho on her. But his statement flew her back in time, before she'd known she was heading off. She'd been assigned campfire duty at the girls' camp, which meant she had to be the one who stayed around to make sure all flames were out, and all campers made it back to their cabins. Blade had wanted to sneak over and make sure the fire was out. He hadn't wanted her to be standing out there all alone in a clearing surrounded by woods in the dark. Which was ridiculous since the firepit was in the middle of a circle of wooded cabins and other counselors would be out doing cabin checks.

"I'm an expertly trained former FBI agent, Blade," she said, maybe more sternly than necessary. A reaction to the warmth that had momentarily entered her system. "I think I can drive around Rocky Springs at night." She finished with, "I'll be going out alone, otherwise. I need to eat."

And still hadn't landed on a room service menu.

"I'll have dinner delivered," he said then. A compromise. She got it. She wouldn't be out and about making stops.

An unnecessary choice that would cost him a delivery charge. But when he asked her for her preference, she gave it to him. A dinner-sized chef salad with French bread.

And left him to figure out where and how to make that happen.

Blade knew he'd hear from Morgan again. He was the way to her justice. Just as she remained his absolute best shot of clearing his name. He hadn't expected a dinner invitation.

And couldn't find a restaurant in Rocky Springs that served both chef salads and French bread. He ordered the salad, along with his glazed pork loin and vegetables, and then, with only minutes until Morgan would be arriving, he made a quick trip to the grocery around the corner and got the bread. Had to buy a whole loaf. So be it. He wasn't going to give her reason to find fault with him.

A small part of him, remnants from the past, didn't want to disappoint her. Now that he knew that excess baggage was there, he'd get rid of it. He'd promised himself that the past was not going to pollute his future.

And was closer than ever to ensuring that he kept that promise. As unwelcome as Shane Wilmington's dead body had been in his pit the night before, it had brought a whole lot of attention to his case. Expert attention.

More eyes looking for the truth…

He saw Morgan was parked at the light, waiting to turn into his neighborhood. He was coming up the street she'd turn on—the access to his road—from the opposite direction. They'd be turning on his street together. The light change would determine who followed whom.

He was sending strong thoughts for his light to stay green—keeping her stopped, waiting to turn—long enough for him to beat her to his place. Suddenly, he lost all train of thought.

The black sedan a few vehicles behind her and in the straight lane…expensive-looking, tinted windows…he'd seen it before. That morning, parked at the crime scene. The scratch in the tinting on the passenger side had caught his attention. Because he'd been looking for something trivial to concentrate on while he fought the panic that had been threatening his ability to think clearly. He'd succeeded. In seconds. And later, when he looked for the car again, it had been gone.

Turning onto his street while Morgan's light remained red, he took note of his victory, while trying not to over-think the situation.

Only authorized cars had been allowed on the lot. That black car, in his neighborhood…so they were watching him. He'd expect no less.

But the long light allowed him to get his truck into his garage and have the automatic door down before Morgan pulled onto his drive. He met her at the front door after she rang the bell. Ready to take her on.

Until she looked up at him with worry in her gaze, passing him to enter the impressive foyer with shelves built into the wall, one of the home's extra touches that he'd built himself. "Someone's following me."

Her greeting locked up his gut again. "Black sedan?" he asked. He knew better than to look on the bright side of anything he noticed out of the ordinary. You only got kicked in the balls when you expected the best.

She turned, not seeming to notice his house at all, as she held on to the top of the large satchel hanging from her shoulder with both hands. Almost as though she was hugging it, or herself. "And a tan one. I've been telling myself I'm overreacting, but…" She stopped, beige dress pants and white cotton blouse giving her an air of professionalism as her eyes pinned him in a most decidedly nonfriendly way. "How did you know it was black?"

Door locked and bolted behind her, he slid his hands in his pockets, fine to meet right there where he could show her the way out quickly, and said, "Because I saw it on Bellair, a few cars behind you when you were stopped at the light." And then noted her body language was more than mistrustful. He computed the words she'd actually said. "What do *you* mean 'and a tan one'?"

He walked as he spoke, needing to get them to the large dining room table, in what would have been a formal dining room. From day one, he'd pegged the square footage as his case workspace—complete with a wall of corkboard filled with pretty much every photo, every picture he'd ever had of the original crime scene, and the people who'd been at camp that godawful night.

It was also, unusually, a room with no windows. He'd removed them from the floor plan.

"Wow." Morgan stopped at the opened, double-doored entrance, her gaze moving around the room.

"It's the ten-foot ceilings," Blade spewed forth inanely. The entire first floor had them. As she, an expert detective, would have already noted.

Still holding her satchel, Morgan moved slowly around the room. Seeming to study every single poke he'd ever made in the walls. Saying nothing.

He left her to her ruminations, feeling exposed. And willing to take on the discomfort, too. Anything to get the answers he needed.

When she made it back to where she'd started, she turned to the table, moved toward the empty space he'd cleared for her on one end. Set her satchel there. "This is impressive," she told him, including a sweep of the room in her glance.

"It's desperation," he corrected. "Now, back to that tan car?" He didn't remember one at the crime scene.

And grew more and more uptight as she told him about the black car following her to the restaurant that morning, the tan car behind her all the way to Detroit and back.

"I can't be sure it was the same car," she finished. "It was the same model. Same color. Considering that Detroit is the automakers' hometown…"

She met his gaze, and he held on. "You know it's the same car," he said.

She shrugged.

"Had you seen either car before today?"

"No."

Standing upright, Blade made a decision. "You're fired." There was no doubt in his tone. His posture, every sense he had, was filled with conviction.

"What?" She didn't quite yell. The one word came out more like a squeak. Her gaze threw bullets at him.

He wasn't the least deterred. "No way, Morgan. First, I get that text about your dead sister, and now you're being followed? No. You need to leave. Immediately. Don't come back and don't call me. Period. I will not have your blood…" He felt his face drain as adrenaline left his system.

He already had her blood on his hands. Because he carried Maddie's with him every single second of every single day. Not because he'd killed her, but because he'd left her at that party. And hadn't checked to make certain Shane hadn't gone back. Neither of them had been his direct responsibility but reporting the party had been.

As soon as he'd found out about it. And he hadn't done it.

"Here's what I know about threats." Leaving her satchel on the table, Morgan took a couple of steps closer to him. "They're made by people who are afraid of losing control of a situation. If you give in to them, you feed that sense of control, which emboldens them, and they become more dangerous."

"Fine, I'll take that chance. Face the danger. But not with you."

"Then, okay, I'm fired. And we'll work the case separately." She walked back to her satchel.

No. "Wait."

She shook her head. "I've been working to solve my sister's murder for seventeen years, Blade. If you think you have the power to stop me, you're just…"

What? He was what? He wanted to know. And didn't need to.

"…just wrong," she finally finished.

She was right. He hadn't brought her into the situation. Or even called her to town. She'd go forth with or without him. "Someone's playing with me," he said, feeling a smidgen of his usual calm settling over him. "Baiting me."

"Someone who knows that we once hung out together," she added, her brows creased, as though she was studying a difficult puzzle. "They had to know that making a threat to my life would hit you where it hurts."

Maybe. A part of him liked that they were talking about what they'd once said they meant to each other. Making it a thing. As though it had really existed outside of their hormonal teenage existence. Setting it apart as real enough to still call to him, be meaningful enough to serve as a threat, all those years later.

Not because he saw her current point, but because she'd seen it.

"It doesn't have to be someone from the past," he said slowly, watching her. "It just has to be someone who knows that I was the suspect in your sister's murder and have paid for it ever since. Someone who's warning me that the past might repeat itself in the present, with the other twin."

The words were cold. Harsh. Because the truth was.

That was the world in which he lived. The world in which she was currently standing.

But he got her point.

"And whether we work together or separately isn't going to make a difference, in terms of the threat, is it?"

He posed the thought as a question, but he didn't need to see Morgan's headshake to know the answer.

Chapter 7

She'd made a mistake, agreeing to meet in Blade's home. Searching it had been in the plan from the beginning, but having dinner there? Working with him?

What in the hell had she been thinking, suggesting that the phone threat that had come in had been of a personal nature, based on their youthful romance seventeen years before? She blanched at the thought of having said such a thing.

Was beyond embarrassed that her client had had to point out the more likely scenario to her.

He'd been publicly held accountable for Maddie's death. Anyone who knew about the case, had read about the case, could conclude that he wouldn't want the other twin to show up dead. Most particularly not right after the deceased twin's boyfriend had been found murdered at his feet.

"We can't get you out of danger." Blade spoke as though they were no more than professional associates. "But we need to take precautions to minimize your exposure to life-threatening situations."

The statement, while sweet, made her smile. In a professional-only way. "Again, ex–FBI agent here," she said. "I've spent the past fifteen years making enemies of the worst kind. And I'm trained to protect myself."

"So you've reported the tan car? And the black one?" he asked, and any response Morgan might have made froze on her tongue.

She'd given the information to him first...had entrusted it to him before taking it anywhere else... What did that mean?

And even if it meant nothing, what would it mean to him?

She couldn't have him drawing any false impressions about why he was there. Or in any way insinuate that the things she'd thought she'd felt for him in the past were real.

"No. I haven't been able to get license plates. Which is what really bothered me the most. It's like whoever is doing this, if there really is someone, is good enough at it to know how to position himself so that I can't ever get a look at the plate." She came up with the valid answer in time to save face.

Blade sprang into action as soon as she'd finished the words. Taking a step toward her. She backed up, heart pounding, feeling apprehension, not fear, until he turned and grabbed a television control off the table. Clicked it toward a large screen hung on the far wall of the room.

"That black car was on the lot after it had been cordoned off as a crime scene," he was saying as he clicked and scrolled.

She stared at him. Somewhat aghast at his sudden intensity. Not fearful, but not sure about him, either.

"There's a long thin scrape in the tint on the front passenger window," he added.

She continued to stare. Either the man had lost all cognitive ability, or he was about to impress her.

"When I saw the car behind you at the light, I thought it was there because of me. Watching me. I'm home, so it makes sense that they'd be keeping an eye on my neighborhood." He'd brought up security camera screens. She recognized the crime scene. Remembered that the lot was currently under the control of Carmichael Construction. Realized that the cameras she'd seen there were his. Not the landowner's.

He glanced over and said, "I was found with a dead body at my feet, with only my word to verify that I didn't put it there. When everyone started questioning me, I zoned out for a couple of seconds. Stared at the damaged tinting on the window." He didn't even pause for breath as he continued, "The evidence is circumstantial—no one can prove I didn't put it there, or, more importantly, prove that I harmed Shane Wilmington. But, just like in the past, a lot of people will be convinced that I made history repeat itself. That I found a way to commit murder a second time without being charged." His green eyes stayed focused right on her without a flinch.

Morgan, feeling the blow of the words, had to school herself not to show any reaction. Not to recoil.

He was including her in that community of opinion who believed him guilty, not only of her sister's murder, but also of Shane's. She'd spent seventeen years with the knowledge that he'd killed her twin. And wouldn't be honest with herself, or be any kind of decent detective at all, if she didn't consider that the second murder was also on him.

"I can't figure out why you'd kill Shane and stand there with his body and call the police." The words came out of their own accord. A truth that she'd have chosen to withhold at that point, had she been at the Bureau, in an interrogation room or even a conference room.

As opposed to being in the home of the man with whom she'd once thought herself forever in love.

Her past association with Blade, what she'd thought she'd felt, what she'd promised, didn't matter. Had no bearing.

So why did they keep rearing up to blindside her by throwing shadows on what should be clear?

"Why would I kill him at all, after seventeen years of getting away with murder?"

The question came quietly. Introspectively. A question Jasmine might have asked her, putting herself in the perp's mindset as they tried to figure out a case.

Blade's words drew her gaze to him, kept it there as she said, "What if he knew something that could prove that you were guilty of murder? What if for some reason he suddenly decided to confront you with it…some change that compelled him to come forward…say, a real estate deal? There would be a lot of money to be made if the right contractor would take the job and be willing to skate on certain inspections…" The words flowed as they came to her. Holding sound logic.

Believable motivation. Pieces falling together.

But for the first time in her career, Morgan didn't want to follow them to see where they'd lead.

Her words reminded Blade of ones he'd issued to her earlier that day. But somehow they didn't carry the sting they might have. He didn't dwell on the realization. "So what is my reason for calling the police with the dead body in the pit at my feet?" he parried when Morgan fell silent.

She stared at him a minute. And then, eyes opening wider, said, "To throw suspicion off you. Who'd call the police on themselves, and then not confess, right? But that doesn't really work because in your line of work you could so easily dispose of the body in a pit, pour cement for a foundation and be done with it."

For a second there, he was shocked, hearing the words come from Morgan Davis's mouth. And then he was glutted with guilt. The change in her...that a mind that had once danced with butterflies and stories of happily-ever-after would be so quick to fill blanks in dark worlds...just seemed...criminal.

"So why else might I have done it?" he asked, drawing his own mind back to the real world. The question was rhetorical. And yet...not. If he knew what she was thinking, what others would conclude, even if he couldn't get a step ahead of them, he could at least keep up.

Morgan's gaze was different. Not soft, but open. "You tell me," she said, dropping down to a seat at the table.

He sat as well. Taking a second to figure out her new tactic. Decided to take her at face value. To give her what she wanted.

So she could deliver what he needed. The truth.

"The only thing I can figure is, he showed up on-site—and would have had to climb the fence because I'd locked the gate behind him—threatened me somehow. I don't know it's him, I'm not expecting anyone, and suddenly there's a guy there. I pull my gun...he lunges toward me, I shoot. He's still coming at me, I knock him down, put my foot on his neck to keep him down...and panic and call the police..." It all fit.

And Blade, hearing his words replay in his head, felt sick. In body, heart and mind. What in the hell had he just done?

"Why would you have pulled your gun?"

"I did, actually, when I heard the noise up above. That dragging-on-the-gravel sound."

"So a guy's above you, has you trapped in a pit with all kinds of heavy equipment around that he could have used to hurt you, and instead, he stands there and lets you pull a gun and remains in your line of fire to let you shoot him?"

"He came down into the pit to confront me," Blade said, compelled by her attentive look to play along with her.

"Or, what if you weren't in the pit when he confronted you? What if things happened as you say, but aboveground? And then, when you realize what you've done, you drag him as you claim happened, dump him in the pit and then climb down and call the police?"

He shook his head. "I'd been taking photos in the pit. They're time stamped. I was definitely in the pit."

Morgan stared at him. "And he'd only been dead less than half an hour, based on liver temperature."

"Right." Didn't mean Blade hadn't killed the guy, just as he'd hypothetically described. He had photos from ten minutes prior to the body landing at his feet. He hadn't had his maps and location system on. Had no way to prove that he'd been on-site for more than half an hour.

She looked at him, oddly, as though he had something more to tell her. Something he wasn't saying. "So why did you call the police?"

"I had a dead body at my feet." He gave her the only explanation he had.

"Exactly." Morgan stood, paced around the table. He watched. Reminding himself of the one truth he'd always had. He was innocent.

When she sat back down, she did so right next to him. Facing him. Leaned forward until her gaze was only inches from his. "I'm not betting my life on this one, Blade. But if this were any other case, I'd risk my career on it."

"On what?"

"You didn't kill Shane."

He sat there, watching her, a bit confused. Looking for

her angle. Ready to meet her head-to-head as soon as he figured out her direction. And when he couldn't catch up soon enough to suit him, he asked, "How do you know that?"

"Because a man who just murdered someone, most particularly if he'd been surprised by an intruder in the dark, would be in panic mode. Locked on his own job site, down in a pit, he'd conceal evidence, at least long enough to think. And if he was someone who broke laws, who skated on inspections, or had anything to hide, he'd sure as hell at least think about hiding that body. An honest man, on the other hand, one who, for whatever reason, has lived an exemplary adult life, without even so much as a speeding ticket, would automatically dial the authorities."

He looked for the trap she might be setting. To see if he'd fall into it. Didn't see one. Didn't mean there wasn't one. She was an expert. "What about the whole plan to make myself innocent by calling in the body? A ploy to draw attention away from myself?"

Her headshake brought a frown to his brow. "A man who's in panic mode doesn't have the wherewithal to come up with such a plan in the space of time between your last photo and your call to the police. And all of that aside, there was no blood found at the site," she said, reminding him of something he'd known, but they hadn't discussed. The wound hadn't been fatal. Someone could have shot Shane, stemmed the flow of blood, kept him alive for an hour or more, before breaking his neck and hauling him into Blade's pit.

"So I shoot him, wrap him, he's still alive, I bring him to the pit, I break his neck, and then call the police," he said, needing to see it all. What the police might see. Detectives. Anyone and everyone who were going to need to prove that he was responsible for both murders, since the two people dead had been in a relationship years ago.

"And take pictures with his body just hanging out?" She rewound footage he'd paused on the screen—the black car. How had he let himself get distracted from finding the plate?

He had to get the woman out of his house.

She'd stopped the scroll on the screen. And he saw himself, in the pit. Taking photos. No body there.

Weary, he continued to play along until the end. "I left the body up top while I took pictures and then…" His words dropped off as she scrolled again. And stopped the footage. Scrolling forward, and then back, several times.

"Do you see that?" she asked.

Now what? He watched the screen. Once…twice. Paying more attention as she waited for him to figure out which tangent she'd jumped to.

And then sat up. "There's a break in the footage," he said. "The clock shows no break, but right there, it's like…"

"The camera was somehow stopped and restarted, without the clock showing a discrepancy," Morgan said softly. "You could very well have stopped the camera yourself, to allow you to move the body over, and somehow manipulated the timing afterward, but before…there's no break in the clock from the time your men leave until you arrive. And after you arrive, where there's the break in footage, you have time stamped photos on your phone to prove you were in the pit. Not aboveground…"

Glancing over at her, meeting her gaze, Blade started forward, to pull her into his arms. Stopped just in time, but couldn't quell the emotion glazing his eyes for a second, as he heard her say, "You did not kill Shane Wilmington. And neither, by the way, did I."

With that she stood up, walked to her end of the table and started to remove files from her satchel.

Morgan had to retreat to her corner while she tamped down the flood of relief flowing through her as she allowed herself to accept that Blade hadn't murdered Maddie's boyfriend. She'd been struggling to see him responsible for it. Had needed the proof.

And had to get herself in check, too, if she was going to do her job. A job for which he was paying handsomely.

She'd wanted to take his hand as she'd watched truth dawn on him. She'd cared. Personally. And couldn't let that happen, period.

If she found proof that Blade thought she'd never find, that he'd killed her sister, she'd be in the front row in the courtroom, giving testimony as to why the man should be put away for the rest of his life with no possibility of parole.

The doorbell rang. She didn't even look up as he left to answer it. Nor did she intend to move anywhere else to eat. She'd take her salad with files, thank you.

She had to find justice for Maddie. She had no future without it.

And whether she liked what she found or not, she had to be able to see the elusive clue when it presented itself. She had to be 100 percent.

By the time he returned, placing a bag next to her and taking another to his end of the table, she had her focus back on the television screen, going through frame by frame, as she watched for the black sedan to appear on-screen.

The reason he'd turned on the cameras in the first place.

Glancing up at the screen, as though noting what she was doing, he said, "I have wine, tea, coffee or beer."

"I'd like water," she told him. Maybe to be querulous,

to put some walls between them, but also because it was what she really wanted with her dinner.

And by the time he returned with a tall glass filled with ice and water, and a full French loaf overpowering the small cutting board that the bread and a knife sat on, she had the image on the screen frozen again. Pointed toward it, rather than acknowledging that she'd been served.

"Look. I've been through the whole thing. There's no front plate, and the car backs into the parking spot at the edge of the lot, right in front of a line of trees. When it leaves—" she scrolled more "—it pulls forward just enough to back out of the lot onto the street, at an angle that precludes the cameras from catching the plate number."

"A coincidence? Piece of bad luck for us?"

Us. Just hearing the word come out of his mouth, referring to them… No.

Just. No.

"More likely we're dealing with a professional." She focused on what mattered most. Finding the answers that would end one part of a seventeen-year nightmare.

"Everyone had to have credentials to get on the lot."

"I drove in. My credentials weren't checked until I approached the scene. And…to your point, you thought law enforcement was keeping a tail on you. We don't know that they aren't."

Sitting at his end of the table, opening a container that released mouth-watering aromas, he looked over at her. "The black car followed you to the restaurant, and probably here. And the tan car, possibly following you to Detroit and back?"

She shrugged. "As you said, I show up at a crime scene, with no formal invitation, just after dawn, from across the state. The dead man happens to be the pseudo-boyfriend of my deceased sister, and the potential suspect is the man long suspected of killing my twin. I've recently walked off a prestigious job with the FBI—albeit to join an equally prestigious private firm of experts—and it's well-known that I've been investigating Madison's death privately ever since it happened. I'd almost fault the local police if they didn't keep some kind of tabs on me. If for no other reason than to make certain that when I find who did this, I don't go rogue and take justice into my own hands." Hearing her words, listening to reason, Morgan felt some of the immediate tension draining out of her. Opened her bag and pulled out the largest, loaded chef salad she'd ever seen, with meats that were clearly fresh cut, and tomatoes that shone with ripeness. "Where did you get this?" she asked him, figuring she'd visit the place again, if she ended up in town long enough.

"Ruby's," he told her. "On Main Street. I ordered the family portion."

Of course he had. Blade Carmichael had been the guy everyone went to when they needed something. At least among the counselors. He was the always-prepared guy. If he didn't have something, he'd figure out a way to make do with something else.

Which had intrigued her no end. The way he always seemed to have what they needed or come up with alternative solutions. The single most important quality that had drawn her to the younger version of the man. Even more than his steaming-hot looks.

The trait had definitely led him to impressive professional accomplishments. Just looking at the little bit she'd seen of his home, she could understand why Carmichael Construction was such a huge success.

And always-prepared guys, who could figure out ways

to get things done in various ways, would fit the profile of a man getting away with murder.

Ignoring the big loaf of bread for the moment, she took a bite of her salad. Had difficulty swallowing.

Now you know how it feels.

Her gaze moved up and out, landing in his direction without her full consent. He had an empty fork in hand. Was watching her. Frowning. But looked more bothered than angry.

Wouldn't a guilty man get angry when he couldn't convince someone of his innocence? Because that suspicion hanging out there meant he wasn't succeeding. Not well enough.

He looked away. Grabbed a napkin, dropped it—on his lap, she surmised—and took a bite.

"I'm not sure you didn't do it." As soon as she said the words, she wanted to take them back. Hoped that she'd said them softly enough he hadn't heard.

The way his gaze shot back to her put the death to that hope. "Shane, you mean?"

She shook her head. "My current theory is that you did not kill Shane. I don't believe you did," she further enhanced her response. She wasn't positive he hadn't, because she couldn't be, not without the proof.

Which left only one other option. The one that had broken them apart, and because of that, would always be between them. Separating them.

Just because she now knew how it felt, to be suspected of something she hadn't done, didn't mean he hadn't done it.

And still…

"I'm sorry that I didn't at least listen to what you had to say." She put down her fork. Wasn't the least bit hungry.

Picked up the bread, yanking an end off the loaf with her fingers. Needing to get back to work.

To have her focus only on the job. Where it served her, and others, in a positive manner.

Dwelling on the past…sitting with an ache that would never die…weakened her.

Apparently not nearly as off his game as she was hers, Blade continued to eat. Seemingly engrossed in the food, the experience. He hadn't looked up at her at all.

Morgan took small sips from her glass. Letting the cool, clear fresh liquid slide down her throat. Soothing it. Ripped a small bit from the piece of bread she held. Found a note of pleasure in the homemade taste as it rested on her tongue.

"You went to the party when you told me you weren't going to." There. That.

A pain that still had the power to undermine her determination to let it go. She sounded like a jealous high schooler, not a renowned investigator who'd put serial killers in prison. In those moments, some of the things roiling through her, she felt a little like that teenage kid.

Because he'd broken her trust. In himself, and in her own heart, too. A result that didn't live just in the past, but was a very real part of every minute of her life since.

Joining forces with Blade Carmichael had been a logical, professional choice. Clearly not a good personal one. The surge of feelings, of young doubts, of broken trust… she hadn't expected them. Didn't have a plan in place to deal with the onslaught.

Distraction, focusing on the case, her usual cure, wasn't working. Not with Blade sitting there eating in his usual constructive way. One bite at a time. Making his way through his meal to reach a clean-plate accomplishment.

Or a full-stomach one.

He had a reason for everything he did.

So why had he approached her that morning so long ago, reaching his arms out, looking as though he'd seen a ghost?

To beg for her forgiveness?

Or…

Or what? Tell her he hadn't done it? Clung to her as the only person who'd believe him? Because if he hadn't killed Maddie, his entire, well-ordered, constructive world had been crashing around him and he'd had no one who cared to hold him up. To stand in his corner. To vouch for him in any way.

Shaking her head, denying the images springing to mind, she dropped the bread. Picked up her fork.

Didn't matter what he might have said. She hadn't given him a chance to speak.

Maybe if she had, he'd have uttered whatever had been on his clearly stricken heart. He'd have let loose that elusive small clue that could solve her twin sister's murder.

Certainly, if she had, she'd have a key to dealing with the man in the present. Maybe even a smidgen of his trust, something that would lead him to let his guard down.

And maybe, if she hadn't been so filled with dreams of Blade in the past, her first and only love, she'd have noticed that Maddie hadn't been at all her usual, winding-down self when they'd met in the large girls' bathroom to brush their teeth that night. She'd have paid more attention when Maddie hadn't seemed to notice two of her campers hiding in one of the showers, sharing an extra snack, a candy bar, after the no-more-sugar hour had passed.

Maybe, when they'd told each other "Good night, sleep tight," she'd have known that Maddie was planning to sneak out of her cabin as soon as her girls were asleep, not go to bed herself.

Maybe, if she could get her head out of her ass, she could find justice for all of them and put the past behind her.

Chapter 8

Blade finished the meal he cared little about. He'd paid for it, would be hungry if he didn't consume it, and it wouldn't be good reheated.

And then he looked over at the woman he'd alternated between needing and hating during the first couple of years after his life had blown up in his face.

She was eating, but judging by the amount of food left in front of her, she'd barely touched the dinner he'd provided. To her specification. Down to the dressing.

Perhaps there was some lesson in that for him. If he wanted to bother to unravel it.

He didn't.

"I apologize for my parting shot as you left the office this afternoon." He said what had to be said. They weren't teenagers.

And her sister's death, and his having been pegged for the crime, were in no way her fault.

The rest…that was personal.

And they, in their modern-day manifestations, were not.

She'd stopped eating to look over at him.

"It was unprofessional," he said, putting the period on the topic.

He wasn't close enough to be sure about the emotion he thought might have flared in that striking blue-eyed gaze, but found himself hanging there, waiting for her response, when the pealing of her ringtone crashed into the moment.

A move clearly designed by fate, Blade determined as he left her to her conversation, taking his empty dinner container and iced tea glass into the kitchen to dispose of them.

He ended up taking the container, and the bag it came in, to the bigger trash receptacle in the garage, so he wouldn't overfill the smaller kitchen one.

So he could get out of his house, out of the confusion slithering through his world, for a second.

Morgan was still on the phone when he returned. He couldn't make out her words, but the tone of voice didn't sound good. Short. Tense.

Angry? He couldn't tell.

And figured he'd best get back into the dining room and find out. The call might not be about their joint efforts, at all. She had a life.

But it could be...

He got no farther than the double door opening to the room, had a glimpse of Morgan's tight lips as she paced, when there was a loud knock on his front door, followed by the ringing of the bell.

For some reason, a glimpse of Morgan's generous-looking uneaten salad accompanied him as he answered the summons.

Something big was going on.

Dread filled his gut, hardened it as he pulled open the door.

Saw the two Rocky Springs detectives standing there, their faces grim.

And knew better than to turn around, to seek any kind of information or understanding from the woman he heard coming up behind him. That phone call...

Had she known they were about to have visitors?
And hadn't warned him?
Did it matter?
The cops were at his home.
And once again, he was on his own.

Shaking inside, cold, but managing to find her professional distance, too, Morgan followed as Blade led the investigators, one male, one female, into a formal living room she hadn't yet seen. The furnishings, dark leather, were offset by the light-colored porcelain flooring and lighter-colored wool rug. Tasteful. Elegant.

And seemingly completely unlived in. Other than a little dust, she saw nothing that indicated any form of life took place in that room.

There wasn't even a television set.

A shame, too, as it had a lovely bay window overlooking the front of his property, which, she knew, was lined with pine trees. In the dark, the window looked out over darkness and shadows.

Darkness and shadows. Like Blade's life?

As precise as he was about all his choices, she couldn't help but wonder if the design was purposeful. The back of his property had a beach view.

Looking from the window to the man who'd obviously built his own home, she kept her mind as blank as she could. Needing to hear facts, to assess truth, to make sense of a situation escalating so far out of control she couldn't find a starting point. A place to begin investigating.

"Have a seat, Blade," James Silver, the male detective, said. Inviting a man to sit in his own home.

Blade didn't question the police presence in his home. Didn't react to being ordered around there, either. He simply sat. On the chair closest to the room's exit. Facing the window.

Standing back, also close to the door, but within view of Blade's face, Morgan itched to pull out her phone, to record the coming moments. To be able to watch them later. She had no permission to do so.

Life wasn't an instant replay.

The female detective—Kaycee Blakenship, her badge read—took a seat on the couch, the corner closest to Blade, while her partner sat down beside her. Morgan spared both of them a brief glance. Didn't recognize either from the crime scene.

James had called Blade by his first name. Meaning they knew each other?

Wasting less than twenty seconds of her attention on the detectives, she returned her full focus back to the man who was paying her to be there. He wanted her to find the truth.

He could be underestimating her ability to do so. Figuring she wouldn't get to it and would, thus, keep him out of jail. But she wasn't feeling it.

And feelings weren't truth. She couldn't trust them.

"We need to know your whereabouts this afternoon, Blade," James spoke first.

Morgan watched Blade—his face, his hands...looking for any sign body language might give her. She knew what was coming. The next minutes were critical.

"I was here," Blade said. Then, when he glanced between the three investigators who were all looking at him, said, "I left the crime scene, came home to shower and then met Ms. Davis for breakfast." He named the diner. "I was there for fifty-four minutes, left and drove straight home, parking my truck in my garage. I came in, put a load of clothes in the washer, waited for the cycle to finish, put the clothes in the dryer and took a nap. I'd been up almost twenty-eight hours…"

"You washed clothes?" Kaycee's tone wasn't unkind, but it was clearly pointed.

"I did, yes," Blade said. And for the first time, he looked down for a second. Broke himself away from the interrogation he'd been unexpectedly shoved into. Morgan's heart rate doubled. A rapid tattoo spelling horror.

"Mind telling me what you washed?"

Blade didn't have to answer any questions. Hadn't had to let the investigators into his home. He could lawyer up at any point.

In that second, Morgan wanted him to do so. Had to physically restrain herself from interrupting to tell him to do so.

He looked over at her. To get her advice? She took a step toward him, but he'd turned back to the suited detectives on his couch. "My underwear," he told them.

And Morgan stepped back.

"Your underwear." Kaycee's tone held…doubt.

"Yes."

"One pair?"

Oh God, the man had soiled himself during the night's events and this woman was going to drill him about it?

"No." Blade's chin tightened. "The week's worth that were in the laundry."

"You washed only your underwear."

"Yes."

"Mind telling us why?" James's tone was softer. More curious than antagonistic.

With a raised brow, Blade glanced straight at the man. "Because I'd just hired Morgan to investigate every aspect of my life. She'd mentioned going through my dirty laundry, and I washed the underwear." He shrugged. Threw up his hands. And sat there. As if daring any of the three of them to have a problem with his choice.

Morgan had a problem with him sharing it. Most particularly when the other two detectives' gazes turned, simultaneously, to her.

What could she say to defuse the situation? That she'd used the dirty-laundry analogy figuratively? That he was on his own? That she'd had nothing to do with Blade's activities that day?

That she could vouch for him?

Tell them to leave?

With another dead body out there?

She threw up a hand, tilted her head and kept her mouth shut.

She held no keys to the truth.

But Blade might.

Blade heard the newest development from the two detectives, each taking turns, back and forth, with their details.

While he sat in stunned disbelief.

Mark Hampton was dead.

Dr. Mark Hampton. Camp therapist, and kayak coach. One of the few personnel who worked both girls' and boys' sides of camp.

He'd been found dead, slumped over an opened drawer of his desk in his office. Poisoned.

With a ripped Carmichael Construction business card just out of reach of his outstretched hand. As though he'd been reaching for it when he'd passed out. Had been trying to let law enforcement know who'd poisoned him.

A used syringe had been in the trash, with no fingerprints. And the angle at which it had gone in the man's neck ruled out suicide. Death had been almost instantaneous.

There'd been no sign of a struggle, leading authorities to believe that the doctor had likely known whoever had killed him.

"I've never purchased, nor used, a syringe in my life," he said quietly, when the two finally stopped talking.

"A twelve-pack box of the kind used, with one missing from the package, was found in a Carmichael Construction dumpster an hour ago," James Silver advised, his tone somber. Blade knew the older man. Had built a shed for the guy with his own hands when he'd first been starting out.

"That's a little convenient, don't you think?" he asked, refusing to look in Morgan's direction. Unwilling to see those vivid blue eyes sparking with accusation again. Been there done that. And the memory of the first time, the vision he'd never been able to wipe from his mind, was enough to last a dozen lifetimes.

Put that in a syringe and shoot it.

"Sierra's Web thinks so." Morgan's voice, not tentative, but not filled with determination, either, sounded off to his right. "We've got Blade's home security camera feed on tape, as well," she added, surprising the hell out of him. Not regarding the camera feed; he'd willingly turned it over to her firm of experts. But that she sounded as though she was defending him…

"We see him arriving home this morning, as stated, and then no movement from the garage camera until he left for work late this afternoon, also as stated. I also, um, just checked the laundry as you two were speaking. Several days of dirty clothes in the basket. No underwear."

If it were possible for Blade to feel any more humiliated,

he didn't want to know about it. But wasn't going to cower. Or make any mistakes, either.

Life was exploding out of control. Two deaths in two days? Both pointing at him?

Both connected to that godawful summer camp?

Panic sluiced through him, but he tamped it down.

He knew how to play the game. Stay calm. Pay attention. Show them as little as possible and get as much information as he could. All of which would be carried straight to his dining room as soon as he was alone.

"Blade could have left this afternoon, on foot, through a window not covered on camera," Detective Blakenship was pointing out. The fact had been hanging there. Had to be said. "The cameras are his. He'd know exactly where and how to escape."

Blade continued to watch the detectives, as he'd been doing since they'd started talking. Morgan had left the room…had been going through his laundry basket…while he'd been put on notice that yet a third murder was being planted on his shoulders. The fact stung. All parts of it.

But she'd returned. To point to the possibility of his innocence.

Nice. Still, no reason to rejoice.

He was paying her firm a hefty sum. And they had a team of expert lawyers. They were doing their jobs. He couldn't let himself believe Morgan's words were anything more than that.

He'd broken her trust. She'd as much as told him so, earlier, right after apologizing for breaking his.

"Am I under arrest?" he asked, when the detectives glanced in his direction. They didn't have enough to charge him, but they had enough circumstantial evidence to hold him for a day or two.

Blakenship looked at James, who shook his head and stood. "I agree with Ms. Davis, for now," he said. "There's evidence that you're telling the truth. And while other evidence points at you, it doesn't necessarily touch you. But I have to ask you, for your own sake, please don't leave town."

He had no intention of going anywhere.

Not unless he had to, to find Madison's, Shane's and Dr. Hampton's killer.

Morgan left soon after the detectives did. Blade's suggestion, and one she felt she had to honor. He'd closed himself off.

A move she understood.

If he remained uncommunicative, she'd take herself off the job. There was no point in working with him if he wasn't going to be open with her.

But the third death—and pointing at him—it just didn't make sense that he'd done it.

He could be some kind of mentally disturbed individual who was playing them all, but she didn't think so. There were no signs at all of erratic behavior.

And no absences in his daily routine. Sierra's Web had been through his finances. His credit card usage was conservative, predictable and regular. The man hadn't taken a trip in years.

He owned a boat, docked at the marina in town. That had been news to her. Something that lightened her load for a second as she'd heard Glen rattle off, with no inflection in his voice at all, the information the firm had gleaned that day. Right after he'd told her about Hampton's murder—the purpose for his call.

Blade had always wanted a boat. His father, who'd had enough money to buy him ten, had chosen to rent vessels on the few occasions they'd been out on Lake Michigan. He'd preferred flying, traveling to far-off places. Just as Maddie had always talked about wanting to do.

While Morgan and Blade…hadn't.

The cabin cruiser was a decent size and had been searched that morning by the Rocky Springs police. Glen had forwarded all reports to her, another reason she'd left Blade as soon as he'd asked that she do so. She needed to get back to the hotel, to assess everything Glen had sent, without Blade looking over her shoulder. Filling in any blanks, filling her mind, before she had time to assess for herself.

She'd draw her own conclusions, come up with her own theories—and then listen to his. Put them in the mix.

Something very clearly wasn't adding up. Why, after seventeen years, had there suddenly been two new murders? Were they connected by the killer?

Or something else?

Were they looking at only one killer? Detective Silver hadn't seemed any more sure of that than Morgan was. Even if Blade had killed Madison, why would he suddenly start killing again?

And do so in such a way that put him in the spotlight?

Unless he wanted to get caught? Couldn't live any longer with the guilt?

But then, why not just turn himself in?

He could be playing them all. The possibility was there. The man was quiet. Somewhat of a loner, other than his work. His employees, his crews, all spoke highly of him, she'd been told. He paid better than average wages. Ran a tight ship, but was clear in his expectations, and fair. According to what Glen had told her, he had an army of supporters at Carmichael Construction.

A revelation that she'd been pleased to hear. For the case, yes, but for him as well.

So…was she softening toward her sister's killer?

The thought had Morgan on the car's audio system halfway through town, instructing the female voice to dial Jasmine. If they were looking at a serial killer, her ex-partner should be on the case. Could take over jurisdiction.

Morgan didn't trust easily, if at all, but Jasmine was someone she'd learned to rely on more than anyone else when something wasn't clear to her.

Her friend picked up on the first ring. Was relieved to hear from Morgan. Agreed that, at least with the two recent kills, they could have a spree on their hands, said she'd look into the case and get back to Morgan in the morning.

Her tension easing, though she hadn't mentioned that she might be swaying on the idea that Blade Carmichael was her sister's killer, Morgan pulled into the hotel parking lot. There'd been no sign of a black, tan or any other color vehicle following her. Relieved, hoping that Blade had been right and the local police had been keeping an eye on her, she pushed the button to turn off her car, and gathered her satchel, putting it over her shoulder before getting out.

If the police had suspected her in Shane's killing, Hampton's death should have eased their minds on that one. She'd been east, in Detroit, and then at her hotel during the time frame she'd have been needing to drive an hour straight north to kill the doctor. As they'd know if they'd been following her.

The satchel was heavy, but Morgan, while mourning for the doctor she'd barely known, felt lighter, walking toward the hotel, glancing off at the marina lights in the distance, curious about Blade's boat.

He'd wanted three of them. A pontoon, for larger gatherings. A speedboat. And a cabin cruiser. According to Glen, he'd ended up with just the last choice. Which, considering how his life had changed so drastically that last morning she'd seen him, made sense. Blade in his current state didn't seem the type to need high-speed thrills or do much par...oomph.

A grasp out of the darkness, the back of her arm...

Morgan spun on instinct, ducked, grabbed body parts and swung. Only realizing what she'd done when she had a dark-clothed body on the ground, her low-heeled dress shoe planted in the middle of the guy's stomach, right between the ribs, and her gun pointed at his head.

"Move and you're dead," she said, letting her anger spew through her tone, as, adrenaline pumping through her, she grabbed her phone with her free hand and dialed 911.

Her pulse was jumping as Morgan ended the call, but she didn't budge a muscle from her stance. Wouldn't hesitate to use her weapon if the guy dared to move.

Seventeen years of training, of being on guard...of waiting.

Could it really be as easy as a single flip to the ground to catch the guy? The young kid staring up at her with wide eyes and a bit of a nervous look about him wasn't the killer. He couldn't be more than eighteen or nineteen, if that. Certainly not old enough to have been at camp or killed Madison.

But he could be someone hired by the killer. Whether the guy's job had been to warn Morgan off, kill her or kidnap her, she didn't know. But as she stared silently at that face, her foot rising and falling with the guy's frantic breathing, she knew she wasn't going anywhere until she found out.

Chapter 9

Blade was still sitting at his dining room table when he saw James Silver's name pop up on his caller ID. He considered hitting End Call. Sending the summons to voicemail.

He could be in bed. Could turn his phone off, or sleep through a call.

But he didn't. Avoidance was not the answer.

"Yeah," he answered, bracing himself for whatever new evidence had shown up in the Hampton case, pointing at him. Reminding himself that every piece of bad news was really a clue that would lead him closer to the true killer.

Or killers. He couldn't get it out of his head that there might be two of them. That someone from the past was, for some unknown reason, resurrecting Blade's nightmare, for some completely unrelated reason.

Maybe a predisposed killer who preyed on those who'd seemingly gotten away with murder? So that *he* could? Do the deed with deflected blame…

His mind had been in high gear since he'd seen the detectives at his door, processing even as he'd drawn inside himself, but the second he heard what Silver had to say, that Morgan had been jumped in the hotel parking lot, Blade was grabbing his keys and heading for the door.

"I'm on my way," he said.

"She's fine…just…" Silver's voice grew faint and then abruptly disappeared as Blade ended the call.

He had Morgan on the line before he was in his truck. Heard for himself that she was fine—in her hotel room without a scratch—and told her that he was on his way.

He didn't wait for her to tell him not to come. Didn't give her the chance. He hung up as he started the truck and took every ounce of self-control he had in him to keep to the speed limit as he made it across town. If her life had been at stake, he'd have justification for speeding.

Knowing that she was fine, he had no excuse.

Adrenaline and a lifetime of suppressed emotions pushing to the core were not reasons to break the law.

But as soon as he'd parked his truck in the first spot he came to on the hotel lot, he was out and running for the entrance. Taking the stairs up to her floor two at a time. No way he was waiting for an elevator.

But as he opened the stairwell door to enter her floor, and his mind's eye got sight of himself, he stopped, took a couple of deep breaths, before walking more calmly to Morgan's door.

He rapped twice. She opened the door almost immediately. Let him in and quickly closed it behind him. Still in the beige pants and white top she'd had on, same beige pumps, too. He had to agree with James Silver—she looked none the worse for her ordeal.

Blade smiled.

"What?"

"Whoever would have thought you'd grow up to take down grown men like it was a walk in the park?"

Her gaze darkened and he realized the mistake of his words too late to take them back. She hadn't simply grown up to be a superhero. She'd been changed and completely shaped by her sister's death.

Which hung there between them, again.

Always.

Didn't diminish how much he was impressed by her abilities, though.

Two steps farther into the room, he recognized his second mistake. The place was small. Minuscule. A mouse house. While he was standing there at any rate.

For hotel rooms, it was pretty standard.

The bed. A love seat. A desk and large counter with refrigerator and microwave. A closet and bathroom. A big mirror on the side wall that pretty much showed the whole place and everyone in it.

He'd hung up on her before she'd been able to tell him not to come.

"I picked up some beer downstairs," she told him, grabbing the handle of the refrigerator door. "I don't know about you, but I could use one after this day." She took a can, held one out to him.

No way he could stay in that room and drink a beer with Morgan Davis. Even the can of light stuff she was holding out to him.

He apparently didn't have it in him to refuse her, either. He took the can. And before he could do anything further to misstep, she walked away, toward the wall of curtains, throwing the sheer open to reveal a door handle. She pulled, and when he realized there was a balcony out there, Blade practically ran to accompany her outside.

Not really. He maintained his outward decorum. Managed his stride.

But he figured that door as his get-out-of-jail-free card.

The Morgan Davis jail he'd have been in had he attempted to sit on that bed and drink a beer with her.

He wouldn't have touched her.

But he didn't trust himself not to have blurted out something inappropriate. Like how he'd never found anyone even remotely like her…

Or how glad he was that she was working with him to find the truth.

How having her there was bringing him new hope—even as whoever was committing the current murders was squeezing the breath out of him.

He'd escaped charges in the past. There was no guarantee he would again.

The balcony was more spacious than he'd expected. And the sound of the waves, racing up on the beach and receding…he couldn't have scripted a better next step.

Dropping to the seat Morgan had left remaining when she sat on one side of the square table, he opened the beer. Took a drink. And held the can in both hands at his belt as he looked out into the night, letting the breeze, the night, wash away some of his tension.

But only some of it. They'd "discussed" their good news. She was fine.

They had a lot more business to discuss. None of it good.

"So who is he?" he asked, after just one more sip.

"You don't know? Silver said he was calling you."

Yeah, well… "As soon as I'd heard you were attacked, were okay and in your hotel room, I hung up and called you."

His words were revealing. He said them anyway. He'd promised her the truth.

"He's a homeless kid," Morgan said, her tone professional. Acknowledging nothing off about his proclamation.

"Said some guy approached him on the beach just before I got out of my car, said he'd heard that the kid was a pickpocket, purse snatcher, and let him know that there was a woman staying at the hotel with a lot of cash. Said he described me and my satchel..."

"What?" Blade sat forward, looking over at her. Morgan was looking at him, too. Her eyes glistening pricks of light in the darkness.

"I know."

"Why would someone do that? Did he make a deal for half the money?"

"You'd think so, but no. The kid was clearly in need of some cash, new to the beach, and the guy said he wanted to help him out."

"Did he get a description, I hope?"

He should have expected Morgan's headshake. Her entire demeanor had already told him what he'd needed to know. He just hadn't been on the right page.

He'd been thinking she didn't want him there.

He'd been making it personal.

"He said it was dark, the guy was dressed in dark clothes, wearing a hoodie. Had a blanket around his shoulders so he couldn't tell much. Figured he was homeless, too, because he was barefoot, though he didn't know if he'd seen him around before. Didn't recognize his voice or think he'd talked to him. The kid had been lying down behind the public restroom, and didn't stand up until after the guy was gone. His parents are in Chicago, have been looking for him and are already on their way here," she finished.

He got the feeling she was ready for the conversation on the subject to be over as well, though she wasn't rushing through her beer, or seeming in any hurry to get up from her chair. She'd kicked off her shoes, pulling her knees up to her chest. Was hugging her shins.

Something he'd teased her about doing in the past. Telling her that he was jealous of those appendages.

Why was he even having the thought?

He couldn't remember so many details of the night of her sister's murder. Of the party. Hadn't been able to tell police definitively who'd all been there. Or what exact time he'd returned to his cabin. But he could remember a sixteen-year-old Morgan hugging her shins?

Her legs had been bare. She'd had on shorts…

Glancing from her hands to her face, he said, "You know someone is warning you off," he said. "The text to me… being followed… Someone had to have known you were just arriving back at the hotel and had gone down to the beach to find this guy."

She nodded. Her face seeming tense as his eyes adjusted to the dark.

"Question is, did he want the kid to kill me, hurt me or kidnap me?" she asked, turning her head toward him. "Silver said the beach has a regular homeless population, though they do their best to get everyone places to sleep for the night. But early evening, there are always people out there. So this guy, our perp, he knows that. And just gets unlucky enough to approach a kid on the beach who was too far gone to follow direction?"

He shook his head. "Wait, didn't you say he told the kid he knew he was a pickpocket?"

"Yeah." Morgan's tone was as calm, as lacking in inflection, as he'd ever heard it. He noted the moment for later assessment. "And it turns out the kid has a few priors for just that. It's how he supports his drug addiction. He's been on the streets on and off for a couple of years. Give or take stints at home with his folks while they try to help him."

Blade sat forward. "You're telling me this guy *knew* he was a pickpocket?"

"Yeah," she said again. Took a sip of her beer, casually, as though watching the moon rise up over the lake was all that mattered. Like she had all night to do it, too. "Which means very little," she said after she'd put her can back down on the table. "People who frequent the streets figure out who's who and what's what pretty quickly…"

"Law enforcement, people who work in the system, the courts and jail…they'd know, too," he said, having lost every hint of relaxation. "Someone wants you off this case pretty badly," he said then, staring at her.

Daring her to see the danger chasing right behind her.

Her nod didn't ease his stress any. "Which is the only good news that's come out of tonight," she said.

"Come again?"

She glanced at him then, shrugged, and said, "I'm obviously making him nervous. Which means we're getting closer to finding him."

He didn't disagree.

But he wasn't willing to see her killed just to clear his own name.

"There's a killer out there, Blade." Her words fell softly on the night air. "It's my job to find him."

Didn't matter if he fired her or not. She wasn't going to quit looking.

"If he wanted me dead, he wouldn't have used a homeless guy on the beach to do it."

She had a good point.

"He's warning me off, but not hurting me."

"Yet."

She acknowledged the point with another sip of beer.

"There are two dead bodies to attest to this guy's threat, Morgie." The name slipped out. He heard it. Couldn't take it back.

"Yeah. This guy has killed at least two people in less than two days," she said. "So why not me? It has to have something to do with that summer at camp," she continued as though they were discussing a book they'd both read. "My sister's death. Your seeming culpability, coupled with a lack of charges. Then all these years later, Shane's dead at your feet, and the very next day, Dr. Hampton is poisoned with your business card near his hand when you don't have an alibi. And I'm merely being warned off."

She looked at him. "Why?" she asked.

"He doesn't blame you." The obvious answer came to Blade. One that rang true to him. Personally. Every time he thought about that summer, the one person he hurt for the most had been Morgan.

Even after she'd betrayed him.

The look on her face, the sheer panic, horror, heartbreak, all mingling into tears and screams and convulsions…

Sitting there with her on her balcony facing the beach, watching her in the darkness, the past came back to him, in a different way. With a clearer understanding.

One that changed no facts.

But altered him.

That morning, when they'd both been woken up to a nightmare that was about to steal their youth, and irrevocably rewrite their futures, he'd been in danger of losing his freedom.

But she'd just lost the other half of her soul.

* * *

Morgan was drinking faster than Blade was. She wasn't driving.

And needed a minute.

While she'd handled the situation well that evening, handled it exactly as she'd have expected, she still didn't relish being attacked from behind.

"He never should have gotten close enough to me to warrant a flip," she said as she emptied the last of her beer and, stepping around Blade, went inside for a second one.

She'd let down her guard, alone, at night, in a parking lot, while working a case. Having been followed throughout the day.

She'd known someone was watching her.

Back outside, she didn't stand at the balcony as she might have done had she been alone. She dropped down to her chair again, setting the beer on the table. She'd take the second one slower. There were hours left in the evening and she had work to do.

The day's reports from Sierra's Web to digest.

And should eat, too. Blade had insisted she bring back the salad and bread she'd hardly touched...

"You berate yourself for not having eyes in the back of your head?"

She looked over at him.

"Letting him get close." He tilted his head toward her as he spoke, his words seeming intimate in the night air they were sharing.

Forcing herself to stare outward, not at him, she said, "I was preoccupied. I never walk in the dark without paying attention to my surroundings. Front, back and sides."

There was so much they had to talk about. All vitally more important than her mental stumble in the parking lot.

She hadn't irreparably damaged the kid. Just knocked the wind out of him. And scared him half to death. All of which he'd deserved.

"You had another death on your mind, Morgan," he said, sounding as though he was trying to reason with someone who should have already gotten the message.

His tone rankled. For no good reason. "No, Blade," she said, looking over at him. "I had your boat on my mind. I was looking over at the marina, not minding my own business."

Whether it was her tone, or the fact that she'd mentally trespassed on his private property, she didn't know, but Blade shut up.

Which disappointed her.

His boat. He'd named it the *M & M*. People thought it was for the famous chocolate candies. Maybe because he always had a bag of them in the refrigerator aboard.

M & M. Morgan and Madison.

He'd let them both down.

And they'd let him down, too.

Maddie, refusing to listen to him about staying away from Shane Wilmington. Blade couldn't prove that the womanizing high schooler had left his cabin of boys again that night. That Shane and Maddie had met up again after the party was over.

But his gut told him that's what had happened.

And Morgan... Well, he understood more clearly how she hadn't had his fear, his possible incarceration, his innocence, on her mind that morning.

Her sister had been the other half of her.

He'd just thought...for a few hours there...that he'd become Morgan's other half. That she'd somehow just know that he'd never, in a million years, have done anything to hurt anyone. Least of all her or her twin.

From the first moment he'd set eyes on Morgan Davis earlier that summer, he'd been filled with a need to protect her happiness. Juvenile, probably. But there it was.

Whether she was interested in him or not. There'd just been something about her that had called to him.

Gaining her attention and affection for himself had been a great bonus. For a split second there, he'd believed her when she'd said that she'd felt the same instant connection to him as he had to her.

Truth was, they'd probably both just been hit by hormones brought on by an intense physical attraction.

"I lived on the boat for a year while I built my house," he told her, leaving the part of the past with her in it where it belonged. Gone forever. "It's got a queen-size berth, and thirty feet of living space down below."

He told her because she'd talked about wanting to have an extended stay on a boat on Lake Michigan. Had wanted to take time to explore her 1,638 miles of shoreline.

He'd told her they'd do it together.

The same night he'd told her he wasn't going to attend the unsanctioned counselor party.

"I went to the party because Shane was going and told me that he was meeting Maddie there." He repeated what he'd told her earlier. "It wasn't like I could run over to the girls' camp and warn you." And back then, cell phones hadn't been allowed at camp. Counselors all had radios that they were to have with them at all times, to communicate in case of emergency. "I threatened to report the party, but he pointed out that if I did so, a whole lot of counselors would be out of jobs. So many that they might have to shut camp down early for the summer. Which meant I wouldn't have had any more time with you." Which was exactly what *had* happened. After Madison's murder that summer, the camp closed, and to his knowledge, never reopened.

His words drifted in the breeze. He and Morgan...they'd been speaking at each other—not to each other—since she'd shown up at the crime scene early that morning.

Which was as it should be. They were clearing air so they could better work together. Period.

Chapter 10

Blade's words conjured up things Morgan couldn't deal with. For seventeen years she hadn't believed in her ability to discern where personal relationships were concerned. She'd lost her ability to trust.

And had grown comfortable with that part of herself.

She wanted to believe that the warmth flooding through her, mixed with a few degrees of relief, was due to the beer she was consuming on a mostly empty stomach.

Blade hadn't lied to her. When he'd told her he wasn't attending the party, he hadn't been. Circumstances had changed, but he didn't get the chance to tell her. He hadn't joined the other rogue counselors to party. He'd attended as a chaperone. Her sister's chaperone.

The fact didn't change what ultimately happened. Nor did it change any of the facts of the three deaths she was investigating.

So she let it lie there, and said, "I'm convinced that you did not kill Dr. Hampton. You were exhausted when I left you at the restaurant this morning. This afternoon at your office, you weren't. No way you could have driven an hour each way, killed a man and been rested."

There was more. She just couldn't believe that Blade would deliberately take another life. She'd figured all along that Maddie's death had been an accident. A fit of rage, maybe, or jealousy. The result of overactive teenage hormones. Not a deliberate choice to take her life.

But Shane and the doctor? Those two acts had not only been deliberate, but clearly planned.

"You're frowning," Blade said, drawing her gaze to his. The moon had risen like a spotlight on the balcony. One that lit and left shadows at the same time.

"What if we're working with a team of killers?" She asked the question aloud as it occurred to her. "It's just not likely that one person would make a plan to pull off two murders, in separate towns, within twenty-four hours, with completely different methods of operation," she said, her FBI training coming to the fore. "At least, not feasible that he'd be able to execute the plan without a flaw. You don't just decide to murder someone and go do it perfectly... and to manage it twice without time for rest, or to glory in the spoils..."

Blade's gaze stayed with hers, as though they were thinking the same thoughts. "But if you were a team, had taken time to plan, with the goal of not only killing, but framing someone else for the murders, you'd each have taken your kill method of choice, would have researched, bounced ideas off each other, probably done trial runs, timing everything perfectly. And working together you'd feed off each other's adrenaline. You wouldn't want to let your partner down..."

"Maybe they're siblings!" The thought only occurred as she opened herself up fully to the scenario he was painting. "We've got to go over that list of campers again." Morgan jumped up. Went to the desk, to her computer, had it on and was typing before she sat down.

Carrying in a chair from outside, Blade sat down beside

and slightly behind her, leaning forward, his elbows on his jean-clad knees as he watched her screen.

"There," he said, reaching forward an arm, almost brushing her cheek, as he pointed.

"Alex and Josh Donnelly," she read aloud. Pulled out her phone and sent a text to Glen Rivers Thomas. Then looked back at the list. "I don't remember them," she said.

Sitting back, Blade shook his head. "I don't, either. They were twelve and thirteen, in with the younger kids…"

Morgan turned, felt Blade's closeness too acutely and stared back at the computer. "If you didn't have any interaction with them, why would they have it in for you to the point of framing you for murders you didn't commit?"

"What if something happened that summer? Something Hampton knew about, or something Shane did to them? What if it's affected them ever since? Maybe one of them took it harder than the other…"

"…and the dominant one," Morgan took over, "fearing for his younger brother's mental health, his ability to ever have a normal healthy life, concocted the idea to get rid of the people involved—thus empowering them both. Taking back the self-esteem they'd lost…"

"And they're framing me maybe because I was technically in charge of Shane, and also because they would have seen what happened the morning after Maddie was killed. I was clearly ostracized. I'm the obvious scapegoat… It's twisted, but clearly whoever is doing this is working with a skewed mental outlook." Blade stood, pacing the room.

With him putting feet between them, Morgan could turn to face him. Looked up at him, her mind flowing at its best. "For all we know, these aren't the first two deaths," she said. "It's possible that they started out smaller, an animal maybe. They could have preyed on someone vulnerable." Picking up her phone, she called Jasmine. Giving her friend a rundown on the theory, including the fact that Sierra's Web was already looking into the Donnellys in all ways they legally could. She needed Jasmine to check out arrest records, databases the FBI had access to. Looking for any unsolved missing persons, or homicides in the cities where either of the brothers had been over the past seventeen years.

"I'll get on it immediately," Jasmine said, her tone warm. Engaged. Just like always. She sounded glad that Morgan had called. "Approval just came through for the FBI to take jurisdiction of the case," she continued. "James Silver will be assisting us."

Relieved to have her ex-partner and friend fully involved, Morgan stared at the computer, not the man behind her, and said, "I'm happy to hear that." Wishing she was free to tell her friend how much she needed her on this one.

"I'm just getting started, but the one thing I can tell you for sure is that you need to steer clear of Blade Carmichael," Jasmine said, her tone carrying more friendship than professionalism. Talking to her as they'd spoken to each other over drinks after hours when they were on the job together.

Morgan's heart thudded. She trusted her friend. And… the man right behind her…she couldn't walk away from him right then. Not in the room, but in that moment in time, either. "I'll do my best," she said, keeping her tone on a squad room level. Suddenly needing the call she'd instigated to end.

"I'm dead serious, Morgan." Jasmine's words held definite warning. "Your reputation, your entire career, is at risk if you associate with, work for, the number-one suspect in a serial killer case and he turns out to be guilty."

Chest tight, Morgan took a breath, looking for the right

words to reassure her friend and end the conversation, too. But before she came up with anything, Jasmine added, "I'm worried about your emotional state, Morg. Worried that you're too intimately involved in both the murder and your past feelings for this man to be objective..."

The woman was most definitely trespassing where she had not been invited.

Had Morgan been alone, she'd have told her ex-partner right then that her mental and emotional health was always on her radar, on every case, and if she thought, for one second, she couldn't do the job, she'd pull herself off from it.

She'd have used her quick instincts in taking down her attacker that evening as proof of her ability to be focused when she had to be.

And then she'd have told Jasmine that she knew Blade hadn't committed at least one of the current murders, and believed he was innocent of both.

As it stood, with Blade pacing by the opened sheers on the French doors of her hotel room, she said, "You've got absolutely nothing to worry about there. Call me when you have something and I'll do the same." She wished her friend well and hung up.

She'd just given her loyalty to Blade, over her ten-year FBI partner and friend.

Neither of them knew that.

But she did.

Just as she knew that while she and Blade were both most definitely too involved in the murders to be completely objective, they were also the two people with the best chance of solving the case. Because they had both spent seventeen years working on it.

That case was the life they'd inadvertently shared, rather

than getting married, making babies and starting a family as they'd both once dreamed they'd do.

Blade couldn't help but notice Morgan's energy drain as she spoke with her ex-partner. Obviously, the conversation hadn't gone as she'd expected it to go.

"She didn't buy our theory, huh?" he asked, wondering how much impact Agent Jasmine Flaherty would have on Morgan's take on the case.

Her shrug didn't seem too threatening. "She's going to look into the Donnelly brothers, but she didn't seem to find as much merit in the idea as we did." She paused, glanced up at him and then said, "And I get it. We find a pair of siblings, know absolutely nothing about them and concoct an entire scenario around their names, making them guilty of two murders."

He nodded. "Yes, but isn't that how this works?" he asked. "You didn't call to have them arrested. Or to alarm anyone. We're just following through on a theory." He couldn't lose her. Not when they were finally working together.

The Donnelly theory could be completely bogus, but it was a starting place. A logical one, with everything fitting into place. The first one of its kind he'd had in seventeen years.

That still didn't explain Madison's death. And if Shane had killed her, as Blade believed, he might have just lost his chance of ever living free from suspicion.

A fact he'd take on when he had to. Not before.

"If the Donnellys killed Shane, they might have information regarding Madison's death," he said aloud, forgetting just for that instant that he and Morgan weren't a team on the same page.

"What if it wasn't siblings?" she asked, frowning, as she went back to her computer and started typing.

Noting that she'd ignored his statement about her sister's death, Blade went out to gather their beers. He sipped his tepid one, set hers on the desk beside her and took his own seat.

Rome hadn't been built in a day. Nor had it crumbled in one.

"Alex and Josh Donnelly might lead successful, law-abiding lives," she continued, "but the theory best explains what's going on. At least as far as we see it right now. Two different cars were allegedly following me today. Partners, taking different jurisdictions. One in town. One outside of town. Maybe one of them lives here, one doesn't…"

"The one who lives here would be familiar with the homeless people hanging out at the beach." Blade leaned in further, looking at names. Trying to remember faces, and more importantly personalities.

"Mark Hampton's death puts a whole different spin on this," Morgan said. "It makes sense that we'd be looking for someone who'd gone to him for counseling…"

Blade's excitement ramped up again. "Or someone who should have but didn't. Maybe blaming Hampton for not noticing. Or trying to help."

Morgan's glance over her shoulder at him put their faces within inches of each other. He noticed. His gaze dropped to her lips. When he realized he was lingering there, he quickly pulled his eyes back up to focus on hers. She was looking toward his lips.

Remembering? As he'd just done.

Their first kiss that summer had been her first. She'd been tentative in the beginning, to the point that Blade pulled back, fearing he'd made a mistake, read her wrong, that she wasn't wanting to make out with him.

She'd quickly righted his thinking on that one. He started to get hard in real time, and immediately brought Shane Wilmington's dead body to mind.

He would not disrespect Morgan, himself or the search for Maddie's killer by falling back into memories built on a fantasy.

Life had quickly shown him just how difficult, how real, it was going to be.

"There has to be something to this theory." Morgan's words threw him for a second. Sometime during his mental blip she'd turned back to the computer. Glancing at the screen, he didn't see anything new there.

Just the same list of camp attendees they'd been scrolling through.

"How do we know that the partners are even from the same year we are? Dr. Hampton was there for years, and Shane had been attending as a camper since he was twelve," she continued. "Say this duo attended during the previous year, and because of what happened they didn't come back the year we were there? The news of Maddie's death was all over…"

"As was the fact that I was the only suspect," he added, underscoring the part that he'd lived with ever since.

"So, they didn't have to be there when we were, just had to have attended at some point." She pulled out her phone, sent a couple of texts.

He didn't ask where those instant missives were going. She was doing the job she'd been hired to do. He was there because she'd demanded access into his entire life. Including his mind.

They weren't partners, a team working together.

"I'd like to run something by you," she said then, taking a sip from her beer, holding the can between their faces, as she turned to look at him.

Scooting his chair back a few feet, he nodded. Instinctively prepared to hear something he wasn't going to like. Ready to find a way to work with it. He'd put up with whatever hell was necessary to get to the truth.

"You remember Remy Barton? He was a camper, a couple of years younger than us." The question startled him. He hadn't been expecting a trip down memory lane. At least not one that carried a smile.

"Of course. He'd been afraid of his own shadow when he came to camp, but was determined not to let his fear stop him. He learned to swim. To kayak. Rope climb…"

"Did you know his mother had passed away just a few weeks before camp?"

He sat up straight. "Hell, no! He never said anything, never." But when he thought about it, he'd seen the kid go mellow a few times. Had put it down to homesickness. Something a fourteen-year-old boy would rather die than admit.

"I knew only because I caught him crying late one afternoon. He'd been down at the stream that divided the girls' camp from the boys' camp, and I'd just been coming back from my weekly evaluation with Maggie."

The camp manager. Blade hadn't thought much of her in years, either. Other than to resent how quickly the woman had believed what she was being told, that Blade was guilty of murdering a sixteen-year-old girl…

"Anyway, after Maddie's death…" Her pause was minute, but Blade felt it to his core. "Remy stayed with me that morning until my parents came. He didn't say much. Just hung around, making sure everyone else left me alone. We ended up staying in touch…"

If she was about to tell him that the kid had grown up to be her lover, he didn't need to know. Not unless it had to do with the case.

"He's married now. Has three kids, a daughter and a set of twin sons. He's also a psychiatrist who specializes in troubled youths. He's helped Jasmine and I on a couple of our cases. Since he was at camp more years than we were, I was thinking maybe we have him take a look at the camper rosters, and Sierra's Web's further investigation in the lives of the campers, and see if he has any insights for us. I already talked to Kelly Chase about him…"

The Sierra's Web psychiatric partner, he knew from the research he'd done that afternoon. "Kelly thought it was a good idea, and I'd like to ask Remy for input on your behalf," she said then. "I'm asking because he'd be officially brought into the case by Sierra's Web, which means you'd be paying for his time."

That was it? She wanted the grown version of a kid he'd admired to help them? "Do it," he told her, reaching for his beer. Hiding his relief in a swallow.

And maybe drowning a bit of hope there, too.

Morgan was going all-out—bringing in the best of her best to help. To find her sister's killer, he knew. But she was also sitting alone with Blade, giving him beer, in her hotel room.

Was it possible she was finally starting to believe that he wasn't the one who'd murdered her sister?

That he wasn't a killer at all?

As much as she was eager to get as many balls rolling at once as she could, Morgan did not text or call Remy yet that night. A family man, he cherished his home time with his wife and kids. And until Sierra's Web and Jasmine's FBI team did their legwork on the lists of camp attendees, Morgan didn't have enough to give Remy to warrant the evening call.

Buzzing with a need to delve deeply into the reports Sierra's Web had already sent, and to continue going through the seventeen years of information Blade had made available to her that day, she didn't say so.

Out of character for her.

She'd be up a good part of the night getting through it all and taking a fresh look at her own files in light of the new death—the possible connections, the floating theories.

And she'd been jumped in the parking lot less than two hours before. By a person who'd been manipulated by someone who was organized. Intelligent. Someone who was executing, or helping to execute, a meticulous, intricate, well-thought-out plan.

Someone who could be right there in the hotel with her.

Or just outside watching.

It wasn't that she was scared. She'd lived through far worse situations. And didn't spend time worrying about death.

She just wasn't ready to be alone with her jumble of facts and missing truths.

Not when Blade was showing no signs of leaving. He had to know something, even if he didn't know he knew.

And if he did?

Maybe she was the one to figure out what it was. If not directly than in other ways. As soon as she figured out what those ways were.

Drinking beer had not been the best idea. She'd been up since four the previous morning. The clock was heading toward nine. And the day, all that it had held…she felt like she'd lived months, not hours.

She wasn't at her sharpest. Most particularly not to face the culmination of seventeen years of searching. She'd come face-to-face with her obsession and couldn't turn away.

He was sitting back in his chair again, his brow furrowed, as he stared toward her computer screen. If he was deep in thought on the case, following some kind of memory, she didn't want to interrupt.

And almost as though he'd read her mind, he looked at her. Caught her watching him.

She couldn't look away. He didn't. The moment escalated, sending her places she couldn't go. Just like in the parking lot that evening, she had to act.

To do.

To save and protect.

To question.

To know.

"What if you were out that night, checking up on something, making sure Shane was still in his cabin, sleepwalking…" She stopped. Waited for his rejection.

He hadn't moved. Not his body. Or his gaze.

"What if you saw Maddie, thought she was me, grabbed me up to kiss me…"

He started. His eyes seemed to blaze with emotion. But he stayed right there, holding her gaze. And she sat there, tongue-tied. The moment, or the picture she'd painted, hanging there.

Encapsulating them.

She'd had the thought so many times. Needed to know.

And couldn't go any further with it. Because what came next was Maddie, thinking she was being accosted, striking out at him, kicking him maybe, and him, reacting, hitting out in defense. Or even trying to grab her arms, to calm her down, maybe stop her from screaming. She could have moved, his strong grip could have slipped.

Her twin had died from one blow to the side of her head. There'd been bark in the wound, but she'd been left in the dirt and leaves to bleed out. Had been found lying on a branch, a partial mark from which had been embedded in her head. The medical examiner had thought the indentation could have come from the fall, but that the initial blow would have had to have been much more powerful than a mere fall.

Blade wasn't talking. Leaving. Or even looking away.

She couldn't find words. Or turn around and get to work. He was her worst enemy. The face she'd carried, hated, for seventeen years.

And after the day they'd had—the things they'd said, being in his presence—he was more than that, too. She just didn't know what. Couldn't unravel all the messages her senses were sending her.

"Earlier, when we talked about the Donnelly brothers, it was just a theory." Blade's words were a lifesaver. And, somehow, a death knell, too.

"Right." Was he about to tell her the words she'd just uttered were more than that? Not just one theory, but fact? Had she inadvertently hit on the truth?

"The Donnelly theory was based on our reasonable assumption of what could be probable fact."

Why did she suddenly feel as though she was in a courtroom? She had experience in the venue. Training. Knew to respond with truth and utmost brevity. "Right."

"By what probable fact do you base the theory you just proposed?" He was frowning. Sounding more confused than accusatory—as a defense attorney might have done.

Unless he was playing nice to lead her into some kind of hole that she'd fall into, never get out of, and he'd walk free.

Shaking her head, Morgan recognized the absurdity of her thoughts. At the same time, every instinct in her body warned her not to fall prey to emotions where Blade Carmichael was concerned. She'd trusted him with her life, her sister's life, telling him concerns—worries—she'd had where Maddie's wild streak was concerned. And her sister had ended up dead with all proof pointing to him.

She needed the truth. And had sworn to speak it.

If a theory she'd carried through the years was correct, she had to know. "I base it on the fact that I almost suggested that, while the party was going on, after all our kids were asleep, we meet, at the river. I laid in bed that night imagining what it would be like…"

Her standing there. Him running up, grabbing her off her feet. Passion doing what it so desperately compelled them to do…

He'd glanced away. Toward the still-open sheers.

She couldn't take her gaze off him. The tension biting in his jaw. The vein in his neck, looking ready to pop.

That wave at the back of his hair, recognizable even with him wearing it shorter.

"I base it on an assumption that you were feeling the same way I was, thinking like I was. I figured, lying in bed that night, that I could get to the boys' camp via the river, could approach your cabin from the back, and then push the radio button for a call, and just not speak. I knew the static sound would wake you up…"

She'd been an idiot. Hearing the words aloud, the convoluted intricacies involved…

His jaw clenched again. Telling her that what she was

saying was affecting him more deeply than any other thing they'd shared with each other that day.

Spurring her on...filling her with horror...

"If you'd had the same kind of thought, were out looking for me, and Maddie had been sneaking back from the party alone, since everyone testified that Shane had left before her...if you came upon her at our meeting place..."

It could have been an accident. He'd still most likely go to prison, but for much less time. Involuntary manslaughter, or even straight manslaughter...

With a nod, he turned in his seat, facing her again. His gaze holding hers as though he had it imprisoned. It felt to her as though he did. "This is what you've thought all these years?"

She shrugged. Needing to search her mind. To stay truthful, in order to have any hope that he'd end almost two decades of a struggle for the answers that might free her. So she could have a future filled with a personal life to balance her professional one.

Wanting, instead of answering him, to promise to visit him in prison, if he ended up there. Which made her uncomfortable.

"At first, I thought I'd completely misjudged you. That you were some kind of evil being," she told him honestly, swallowing hard as she maintained eye contact with him. "But as I matured, studied criminology and let myself remember the young man I'd known...this is the only theory, or a rendition thereof, that seemed plausible to me."

"You didn't stop to wonder why on earth I'd hit her, leave her lying there to die, put the cross you'd given me in her hand, and then put her class ring in my pocket and go home to bed?"

Her eyes stung. She could feel a surge of moisture.

Forced herself to hold his gaze. "I figured you got scared and ran. Maybe didn't know she was even badly hurt. The class ring…" She shrugged. "Classically, it would be considered a trophy, but then you'd have to have known you'd done something for which you'd want a celebratory memorial…or…it flew out of her hand as you hit her, you saw it in your path as you ran, grabbed it up intending to give it back to her. Or maybe you found it as you were leaving the party, pocketed it for the same reason. Could be you saw Shane with it, told him it was against the rules, because you knew what I'd told you about my sister's weakness, and maybe you forced him to give it to you, to give back to her. Or to me to give to her. And the cross…when she struck out at you, if you still thought she was me, that one was simple. You figured I wasn't the girl you thought I'd been and gave it back."

There were holes in the idea. Things only he could fill in. Happenings of which she was unaware that had led to actual outcomes…

She'd begun to hope, at some point during the day, that it wouldn't come down to Blade being the doer. Her heart had apparently come back to life so quietly, she hadn't realized what was happening in time to prevent the rebirth.

But they still had two deaths to solve. And if they could have the past resolved, open on the table, the rest would…

Fall into place.

Leaving her young girlish hormonal heart forever cracked, but maybe not completely, irreparably broken.

Chapter 11

Hope was a curious thing. Blade sat there with Morgan, finding immense relief in her story regarding his supposed guilt.

A small tendril of belief sprouted from his barren surface, refusing to be trampled by seventeen years of disappointment and experience.

When they'd been teenagers, he'd wanted her to just know he hadn't done it. If they'd been the soulmates she'd claimed, she would have known.

Or at least stood by him long enough to reason things through.

And with his new insight into how that morning had gone for her, what it had done to her, ripped from her...how could she access a soul that had just been destroyed by unimaginable loss?

But over the years... Morgan—the woman who he'd taken to be a soulmate when he'd never before even believed in such things—had had to revise the base judgments she'd made that morning. Factoring in the person he really was.

She still thought him possibly culpable, but only accidentally so. So much of what she'd just said...him making Shane give back her sister's ring...could so easily have happened. She'd seen that in him.

And was sitting there studying him, looking as though her world had just ended.

While he felt like his might just be beginning again.

Leaning forward, his elbows on his knees, he glanced slightly up to meet her gaze. "I didn't do it, Morgan," he said quietly, his eyes as steady as they'd ever been.

Moisture filled her eyes. She blinked, but her gaze was brimmed full. No tears fell. Nor did she offer any words.

She studied him intently. She nodded. And she turned her back to him.

Giving her focus to the case on the screen in front of her.

Blade stood, poured the remainder of his beer down the drain by the refrigerator and quietly let himself out.

She watched him go. Staring at his back, needing to be there, waiting, if he looked back. He didn't. Morgan knew a sense of relief as she heard the lock click automatically into place behind him.

There was more. A boatload of emotions that defied all tides, coming or going, that just remained there, filling the room. And spaces inside her where she never went.

Ignoring it all, she closed and locked the balcony doors, pulled the shades, poured out her mostly full second beer. Opened a third, cold one, and brought out the salad and bread she'd barely touched at dinner.

Carrying the sustenance to the desk, she sat down at her computer, starting at the beginning of the files Sierra's Web had sent—research and backgrounds, life events and current status of key players. Police reports. Forensic evidence would come later. The next day, hopefully, as things from the construction crime scene, as well as all evidence from Madison's murder, had been flown to the firm's state-of-the-art lab in Phoenix for a quicker turnaround.

A man had died that day, and she was mostly numb about it. She'd known who Mark Hampton was. Had sat on the shore while some of the girls in her charge had taken kayak lessons from him. She'd seen him approach the morning she'd found out Maddie had been killed, but she'd twisted around so she couldn't see him. Had tearfully begged the female camp counselor coordinator who'd been sitting with her to make him go away.

It hadn't been anything against the therapist. She hadn't wanted to talk to any man at that point. If Blade could fool her, any guy could.

Still, she'd respected him. Had thought, throughout the summer, that he was patient and kind. She had no reason whatsoever to think that he'd deserved to die.

But what did she know, really know, about what had happened that summer at camp? She'd been so lost in her own little reality—having her soulmate appear before her. Falling in love.

Going through Blade's financials felt wrong, but she pulled them up as she tore off bread and dug into the salad. She'd had an oral report on them.

She had to see it all for herself. Mentally catalog things in the way she did that would allow them to spill back at her in just the right moment, with just the right catalyst to bring them forth. It was like an art form, the way her mind took in details and then gave them back to her in full picture forms that she'd used time and again to solve cases.

She'd barely made it through the list of accounts, hadn't opened any detail pages, even the summaries for each account, which would give her totals. Incoming. Outgoing. Remaining. And was interrupted by her phone's text message tone.

Figuring it for Blade, letting her know he was home—

though she had no reason to think he'd let her know that—
she picked up the device. Pressed to open the app.

And saw five digits instead of a full number. Pressed for
the conversation. The screen was blank, other than a terse
sentence.

Get out of town, and off the case, before something really
bad happens to you.

Where the sixteen-year-old Morgan who'd been trying to
push her way in would have panicked, dropped the phone,
Morgan texted back, Who is this?

And then, with a few presses of her thumb, sent the text
on to Hudson Warner at Sierra's Web, and then, in a separate text, to Jasmine.

If she could keep the sender engaged, either of the two
agencies would have a better chance of at least pinging the
tower from which the text came.

Adrenaline pumped through in healthy spurts as she
waited. The killer was right there. Reaching out to her.
Closer than he'd ever been before.

At least the current killer was. Which was closer than
she'd been to anything dealing with her sister's case since
the morning she'd ceased being a twin.

Not only was he close, watching her, but he wanted her
gone. Which meant that she was posing some kind of threat
to him. She was poking her nose where he didn't want it.

She was learning things.

After a minute passed, with only thumbs-up responses
from both of the people whom she'd just texted, she started
eating again. The salad was delicious. As was the bread.

Beer was her wind down. She'd relax. Take in as much

information as she could reasonably expect to process, and then, lie down and get some sleep.

With her loaded gun right beside her. A split-second hand grab.

She wasn't ignoring the very real threats coming her way. Nor the fact that they were escalating. She just wasn't letting them have the desired effect. Rather than letting them unnerve her, she'd use them to her benefit.

Cowards bullied. Good investigators found ways to use their perps fear to get them to make mistakes.

Three and a half minutes after the warning had come through, her phone pinged again. Jasmine, or Sierra's Web, were her immediate thought, letting her know the message had come from a burner phone. That one was a given.

It was Blade.

Home. Breakfast in the morning? To exchange notes.

He'd be spending the next few hours doing what she was doing. She didn't have to be told to know that.

Fine. She hit Send.

My office? Your hotel?

Not his home, she noticed. Though she still hadn't searched the place, as he'd agreed to let her do.

Here. And pay attention to the road. We need to know, am I the only one being followed?

She took another bite. A sip of beer. Scrolled on the computer.

Feeling a new burst of energy.

She was working late, on the same case she always took to bed with her.

But for the first time in her life, she wasn't working alone.

Something thudded on the balcony.

Instantly awake, alone in her room, Morgan moved her hand a couple of inches, wrapping her fingers around the grip of her pistol. Using her thumb to release the safety and positioning her finger on the trigger.

In one motion, she swung up, pointing her pistol, and saw the small blaze of red, within a haze of smoke.

Keeping her gun pointed, she reached for the hotel phone with her other hand. Dialed for security and reported a fire on her balcony, and then, setting her gun down right beside her, keeping an eye on the balcony, on a red blaze that wasn't growing, she quickly grabbed the top pair of pants from her opened roller bag, snapped on a clean bra, throwing in the dirties she'd changed out of before her shower... was it only three hours before? She ran to the closet and pulled a shirt off the hanger. Kept the balcony in sight, watched more and more smoke furl into the air. Fastening one button to keep the short-sleeved shirt on, she rushed for the desk. Grabbed up files and computer, cords, charger and her notepad, stacking them on top of each other and cramming them into her satchel.

Since the fire hadn't yet noticeably grown, she left her suitcase open as she pulled it toward the room's outer door, stopping at the closet to grab the rest of her shirts, and at the bathroom for her toiletry bag, and, just as she heard the first sirens—less than two minutes from the time she'd awoken—she was out the door.

Heading for the stairs.

* * *

Blade was asleep in his recliner—a place he spent the night more often than he should—when his phone awoke him.

Morgan? At four in the morning?

"Are you okay?" he answered, pushing down the footrest to head to his bedroom for jeans and a shirt.

"Yeah. You feel like a drive to Detroit?"

At four in the morning? "Of course, but are you okay?" he said, heart thumping as he moved his phone from one hand to the other, sliding his arms into a dress shirt he'd just yanked off the hanger, grabbing for jeans off the shelf and holding the phone with his shoulder and chin as he stepped into them.

"I'm fine. Someone threw a flare up on my balcony," she told him. "It exploded, caught fire, but only the chairs burned. If it had been a couple of inches further in, the glass in the door would have exploded and my carpet would have gone up in instant flames."

She sounded like she was discussing a breakfast menu. He stepped into his work boots.

"I need you to pack up your dining room table, bring everything along," she told him. "And get good pictures of every inch of the walls." She went on to describe particular shots she wanted him to take.

He stopped only long enough to throw a change of clothes into the duffel he kept on the floor of his closet, scooping toiletries into it, and was on his way to the dining room as he said, "Where are you?" She lived in Detroit. The FBI office was there, too.

"The police station."

And it hit him…she thought he'd tried to catch her room on fire? The flame of fear shot through him, but only for the second it took him to process and dismiss it. "I've been here, working, most of the night. I have time-stamped documents, emails I sent to staff members, to verify that."

"No one's asking." He had her on speakerphone as he gathered up his files and loaded them into one of the four boxes he had on the case. "The flare came from the beach," she continued, sounding completely professional. "No distinguishable footprints. No fingerprints."

"The make of the flare? Was it sold in town?"

"The local police, headed by Silver, are getting to work on that. Silver was at the crime scene." He thought he might have detected a slight catch in her voice with those last two words—the crime scene which had been her hotel room—but he wasn't sure.

"His warnings to you are escalating," he said, stating what she had to already know. "You didn't heed them. He's getting angrier." It didn't take a profiler to figure that one out. A simple understanding of human nature led to that conclusion.

"Right. Which is why I'm leaving town. Hoping to fool him into thinking he was successful, to buy a little time while teams get to work on the attack earlier tonight, the phone threat and the flare."

She delivered the last like they were a grocery list. Morgan, who'd been the most softhearted girl he'd ever met. He brushed past the change to say, "You want him to follow you home."

"No. We're going to leave my car at the hotel. And your truck at the police station. If he concludes that you're in custody, great. He'll figure out, quickly enough, that I'm not in town, but the plan is for us to take a rental to Detroit, back roads, now while it's dark. We'll have an escort until we're certain we aren't being followed. Hopefully, by the time we're at my place, we'll have come up with our next steps."

He'd finished packing boxes, was using his phone to snap photos while they spoke. "I'm actually part of a law enforcement plan to accompany you to Detroit?" he asked, deadpan. While consciously trying to contain the sense of freedom, of victory the knowledge gave him. To not only be off the radar, but to be a legitimate part of the investigation...

He got no further before she said, "You're my client. Part of the deal, on my side, is my access to you. I'm not leaving without you."

Reality hit again. In raw places. Harder due to his momentary letting down of his guard.

"We're too close, Blade." Her voice fell into the silence left by his lack of response, while he accepted that he was only a part of things because she didn't fully trust him. Was he also imagining that her tone was softer than he'd heard since they'd reconnected? "We're on the verge of getting him. We can't back off now, and we both know the way to do this is together. We were the ones most affected by what happened that night at camp."

He was out the door before she'd finished speaking and kept her on the line during his short drive to the police station.

Even if no one was ready to unequivocally believe, yet, that he hadn't killed Madison Davis, he was being given a second chance.

No way he was going to miss one second of it.

Or mess it up, either.

He was going to be right there, facing whatever he had to face, to bring the killer, or killers, to justice.

Blade offered to drive. Morgan refused the offer. She was trained for surveillance, trusted herself to be better able to tell if they were being followed. And needed her rearview mirror to best do that.

And she'd had more sleep than he'd had. As soon as they'd headed out of town in the blue rental sedan, and she'd heard he'd only been out about an hour before she'd called, having spent much of the night doing his own internet research on the lives of others who'd been at camp with them that horrible summer, she suggested that he use the driving time to get some rest. They could count on a full, taxing day ahead of them. She needed him in top form.

Mostly, now that he was back with her, she needed time to gather herself. To relax into who she was, what she knew, and do what she did.

To tune in and find herself while her entire life's work was exploding around her, to catch as many pieces as she could, and put them together into their final, rightful, resting place.

The fact that Blade's presence helped *her* was not good news. But recognizing the truth, she didn't fight it. Not when it meant she was getting closer to proving who'd killed her sister.

While she drove, remaining on edge with facts and impressions, with replays of the near escapes she'd had over the past twenty-four hours, coming to terms with the fact that she was the target of a smart, organized and determined but elusive killer...Blade Carmichael almost immediately went to sleep.

His relaxed form and even breathing might have made her smile in another lifetime.

Funny, most definitely not in a smiling way, she never in a million years would have figured his first time sleeping with her to play out quite like that.

A thought that brought a swell of emotion that had nothing to do with the case and put her on guard. To the point that she spent the entire rest of the almost-three-hour drive with all the route switches not only watching everything around her, but watching herself, too.

No more lapses into the past.

Even if it turned out that Blade Carmichael was not her sister's killer, he wasn't the man he'd been when she'd known him. And more importantly, she was most definitely not the girl he'd thought he'd fallen in love with.

Finding Maddie's killer would settle a huge load of tension inside her. It would allow her to keep her promise to her identical twin to not let a day go by without working on finding Maddie's killer and seeing him brought to justice. But it wouldn't bring Maddie back.

And living without the other half of her identity, being in the world without the one person who was so connected to her she could sense Morgan's moods, read her thoughts…

She'd do it. Had been doing it for seventeen years.

And doing so had changed her. Period.

It had robbed her of her deepest sense of self. Of her ability to love openly, freely. Of her ability to trust. Of her belief in happily-ever-after.

Forever.

Chapter 12

Blade was wide awake when Morgan signaled a turn before the intersection she'd indicated they'd be driving through to reach her condo on the next block up. He looked in his side mirror, out his window, hers, as she turned again, and then a third time, taking them out to the expressway.

"I'm assuming we were being followed?" he asked, surprised at the calm with which he approached the news.

Living seventeen years with the feeling of being hunted, he'd have expected a bit more distress. With every muscle tense, prepared to spring into whatever action presented itself, he wasn't afraid.

He was ready.

Had his legally registered gun clipped to his belt.

With another couple of glances in her rearview mirror, and both side mirrors, Morgan shook her head. "No, not that I can see, but that tan car…it was parked three driveways down from mine. Opposite side of the street."

"He's got someone planted there, to notify him if you go home."

She nodded. And he was confused. "I thought the idea was for him to think you'd quit and gone home."

"With you in the vehicle with me?"

"I'd duck down until you pulled into your garage."

Morgan shook her head, signaling and moving over into

the exit lane. "My plan was not to let him know I'd quit," she said then, and thinking back, he realized that she'd only mentioned the killer thinking Blade was in custody, nothing about her. He'd assumed...

"My quitting gives him a sense of victory," she said, exiting the freeway, taking the far lane, signaling a right turn as though she knew exactly where she was going.

"Mind telling me what we're doing now?" He could put a little more strength in his tone. He wasn't her prisoner. Could speak up for his right to be an equal partner with her. Clued in at all times. Remind her who was paying the bill.

But it wouldn't serve any good purpose. While he didn't appreciate being kept in the dark, at all, for any part of Morgan's investigation, he was getting exactly what he wanted.

Her giving her all, working diligently, to find the truth.

And only a fool put his foot in his mouth when there was good stuff cooking.

"We're heading to FBI headquarters," she told him. "Jasmine's giving us a conference room to go over any new developments. She wants to interview both of us, and has agreed to keep me apprised of anything she finds. With Sierra's Web officially on the case, we're all working together..."

A conference room at FBI headquarters. Not exactly what he'd have chosen for himself, personally, but for Morgan...to know that she would be out of harm's way, fully protected, for the next few hours at least, relaxed him a smidge.

"Mind if we get some breakfast before we head in?" he asked, his tone congenial. While his mind played over what he'd learned since Morgan's phone call had awoken him that morning. Putting it together with things he'd gleaned the night before. There'd been a girl at camp...

He hadn't thought anything of Emily. Not until the night before, when he'd come across her name and had looked her up...

If he didn't have to answer to Morgan, he'd have already been heading in the other woman's direction. To follow up on a bad feeling.

Instead, he was going to have to cough up some more difficult facts.

In search of the truth.

She didn't want to sit openly in a restaurant. Since she couldn't be absolutely positive the killer didn't have a way of tracking her, Morgan didn't want to put any more people in danger than absolutely necessary. She'd planned to leave her cell phone at her apartment. Had turned it off as soon as she'd hung up from Blade at the Rocky Springs police station. Was already using one of the burners she'd brought with her, just in case.

Instead, she'd be leaving her cell with Jasmine. Having it monitored. And if it was clean, returned to her. "I'm going to need your cell," she said as she pulled up to the newly installed drive-through window to collect their food order from a restaurant that, until a few years before, had been dine-in only.

And one of her favorite breakfast places.

Blade's instant frown, his clear tension, relieved her some. He'd been so...agreeable, to the point almost of docility, that she'd been on edge with him. Because he hadn't been giving her his true self. "My cell?" His challenging tone matched his body language.

"In case it's being traced," she told him. Pulling out her own burner phone. And her dead cell. "I'm leaving mine, too. We'll get them back after they've been analyzed."

With a nod, he mentioned the pictures he'd taken that morning, at her request.

And in between chatting with the woman at the window, paying, asking for extra syrup, she let him know the burner had a memory card and he'd have time to move over anything he needed.

Not because it was the truth and right to let him know what was ahead.

But because she wanted to keep him happy.

And that was most definitely not a good development in the case.

Blade knew the second he met Morgan's ex-partner that Agent Jasmine Flaherty did not like him. The woman was polite. He couldn't find any real fault with her treatment of him.

But as he left the room she'd invited him into for a one-on-one chat, he could feel the chill emanating from the other woman.

He made a mental note to himself of the less than positive reception, along with a footnote to keep his impression to himself. Agent Flaherty had worked alongside Morgan for more than a decade. It didn't take a genius to figure out that the FBI agent-in-charge's opinion of him had been influenced by that partnership. And had been years in the making.

Another reminder of, and insight into, the grown-up version of a young girl he'd once known. Every time he told himself he was seeing a resemblance between the two versions of Morgan Davis, he was being foolish.

A luxury he most definitely could not afford.

But the whole come-to-truth moment made it a bit easier

to sit down in the conference room, alone with Morgan, and take charge of the conversation.

"Regarding our next plans," he said as he held two cups, one at a time, to an in-room coffee portal, then slid the first toward her. "If I was working alone, I'd be heading upstate right now. To a little town just east of Reed City."

His own cup filled, he sat down a couple of seats away from her spot at the head of the table. His stuff was there.

Hers wasn't. Her satchel currently hung over the back of her chair, as though she hadn't been planning to stay long.

Which was just fine with him.

As though she'd read his mind, she turned, reaching behind her into her satchel, pulling out a stack of folders, along with her laptop, as she said, "Why Reed City area?"

And he opened the smallest of his four boxes. The one he'd packed from his table hours before. Taking out the folder he'd put in last.

Opening it, he grabbed the photo on top. That of a seventeen-year-old girl. Pushed it across the table, within Morgan's reach. "You remember her?"

With a frown, she studied the grainy, computer-generated-and-printed photo. Then nodded. "Yeah, that's Emily Kingsley, right? The kids' camp music director."

He nodded. Waited for her to look up at him.

"I came across her name last night and remembered something."

Her gaze sharp, her jaw taut, she asked, "What?"

"She was seated next to me in orientation," he relayed without hesitation. There would be no secrets between them. Not until they found the person who'd murdered her sister. "She was friendly," he continued, remembering back, trying to give her as clear a picture as he could. Checking to make certain he wasn't sparing himself.

"Knowing no one else there, I was friendly back," he continued, looking Morgan right in the eye. If her blink right then had been any more than a natural physical happening, he chose not to deem it as such.

"You two were flirting," she said, in that professional tone he was beginning to dislike. A lot.

He shrugged. "Maybe. But I honestly didn't put any stock in it," he told her. He'd done his soul-searching the night before. "It was before camp started. I'd read the rules. No fraternizing between boy and girl camp counselors. Before I knew that, behind the scenes, it happened all the time."

"It wasn't her first year there," Morgan said, glancing at the photo again. "She'd have known."

"Right, which is part of what came to me last night…"

"Did you date her?"

Morgan's tone had changed. Reminding him of one other sentence she'd said to him the day before. *You told me you weren't going, but you did.*

"I did not," he got out there with full confidence. And then followed his strong words with, "I helped her move music equipment, though. On move-in day. She said something about us hooking up later, and I nodded. Thinking we'd see each other at the first-night barbecue."

Which was when he'd met Morgan and Madison Davis.

"Not that we'd be hooking up in any kind of real-world sense." He continued speaking, as though he could dissuade her thoughts from traveling down channels that wouldn't be good for him.

For them.

"Since I worked with the older kids, I didn't see her much after that." He moved right along with his story. "But last night, when I first got a look at her face, I remembered something."

He paused, taking stock of Morgan's countenance. Finding nothing there but a detective in a cream-colored button-down cotton dress shirt with her long blond hair clipped up in some kind of do at the back of her head.

"Ice cream social night," he said then. A function for camp counselors and teenage personnel that took place during family night at camp.

"We were together that night." Morgan's tone, lacking any emotion at all, didn't bode well.

"Yes, we were, and even walked back to the river together, waving goodbye as we each went to our own respective areas." He found himself painting a part of the picture that wasn't necessary to the case.

Hearing his words, he quickly reverted back. "But when we were waiting in line for the hot fudge...she was across from us, in line for the topping table. I was just glancing around, seeing who all was there, and I caught her looking at me. Her gaze... She looked...mad."

Morgan sat forward. "Mad?"

"Yeah," he said, meeting her gaze head-on. "But it was weird because when she saw me looking at her, she gave me that flirty smile, and raised her eyebrows, as though letting me know that—"

"I know what she'd been letting you know," Morgan interrupted, her tone brisk. "You're sure she looked mad?"

"Yeah. At the time I figured she hadn't really been looking our way, hadn't seen me, but, rather, had been off somewhere in her head. I figured she'd had a fight with someone. Or was in trouble for something. When she saw me, and immediately changed, I figured it wasn't about me and completely forgot..."

Morgan had her computer plugged in and on in seconds.

Was typing. And scrolling. "I've got it all here," he told her, pushing the printed file in her direction.

She reached for the file, opened it to the first page, an incidences listing. In chronological order.

Domestic violence occurrences. With Emily as the perpetrator, every single time.

"The fifth charge down, it was dropped, but was against a roommate she claimed had been hitting on her boyfriend. She claimed the woman came at her and it was self-defense."

Her chin tightened as she read, but when she looked up at Blade, he saw something mixed in with the anger and determination gleaming from her eyes.

He saw what looked liked despair.

Bile rose inside Morgan. Her stomach knotted so tight she almost doubled over with it. So many times…from that very first day…most particularly with Blade as the suspect…there'd been the dreaded fear that her identical twin sister had died because of her.

And, oh God, was she finally on the cusp? Would this day—out of thousands of them that had passed between then and now—be the one that brought Maddie justice?

"I need to talk to Jasmine." She spoke aloud, not consciously, but just doing so, as she stood, heading toward the door. "She can do a deeper dive, possibly get a warrant to look at financials. We have to find out if she's been anywhere near Rocky Springs, or contacted Dr. Hampton. We need to know if she's withdrawn sums of money from her accounts and get her photo around the beach at Rocky Springs. See if anyone who hangs out there has seen her…" She broke off as Jasmine, seeing Morgan in the open doorway, came toward her.

And ten minutes later, she and Blade were on their way up north to the little town of Everson. Law enforcement needed warrants, had to go through specific channels, but as a private detective, she was free to knock on doors and ask people to speak with her. She couldn't legally compel them, but there were other ways of getting people to talk.

While Jasmine and Sierra's Web did the deep diving, she could do what they could not. And Blade... Bringing him along could be a catalyst, if they actually ran into Emily.

"If we're correct in our theory, seeing us together might set her off," she warned as they drove out of town just after nine that morning. "We could be heading into a minefield." As she said the words, Morgan pulled off to the shoulder of the road.

"I can't do this, Blade. I can't take you." The investigation would go better with him there. He knew more about his summer with Emily than anyone. Might remember something more. And the rest...of course he knew more. But... "If something happens to you... I can't take that on, too."

The weight of her sister's death was weighing her down so heavily she wasn't sure anymore that justice was going to free her from anything. How did you build a future if you'd been responsible for the death of your other half?

Blade's gaze, as he looked at her, was not at all congenial. Or cooperative. Instead, he was clearly a man who was going to do what he was going to do. But his tone wasn't combative as he said, "You can drive up on your own, but you can't stop me from also visiting Everson today."

No. She couldn't. But...

"My life, my choice," he said.

She didn't want him going out on his own. Possibly even

going rogue. They'd be safer together. She'd have more chance to protect him if she was with him.

And…he'd have her back, too. She was strong. Capable. Trained. And only human. Not invincible.

Not that she'd cared all that much, either way, since Maddie's death. If she died, she'd be whole again.

She wasn't living with a death wish. She just hadn't feared her own death. Hadn't given it much thought. Hadn't cared a lot.

So why, sitting on the side of the highway with a man who was still a suspect in her sister's murder, was she suddenly wanting to stay alive?

With one last glance at him, but not another word, she pulled back onto the highway.

I can't take that on, too. Morgan's words continued to reverberate with Blade. His perspective of the occurrences that had robbed him of his future shifted again. Being with Morgan, he wasn't just experiencing things through his own life. It was as though he could feel her, sense her, something. At the very least, he was gaining new understanding—outside himself.

I can't take that on, too.

Too. As though in addition to what she'd already taken on. And while she could have been referring to her sister's cold case, combined with the two new murders, he didn't think so.

She couldn't be responsible for his death. Too.

Meaning she felt responsible for Madison's. The thought hit him harder than a ton of bricks. Hit him in a real way. All those years…she'd been blaming herself?

And why wouldn't she, since she believed her boyfriend had been the one to kill her sister? And with the scenario she'd given him the day before—her thinking he'd mistaken Madison for her—he'd been so busy digesting the fact that she'd had serious thoughts about meeting him after hours, down by the river...

Because, yeah, he'd had those thoughts, too.

But the key point was, the two of them...they'd known better than to trade one night for their integrity. They'd been given a set of counselor rules for good reason. And other than the one instance of following Shane to the party, and staying until the guy had left, he'd never broken one of them. The one he had broken had also been for good reason. Looking out for the safety of others. Not for his own personal gratification.

And while he had no desire to point fingers at the dead, neither could he sit in the silence that had pervaded the car since she'd left the shoulder of the road.

"No matter what we find, if it *was* Emily, Maddie's death was not your fault, Morgan." He'd been vacillating between present and past so much he'd almost said Morgie. Caught himself.

She didn't even look his way. Just kept driving. Her face schooled into the professional expression he was growing to dislike a lot. He was fine with her keeping walls up between them—mostly fine, at any rate. He understood that. But to cement even her normal daily expressions...

They weren't strangers. And the circumstances that had brought them together...

"Madison chose to break the rules," he said then, whether it made her mad or not. If she'd been living in a torturous hell of her own making, with no one to help her see her way out...if that was the only good thing having him back in her life did for her then it would be worth her anger. "She chose to attend the unsanctioned party. To meet Shane there.

And she chose to be in those woods late at night. There was no sign of a struggle at the scene. No sign of anyone being dragged or trying to get away. No signs of restraint or defense wounds on her body. She was there because she chose to break the rules that were in place to keep her safe. And she chose not to tell you, to even give you a chance to watch out for her."

There. Whether she allowed him to help her or not, at least the words were in her brain. She'd have to play them through. And knowing her as he was beginning to believe he still did, believing that the Morgie he'd known hadn't been completely obliterated by that summer's events, he'd bet money that every time she blamed herself, she'd at least think about what he'd said.

Not because he was that important. Or that smart. But because she was a person who considered all sides of a situation.

When she had access to them.

He'd merely given her access.

And had one more thing to say about it. "Just like today. If something happens to me up there…it's on whoever does the damage. And would only be a really unfortunate result, a consequence, of my choice to visit Everson."

Because Madison Davis had most certainly not deserved to die that night. Her death hadn't been her fault. At all.

She'd paid horrible consequences for a choice she'd made.

And that was that.

Morgan instinctively rejected Blade's attempt to absolve her of any guilt in her sister's death. If Morgan had be-friended someone, brought them into Madison's life, and then Madison died as a result, there was culpability.

But for a second there, her chest had lightened. She'd felt a flutter in her stomach. Had felt like a cupcake with buttercream icing. And it was nice.

She'd thought all deep, good personal sensations had died right along with her sister. They'd shared feelings. An ability to feel what the other was feeling. People had scoffed at the possibility. People who weren't identical twins and hadn't ever felt that sense of being an intricate part of another.

It's on whoever does the damage. Madison had made the choice to break the rules that were designed to keep her safe.

The thoughts presented a second time as they left rush hour city traffic behind, and she upped her speed. And again…that lightening in her chest…a fresh clear breath… came. And went.

When she needed to be focused completely on Emily Kingsley. "Tell me what you know about Emily's current daily life," she began, breaking the silence that had been trying to hold her in a world where Maddie's death wasn't on her.

"She's…" Blade's words were cut off by the ringing of Morgan's burner cell. Only people on the case had the number. She'd paired the phone with the car's audio system. Recognizing Kelly Chase's number, she let the psychiatry expert know that she was on speakerphone as she answered.

"Remy Barton has agreed to advise us in any way he can," Kelly reported. "I've looked over his portfolio, and after speaking with him, I think you made a good call, bringing him to our attention," she told Morgan. "I brought him up to speed on everything, sent over reports. He said he'll be back to me later this afternoon, and I'll let you know as soon as I hear anything from him."

Morgan would have liked to be in touch with Remy herself. Just to connect with her good friend, to hear what he had to say to her, personally, regarding the drastic turns her life had taken in the past two days. But for that reason, she hadn't texted him. She wasn't ready to talk about it.

Not even to Remy, or Carrie, his wife. Or Jasmine, either. Her friend had tried to get her alone, had managed to issue a small reminder warning in the hallway, stating she should think about stepping back and allowing the FBI to bring the killer in, but Morgan had managed to sidestep any response and then they'd been joined by Blade and any further chance for conversation on the subject had been forfeited.

On some level she knew that Blade was the reason she was distancing herself from the people who'd been her support group over the past many years.

She couldn't let herself dwell on that, either. Not until the work was done.

As soon as they hung up from Kelly, she asked again about Emily. Heard the rundown of what he'd found the night before. The woman had a degree in marketing. Had bounced from firm to firm, mostly worked from home, but had never seemingly been out of work. She'd been married three times, had no kids, was currently going through a divorce, and her home was on the market. From what he'd been able to find in public records, she didn't appear to have any family in town.

"Maybe the third divorce, especially if she's being forced to sell her home because of it, is her stressor and she went back to what she might think started it all," Morgan said, looking for the rationale behind what they were thinking the woman might have done. "She's blaming you for not wanting her, me for taking you away from her. Framing you. Trying to get me out of the picture…that part makes sense."

"But why Shane? And Hampton?"

"Maybe the who doesn't matter as much as they were at camp. For all we know she had sessions with Hampton over something at camp, or in her home life. And Shane? Maybe she went after him, too. Or, more likely, he went after her, and then moved on…"

Blade shook his head. "I don't remember Shane ever chatting her up, or even making booty call remarks about her…"

Still didn't mean it hadn't happened. It wasn't like the two guys had been buds. They'd just been counselors, in adjacent cabins, and so involved in a lot of the same activities with the same people.

"It's possible that she has nothing to do with the current murders," Blade said as the miles whizzed by in the shapes of Michigan wilderness in the summertime. Woods thick with green leaves, farmers' fields filled with corn, soybeans and asparagus. Small towns sparsely spaced around them.

Morgan glanced over at him. "You think she's the one who killed Madison, though?"

His shrug didn't tell her enough. And it occurred to her it could be because he might really and truly be as much in the dark as she was.

With as great a need to know.

His being there with her, having spent much of the night following up on a flash memory…felt more like compulsion than deflection.

He wasn't deliberately trying to steer her wrong.

She had no proof of that. And could already hear Jasmine telling her that thought right there was why she needed to pull back.

And maybe, if she was the agent in charge on the case, a member of law enforcement being entrusted to solve three murders, she would consider having someone appointed in her place.

As it was, she was helping those officially assigned to find the killer. And being paid to do so. Blade had legally and officially hired Sierra's Web, and in particular her. She was doing the job she'd signed on to do, with everyone involved fully aware of her personal attachment to the case.

It was that exact attachment that made her the one for the job.

And… "It seems a bit too coincidental that these murders happened, after all these years, within twenty-four hours of each other, involving you, if they aren't connected," she put out there.

"Any word on the Donnelly brothers?" Blade asked then.

And she shook her head. "Sierra's Web was still working up full profiles when I talked to Glen after the flare hit my room this morning. He said I should have the report by noon. But as far as he'd seen, there was nothing that stood out. Neither of them have police records. Alex had a speeding ticket, which he paid, four years ago. Last known address for both was Grand Rapids. Hopefully with techs sending current images of them through security camera footage, we'll be able to see if they've been in Rocky Springs recently."

Nothing that had turned up so far had definitively ruled them out, but there was nothing that made them suspicious, either.

And truthfully, the Donnellys had been a crapshoot. Names culled merely because they'd been siblings at camp. The rest had all been theory.

Good storytelling.

Like her relationship with Blade Carmichael had been all those years ago? A fairy tale she'd created in her mind?

And if so, what did that make him in the moment, in her car?

A suspect? A man she was keeping a close eye on? Her closest tie to what happened in the woods that night?

A co-sufferer? Someone in her same boat who needed what she needed nearly as badly as she did?

The man who'd hired her to find the truth so that he could not just be free but be exonerated in the murder that had been pinned on him seventeen years before? And the ones currently framing him?

He could be any or all those things.

As long as she didn't start creating fiction in her head again and cast him as a friend.

Chapter 13

Unless Emily Kingsley was some kind of supervillain, there was no way she could have killed Shane Wilmington, let alone Mark Hampton. She'd have to have been able to teleport from a divorce court hearing the day before to Hampton's office or create funds out of frozen assets in order to hire anyone.

The woman wasn't happy to see Blade and Morgan together. He got that loud and clear. Her sarcasm about how nice it was to see them together again couldn't be missed. And she'd been pretty much heartless in response to that week's killings. She was not what Blade would consider a nice person, in any way.

But she wasn't their killer.

He and Morgan were out of Everson less than half an hour after they'd arrived. And, at Morgan's suggestion, were heading to Lavenport, to talk to people who'd last seen Mark Hampton. It was what a private investigator did, she said, as though reminding herself as much educating him.

"You want to see if anyone recognizes me?" he asked, not in an unfriendly way, but serious just the same. The more he came to understand her position, what she had to have been through mentally and emotionally, the less he blamed her for doubting everyone and everything.

She glanced over at him as she pulled out onto a side road that would, in an hour's time, lead them straight into Lavenport. "No."

He believed her. The denial felt good.

"And for the record," she continued, "I already told you I don't believe you murdered Shane or Dr. Hampton. I'd appreciate it if you'd keep our relationship professional and quit baiting me."

"I wasn't baiting you," he heard himself say where he would normally have kept his own counsel. "I've lived under suspicion for the past seventeen years," he found himself explaining for the very first time. Would like to have wondered why, in the midst of a double homicide investigation and quest for a seventeen-year-old killer, he decided to open up. But he didn't have to wonder. He knew.

Morgan had that effect on him. In the past, when he'd been falling in love with her, and apparently in the current day, too, as his private investigator.

So be it.

He'd learned a long time before not to fight that which you had no power to change.

Might have shared that insight with her, too, if she hadn't just reprimanded him. The chastisement he could take all day long. For himself. But her uttering it meant that she was bothered. And that was something for which he did not want to be responsible.

The woman had suffered enough.

There'd been no sign of them being followed to Everson. No sign that anyone was following them out of town, either. And nothing new to learn in Lavenport. Everyone Morgan spoke to was shocked at Mark's death. Saying he was well loved. Had no enemies. He'd been divorced for years. His wife had moved away shortly after the split. They'd had no children. He'd never remarried. He didn't drink or hang around in bars as far as anyone knew. No one had seen who'd been in the psychologist's office. He'd had no appointment on his calendar for the time of his death. And no one had gone through reception.

Which meant the doctor had to have known his killer, and let him or her in.

The building, and Mark's office, had no security cameras, as patient confidentiality was a big concern for them.

Pulling over as they headed out of town, Morgan asked Blade if he minded driving. She'd still keep her attention on their surroundings, but she needed some time on her phone. Needed to read reports that had been coming in. She was missing something.

It had to be there.

Once they were back on the road, she read half a page of information from Sierra's Web, regarding campers from that summer, organized by those who had circumstances that stood out as possible homicidal tendencies or stressors, and, after another quick check of their surroundings, glanced over at Blade.

"You know Kyle Brennan, or Tammy Phillips?" Both at the top of the list. She'd known them both by sight and name. Had thought they were nice.

"Kyle was in charge of all the counselors," Blade said. "He was great most of the time, but he had a temper on him. I once saw him trying to hammer a stake in the ground. The stake broke and he threw the hammer so hard it flew into a tree several yards away and stuck."

Shocked, she looked at him. "Did you report it?"

Blade shook his head. "I didn't have to. Mark Hampton

was there. I saw the doctor look over at Kyle and figured he'd get a talking-to."

Tense, Morgan looked back at her page. "Says here that he's been in and out of jail over the past couple of years. He'd had a drinking problem, and anger issues, though apparently had both under control until his son died a couple of years ago."

Blade's gaze swung toward her before quickly returning to the road. The glance had been enough for her to see his shock. "None of that came up in my searches last night."

"It's from police and court records," she told him. "And there's more. He recently lost his father in a boating accident… Kyle was driving the boat. And had an alcohol level above the legal limit."

"Mark Hampton," Blade said then, sending her another urgent glance. "The way I saw him looking at Kyle that day with the hammer. Stands to reason he'd counseled Kyle at least once…"

"What about Shane? Do you know of any interaction between the two of them?"

Blade pulled over then. Abruptly. Stopping the car. Staring at her hard. "Kyle had a thing for Madison." He bit out each word. "It didn't occur to me to… Every guy at camp except for me seemed to have a thing for her—" His words cut off abruptly, as though he'd just realized who he was talking to.

Morgan shook her head, couldn't be bothered with supposed hurt feelings. "You know I was fine being the introverted twin," she reminded him impatiently. "And I knew full well how the guys all gravitated toward Maddie, and how much she loved being the belle of the ball…" Her mouth dropped open as horror surged through her.

"Kyle?" she asked. "You think he followed Maddie from the party after Shane left without her? That he…"

Her words broke off as pieces fell more solidly into place than they had since the entire nightmare had begun…making sense in a way nothing ever had…

Reaching behind them, Blade pulled a file from one of his boxes that he'd put back in the car when they'd left Detroit. "That's a recent picture of him," he told her. The image was printed in black and white on copier paper. Didn't matter. She saw what he wanted her to see.

The man had been at the beach, and the social media caption read, "Just chilling with my homies."

Heart pumping, breath coming in gulps, Morgan was about to ask Blade if he knew where Kyle was living, thinking he'd be the quickest way to the answer, when her burner phone pealed, startling her so badly she jumped.

Expecting the call to be from Jasmine, or Sierra's Web, she was startled to see Detective Silver's number on the screen. Recognizing it from the area code and the last three digits being zero.

Putting the call on speaker without hesitation, she looked at Blade and said, "Hello?"

"There was a bomb in your car." Silver's voice was urgent. "Kaycee went out to move it, and just happened to notice the device because the sun caught the black plastic…"

Blood drained from her face. She looked at the floor of the car. Caught in a sense of unreality as she said, "Tell me she's okay…" And then, eyes wide, looked at Blade.

Kept her eyes pinned on the depth of his as she heard, "She's fine. She made a run for it and got far enough away before it went off, but if she'd sat in the driver's seat…"

She got the picture. If that had been her, if she'd gone

out at night, or on a cloudy day, or just plain hadn't been looking in the right place as the sun shone in...

"He's escalating." Blade's words were sharp. Filled with very clear anger. "This was more than a warning."

She calmed herself as best she could. *Think*, she ordered herself. *Think!* "There's got to be something there that will lead us to him," she said then. "Call Jasmine, get FBI's bomb experts there..."

"Already done." Silver's voice had a tone of compassion in it that time. Something she didn't need. "They want you two in protective custody," he added. "I think..."

Her phone beeped another call. Jasmine's number. With Silver still talking, she showed Blade her screen, her brows raised. He shook his head.

"You'll be getting a call from the protection detail—" Silver was saying.

Ignoring the FBI agent's call, Morgan interrupted Silver to say, "I *am* protective custody. Blade and I are safer on the move, and we'll be in touch," she finished and rung off.

They could trace her call. They had the number. Could even show up wherever she and Blade went next, but they couldn't make her cower and hide.

If someone had to die bringing in Maddie's killer, it might as well be her. She couldn't sit back and let others die when she could be partially to blame. Or, for that matter, ever.

But this time...it was personal.

She was not stopping until the job was done.

Blade had spent seventeen years relying only on himself, fighting to build a life within a wall of suspicion, learning to live with the weight he carried, being on guard for mistrust from others and working to prove he wasn't the man the world had judged him to be.

In the space of one phrase, "if she'd sat in the driver's seat," everything had changed. His reputation didn't mean a whit when weighed against Morgan Davis's life.

Nor did his future. He'd been all in on their investigation from the beginning. His reasons for being so had changed in a blip. As had the urgency of his time frame. He had a lifetime to prove his innocence.

She might not have another day if they didn't get the fiend who was murdering people, framing him, and who was now after her. Seemingly for not heeding warnings to quit helping him.

As soon as she'd hung up from Silver, Morgan dialed Sierra's Web. Blade wasn't pulling back onto the freeway until he knew what the experts had to say.

"I'm putting you on speaker," he heard her say, just after her greeting to whoever had answered. "Blade's here with me."

She hadn't heard what the firm had to tell her yet, but was including him. He was their client.

"I just got off the phone with Silver," she started in. "I need to know what you have on Kyle Brennan."

"Enough to know we're concerned about him," the male voice responded. "Hudson here," the voice then said. "Glen's in the room as well."

Both partners in the firm. IT and forensic experts. Blade recognized the names from the research he'd done.

"And we need to talk about the bomb, Morgan. I know this case is important to you, but it might be better served by one of our other expert investigators. Carmichael, you're there?"

"I am," he answered before meeting Morgan's gaze. He

knew what he'd see there. And while his senses were all pushing him to accept the firm's suggestion, to run with it, to save Morgan from any more danger, his mind knew differently.

With one more glance at Morgan's emotionless, hard-rock stare, he glanced out the front windshield. "And I disagree that someone other than Morgan would be better for the job." The words were like death in his throat. But he continued, "Not only does she know the case better than anyone, but she's going to work, by herself, or with all of us, and she's safer with all of us than she would be alone."

He glanced at her as he finished, saw the firm set of her chin, the tightness in her jaw—denoting her anger.

But he saw something more there, too. The softening in her eyes.

And guessed she didn't have any clue it was there, as she looked at her phone and said, "What do you have on Kyle Brennan?"

"I had my team start on him as soon as we had the compiled list we sent you, Morgan," the man continued. "He has a home in St. Joseph…"

A beach town only ten miles from Rocky Springs. Blade's gut grew tight.

"Local police were there this morning. No one answered the door. Nor is he answering his last known number."

Morgan glanced at Blade, and he nodded. Pulled out onto the freeway, looking for the next exit so he could head back the way they'd come. They had to get to St. Joseph. Unlike local police, Morgan could talk to anyone, and ask anything. They just didn't have to answer. He'd already learned that sometimes the questions she asked gave them information simply by the nonanswers.

"We don't have a warrant for financials yet," Hudson

continued. "We need something more to compel that. But we've been obtaining footage from many surveillance cameras since early this morning. Some going back more than a week. Our people have been going through them and were able to get his license plate number from one of them. From there, they've been scouring the footage for other hits on the plate…"

His mind boggling a bit at the amount of work being done, Blade still grew impatient to hear the bottom line. He had to know what he was up against in his determination to keep Morgan safe.

The only way he had a hope in hell of doing that was to help her catch the murderer who wanted her out of the picture.

Because there was no way she was ever going to agree to quit looking for Madison's killer…

His mind tuned all focus to Hudson Warner's voice as the expert said, "We have him on camera at a gas station at the edge of town, heading toward Rocky Springs, the day of Shane Wilmington's killing. And passing through an intersection yesterday morning, in the direction of Lavenport. In itself, this means nothing, but if we could similarly place him in those towns near the times of the murders…"

"We were just in Lavenport," Morgan told the expert. "No one saw anyone or anything suspicious, which makes me think that Hampton knew his killer and let him in his office. It's either the doctor letting someone in—there's a back entrance for personnel to come and go through—or someone having to go through reception to get to the private offices. Hampton was the only one back there during the time of his murder."

"We've got calls going out right now for any surveillance footage we can get in the town," Hudson said, making Blade extremely thankful for having hired the firm. It would have taken him weeks, probably with no results, to get that information on his own.

"In the meantime, we've got him on camera, not today, but several times over the past week driving by a corner convenience store half a mile from his home…"

"I'm on it," Morgan told the man. "Send me the address…"

The two talked more. Details about Kyle's father's death. Impending charges that were likely going to hit the man within the next week or two.

Which would be why the killings had taken place so soon, one after the other. Kyle was on a mission to complete business before his time was up.

Blade knew how it felt to be driven to finish a job he couldn't leave undone. But Kyle's mission? Killing others?

That was something he prayed he never had cause to understand.

And was more determined than ever to help Morgan find the guy, to stop him, before anyone else got hurt.

They made it to St. Joseph with no sign of anyone following them. The black car and the tan one seemed to have disappeared to the point that Morgan had to consider that she hadn't been followed at all. That she'd been mistaken.

She didn't believe it, though.

"Why would he suddenly stop having us followed?" she asked Blade as they made their way to the convenience store by Kyle Brennan's house.

Barely taking his gaze off the road, Blade threw her a glance, and shook his head. "There are so many pieces in all of this that have never made sense to me," he said. "Until today. Kyle killing Maddie…"

His words dropped off and she glanced around them,

thinking at first that he'd noticed a car behind them after all, recognized one in front of them, saw Kyle…

But her quick, professional scan gave her nothing. And she figured that he'd stopped talking for more personal reasons.

"We're here to find out the truth, Blade," she said, softly. Her gaze on him. The stiff shoulders, that muscle in his neck, the tenseness of his jaw. "I've never been out to prove you guilty. All I've ever wanted, what I need, is the truth."

He pulled to a stop at a red light and his glance her way lasted uncomfortably longer than the previous one. "But those two points, proving me guilty and finding the truth, they're one and the same to you."

His words tugged at a piece of her heart she'd thought dead and gone. Forcing her to look deep before she answered him. And when she had her answer, she met his gaze. "No," she told him. "I believed that the truth would point me to you, but I wasn't looking for it to. Or in any way wanting it to."

The admission cost a lot. Inside her. Where she'd stopped living.

It scared her.

Left her uneasy. Unsure what it meant. What it changed. If it changed anything.

The light had changed. Completely silent, Blade was focusing on the road again. She did the same. There was nothing else *to* do. He was a client.

Someone had just tried to blow her up.

And they weren't just on individual quests to solve a seventeen-year-old crime. They were on the hunt for a current killer. Or two.

The convenience store was deserted when she and Blade walked in. A woman behind the counter, brown skinned, fortyish looking, named Bonita according to her badge, studied the photo that Morgan handed to her, leaving Morgan to wonder, as the perusal went on far longer than a glance or two, if the woman knew something. And was trying to figure out what to do or how much to say if anything.

"Who did you say you were?" Bonita finally asked, looking from her to Blade and back.

Morgan pulled out her creds, held them clearly for the clerk to see.

She was ready to pull her gun as well when the woman said, "I know him, yeah. He comes in here fairly regularly for his morning coffee. He's the guy who's under investigation for the boating accident that killed his dad. It's been all over local news…"

Morgan nodded.

"Someone from the family hire you to check into it all?" the clerk asked, sliding a hand into her short-sleeved, pocketed work jacket. Blade's step closer, putting his thigh against Morgan's, was no mistake. She was glad for his support.

"No, I'm actually…" She stopped, nodded toward Blade. "We…" she corrected, hating that she was happier not working alone after the bomb episode that morning, "we knew him, years ago. At camp. We're looking up people who were there that summer, talking about stuff that happened and wanted to see Kyle."

True. And yet…unless the woman knew more than she was saying, Morgan was mostly nonthreatening. She'd shown her credentials.

"I haven't seen him in the past couple of days," Bonita said then, her gaze clear, as she handed back the grainy photo. "I don't think he was in for coffee yesterday, and I know he wasn't in this morning."

Morgan looked around for surveillance cameras. Saw none. Suggested to the woman that she speak to the owner of the store about getting some in. For their own safety from theft, if nothing else, and was heading out the door behind Blade when the clerk called out.

"You might ask Jessica," she said. "His ex-wife. They split after their boy died, so I don't know if she can help, but they grew up together, so she might know who'd know."

Bonita's knowledge of Kyle Brennan went back a lot further than the few months since his father's death. Making a mental note, Morgan got Jessica's information, thanked Bonita and headed out the door. Feeling heat on her back as she did so.

As though every step she took was being watched.

Out of curiosity? It probably wasn't every day that the convenience store clerk had a visit from a nationally certified private investigative expert. Most particularly not one interested in a summer camp experience from her youth.

And Bonita could know a whole lot more about Kyle than she was letting on. Like the mission he was on—with little time to complete it. She'd clearly had sympathy in her tone when she'd talked about the man.

Because of his losses.

But surely the clerk didn't condone emotional pain as an excuse to run around the state murdering people. The fact that Morgan even considered the possibility gave her a clue as to how jaded her heart and mind had become over the years.

At some point, she'd begun to believe that anyone was capable of anything.

Which was the complete antithesis of what her exuberant twin would have wanted.

The realization sickened her.

Chapter 14

Jessica was an accountant for a small real estate firm housed in a three-story professional building in downtown St. Joseph. Blade pulled into a diagonal spot out front as Morgan finished a call with Sierra's Web over the car's audio system.

Kelly Chase had called to give them an update on Remy Barton's thoughts pertaining to the case. The child psychiatrist had gone over the case files and Kelly was keeping him apprised of new information as it came in. She'd reported that Remy felt certain, as they all did, that whoever had killed Shane had had something to do with Madison Davis's murder seventeen years before. He'd agreed that a recent stressor would have probably instigated the new string of murders. And had pulled Kyle and Tammy Phillips as the two most likely suspects from those at camp that year. He also strongly believed that the same person was responsible for all three murders.

His reasoning for thinking so had been sound enough that Kelly agreed with him.

Remy also felt that Morgan needed to leave town immediately, get herself as far from the case as possible, until law enforcement found the killer. The escalated threats against her were bothering him greatly.

As they were everyone—with the exception, apparently, of Morgan.

"He's a friend," Morgan reminded Blade as the call disconnected. "Of course he's worried. Same as Jasmine."

And her coworkers at Sierra's Web, too, though Blade didn't bother mentioning Kelly's reminder that if Morgan wanted to be removed from the case, they had other proven investigative experts who could step in.

He almost called the firm back and fired her, when she reached for her door handle, and turned, shaking her head, as he grabbed his. "This is an ex-wife, Blade. A woman who lost a son. The father of whom is likely going to be charged with some kind of negligent, DUI homicide in the death of his own father. She's not going to be receptive to opening up with an unknown man in her midst. And if she happens to know about what happened at camp seventeen years ago, which she might since she and Kyle grew up together, she'll probably freeze up completely with you there."

The sense the woman made pissed him off. Put him on edge. Because she was right. And because he did not, in any way, want her walking into that building alone.

He might not be a cop, but he was a licensed gun carrier and knew how to shoot.

"I'm a big girl, Blade. I'm really good at what I do, and know how to watch my back." Morgan's odd tone hit him in a very personal way. Was she attempting to...comfort...him?

Because she was a professional, and right, he nodded. "I'll stay right here," he told her, his tone firm. "And wait..."

He stopped her with a hand on her arm before she got out of the car. "Put me on speed dial," he told her. "And keep the screen on so you just have to press once."

The glance she gave him, like she wanted to smile, or was about to reach over and give him a quick, reassuring kiss, shook him far more than it should have done, as she slid from the car.

But before leaving him, she paused long enough to set up a speed dial icon for him on her phone's front screen. Held it up for him to see. And then bent down. "If I'm anywhere near as good at my job as I'm told I am, I'm probably going to be a bit," she told him. "Maybe you could use the time to visit a few of the bars near Kyle's house? Show his picture around? Ask if anyone has seen him?"

With a knot in his gut, Blade nodded.

While she'd escaped the explosive planted in her car that morning, they were clearly sitting on a time bomb that was ready to go off. They couldn't afford for Blade to sit around and play babysitter.

But he watched her safely into the building, saw her show her credentials to the security guard, saw the uniformed man check her gun and hand it back to her, before he drove off.

As soon as Jessica Brennan heard Morgan's name, her face changed from questioning to almost warm and she gently ushered Morgan down the hall to a small conference room.

Morgan turned as Jessica shut the door behind them. "I'm sorry just to show up like this, but…"

Jessica cut her off before she could finish. "Oh, don't apologize. I've wanted to meet you forever. I just have to say, I'm so, so sorry about what happened to your sister. I've thought about you so many times over the years. The way that summer changed Kyle…he was so much more aware…more vulnerable, maybe…letting people know he cared about them…and I can't even imagine how it changed your life. I just…please know that your pain is shared…"

Jessica's words broke off as tears filled her eyes, and Morgan, fighting her own rush of emotion, nodded. Took a deep breath. She was there to work. To focus.

Not to feel.

"I was sorry to hear about your son." The words slid forth because they were right. Not because she was working.

Blinking, Jessica nodded again, motioned to a couch along the back wall, took a seat at one end and when Morgan sat on the other said, "The day after he returned from camp that summer, Kyle asked me to take a hike in the woods with him. He told me all about that horrible morning, when Madison's body was found…"

Another force hit Jessica. Chin trembling, she kept her lips together and nodded.

"He told me how much he loved me and asked me to marry him. He said he didn't want to wait another second for me to be his wife and wanted to elope. And…we did…" The woman's smile was bittersweet. Completely lacking in anger or resentment.

And she hadn't yet asked why Morgan was there, suddenly showing up out of the blue.

Morgan took on the sweet woman's pain, pushing away her own, forcing her mind to kick into gear. Kyle's eloping as soon as he got back from camp, after having been clearly interested in Maddie, spelled one thing to her. Guilt.

"He was so angry that summer. He'd talk about everyone who hadn't protected your sister. The camp psychologist, Hampton he said his name was…he just kept going on and on about the man's incompetence, said he was serving his own self-interest and not watching over the kids in his care. Said Madison would still be alive if not for him…"

Morgan didn't tell the woman that the psychologist was dead.

"He's kind of been that way ever since," Jessica said then, her face shadowing. "Always taking it to heart when someone hurt someone else. Not long ago he risked his job as director of technology at Bloomington's." The woman named the national chain of clothing stores. "He actually went to the CEO and threatened to go public with workplace inequities over what he thought was poor treatment of a store manager."

Jessica sounded as proud of her ex-husband as she did worried about him. Maybe more so.

"Have you heard anything recently about the summer that started it all?" Morgan asked, willing herself to stay above water with the compassionate woman. She couldn't afford any sympathy for herself at the moment. Couldn't let the grief take hold. "I was hoping to talk to him, but haven't been able to reach him. The woman at the convenience story thought you might know where he is."

Jessica shook her head. "I've made a point to check in with him regularly since his father's death, and he hasn't said anything about that summer. Hasn't mentioned it in years. But he's in bad shape. I'm really worried about him. I haven't talked to him in a few days. I've been working long hours for a midyear close of books, and I'm worried that I haven't been there enough for him. I tried to call him last night and again this morning, but there was no answer."

Clearly, while the woman didn't want personal involvement with her ex-husband, she cared about him.

And Morgan knew what she had to do. Without telling the woman the ramifications, she suggested that Jessica call the police for a welfare check, and then, if they couldn't find him, place a missing person's report. And sat there beside her as Jessica made the call.

Well over an hour had passed by the time Morgan texted

Blade that she was on her way downstairs. And the first thing she told him, when she climbed into the car, was that she feared Kyle might be suicidal.

If he thought he'd finished his business…he had nothing left for which to live.

"If his last act was to kill me, and he didn't know I'd given my car keys to the police, he'd know that the bomb went off and might think me dead," she told him.

"I'm willing to hope for that," Blade said as he pulled out into traffic.

And then she told him her bigger news. As soon as a missing person's report was filed, they'd have access to Kyle's bank account and credit card statements. She'd already texted Sierra's Web and Jasmine to be on the watch for the report.

The quick look he gave her felt personal as he said, "You *are* impressively good at what you do."

When Morgan felt herself sliding into the warmth his words sent through her, she quickly forced her mind to the job at hand. Asking Blade if he'd found out anything new. And then paid attention, listening between the lines, as he told her he hadn't found out anything new during the hour. Listening for anything that might not seem important to him, but that clicked with her. He'd visited a couple of bars. Kyle hadn't frequented them. Someone from the grocery store closest to his house recognized him but didn't even know him by name. The manager of the bank in his neighborhood said they couldn't give out information to anyone without a warrant, even as to whether Kyle was a client or had been in recently. Blade had posed as an old friend as he'd approached the man's neighbors, but only a couple had been home, and no one had seen him in the last day or two.

In a way, the news was good. Kyle's seeming disappearance could mean that they were more likely on the right track.

But she was too aware of how the world worked, too seasoned at her job, to sit around and count on that. She called in a full report to both Jasmine and Sierra's Web, heard praise from Jasmine and Glen Rivers Thomas regarding the missing person's report—and then, with Blade's full buy-in, told both teams that she and Blade were going to head northeast, toward Flint, to see if they could get an interview with Tammy Phillips. The woman was older than she and Blade, so neither of them had known her well. She'd been in charge of camper special activities—drama and camp photos was all Morgan remembered—taking kids a group at a time, and the counselors had most often just dropped off their charges and come back later to get them.

She'd been someone Morgan had looked up to. Had never, to Morgan's knowledge, ever given anyone reason not to trust her.

But Tammy had been in and out of trouble ever since that summer. There'd been a pregnancy that next year, with the baby placed with child services, to eventually be adopted out. After that she'd done time for a number of things, including petty theft, prostitution and purposefully running her car into a male boss who'd fired her. The man's injuries hadn't been serious, and she'd been out of jail almost a year. But her family members had all refused to take her back in, so she was sharing an apartment with another former prostitute. She'd just, the week before, been fired for the third time since her release—a job stocking shelves at a discount store—for losing her temper with customers. From what Sierra's Web had found, there'd been talk on social media about her having threatened a customer, but no charges were filed. Tammy had claimed that the guy hadn't filed because he'd deserved what she'd given him.

It could all add up, the final stressor being the most recent job loss.

"But what would any of it have to do with Madison's murder?" Morgan asked herself as much as Blade, thinking aloud as they sped across highway miles. "Or Shane's or Hampton's? I don't remember her ever having any kind of crisis at camp."

"Shane never talked about her, either," Blade added.

So maybe they were on the wrong path. But she had to keep looking, anyway. Two expert teams of professionals were working the case. Morgan's job was to go underground and find out what they couldn't.

To find the one small crumb that could bring it all together.

Something for which she'd been searching, unsuccessfully, for close to two decades. But there were so many more pieces now. Which meant a lot more crumbs that could be languishing out there, never to be found if she didn't look all over. Overturn every single rock.

No matter how unlikely it might be to tell her the truth.

At Morgan's suggestion, they drove through a well-known high-quality sandwich shop on the way toward Flint. And at his own, ate while he drove. As unbelievably busy as Blade had been over the past few years, as his company reached heights of success he'd failed to dream of, he'd taken to using the time driving from construction site to construction site as his lunch hour. And lately, his dinner hour, too.

Whether by some kind of telepathic agreement, or just because they were both filled with thoughts and impressions pertaining to the past forty-eight hours, he and Morgan were silent for most of the way to the little town just before Flint, Tammy Phillips's last known address.

Unlike their attempts to locate Kyle Brennan, they had no trouble finding the woman. Though two minutes into the interview in the small living room of her rented apartment, Blade was beginning to wish they hadn't been so lucky.

"I wouldn't have thought it possible for you to get any sexier, Construction Man," the woman purred, taking a seat right next to him on the couch. With the whole couch stretching out bare beside them.

While Morgan sat in the armchair perpendicular to him.

Construction Man. The woman had kept track of him?

"But look at you, you have," she finished, touching one finger to the top of his hand.

Blade didn't even chance a peek at Morgan. Didn't want to know, either way, if she was at all bothered by the camp activities director's familiarity.

As though they'd known each other far more personally than he'd told Morgan they had.

What he knew was that he was a distraction, getting in the way of the job.

He stood and asked if Tammy minded if he used her restroom. Even though she made a point of telling him that he could use the one attached to her bedroom down the hall and to the right, making a point to apologize for the little bits of lingerie she'd left out, he quickly excused himself as though he couldn't wait to find out for himself what was there.

And scoped out a different half bath, first door on the left.

To give Morgan time to do her job so they could get the hell out.

Since he was in the little lavatory, he actually took a

few seconds to pee, but then, second-guessing his choice to leave the room, hurriedly washed his hands and made a beeline back to the living room. Morgan was trained. Armed. And capable.

Blade still didn't like leaving her alone with a murder suspect.

Morgan was standing by the front door when he returned. Tammy, still on the couch where he'd left her, stood as soon as he appeared, and walked toward him. "You don't have to go so soon, do you?" she asked, touching her arm to his as she glanced up into his eyes.

He glanced over at Morgan, who didn't say a word.

"I can always drive you where you need to go afterward," Tammy said softly, her tone loaded with innuendo, at which point Blade's tolerance ran out.

"I'm with Morgan," he said, quite clearly, glancing at the investigator he'd hired as though there was a whole lot more between them than work.

Doing so convincingly enough that Tammy stepped back, a sullen look overtaking her lined and used-looking features. "Well, who'd have thought?" she said, her accommodating sexy tone suddenly filled with sarcasm—and bitterness. "He gets the girl, kills her twin and then gets the girl again?"

"Let's go." Morgan's tone was an order.

By the time she'd finished uttering it, he was at the door, pulling it open. Trusting that she'd managed to get all the information she'd needed during his minute down the hall.

Neither of them spoke until they were back in the car. He'd started the engine and was pulling away, trying to find a way to get Morgan to believe that he'd never had a single personal conversation with Tammy Phillips in the past, when Morgan said, "I sent a text to everyone while

I was waiting on you. Tammy's just joined Kyle at the top of our suspect list."

He'd been in the bathroom no more than a minute, two tops. Glancing at Morgan, seeing the tension in her jaw, he asked, "Why?" Praying it didn't have anything to do with him.

They were running out of time. He had to keep Morgan alive. And would be much better able to do so if she could trust him a little.

"That baby she had? The one that ended up being adopted out? It was Hampton's."

Blade pulled to a quick stop at the end of the street. Stared over at Morgan. Shook his head and looked again. "What?"

Throwing up her hands, she said, "According to her, at any rate. I've got everyone following up as we speak."

"How did that...? What did you...?" He'd known she was good, but, in less than a minute she'd managed to get so much information.

"I asked her how well she knew Mark Hampton," Morgan said. "She told me, 'Well enough to have his baby.' And then, when my mouth fell open, she told me that they'd had an affair all summer. She'd thought they had a future. But when Maddie was killed and summer camp came to an abrupt halt, she asked him about their next steps and he told her there weren't any. He was married. Apparently, she went to his wife, told her about the affair, about the baby. She took great delight in letting me know, without taking a breath, that the marriage ended less than two years after that."

"And the baby?"

"She claimed Mark signed off on the adoption. Oh, and...that the drugs in the baby's system were ones Mark gave her to help regulate her emotions."

"You believe her?" Blade asked, glancing in the mirror to make certain there was still no one behind him.

Morgan's shrug registered right about where he was landing. Turning the corner, heading toward the town's Main Street, he said, "We'll wait to hear what Sierra's Web reports back on that one."

And when Morgan said that she'd like to speak to Tammy's last employer, the manager of the discount store they'd passed on their way to the apartment complex, he headed in that direction. Trying like hell to tell himself that there was no change in Morgan.

No new doubts in her mind.

But with several glances in her direction, couldn't get a feel for where she was at. On anything.

And before he'd even decided to speak, he heard himself blurt, "I knew Tammy like you did in the past. Period. She was someone I dropped the boys off to. I swear to God, she didn't even seem to notice me, and even if she had, I sure as hell didn't notice her. Not in that way." He sounded like he was some kind of geeky high school kid trying to impress someone.

Rather than the wealthy, successful contractor he'd become.

Because he didn't see himself as successful. And didn't give a damn about the money. How could he when he lived under the shadow of an unsolved murder that had his name on it?

When he stopped at the next light, and turned to look at Morgan, she was studying him. He couldn't make out her expression but didn't feel arrows coming at him. "I swear to you, Morgan." The second he'd seen her, talking to her twin, trying to get Madison to listen to her about something while Maddie had been busy watching Shane, he hadn't looked at any other female without having the other come second.

Which was why he was still single.

That, and the shadow he lived under.

When it felt like Morgan was going to just sit there, not talking to him, forever, the light changed, and he pulled forward. Fully aware that he wasn't going to convince her of anything.

She needed the proof they didn't have.

Tammy's employer, and the bartender at a bar around the corner from her apartment, both painted the same picture. Tammy Phillips was a bitter woman with anger issues who blamed men for everything bad that had ever happened in her life.

And she was a woman who couldn't seem to live without men, too. She flirted with any guy she thought had money, and then, if he slept with her and ditched her, she targeted them. The bartender knew of two different times she'd told men's wives that she'd slept with them.

Both times, she'd been telling the truth.

The information by itself didn't make Tammy a killer. But the way she'd homed in on Blade when he'd made it clear he had no interest in Tammy—blurting out about killing one sister and still getting the other one...

She'd been reminded of things she'd heard the summer Maddie had died. Maybe not the exact words, but the tone of them, the content...

Her parents had tried to keep her away from all the publicity, but they hadn't been able to keep her off the internet. She'd read everything she could find.

Desperately searching for answers she still hadn't found.

And if Shane Wilmington's and Mark Hampton's deaths

remained unsolved, she would still be seeking. The quest had no end without the answers.

The bartender had brought up a self-defense instructor Tammy had mentioned, someone who could feasibly have taught the woman how to kill with pressure to the neck, among other things. She'd also said that Tammy, who was usually in every night, hadn't been at the bar the past couple of nights. The FBI team and Sierra's Web were already checking into Tammy's activities as much as they could without a warrant.

Any information Morgan and Blade could add would speed up the process. Until someone came up with enough for a warrant to bring the woman in for questioning.

She glanced over at Blade as he drove a few miles out of town toward the business address of the self-defense instructor. She couldn't talk to him about the confusing emotions roiling around inside her where he was concerned—couldn't let her focus be sidetracked right when she was on the cusp of something huge. But knew she had to get one thing out.

"I believe you," she said, only realizing it was a sentence hanging there out of the blue, when she came out of her own head enough to hear herself. She'd given that statement no modifier. Believed him about what?

But when he glanced over at her, his green eyes alive in a way she'd missed so much, giving her a nod before returning his attention to the road, she figured he understood.

And felt better.

Chapter 15

Donna Abigail, the self-defense instructor, hadn't been willing to speak with them and Morgan hadn't pushed.

"A hostile witness is likely to go straight to the suspect," she told Blade as he pulled out of the driveway and, taking Morgan's next suggestion, to try to see if Tammy's mother, who lived in Flint, would talk to them, he headed back to the highway.

She knew he was frustrated. Seemed to be seething with an overload of the tension that was consuming her, too, as her mind took her on yet another rundown of the case.

There'd been nothing from the coroner on either body that could tell them anything except how Shane and Hampton had died, and approximate times of death.

No fingerprints. Nothing even that tied Shane's and Hampton's deaths together.

The bomb in Morgan's car had been flown to Sierra's Web and was being analyzed. She was hoping that it would give them a clue. At least a place to search next.

"Unless something changes, I think we need to find an out-of-the-way place to spend the night tonight." She dropped the suggestion into the silence that had fallen in the car. Dinnertime was approaching. A couple of hours after that and darkness would be upon them.

The second night since Shane had landed at Blade's feet in the pit.

"Just in case whoever put that bomb in my car thinks it killed me, I'd like to stay out of sight of Rocky Springs, and Detroit."

It meant they'd be spending the night, if not in each other's direct company, at least very close.

"Agreed."

"Your duffel and my go bag are already in the trunk, and we can stop for anything else we might need."

He'd shown no reaction, no indication of any emotion at all attached to them being out overnight together. She should be thankful.

Ironically, his lack of care to something that, at one point in their lives, would have been the most major experience of a lifetime, left her a bit peeved.

Her response was so unacceptably unprofessional that she brushed it away. "I'd like to have Sierra's Web secure an overnight private rental for us so it can't be traced to either of us," she continued. "Small-town-getaway kind of thing. We'd be just another couple of strangers, and yet, in a place by ourselves in case Kyle, or whoever, discovers us. I don't want anyone else hurt, like they could have been with that fire on my balcony last night."

He didn't even glance over at her, his gaze trained on the road, as he said, "Fine. The safest place they can get where we can blend in undetected. Whatever it costs."

Ten minutes later, with the firm promising an overnight destination within the hour, Morgan was once again silently going over case information. She needed more space than her phone to see everything together. She needed Blade's dining room, his wall.

And until she could get out of the car and spread out to

get a more complete picture all at once, Morgan focused on the road, the woods and farmlands they were passing, every part of their surroundings, looking for anything that sparked her. She mentally reviewed the verbal report Sierra's Web had just delivered to her and Blade over the car's audio system.

The flare on her balcony the night before had been a dead end. Any identifying information had burned up. But based on size and what forensics had determined as content, the thing could have been purchased anywhere, most likely online. Silver's men had checked local places and had gotten nowhere.

Same with the bomb in her car that morning. Glen's team was still working on it, but from what they could determine, the thing could have been made in any kitchen. Hudson's team was checking internet searches for bomb creation tutorials made by Kyle, Tammy, the Donnelly brothers and Blade, and would then be doing the same search for the entire list of camp names starting with those their research led them to believe were most likely to commit a crime. Based on past criminal history—other than Kyle and Tammy, there were only some minor infractions— combined with any known life changes that could be stressors. From there, they'd go from oldest campers to youngest, as Maddie's death had been blunt force trauma and therefore more likely caused by someone big enough, strong enough, to deliver the blow. They'd also be doing searches of any of the common household chemicals contained in the bomb and comparing them to any possible flare purchases.

Local law enforcement would get warrants for financials where they could, which would allow Sierra's Web to pinpoint their searches more rapidly.

Shane's autopsy overview by Sierra's Web concurred

with the medical examiner's report. Cause of death had already been determined, and both examinations had concluded that the man's body had shown no defensive wounds, leading everyone on the case to believe that he'd known his attacker. His clothes had all been put through forensic testing and there'd been nothing on them to point to the identity of his attacker.

The pressure on his neck had been applied by some kind of smooth surface. The bottom of a shoe with an unmarked arch sole, or anything else that was smooth and four or so inches in width. The break had been smooth. Probably just one quick snap. With the gunshot wound being postmortem.

"Why would someone shoot Shane after he was dead?" She asked the question aloud. It bothered her. That bullet. Mostly because it made no sense.

Which meant she was missing a piece that would explain the action.

"I'd say to frame me, but that means whoever killed him would have to know that I have a license to carry, always have my gun on me, know at least the approximate caliber, know me well enough to know that, given the circumstances that night, I'd shoot. But you'd figure the killer would know that the coroner would be able to tell that the bullet didn't kill Shane, so it doesn't really make sense, does it?" His frown was half in shadow as the lowering sun cast a beam across him.

"The caliber of bullet does," she answered him honestly. "And if you did shoot him, knew he had a gunshot wound, shooting in the air that night could easily be explained as your attempt to make it look like self-defense. But...why? Why make up such a ruse, if you didn't need to shoot him at all because he was already dead, which you'd know if you'd killed him?"

"Unless I didn't know whatever I did to his neck had been fatal. What if he was still breathing?" Blade's tone held none of the fatigue she'd heard from him two days before. As though…he wasn't feeling the weight of suspicion on himself, but, rather, was putting himself in a killer's position.

He was right there with her. Committed to the truth, just as he'd told her he'd be. Her heart swelled, her admiration for him grew more than she'd ever have thought possible it could, as she looked over at him.

"From what the ME said, the break was in the upper cervical spine and resulted in instant death," she said slowly. "Breathing would have stopped instantly. There'd be no pulse. So why shoot at close enough range for the bullet to go completely through?" Depending on how long after death that shot had been made, there wouldn't have been any blood spatter. But, still, why shoot at all?

"If someone knew you carry a pistol, but wasn't sure of the exact details that would show up in forensics, and was trying to frame you…"

But that still didn't fit. Anyone who'd go to all that trouble, who knew that much, particularly someone who knew how to kill a person with quick pressure to the neck, would know that an ME would discover the shooting had happened after death…

"It has nothing to do with you," she said then, staring at Blade. Catching his gaze briefly as he glanced over at her and then back to the highway. "It's overkill. Whoever killed Shane already had the plan in place to frame you, by dumping the body with you alone on a locked site. The gunshot, that was just for himself…"

Silver and his people were already working with Jasmine to interrogate everyone who'd had access to Blade's schedule, who might have known that he'd be at the site late at night alone. But the killer could also just have been following him, like he'd had Morgan followed the day before…

And if the killer was Kyle, who lived just minutes away from Rocky Springs…who could make the kill, and the dump, and be home in bed within the hour…

"If I'm Kyle…" Blade's voice drew her gaze back to him, her mouth slightly open. It was like he'd read her mind, that he'd known what she was thinking…something that had happened in the past. The one thing that had convinced her that what she felt for him was real.

Because he'd been the only other person in her life, still was, other than her identical twin, who'd ever done that…

He was still talking, and she quickly focused, catching up with his description of how he'd feel as a senior camp counselor falling for the most beautiful, vivacious girl at camp. "And I think I had the girl first, I've made it clear she's the one for me, and Shane, the womanizer, who didn't really care for anyone but himself at that point, comes along and steals her away, just to play with her…"

She nodded, energized in a way she hadn't been in a very long time. Kept her eyes on Blade as she took over. "He has trouble controlling his temper," she said. "He's furious when Shane goes to the party to see Madison, waits around, thinking he'll charm some sense into her after you make Shane leave. But she's thinking she's in love with Shane at that point. She starts to scream, and he lashes out. Meaning just to quiet her down, but…the way you said he threw that hammer, an instant reaction that could have been deadly… he just used more force than he meant to on Maddie. She dies on him. He knows no one knew he'd been out there and takes off, leaving her there to die. The next day, when he gets away with it, it's like a new lease on life for him. He marries, keeps himself in check. Until his son dies…"

"He starts drinking heavily…his wife leaves him…he's out with his dad, the one person who probably stuck by him…"

The words caught at Morgan and she stared at Blade's profile. Needing to know…had his dad been there for him? After the suspicion in their small town had ruined the older man's business?

None of *her* business.

Blade's conversation was and she tuned in to hear "…and he goes after Hampton because the guy talked to him about his anger issue after the hammer incident, but didn't intervene? Didn't get him fired and into an anger management program? He's blaming everyone else for the hell his life has become?"

She drew air in sharply, unconsciously, as something else occurred to her. And drew Blade's gaze to her, too, before he quickly returned to the road.

"And he blames you for making Shane leave the party," she said. "And since you were already a suspect, he's hoping to make you pay as he expects to…with an indictment and long prison sentence."

"And you?" Blade asked, glancing at her one more time. "Why does he want you dead?"

She'd thought because she was getting too close to catching him, but that look in Blade's eye, as though he expected more from her…

"Because I'm not Maddie."

Blade's slow nod, that intense look in his green eyes, the grim set of his chin, told her, more than anything past or present, just how much the imminent threat against her life was affecting him.

They told her that he still cared.

Even if he didn't want to.

* * *

Blade had thought fate an enemy in the past. But the ironic twist of cruelty hitting him between the eyes as he drove was beyond the pale.

He'd grieved for Madison Davis. And for Morgan. He'd never recovered from that summer at camp. And not just because of his suspect status. He'd hurt because Morgan was hurting. Had never gotten over the loss of the future he'd thought they'd have together.

And he was now not only being framed for more murders, but he was also facing an unknown fiend trying to kill Morgan, too?

Kyle Brennan, Tammy Phillips or someone they didn't yet know. They could be sneaking up on them that exact second, on that very road. How could Blade possibly hope to beat what he didn't know? What he couldn't prepare for?

He couldn't let her die. There'd be no life left inside him.

When Morgan's phone rang, he felt the sound reverberate through every nerve in his body. Hoped to God they were about to hear that someone had caught Kyle. That he'd had definitive proof on him to nail him for all three murders.

And remembered that he'd given up on hope as soon as he heard Agent Jasmine Flaherty's voice come over the car's audio system. "Take me off speakerphone." The tone brooked no refusal.

With a glance at Blade, maybe with some apology in it, Morgan did so. And then signaled him to pull over.

Heart pounding with dread, he did so immediately, getting to the shoulder, and putting the vehicle in Park so that he could turn and glance all around them.

No, that didn't make sense. The FBI wouldn't be having them pull over if danger was coming up behind them.

Must mean it was in front of them…

Morgan's ashen face stopped his train of thought. She glanced at him, stared at him rather, her expression full of emotions he couldn't decipher, and then looked out the front windshield as she said, "We're on our way," and hung up.

Then, staring out the windshield said, "We have to head back to St. Joseph. You're wanted for questioning."

Blade's gut, his entire being, steeled into numbness as his mind took over. He stared at Morgan. "For what?" But he knew. Another body.

Who?

And how many more people had to die before…

Morgan was a talking statue. Sitting straight, staring straight. If not for the blinking of her eyes he…

"Gary Randolph was found an hour ago in the dumpster behind the office building where Jessica works."

He felt a prick of emotion. A flash of the man's face appeared and was gone. "He was our boss," he said slowly, sitting there in the driver's seat, going nowhere. But back. "He hired all the boys' camp counselors. Was the one who…" His words faltered as he slid back in time, felt the stab of panic, and then, forcing himself out, finished his sentence. "The one who hauled me out of bed that morning. The first person who asked me if I'd killed Maddie." Throat tight, he swallowed. Shook his head.

"He's dead, Blade. He died fifteen minutes after they found him. He'd been shot, had lost too much blood."

His brain started to catch up with the present. "In St. Joseph?" The city they'd just left. *He'd* just left. Behind the building where he'd dropped off Morgan, and, an hour later, had been texted to come pick her up.

"Time of dumping was within the last three hours. And based on when he was last seen…"

"…he was shot when you were with Jessica Brennan,"

he finished for her. While he'd been heading around town. Building an alibi of people, a few of whom would say they'd seen him, but none of whom could speak for what he might have done in between those short visits.

And Morgan wasn't looking at him.

Getting out of the car, he headed to her door.

She was out of the vehicle before he'd made it halfway around the hood, passed him by and was already behind the wheel before he got in.

He could make a run for it. She didn't know he wouldn't.

He'd pulled over beside a forest of pine trees. Something Michigan was famous for. A world within which, with his skills, he could survive, and keep hidden, until they quit looking for him.

A cornered man would run.

A guilty man would.

And Morgan wasn't doing anything to make sure he didn't. She just sat there, car running, waiting for him to get in with her.

She had to think like a professional. To remain fully on the job—mentally and physically. Morgan couldn't look at Blade. Couldn't bleed with him. Emotions would cloud her judgment. Make her weaker than either of them could afford.

When she felt him drop beside her, and her peripheral vision caught his hand closing the door, she put the car in Drive and took off. Looking for the first available turnaround.

Even as she did so, everything inside her tensed at the idea of getting anywhere near St. Joseph. Jasmine had told her that they wanted her there for her own safety. Thinking that Blade had been responsible for the warnings to her to back off. For the flare on her balcony that hit after he'd been in her room that night. Would know exactly where and how to aim. And a contractor would most definitely have access to flares.

The bomb…he'd been with her more than anyone. Could have planted the thing when he'd arrived at the police station that morning.

Her friend had had a supposition that fit. Made sense.

But it didn't ring true to Morgan. And she was done believing what other people told her.

She'd left the FBI so she could do what she had to, within the law, to follow her instincts and the clues to the truth. Not just to a confession. But to provable truth.

Jasmine didn't know Blade. Hadn't known him in the past. Didn't know about the careful way he watched, making sure everyone was okay, even as he joked and played around. Hadn't heard about his hopes and dreams for himself and his family. His love of Michigan.

And she hadn't spent any time with him in the present, either. Hadn't seen his reactions as each piece of evidence came in. Or witnessed him not jumping to his own defense, as a guilty person would have done.

Turning her back on the confidence her one-time partner had given her, she had to tell him, "I'm concerned that the killer is setting us up." From there, free thoughts just started pouring out. "I'm afraid because he had to know we were just in that town. Or had known we were heading to it. That he's been following us all along, and we just haven't caught his tail. Maybe he got close enough to put a tracker on something we carry with us…"

She swerved before the words were even fully out of her mouth. Pulled off, stopped so abruptly she and Blade were both projected forward against their seat belts.

And looked over to find him unhooking his belt. "I'll

take the trunk, and exterior, you handle inside," he said, already climbing out.

She checked the OBD II diagnostics port first. Under seats and floor mats. Glove box and console. Then dived for the items they'd carried into the car with them. They hadn't noticed anyone following them since before they'd changed vehicles.

After a search, she used her phone to run a manual tracker alert, came up with nothing, and exited the vehicle to run the scanner under the bumpers and hood.

"Check the wheel wells," Blade, who'd been going through their bags in the trunk, said as she passed by him.

She did so without comment. Conscious of everything around her, and on the journey ahead. As soon as they were back in the car, buckled in, she put the car in gear and sped off, spewing gravel behind her. "We have to show up," she told him, her gaze glued to the road, and the mirrors. Specifically, not running into Blade. "It's an official law enforcement request. But we need to be prepared that the killer is counting on that."

Her mind was in full gear. He'd paid for that service.

She'd give it to him for free.

The knowledge should have landed with a severe blow to her equilibrium. Taking her breath. Instead, it settled upon her with the peacefulness of truth.

"When I'm being questioned, he'll have a trap for you," Blade said, again sounding more like a work partner than any kind of suspect she'd ever interrogated. He hadn't even asked why he was wanted, what evidence they had against him.

Nor had he questioned their turning around.

Or made a noise about the fact that she had to drive.

It was when she realized that, that she glanced at him. "This has been your life...for seventeen years...you've lived with the doubt of others, the questions coming at you again and again, out of the blue…"

He shrugged. She only caught the move peripherally. Didn't think he'd even glanced her way.

"He had one of your business cards in his wallet. And a call, not from the number we have for you, but in a voice message that says this is Blade, on his phone…before the call was cut off. He also had a meeting scheduled with you on his calendar for this afternoon." All of which could have been done by the killer. Or, Blade could have used a burner to call the man as soon as Morgan had entered the office building that afternoon. Could have met up with him, shot him. Could have, as Jasmine speculated, been rushed when Morgan had called to say she was ready, and been forced to dump the body, still alive, in the dumpster.

"There's a record of him calling your number, Blade," she said then. "This morning." The statement should have been in question format. Or at least in challenge.

Instead, she felt the warning in her words. Her warning him to be careful. Not to say anything that could incriminate him.

He was being set up. She was certain of it. Would take the belief to her grave if it came to that.

But she had no reason to think he'd believe her.

He wasn't pulling out his phone to check incoming calls. "What time?" He'd asked the right question at least.

"Eight twenty."

"We were at the FBI office. I had it on silent." That's when he pulled out his phone. Pressed and scrolled. And then held it up.

She grabbed the phone. Glanced at the screen.

The incoming call was there. A missed call. It was the

only listed in recent calls by that number. "And you didn't wonder who'd called?"

"I get robocalls all the time, just like everyone else. I didn't recognize the number. There was no voicemail."

Good. The answer was a good one. No one could argue with it. If he kept that up, he'd be fine.

She couldn't check outgoing calls while she was driving. Blade pocketed his phone without doing so. Because he knew he hadn't made one. The thought came to her and was brushed aside for more important business.

They'd lost precious time searching for trackers that hadn't been there.

If she didn't get him in for interrogation soon, she could be thought to be compromising her working relationship with the FBI and making herself a suspect in collaboration with a killer.

Pressing a little harder on the gas, figuring if she got pulled over, she'd have an alibi proving they were trying to get there quickly, Morgan kept both hands tightly clenched to the steering wheel as she gave him the worst. "He muttered something as he was dying," she told Blade. "A bystander got it on video. Parts were indecipherable. Sierra's Web has the recording and is breaking down the decibels to see if they can get more. But…he clearly said your name, Blade."

That's when the man next to her turned his head, forcing her to make a quick glance over, and with that brief glimpse of emotion in his gaze—was slammed back into the past.

She'd seen the look before. Seventeen years past. The morning after Maddie's death. Blade had come toward her.

And she'd called him a killer.

Screamed at him to get away from her.

And there was no way she could take that back.

Ever.

Chapter 16

She wasn't screaming at him. Or trying to get away. Blade held tight to that thought as he repeated what she'd said. Something he'd already been thinking. "It's a setup. You have to turn back around, Morgan. We already know he wants me locked up, which is fine, but he needs you dead before he goes to prison. He's setting a trap to kill you and you're driving straight into it. He needs to know that no part of Maddie is still out here."

"If it's Kyle." She wasn't arguing the setup.

And if what she'd just put him through was her idea of an interrogation, she wasn't nearly the expert she'd been cracked up to be.

He knew that she was, though. Which meant...

"You know I didn't do it." The emotion that came up in him as he finished the sentence overwhelmed and shocked him.

"Yes."

He couldn't leave it at that. "You believe I didn't kill Maddie."

Her chin puckered, and her lips tightened. "Yes."

Blade blinked back the emotion welling behind his lids, gritted his teeth against it and focused on keeping Morgan alive. He couldn't afford to get weak.

Not even with relief.

There was no good news until he knew Morgan was safe.

"You have to turn around."

She shook her head. "I can't, Blade. If I do, you become a fugitive. And I'm one with you."

"Only until we find the truth."

"Without help?" She sent him a quick glance, a look in her eye he hadn't thought he'd ever see again. That look... it had carried a wealth of feeling.

Aimed at him.

That wasn't hate.

That was, in fact, the opposite of the grief-filled words she'd hurled at him during their last meeting so long ago.

"You and I have been working on this thing for almost two decades, Blade. We're both intelligent people. And more determined than anyone else will ever be. But alone, doing it ourselves, we've failed. With the new murders, we have the best chance here we're ever going to get. We have to do this the correct way."

He knew she was right. Didn't want to accept what that meant. "We haven't failed." He told her something he used to tell himself, when he got so tired he'd start to wonder why he bothered. "We just haven't succeeded yet."

As long as he kept trying, he was on his way to success.

Which meant they were going to have to head back to St. Joseph.

But not without a plan.

One that, even if it failed, ensured that Morgan Davis stayed alive.

"Take me to the beach, at the edge of town," he told her then. "There's a marina, a guy I know, a friend of mine. He'll get you across the water to my boat. It's not the one that's registered in my name. It's registered under an alias with a post office box. It's legal, can be traced back to me, but not without effort and probably warrants. You get on that, take it out and wait for me to call." He gave her the details as they came to him. Names. Where to find keys. Made sure she still knew how to drive a boat. "The boat was Michael's idea," he said, naming his friend. "Said I didn't have to use it but having it there would give me peace of mind if I ever felt the walls closing in on me. Did I mention that he's a retired therapist who counsels victims of various forms of PTSD?"

And before she could get a word in edgewise, he continued with, "I'll drive myself into the station. And when I'm done there, if Sierra's Web has done their job, we'll have a private rental with a dock for the night."

"They're not looking for a rental with a dock," she told him. But he noticed she was staring ahead, driving steadily. Not frowning at him. Or shaking her head.

"They will be," he told her, and pulled out his phone.

She couldn't leave Blade to drive himself to the police station. There were too many unexplained actions hanging over them. She couldn't desert him.

But she liked the boat idea a lot. And a rental with a dock. She heard Blade on speakerphone talking to Glen Rivers Thomas about having someone there get them one for the night. And she inserted, "When you get an address, call Blade or myself with it. Don't put it in writing. And don't tell anyone else about it."

Blade's gaze shot to her. And he continued to watch her after he hung up.

"I don't like that we didn't find a tracker," she told him.

"You think someone on the case is involved in this?"

"Do you have any other explanation for how someone knew we were in St. Joseph, at the exact time we were there, when we only decided to go on the spur of the moment, and only the teams working the case knew about our where-abouts? How could anyone have framed you without knowing exactly when we were there?" She ended with where she'd begun. Repeating the question that had been hanging there bothering her since she'd first heard about Randolph's death.

"The fact that we were only there for such a short time, and no one knew we were there, makes it look more like I did it."

Yeah. She got that. Had understood it since her phone call with Jasmine. And to that end…

"Jasmine…we were partners for years… We'd grown re-ally close, like sisters, I thought. But when I quit…she was glad. Relieved. And at my shock, she explained that no lon-ger being partners meant that we could pursue a personal relationship. I swear to you, I had no idea she had feelings for me. She'd never let on. And I let her down gently. Told her my heart was dead in that area, but… She's been ada-mant about wanting me off this case and every time I talk to her, she gets more and more uptight. This morning, she ac-tually pulled me in for a hug before we left. Told me that she loved me. And what if she's lost sight of the case because, she's seen, with you back in my life…she knows that my heart wasn't dead? That it had been in your possession all along? Locked up with all the other truths I couldn't find?"

She continued to push the pedal nearly to the floor as she spoke. Her hands sweaty on the steering wheel. But…they were likely driving into some kind of trap. And if she wasn't good enough to get them out of it in time…he had to know.

And even if they made it through and went on with their separate lives, she owed him the truth. She loved him.

She wasn't telling him right out. They were working. But…

Blade hadn't said a word. Speeding along, she couldn't

spare but a glance at him. Didn't dare test herself with even that.

She hadn't been making an avowal to a potential hookup. She'd been speaking a long-overdue truth that a good man deserved to hear.

Working for her client so he had all the facts.

Because if Jasmine was the one who'd let the killer know that they'd be in St. Joseph... "Whoever leaked our location has to have figured out who the killer is," she said softly, into the silence that had fallen. "How else would they have known who to tell?"

Blade glanced at her then. She felt the intensity of his gaze, even before his face appeared peripherally. "It's not like someone who worked the case in the past could be in on it," he said slowly. "The detectives in Ludington...they're all retired. They just sent case files..."

Ludington. Or rather, the huge acreage of camp land just outside city limits, which had been the end of life as both of them had known it.

"I'm going to drive you to the station, Blade. Walk inside it with you. And wait there, surrounded by police officers, for you to finish your business there."

"No." His tone was as harsh as she'd ever heard it. "No. I refuse to go."

"Blade." She could be firm, too. "We have to see this through. He was rushed today with Randolph. Mistakes were made. And I say he, but it doesn't have to be Kyle. You notice how Tammy seemed to know you instantly? And even have information about your career? If she was tipped off, she could have driven to St. Joseph this morning and then have time to get back to her apartment before we did. We stopped to get sandwiches..."

"You're not driving into a trap for me," he said again.

She saw the headshake even from the corner of her eye. "I can't sit here and be a part of that."

"You're right, you're driving," she said. "They need you alive to be their scapegoat, so you'll be safe. I'll be down on the floor. When we get to the station, you pull up to the door, and I'll get out and hide in front of you as you walk in."

"No."

He'd developed a stubborn streak.

"I will not live to see you die, Morgan."

"And I won't live at the cost of your freedom."

"I'm the boss." His tone was sharp.

He was her official link to the case, yes. The one who'd hired her through a firm that was known to successfully assist the FBI in all kinds of cases.

Didn't matter anymore.

She hadn't stood behind him in the past. Perhaps if she had, her life would have turned out differently. Maybe she wouldn't have been alone all those years…

"You can fire me if you want to," she said right back. "I'm not leaving you to face things alone. Not again. You either take us there with me hidden on the floor, or I drive us there in plain sight."

And that was the last she was going to say about it.

Blade's instincts were screaming at him not to go to the police station in St. Joseph. More bodies turning up…the guy was escalating… Which meant to him that there was no way to catch the guy with logic.

Or the bodies were the result of years of planning, and the kills were being executed by more than one person. Perhaps murder for hire? With one person at the helm?

Remy Barton and Kelly Chase both thought they were

dealing with one killer, based on the way the bodies were being deliberately staged, but also the overkill. Though, with Randolph there'd been none. Because the killer had run out of time.

"If there's someone on the inside, and we head to the station, they might just lock me up," he said aloud, stating what was concerning him most at the moment. He didn't give a whit about spending a night in jail. Been there done that. "If that happens, I can't be out here, helping you."

He couldn't keep her safe.

When she didn't immediately respond, Blade pressed a little harder. They were only twenty minutes from town and he was already in the driver's seat. "What if I agree to show up for questioning in Rocky Springs?" he asked. He knew James Silver well enough to trust the guy to play by the book. And the idea was growing on him for other reasons as well. "If there's a trap in St. Joseph, we avoid it," he pressed. FBI Agent Jasmine Flaherty had traveled from Detroit to meet them in St. Joseph. And with Morgan's doubts about the agent…it seemed smarter to be in more of a protective custody when the agent came at him.

And they'd be closer to his boats, both the legitimate and the alias.

The boats were not only his haven; they were also his safe place. Both were built with bulletproof synthetic fiber in between sheets of fiberglass. And were fully stocked with enough supplies to last him for months, if need be, including fishing poles, burner phones and bullets. Dr. Michael Comer had suggested that when he felt panic coming on, he should go to work on something that brought him both strength and pleasure. When he'd run out of things to do on the first boat, he'd started on the second. There were state-of-the-art televisions, closets with clothes for all seasons, life vests and inflatable boats. He could sail if he had to preserve gas…

Morgan had picked up her phone. He saw the Sierra's Web number come up on the dash display. And glanced back at the road to be momentarily blinded by the nearly setting sun glinting off flashes of metal appearing directly in front of him.

"Down!" he hollered so harshly his throat stung as he threw the car into Reverse and floored the gas, backing at breakneck speeds as bullets sounded in front of them.

He heard the shots. Wasn't sure if they'd landed. Tires squealing, he was rounding a corner, and then backing onto an adjoining country road, to back onto another, and then another. Years of backing construction trailers and cranes into tight spaces were serving them well.

Would his efforts be good enough? With the speeds he was traveling, he couldn't look forward to check. Morgan was still in her seat. Had her gun.

"Morgan? Blade!" Glen Rivers Thomas's voice came over the phone.

"Shots fired!" Morgan's tone was sharp. Controlled. "The car's hit, once. We're not."

The succinct words, her tone, calmed Blade some and, as he reached his destination, he threw the vehicle in gear and shot down the beachfront road toward the marina.

"What the hell's going on?" another voice came over the phone. "Talk to me."

"Hudson, it was a trap. Two motorcycles. They appeared out of nowhere onto the road in front of us, a blockade." Morgan's response was immediate. "They had guns. Hesitated before they shot. Amateurs. Young guys. Peach fuzz. Smaller street bikes. One black. The other silver." She named a well-known brand and then said, "I think we have a mole. Maybe Jasmine. Or someone on the St. Joseph force. Someone knows who the killer is. Tipped him off."

"James Silver might help," Blade inserted then as he rounded the last bend before the marina. "I've got a boat. Will get us on it and wait to hear from you," he said then. Giving orders as though he was law enforcement himself. Or talking to his employees.

A contractor taking back control of his life.

A man determined to save the life of the woman he loved.

Chapter 17

Morgan wanted Madison's killer. Had been prepared to do whatever it took to find him. To die for the answers. She'd made it through seventeen years of failure by imagining what it would be like when she finally had the guy in her sights. Imagining the takedown. No way she'd ever seen herself out on the waters of the massive Lake Michigan, moored far enough out to be invisible from shore, in a thousand-square-foot living quarter beneath the deck, watching cameras for anything approaching—with Blade Carmichael.

In the dark.

He had a satellite phone. Of course. They were using it sparingly.

"All this stuff," she said, looking around, at the supplies she could see, and those he'd shown her, hidden away in cabinets and compartments. "Were you planning to go underground? Run? If they ever came after you again?"

The question seemed to dim the light in his eyes as he sat across from her at the small table that folded down into a double bed. But he held her gaze as he said, "It's a mental health project." And then he went back to the pages of evidence he had spread in front of him. Some of them from one of his boxes, others that he'd printed from an email they'd received from Sierra's Web before they left shore. Reports pertaining to people at camp when Madison was killed. Looks at social media, and other records they could access, one search pertaining to known associations between any of them.

She'd hurt him with her question, so she laid one hand over his. "I wouldn't have blamed you," she said softly. "You've been persecuted for seventeen years for something you didn't do. There had to be a way you could promise yourself that enough was enough."

His green eyes rose to hers slowly. And seemed to show her parts of his soul. As she'd been so certain they'd done in the past. "Living on the run would be worse than persecution," he told her. "I've always known that there was a killer out there who had to figure that I'd be looking for him. I think some part of me was always prepared for him to come finish me off, so the threat was no longer there. I just never thought…for one second…that he'd kill other people first."

She wanted to pull him to her. To hold him tight. And felt his hand turn in hers, his fingers threading through hers. She held on.

"They'll catch the kids on the motorcycles," she told him. "And the fact that they were there…tells me the killer is getting more out of control, which means more mistakes. He's desperate. Knows we're closing in on him."

His gaze holding hers steadily, seeming to burn with liquid fire, he said, "He's desperate, and determined. Willing to risk everything. Which makes him unpredictable. This person, if there is just one, has killed multiple people in less than three days. He wants you gone. He will try anything to make that happen as quickly as possible."

He wasn't telling her anything she didn't know. Was

just saying aloud that which neither one of them had talked about since they'd left the car at the Rocky Springs police station. With James Silver's and Sierra's Web's intervention, they had gotten into a local vacation rental van to drive back to the marina in St. Joseph, where Blade's friend Michael had boated them to the marina to get on Blade's alias cabin cruiser.

Only Sierra's Web, their sole contact, and James Silver knew that they were staying on the boat. The expert firm was still working the case with the FBI. And in light of the near ambush, and the fact that neither Blade nor Morgan were under arrest, it had been made clear to the FBI that Sierra's Web had them in protective custody.

Michael had been told that they'd be boating to a vacation rental with a dock. Not because Blade didn't trust him, but because they had to keep those in the know to the fewest number of people possible.

Blade had given a list of the people he'd seen in St. Joseph that afternoon, and Hudson Warner's tech experts had been able to find him on surveillance cameras. That, in light of the attempt on his life, had convinced the FBI to back off an immediate need to question him in the death of Gary Randolph. They didn't have enough evidence to hold him for anything.

Everyone who'd attended camp the summer of Madison's death, other than Kyle and Tammy, had been notified to be extra-vigilant, and get out of town if possible. Tammy was under twenty-four-hour surveillance. Law enforcement was still attempting to locate Kyle.

Darkness had fallen shortly after they'd anchored. They'd had dinner on the deck, take-out pasta and salads that Silver had had in the van for them. But they'd gone down under immediately afterward—with the windows covered with room-darkening shades that would conceal the light—to get to work.

Blade was still holding Morgan's hand as he said, "Something more had to have been going on at camp that summer." As his words ended, he pulled his hand away, shuffling through another set of papers, and grabbing for his phone.

She missed the warmth of his fingers, missed the sense of being held, but knew he was right to keep them firmly on track. They'd need to rest. Neither of them would be able to keep going at the top of their game on the little bit of sleep they'd had over the past couple of nights.

"What if whatever it is, Madison found out about it?" he continued, scrolling through his phone. He stopped at something. Turned his phone to show her a series of pictures he'd taken at camp that summer. She recognized them from ones she'd seen on his dining room wall. Had it only been the day before?

Seemed like they'd lived months since then.

The photo he'd enlarged, so that only parts of it were showing on the screen, caught her immediate attention. She homed in on what she knew he'd meant her to see.

A group photo, arranged by Tammy but taken by their camp photographer. A boys' camp memorial, with so many heads, they were mere dots until you enlarged them. But all three of the murdered bodies in the morgue were in it.

They would be—that had been the purpose of the photo. There was another one, which had been hanging right next to the first, on Blade's wall, filled with girls' likenesses, including all their counselors...

She looked at Blade. "The camp photographer."

Blade nodded. "He'd have hundreds of photos of activities from that summer. Pictures that might have caught something behind the scenes."

Getting energized again, Morgan continued, "Like Tammy and Mark Hampton in intimate conversation. Or Tammy looking at him as a woman looks at the man she loves."

Her words faltered, fell away, as she looked over at Blade. Like any photos taken of her and Blade might have done?

He held her gaze. Neither of them spoke.

And then they both started in at once. "What if…?"

"We need to…"

"You go," he said to her. "We need to what?"

"Call Hud and get them on those camp photos. Hope to God there are still at least negatives of them."

"We need to wait until ten. We agreed, signal off until then," he reminded her.

Fifteen minutes. "So, what do we think might have been going on at camp?" she asked, forcing herself to stay focused. She was tired. Had started the day very early with a fire on her hotel room balcony. Had been home, to her old office, across the state on interviews, had her car blown up, found out another person she'd known had died. Been shot at.

And had admitted that she was still in love with Blade Carmichael.

Shaking his head, Blade kept scrolling on his phone. Looking at pictures, she assumed. "I don't know," he said. "Maybe Madison stumbled on Hampton and Tammy together? And told Shane? Who told Randolph, who went to Hampton with it…"

The chain of people made sense. "Maddie tells Shane about something…whatever. He goes to the guy who's the boss of all counselors, Kyle Brennan, who goes to the next guy in line of command, Randolph. And if *he* went to Hampton, it either had to do with Hampton's affair, or something that Randolph thought the camp counselor should know. Should handle. Like maybe a phone call to parents of whoever was involved?"

Blade nodded. "Unless it had to do with staff. Tammy and Hampton…maybe…but what if there was something going on with the staff?"

"Like a poker game?" she asked.

"Or something worse. Drug trafficking, maybe?"

"Did you ever hear of anyone being high while you were there?" she asked him. She hadn't.

Blade's headshake was short, to the point. "Didn't mean it wasn't happening, though," he reasserted, looking over at her.

The look wasn't particularly personal. Wasn't at all sexual. But Morgan flooded with desire for the man. Sexual, but far more than that.

He was good for her.

Right for her.

Another part of her.

Sitting there with him, speculating, as she'd done with Jasmine and other coworkers over the years, felt like far more than work all of a sudden. She felt like…more.

More alive.

Fuller.

"What?" Blade asked, bringing to her attention that she was staring at him.

Shaking her head, Morgan meant to get back to work, to make a case-pertinent comment, but something deep inside her compelled her to say, "Back then, I felt like we were on the same mental wavelength." As a piece of information. Not a declaration.

He didn't speak. But didn't look away, either. "I still do."

She expected him to look down, to grab a file. To vacate

the conversation. Stayed present anyway, waiting for him to look away. He didn't.

And eventually said, "I do, too."

It wasn't any kind of proclamation.

But it made her heart soar anyway.

Blade had failed to calculate one very critical danger in his plan to get Morgan away from danger. His own libido.

He'd had lovers over the years—most for periods of time. Had enjoyed his time with all of them. And hadn't felt one iota of the burning need coursing through him as he sat in his haven, his refuge, with the one woman who'd taught him that sparks could actually fly between people.

And with her over there, making it pretty clear that she'd begun to feel things for him again, too—first in the car, which he'd managed to avoid and then…right there—how did a guy sit there on fire and not need to extinguish the burning? Even if only temporarily.

He had no experience with that one. *Excuse me while I pop into the tiny head right on other side of that cardboard wall you're sitting by and relieve myself.*

When his satellite phone rang, he knocked it over in his haste to grab up the lifeline it seemed to have just handed him.

If Morgan noticed his fumbling or was aware of his… physical…distress…she didn't let on. Instead, she answered the phone, turning up the volume on the speaker as she said, "Please tell me you have something substantial."

As though she was drowning and didn't know how much longer she could hold on.

Or maybe he was just reading his own state of mind into her tone.

"We've got something," Hudson Warner's voice came over the line as Blade looked at Morgan.

And he knew, by the quick light in her eyes, that he wasn't completely alone in his struggle to keep the two of them away from personal feelings that seemed to be as alive in the present as they had been in the past.

In spite of the age and experience both of them had gained.

"Good work on Jessica Brennan, Morgan," the tech expert said first, and Blade's gaze slid back over to her, right after he'd managed to pull himself away. Pride for her seeped through his skin, despite the fact that she was not his to take pride in. And the split second ended abruptly as the man continued to speak.

"We've got Kyle's phone and financial records, put everyone on them at once."

They'd located Kyle? Blade's mind flashed ahead, his attention all focused on the case again, as he listened with an ear to figuring out his own next move. How he could help. Whether anyone wanted his help or not.

"Whatever money he's spent, wherever he might be staying, he's paid for with cash he would have had to have on hand. There's no credit card activity. No withdrawals from his accounts…"

Blade's energy fell a level. Warner had said they had something…

"Are we starting to think he's a casualty, too?" Morgan's question drew his gaze, more to see her reaction to the possibility. She didn't seem fazed, one way or another. It bothered him a lot. If their best suspect was dead, were they back to square one again?

How many more times could they do this?

"No," Warner's response came slowly, drawn out as

though the man was in thought. "There was a call made from his cell phone this morning. To Gary Randolph."

Blade's enthusiasm dropped a notch.

"Before or after Randolph called Blade?" If she was looking at him, he didn't know. He wasn't raising his gaze from the paperwork in front of him to find out.

"Before."

Before. "That's interesting," Blade murmured aloud. And then, leaned in toward the phone. "He could have been calling to warn me." He could be trying to deflect suspicion from himself. He understood that. But was part of the conversation, had a valid thought, and was damned well going to be heard.

"That's our theory, as well," another male voice said. Glen Rivers Thomas. The forensic guy who'd actually taken Blade on as a client. The man sounded…more alive than he'd heard him in the past. Not just an automaton with a few words doing his job.

Blade sat up straighter, ready to pursue the matter further, when Hudson's voice came over the line again. Mentioning a name Blade thought sounded slightly familiar but couldn't place—Randy Thomaston. "He was the youngest kid in Shane's cabin," Hudson continued, filling in Blade's blanks. "Agent Flaherty's team was notifying everyone from camp to be vigilant and Randy, upon hearing that Shane Wilmington had been murdered, said that he'd seen something the night of Madison Davis's death. Had mentioned it to Kyle Brennan, but the man had said not to speak up. They knew who'd killed Madison and didn't need to cloud the waters any, or point suspicion at an innocent kid, no matter how much of a douchebag he was. A quote from Randy, not my words," Hudson inserted as, heart pounding blood through his veins, Blade's gaze connected with Morgan's and held on tight.

"Thomaston said that keeping quiet has been nagging at him ever since," Hudson continued, his voice seeming to blare throughout the small cabin inside the boat. Overwhelming it…and Blade. He wanted to end the call. Hang up the phone.

Had to know.

He glanced back down at his papers.

Detected no movement from Morgan's side of the table.

"The guy's a light sleeper. Said he woke up that night when Shane left for the party. Woke up again when he got back. Said it wasn't unusual for Shane to skip out after the guys were asleep. Happened a lot. But that night… Shane left a second time."

"Wait," Blade demanded, his tone fierce as he stared down the phone. "What? Shane left a second time?"

His gaze shot up to Morgan's then, stared into those striking blue eyes that were so wide he almost got lost in them.

"According to Randy Thomaston he did."

That was it. A one-sentence confirmation. And then nothing.

A sentence that could change everything, and no one was running with it? He stood up. They had to do something. Go somewhere. Make something happen.

He saw Morgan, still sitting at the table, and took a deep breath. Reminded himself they were still on the phone. Slid back into the booth.

"I assume you're all thinking, as I am, that this lends more weight to the theory that Shane killed Madison," Morgan said, her tone so void of emotion that Blade stared at her. And understood. She was a grieving twin, devastated by a loss she'd never recover.

And a professional seeking justice.

She couldn't be both at the same time.

The realization toughened him up. He'd messed up seventeen years ago, had clearly underestimated Shane Wilmington, should have reported the party. He would not let Morgan down a second time.

"We are," Hudson's voice was just as unemotional.

And Blade found that he shared that space as he heard himself say, "Which begs the question, if Shane killed Madison, why the recent murders? Who stands to gain from them?"

"Who do you know who'd want to see you suffer again?" Glen's voice came immediately. As though he'd been waiting to get the question out. "Someone who carried pain from that summer?"

"Kyle makes sense." He said the first name that came to mind. "Particularly if he told Thomaston to keep quiet about Shane's post-curfew antics." And as he spoke, pictures began to form in his mind. "He was in on it," he said. "I'll bet they covered for each other. They were both womanizers, always talking about who was hot, who'd be the best sex…"

He couldn't look at Morgan. What he'd heard then, what she thought about him, had ceased to matter.

"He knew, the bastard, and let me take the fall?" He stood again. Paced. Needed miles in front of him over which to jog…

"Our theory is that Shane, the killer, has been carrying the guilt all these years. And unlike Kyle, whose life fell apart, he needed to make amends. Starting with you. My guess is, out of respect, he told Kyle first. And that, after his father's death and his own impending charges, was his last straw."

"What if Kyle wasn't the only who called Hampton?" Morgan asked then. Blade couldn't look at her. He felt like he was coming out of his skin.

He checked the cameras that showed him the deck, and the waters around the boat. Felt certain that someone would be out there, ready to attack. To stop them before they all spoke the truth.

"You're thinking Wilmington called, to let the doctor know what he was about to do?" Hudson's voice sounded again.

"Makes sense, now that we know Hampton was also having an illicit affair that summer. It all happened after dark. When the rest of us were locked in at curfew."

"It does make sense," Glen said. "But we've checked both their records and found no calls between them. At least for the two years back we looked."

Yanking on a drawer handle, located by his head, Blade pulled out an unopened package. "They could have been using prepaids," he said. Then dropped the phone back in the drawer.

And sat down on the edge of the bench on his side of the table, too. He had to think. Not react.

"It could also be Tammy," he said then. Reiterating what he and Morgan had already revealed earlier that day. "I could see either one of them making me their scapegoat."

"I could, too," Morgan said, her voice a little softer, drawing his attention to her face. She wasn't mooning over him. But there was a look there.

As though she understood.

And in that look, for that moment, she'd given him everything he needed.

Chapter 18

Morgan's mind raced, searching for evidence within her years' full cache that would help them definitively prove who'd murdered her sister. And who was behind the current string of camp-related deaths.

What in the hell was she missing? One little thing that would help them find Kyle Brennan, and then get him to talk. Something from camp that summer. Remixed with what Jessica had told her that day...was there anything that made sense?

"We've got another theory on the table," Hudson said, bringing her mind back from her instinctive, all-consuming need to get it right, for Madison—and for Blade—to the auditory meeting in which she still sat. "Kelly's here to share it with the two of you," the tech expert finished.

"I just had a long call with Remy Barton," the psychology expert started right in. "He sees merit in the current theory but isn't convinced we're on the right track."

The woman's words caught Morgan's attention full force. She knew Remy. Trusted his judgment. And if they were falling for some kind of red herring, she wanted off the ride immediately. Could that be why she couldn't find the final pieces to close the case? Why she kept feeling as though she was missing something?

As Blade tensed across from her, she kept her focus on the phone, the words coming from it. And the images she had spread before her on the table, all depicting Blade's dining room walls. Giving her the most complete picture of what they knew.

"Dr. Barton believes we're looking for a younger person. He said someone who was sixteen or below, based on adolescent emotional development science. I'm inclined to agree with him. His reasoning, based on actions seeming to be driving a now adult, that appear to be coming out of a juvenile sense of injustice. This conclusion is not only sound, it's scientific."

Morgan felt her muscles tightening, as though she was aware of each one in her body, one by one. She wanted to reach out for Blade, find his hand, but knew she couldn't.

Couldn't afford the chance that she'd be distracted.

She had to keep herself 100 percent at attention. She focused on kids she'd known at camp as she heard the profile she knew was coming.

"We've already contacted the FBI team to get Hampton's patient records from camp and they're working on it. Barton doesn't think our perpetrator is escalating. We're looking for someone who's calculated, with well-thought-out moves. Partly to fulfill his sense of justice, and in part to throw us off course, to show us for fools, due to our previous inability to provide that justice. And, of course, to keep him or herself from getting caught. Different methods of murder could either be a part of this, or they could be about the perpetrator getting his murderer's feet wet, and then growing in power with each successful kill. The hiring of at-risk people to try to get Morgan removed from the case could all be part of the ruse to throw us off, but it could also indicate that the killer is on the fence about whether or not she has to die. Most likely, Morgan, this is someone who knew you. Whether you, as a counselor, knew him or her or not, this could be someone who looked up to you. Who, while he or she now struggles because they hold you partially accountable for so many years of injustice, but who also genuinely liked you. Or, at the very least, feels sorry for you. Probably someone who saw you the last morning at camp. Dr. Barton says that you were held apart, partially with his help. He's spent the past twenty-four hours trying to remember anyone he noticed hanging around, watching you, but said that he was so distraught himself, he can't think of anyone. He's hoping you'll be able to. Or you, Blade. You were there, and also, obviously similarly distressed, but we'd like for both of you to sit down with another long look at camp photos…take time for every face. Close your eyes. Try to remember."

Morgan was already reaching for the file. Blade handed it to her. She threw him a glance, nodded, but wouldn't let herself connect. She needed her mind in the past. Hating him. Because that's where she'd been that morning.

Before she'd even opened the file, Kelly's voice came over the wire again, forcing her to keep the folder closed a minute or two longer. Giving her a major panic-induced hot flash, as well.

"This perp has two teams of experts looking for him, and us appearing to be no closer to finding him is likely feeding his sense of power. Which means we can count on more bodies if we don't get this done fast," the expert said. "Dr. Barton and I both agree that we need to be looking at someone who's insinuated him- or herself into this investigation." Kelly coughed, more like a hard clearing of the throat, and then said, "Dr. Barton also pointed out, without actually pointing fingers or giving his own opinion on the matter, that Blade fits this entire profile. He and Shane were only sixteen. Their camp elders let them down."

The energy in the room shifted. As though it had gone stale. Something they could not afford at that point. Standing, she spun around to the other side of the table, the file of pictures in hand, pushing against Blade with her hip until he moved over so she could sit down.

And then she dropped her free hand to his thigh.

It wasn't the move of a lover.

But she couldn't deny, even to herself, that the touch was conceived in love.

The kind that supported, believed, even in the worst of times.

Blade hadn't been surprised that Remy had mentioned him as fitting the profile. The man wouldn't be doing his job if he hadn't done so. Blade had been counting off every detail as they'd been spoken, seeing himself in every one of them.

The age thing...he'd been sixteen when summer camp had started. Morgan had just turned sixteen. None of the campers had known that he'd had a birthday. He hadn't wanted a fuss.

All he'd wanted was some private time with Morgan, for them to have cupcakes, hold hands and talk about life. They'd made it happen.

He'd been wondering if she'd remembered that, and then there she was, in the moment, shoving him over and...putting her hand on his thigh.

As she'd done that long-ago afternoon.

And that, he hadn't expected.

By the time her hand was landing on his thigh, Kelly Chase's voice filled the room with, "I'm turning this over to Hudson again. You two…above all else, be careful," and Blade couldn't help but figure the message was a warning to him, in particular, to keep his hands, and physical needs, off the table. Literally.

The table they sat at was going to fold down and serve as Morgan's bed for the night.

"Okay," Hudson's voice boomed loudly. "My team is already looking at footage in and around every crime scene, to see if anyone shows up in multiple places, or even more than once, and run any repeat images through facial recognition software. If we find no multiple appearances, we'll run every single face on every single tape through the software. I've also got people working on age progression photos from the camp photos you two will be studying. If this guy or woman is out there, we'll find them."

Blade heard the words. Felt a little…strange…that Warner hadn't also mentioned that they knew already that Blade would appear on some of the cameras. He'd been at the crime scenes. After having insinuated himself into the investigation big-time.

At Morgan's request, of course, but only after he'd asked her for the initial interview.

And begged for her help.

The fact that he was paying the bill had not meant that he was to be overlooked. They'd all stipulated that from the beginning. Glen Rivers Thomas first and foremost.

He didn't like the idea that the firm could be fooled into being convinced of someone's innocence without the proof. Not only had he hired them for the sole purpose of getting that proof, but if he could manipulate them, someone else could, too. Jasmine, for instance?

"I'm turning this over to Glen," Hudson said, bringing

to Blade's attention that he had no idea what the man had said immediately before that statement.

"All right, we have one last report to make," Glen's voice came into the room. Again, sounding just that bit…different. As though the man's emotions had entered the picture. Which made no sense.

"Give it to me," Morgan said, her tone as professional as always, not seeming to notice any change in her boss's demeanor.

Because she knew him far better? Had seen different sides to him?

Made sense, but it didn't ease Blade's tension over the firm's lapse where he was concerned. Jasmine could have left some clue, in some conversation, that they'd missed because they'd been…personally occupied…

He had to tell them Morgan's concerns.

"Wait," he said, leaning over the table. "I think we need to discuss the fact that I fit the profile," he said, starting in slowly, before bringing the firm's possible lapse back to the FBI agent—who'd be a much harder sell than a contractor who'd been a prime suspect in a cold case for almost two decades.

"To that end," Glen started in. "As you both know, my team has been running tests on all the case evidence from Madison Davis's murder," the man continued. Blade's attention, while acute, was acutely split between what the man had to tell them, and the fingers digging into his thigh.

Here it comes, was his first thought. But he knew confusion, too. If they had more on him then why…?

"The class ring found in Blade's pocket…" He heard the words. Started to zone. The ring, the most key piece of evidence, along with the little ribbon cross that Morgan had given to him that had been found clutched in her sister's hand. There'd been no viable fingerprints. How was Morgan going to handle being trapped with him on a small boat too far out for her to swim back to shore…?

Glen was talking about new technologies in forensic testing. DNA advances in particular. Ways to tell male DNA from female DNA. They'd found only one sample of male DNA, and it had been found all over both the outside and inside of the ring. Blade couldn't inhale.

"Over the years, as investigators took a look at the case, mostly at Morgan's continued urgings, the one thing that no one had was Shane Wilmington's DNA. But with his corpse in the morgue, we were able to get a good sample. They prove that the only man who touched that ring found in Blade's pocket was Shane Wilmington."

Blade sat there. Waiting. The ball would drop. Another shoe would fall. He'd take it and keep pushing forward.

"Oh my God!" Morgan's squeal, the way she was suddenly up off the bench, had him staring at her. "They did it, Blade!" she screamed, sounding like the sixteen-year-old sweetie he'd once known. While voices came over the phone, in triplicate.

"Congratulations, you two," Kelly Chase's words came through most legibly.

And Blade sat there.

Morgan pushed her face right up to his. "You didn't do it, Blade!" she said, half kneeling on the bench as she reached her arms around his neck and hugged him.

He didn't do it.

He'd always known that.

But…he stared at her. At the phone. Listened to the voices all talking about the discovery, about who made the connection, running into the office, with the news.

He heard the excitement. But it was Morgan's eyes, gazing into his with the adoration to which he'd once been addicted, that brought the message home to a heart and mind that had been buried too deep to accept a release from the internal prison.

"I know," he said, and then, with tears in his eyes, matching the ones in hers, he pulled her down onto his lap and kissed her.

Long. And then hard.

Morgan half heard her team joking about what was going on in the boat. At the other end of their communication. And then heard an "oh." Followed by a quiet click.

She'd maybe pay later for her unprofessional behavior. But probably not. She didn't care one way or the other.

They had the proof that Blade didn't do it.

They'd found the truth.

He was fully exonerated.

And...he'd pulled back from a kiss that had her wanting to throw an arm across the table to rid it of debris and then climb up on it.

"What's wrong?" she asked as he slid them across the bench, stood and let her go.

Was there someone else in his life?

She hadn't asked. There'd been no reason to discuss their private, personal lives.

Or...he no longer wanted her...in that way.

He wanted her. She'd felt the evidence of that against her hip. But maybe as a sexual partner, not a lover.

Not like the couple they'd once promised each other they'd be.

"We're right where we were when we came on this boat," Blade said to her, breathing heavily, not meeting her gaze. His tone soft.

They weren't a couple just because he'd been exonerated.

"We knew I didn't do it, Morgie. And it looks like Shane did, and framed me, but we haven't proven that yet. Some-one else could have murdered Maddie and convinced Shane—by bribe or threat—to put the ring in my pocket. We don't have your truth yet. And even if Shane killed Mad-die, we can't prove who's out there now, murdering people from camp. And gunning for you." He glanced at her then, his green-eyed gaze filled with a fire she hadn't ever seen.

"I'm not stopping until you're safe," he told her. "My freedom from suspicion will be huge to me at some point. Right now, it doesn't matter when I think about your life in danger…"

He hadn't said *I love you*.

Maybe he never would.

But Morgan heard the declaration anyway. In what he *was* saying.

And doing. He'd slid back onto the bench on his side of the table. Opened the file of camp photos. "I'll sit here, you sit there," he said, nodding toward the bench she'd been oc-cupying most of the night.

"We have to put ourselves back in the frame of mind we'd been in that morning…"

Morgan was already seated before he finished the sen-tence.

She'd go back. She'd feel the horror. The hell.

She had to.

But she would not forget, ever, that she'd just fallen in love all over again.

Kelly had told them to close their eyes and remember every aspect of that morning so long ago. The sun on their faces, the grass beneath their feet, anything that would take them back in time. He sat across from Morgan, watching her look at a picture and then close her eyes, again and again, watching expressions cross her face. All painful distortions of the joy she used to wear so naturally. Blade was resisting his own trip back.

He knew what the past held.

Could figure out the future later.

The present was everything. Because if they didn't keep Morgan safe, neither the past nor the future mattered to him.

And the only way to keep her safe was to figure out who in the hell wanted her dead and stop them.

They had to find the truth.

So he looked at photos, closed his eyes and slowly let himself drift away from the boat to a sunny summer morning that held nothing but horror. Darkness.

And a young face...looking at him with fear. Not the horror and shock that had shot his way from every other face he'd encountered that morning. No one had looked at him for more than a second. That he'd seen. He'd glance at someone, and they'd immediately turn away.

It had felt as though everyone had been staring at him.

And that one face...

He couldn't place it. It hung there, in the air. Just a flash. And then gone. There and not. From photo to photo, eyes opened, eyes closed, he couldn't match the face. The eyes.

That fear.

Was it a younger version of himself he was seeing? He'd gone into the bathroom to throw up. Had brushed his teeth and caught a sight of himself in the mirror.

Had started to cry.

And turned his back on his image—just like everyone else was turning their backs on him.

Was it his own face he was seeing?

Maybe it was.

He didn't think so.

And didn't trust himself to know, either. He'd been a young seventeen-year-old, distraught, terrified kid, who'd fallen asleep in love and woken up a murder suspect. Surrounded by enemies he'd thought were friends. Branded by those he'd trusted.

He'd been in shock.

Boom! Crack! The sounds reverberated outside, and then in. Blade was out of his seat before he fully comprehended what was happening. Morgan, her gun in hand, was right beside him.

Pulling his weapon out of his ankle holster, he stepped in front of her, peering at the screens depicting footage from his security cameras. Heard another blast. Glass breaking.

A screen went dark.

And Blade strode toward a bench a couple of feet away. Threw it open, and grabbed the life raft, along with two waterproof satchels.

"Take these," he told Morgan. "We have to vacate, now."

Morgan, putting the straps of both bags on her shoulders, grabbed for her phone, and said, "They know where we are."

"Leave the phones," Blade barked, as though he was the expert. In a sense, on his boat, and in his life, he was. And saw that Morgan had already put hers back on the table and was reaching for the drawer he'd pulled open earlier, grabbing two new phones, and unsealed one of the bags she was carrying to put them inside.

She started when another couple of shots were fired, ducking, and then moved toward the steps leading up to the deck, saying, "They're on the port side. And still a distance away. Long-range rifle."

Blade had determined the same, based on the faraway sound of the shot, followed a few seconds later by cracks as they hit the boat. He pulled out a couple of wet suits.

"It's going to be too big for you, but you'll need it on," he told her. "Booties first so the water doesn't inflate them." He was already stepping out of his pants as he talked. "Keep your underwear on." He kept an eye on her, only to make sure she got the suit on right, and then, in his own suit, grabbed handfuls of clothes from their go bags, and shoved them into one of the two waterproof satchels he'd pulled out of the bench. He added their guns and with a nod from Morgan, turned off the lights, but when he stepped toward the stairs, Morgan pushed by him.

"I go first," she insisted in the darkness.

There was no time to argue. He started the boat's inflation, pushing in front of her with it, and went up on deck. And then, hiding any glow of human movement behind the growing black raft, he waited for her to crawl to the starboard side of the boat. "Jump in, and hold on," he told her, handing her a rope tied to the boat. Heard the splash as she went over and, securing the life raft, threw it down as well, before rolling himself over the side.

Chapter 19

There were two sets of oars. Morgan's arms ached as she reached and pulled, reached and pulled in tandem with Blade. Fighting waves on the cloudy night.

Focusing on his back in front of her, she tuned out the darkness. No visible moon was good for them. Kept them hidden.

But it prevented her from seeing what was around them. Just ahead. Behind.

How did she protect anyone when she couldn't keep an up-to-the-second assessment of her surroundings? Her ability to take in, to file and hold on to details around her was one of her strong suits.

Blade had told her, before they'd boarded the boat earlier that evening, that both of his cabin cruisers were bulletproof. But the killer had already used a bomb once. If he realized that his gunfire was largely ineffective…

They had to get far enough away from the boat to not be caught by shrapnel if it exploded.

"He's portside," Blade said as they rowed in a line perpendicular to the boat. "As long as we stay starboard, we're safe from gunfire."

And as long as the killer thought they were still on the boat, they were even safer.

Morgan hoped to God that their escape had gone un-noticed.

If the killer knew that they were on an inflatable boat, they were as good as dead. He could already be headed their way.

Shivering, partially due to the sweat building up in her suit as she exerted herself in the seventy-degree summer night air, she forced herself to focus on the job. On the truth she'd promised herself she'd find before she left the earth.

They had their guns out and loaded. And had talked about diving into the water if need be, staying under as much as possible to avoid any bullets that could come their way at any moment. They hadn't talked about how much the relatively light raft would bounce around on the huge lake, even with relatively calm waters.

"We should be good, from here, if he bombs the boat," Blade said twenty minutes after they'd vacated their over-night lodging, leaving all the copies of evidence that it held.

A call to Sierra's Web could replace all of it.

Her mind continued to segue between past and pres-ent. The pictures she'd been studying when the gunfire had started. The memories she'd accessed—many she'd refused to allow to the surface due to the pain they caused.

And the man Blade had become. Everything she'd imag-ined he'd grow to be. And more. His awareness of the pre-ciousness of life, his depth and, based on investigative research, his dedication to staying on the right side of the law, not missing a single inspection or failing to file a sin-gle form in the running of his business…she'd expected him to be a good man.

He'd turned out to be one of the best. At least by her standards.

And, he'd been exonerated. Not that there'd ever been an official charge against him. She still had no idea how the little ribbon cross she'd made in crafts and had given to Blade the evening before Maddie was killed had ended up in her dead sister's hand, but it was easy enough to follow the dots. Shane had taken it from Blade when he'd planted the ring in Blade's pocket.

Whether Shane had given it to her sister before her death or shoved it into her hand afterward might never be known.

But it could be. With Sierra's Web on the case.

Reach and pull. Reach and pull. She was with Blade Carmichael. They were alive. Alone on the lake that they'd both professed to love so much neither had ever wanted to live outside the state. If not for a string of murders and bullets flying, she could be living a dream come true.

Neither of them were speaking much. They had no plan, past getting away alive.

Pulling her oars through the frigid water, Morgan hoped for a bomb with every stroke.

It was their best option.

If the killer thought that their body parts were among pieces of an explosion…they'd have a spare minute to catch the fiend.

"We have to stay off the grid," she told Blade, her voice as soft as it could be to reach him almost a yard ahead of her in the lifeboat.

She'd expected a nod, at best. Instead, he put his oars straight down in the water, slowing them. She ceased rowing as well as he turned to face her.

"I know of an inlet," he said. "Used to be a popular pass-through for boats to the Applethorne River, but both sides were overgrown with cattails, which are protected in the state. For the past few years, it's no longer been wide enough for boat passage. A new passageway was cleared from the lake to the river about five miles downriver. There's a small, overgrown beach area on this inlet. And a two-man tent in the one duffel…" He nodded toward the two bags in between them on the floor of the raft. "I suggest we get there. Build the tent, pull the raft inside and get some sleep. We can use one of our phones to set an alarm to make certain we're up before dawn. From there, it's your call." He talked a little more about the inlet, about the plethora of trees and lack of human habitation.

Had they been in another time and place, the itinerary he was describing would have sounded like heaven to her. So many times that long-ago summer she'd dreamed about a night all alone in a tent with Blade. Doing things that lovers did.

Going through those old photos, closing her eyes with her heart and mind spread wide open, allowed to freely live the bottled-up memories from that summer, so much had come back to her. The way she'd tingled inside, and down below, every time Blade had held her hand. And when he'd kissed her, she'd been on fire there, flooding with warmth and wetness.

In her private moments, every night as she'd fallen asleep, she'd lain there imagining what it would be like when they could finally lie together and she'd know what it felt like to have him actually enter her…

Instead, her sister's life had been stolen away, taking all of Morgan's dreams with it.

Maybe the shots that night were a sign. Reminding her that she had to live every minute while she had it. Not hold off for a future that might not arrive.

Blade's voice had fallen silent. For how long, she wasn't sure.

Morgan nodded. "Let's go," she said.

Keeping the rest to herself.

* * *

As he rowed, steering them toward the inlet half a mile ahead, Blade kept getting hit with mental flashes of that face. Was it him? Showing him his own fear?

He didn't feel afraid. Not for himself, at any rate. His entire being was filled with a cold, hard, steel-like determination to find the man who'd stolen Morgan's future from her, and his, too. Find him and end his life.

Either through arrest, or something more permanent.

He wouldn't kill without provocation. Would not take a life unless it was self-defense. No way he was going to let the bastard make a murderer out of him. He would not let a killer make his own sick falsehoods into truth. Nor ever be the man he'd been living to show the world he was not.

But to protect Morgan from certain death? He was ready.

Would shoot to kill.

No doubt at all on that one.

Having Morgan remove her oars from the water, he took over propelling the boat as he steered them into the inlet, heading back the way they'd come, but on different waters. In the gulf, leading to the river, with land on both sides, there were no waves. But here in the overgrown remains of a gulf, going was slowed by the sludge and weeds that had risen from the ten-foot-deep bottom. Cattails scraped the sides of the raft. But he welcomed their presence. Was thankful for their cover.

Morgan, one oar in hand, had slid in front of him as they entered the gulf, moving from side to side of the raft as necessary, keeping them free from any growth that would impede their progress.

Neither of them spoke.

They didn't need words.

There wasn't enough to say, and too much left unsaid for far too long.

And yet, they worked together as one. Anticipating, delivering, without instruction or question.

She spotted the little cattail-gated beach just as he did, turning to point it out to him, a quarter of a mile from being parallel with the boat they'd abandoned. While he calculated the yards of cattails they were going to need to get through to access land, she used her oar to help pull them closer to shore. "The water used to be about five feet in through here," he told her. If they were lucky, it would be still. They could hike out, carrying the boat above their heads if need be.

As it turned out, with both of them in the water, walking side by side, Blade and Morgan were able to pull the boat behind them. The lightweight vessel slid across the cattails almost easily, leaving Blade's mind to wander over how they must look—maybe to her sister from above—traipsing in their look-alike suits, an hour or so before midnight, side by side.

With a processional behind them.

The horror version of the wedding that never was?

He was shaking the dark thought away, hoping if Maddie was up there, she was helping to keep Morgan safe, when the world seemed to rumble around him.

Not an answer from Maddie Davis.

Jumping, he made it to the small piece of sand-covered shore, and reached to help Morgan climb up behind him, as another, larger rumble hit.

"Thunder?" Morgan asked, but she didn't sound as though she expected to be right.

Blade had a guess. Couldn't be sure. Until he looked in the direction where he knew his boat had been and saw the reddish sky.

An era had just ended.

His refuge had been bombed.

Tears filled Morgan's eyes as she watched Blade stand tall in the darkened wilderness, watching a part of his life going up into a red flare in the night sky. The moon, still mostly hidden, cast enough of a glow for the bomb's rising smoke to seem like curling snakes in the air.

She wanted to wrap her arms around him, hold him to her and never let go. Neither of them knew how long forever would be. Could end that night.

Such maudlin thoughts were not the way she'd become an expert in her field.

Focus on what she could control did that.

Setting up camp was a welcome diversion. Walking a foot into the woods, she stripped off the wet suit and equally damp underwear beneath, donning the clothes Blade had thrown in the waterproof duffel. Underwear. Jeans. A dark button-down shirt. And nothing else. The bra she'd packed with the small bundle was nowhere to be found. Hanging her wet bra on a branch so it would be dry by morning, she stepped back out to see Blade similarly dressed. Jeans. Short-sleeved button-down shirt. Dark color.

He looked…too good to be true.

And she quit looking.

The tent went up easily, and was large enough to fit the entire boat, with the tent's front zippered doors still able to close.

Of course it had, she thought, as she crawled inside and settled back against an inflated side as a backrest. Wishing she had a glass of wine.

Or a beer.

And settled for the bottled water she found in the bag,

along with a supply of dehydrated packaged meals. And a small, battery-powered lantern.

Turning it on, she set it at the head of the boat.

If nothing else, the past had taught Blade to be prepared for anything.

Her go bag was stocked with her own brand of dehydrated food, and other packaged things that didn't have to be cooked.

They might not have spent their lives together as they'd planned, but they seemed to have traveled a lot of the same paths anyway. The realization saddened her.

And warmed her, too.

For the first time in seventeen years, she didn't feel completely alone on her journey.

Her heart jumped, and her belly quivered a bit when the tent flap moved and Blade appeared, taking up what was the rest of the space in the boat-laden tent.

Taking her air, too.

He was…everything.

And she'd existed on nothing for so long. Staring up at him, her gaze glued to him in the dim light, she didn't even try to hide how she was feeling.

He wasn't looking away.

Until he did. "Get some sleep," he told her. "I'm going to sit up awhile…" He'd seemed about to say more, but Morgan didn't wait to hear what it was.

He'd said enough to remind her who she was in the real world.

And who he was.

A client.

A man she used to know.

All that remembering, putting herself back in those moments, she couldn't let them get to her.

Scooting down in the boat, she turned her back to him, tucked herself up into a ball and tried to pretend to herself that she was thankful that Blade was keeping them on the right track.

Only…she wasn't. "What if we don't make it through this?" Her voice sounded small, even to her, as she lay there hunched, listening to crickets and cicadas chirping outside the tent.

"Don't talk like that."

Not the direction she was taking. "It's a viable possibility."

"You giving up?" His voice sounded a bit less…calm. He'd wanted her earlier, at the table. The evidence had been rock hard and impossible to miss.

"The opposite, actually," she said, not moving. "I want to feel fully alive."

There. She'd put it out there. And as the silence continued in the darkness, she knew she'd done what she could. Technically, she was his employee, but it wasn't about that. For either of them.

She'd turned her back on him when he'd needed her most. Had professed undying love and then hadn't even given a scared kid the benefit of the doubt. She'd screamed at him in front of everyone…

"I'm sorry," she said softly enough that she shouldn't wake him if he'd fallen asleep.

"For what?" He didn't sound the least bit sleepy.

"Not opening my arms for you to run into them that morning. I'll regret that for the rest of my life."

"You'd lost your identical twin, Morgan. Your other half. You were in shock, with a shattered heart…"

His words sent her back there again, alone. Frightened. Desperate. "Please hold me, Blade," she said, a young girl and a grown woman on the run for her life, too. "Just hold me? Just for tonight?"

Turning, half sitting, she saw him still upright in the back of the raft, just as she'd left him.

"I can't just hold you."

Oh. *Oh!*

"That's okay, too," she told him. "It doesn't have to mean anything." She heard herself justifying, and didn't give a fig about it. She and Blade…honesty was all that mattered.

"That's just it, Morgie, it would mean something. Too much."

He wasn't ready. Might never be ready. Lying back down, Morgan thought about his words. Knew there was truth in them. And willed herself to go to sleep for the few hours they might get.

Was just drifting off, when she felt his body sliding down beside her, spooning her. And kept herself still, concentrated on breathing evenly, as she waited for whatever came next.

And, minutes later, heard his deep, even breathing.

Satisfied in a way she couldn't understand, Morgan drifted off as well.

His body was hard, on fire, moving instinctively, back and forth, and not getting anywhere. Not going in. The body next to him wasn't open to him.

But her softness…her nipple under his fingers was hard, not soft.

And she moaned.

The sound woke Blade from his semisleeping, half-dreaming state, to find himself riding Morgan's butt like some brainless jerk. He tried to stop, to freeze, his first thought being not to wake her. But her fingers slid up over his hand on her breast, guiding his fingers to the naked flesh.

While his groin shot an immediate message of urgency, she rolled over and planted her mouth on his.

He couldn't stop her. Couldn't tell her no.

Wasn't sure he'd be able to tell himself in any way that would have any effect.

Instead, he rolled her to her back, pulling both of his hands up to cup her face, to open his mouth over her lips and let his tongue dance with hers as it had done in the past.

But with a whole lot more finesse.

He moved. She moved. Clothes disappeared. At a fever pitch, blood pumping through his veins, and his breathing ragged, Blade wasn't sure he'd be able to hold off long enough to bring her all the pleasure he wanted her to have. If they only had one night, it had to be...

Her fingers curved around him. Squeezing lightly. Holding him. He felt himself let go a little bit, but managed to hang on when he remembered... "I don't have protection."

Morgan continued to hold him. And to smile up at him as she lay, naked and spread beside and half beneath him. "For a guy who's more prepared than an entire country of Boy Scouts I find that hard to believe," she told him. Her smile slow, and so sexy he had to kiss it away.

But he found words, too. A minute or so later. If she wanted to play, he could do that, too. Except that he was completely serious when he said, "I don't ever have unplanned sex."

So no need to carry anything extra in his wallet. A reminder to him that he was not a man who was going to meet a woman and get carried away.

And yet, there he was...doing just that.

Except that he hadn't just met Morgan Davis. She'd carried his heart away with her years before. "So, you just… what…stop and buy condoms? Because—" she licked his lower lip "—I know you aren't a guy who expects her to take care of things."

"I have condoms in my bathroom at home," he told her, licking her right back. "And always take one with me for planned sex."

That stopped her. With her arms draped behind his neck, her expression serious, she said, "So you've never had sex, even once, without a condom?"

He shook his head. "Nope."

The look on her face, a mixture of awe and something else, a little sad-looking, she said, "Neither have I. So I guess that means, in a way, we're going to have virginal sex, just like we planned." Her words fell to a whisper before she was through, and Blade caught the last one with his lips. Kissing her long and hard.

But held back when every muscle in his body was urging him to climb on top of her. "You're sure you want to do this?" he asked her.

"My cycle's regular and based on what just ended, I'm not at risk for pregnancy," she told him.

And he felt like a fool, but had to tell her the truth. "I wasn't thinking about that. It's just…not too late to stop."

"Maybe not for you," she said, turning to her side, with her legs open, guiding the engorged muscle in her hand to her private spot.

But he pulled back. Separated them long enough to look her in the eye. "I'm serious, Morgie. If this isn't what you want to look back on…"

She sat up, those glorious breasts right there, his for the taking, except that he couldn't look away from the light in her eyes.

It showed him more emotion than he could decipher. Sadness, need, confidence, warmth…maybe love…whatever it was, he took it in. She grinned and said, "If I'm going to be seeing my sister in heaven in the next day or two, I at least have to be armed with the answer to the one question Maddie will have first. Since sex was always on her mind and she never got to do it. Was Blade Carmichael any good?" Her attempt at levity failed, but the words told him how very much she wanted to finish what they'd started.

Because Maddie had known her innermost heart. Could feel it. Morgan had just given him her sister's blessing to quit thinking and put them both out of their misery.

Without wasting another second, he moved, and so did she, and he slid inside her as she pushed herself onto him. He froze the second he was fully home. To savor. But also to hold on. Seeming to sense his need, she kept her lower body still. And kissed him. Softly.

"Heavenly meeting or no, there's no way I'm ever telling anyone about this," she said, squeezing him.

Her words spurred him too strongly to hold back. Out of control, he pulled, and plunged, their bodies meeting, separating and coming back together with the force of seventeen years of waiting. Of longing. And when her convulsions started around him, he emptied himself of every longing he'd ever had.

Found a satiation he'd never experienced.

Reached heights of pleasure he hadn't known existed.

And was healed.

Chapter 20

Lying in Blade's arms, Morgan drifted, knowing that she'd just touched heaven. That she'd lived a perfect moment. She had to sleep. Wanted to stay conscious, to savor. But she was so tired…

Dark hours of the morning were looming. They were on their own, on the run from a killer they knew, but didn't know who. She didn't want to go forward.

Couldn't go back.

And held herself in a state of dozing as long as she could, half dreaming, but aware of the arms that held her.

Of Blade's even breathing, soothing her, like a mother's womb. Or a sound machine. Waves coming in on the beach…

The beach.

Water.

A river.

Sweating a river…

Morgan sprang upright, hot, rivulets running between her breasts, not sure where she was in that first second.

Eyes wide, adjusting to the darkness. Walls close enough to touch and…Blade.

"What is it?" He was up, pulling on his pants by the time she fully realized where she was. He'd flipped on the little lantern. The night came flooding back.

The bullets. The raft. Fighting waves on the lake. Rumbling earth. A red sky.

The profile. Pictures. Sitting on a bench, waiting for her parents. Stares.

"I don't know," she said, shaking her head, and reaching for her clothes. "What time is it?" Had the alarm gone off? Startled her awake?

He touched his watch and the face lit up. Waterproof, of course. "Three thirty."

Half an hour before they'd agreed to rise.

Three hours, maybe, of sleep.

He was staring at her again. "I think we should get back out to the lake and try to make it to Michael's marina," he said, still watching her as he started to button his shirt.

Her bra was outside hanging from a tree. He was heading out. She asked him to get it. Stood after he left. Put on her underwear. Stepped into her jeans.

The river.

Jeans.

Shaking, feeling sick to her stomach, Morgan dropped down to her knees. Shaking her head. She'd been dreaming. But...

It hadn't been a dream. Her head hurt.

Shivering, chilled, she pulled on her shirt. Buttoned it. Wrapped her arms around herself.

And glanced up, eyes wide, horror filling her as Blade came back in, holding her bra.

She shook her head. Left her bra hanging there from his fingers. "I know," she said.

Sliding down to his haunches, beside her, he was close enough to touch, but didn't reach out to her. "Know what?" His tone was gentle. Soft.

And as filled with concern as his gaze was.

"I know who the killer is. At least… I think I do. I might know. Someone from camp. A younger kid. Intelligent. Controlled. Able to gain the confidence of people at risk, to discern how to play with individual minds and influence them to do things. Definitely involved in the investigation. Something happening at camp. Knew me and Maddie. And you and Shane and Kyle, too."

She tried to swallow. Couldn't. Fought back a wave of nausea. She was wrong. Had to be wrong.

But it all made sick, horrifying sense.

Except, he wasn't sick. She would have known, wouldn't she?

Staring up at Blade, she felt so foolish. And so guilty, too. How could she not have known? It was her business to see, to notice, to figure it out.

"He's been playing us," she said, "and I fell right into his trap…" As much as she needed it all to end, she prayed she was wrong.

"Who?" Blade's tone was sharper. He still didn't touch her. She needed him to touch her. To convince her she was…

"Remy." The word fell off her lips and she almost felt foolish for her thoughts. Except… "I found him down by the river, crying…grief for his mother… He made me promise not to tell… The guys would all make fun of him… I told him to go see Dr. Hampton…he wouldn't laugh. That day, at the river, I hugged him, Blade."

The words felt like a death knell. In a way they were.

The dream hadn't been a dream. It had been long-buried memories, awakened by opening herself up to memories the night before…

"I felt…hardness against my thigh. He was turned on. Attracted to me. I knew what it was, but convinced myself I was wrong. I had no experience, and maybe it was just how a penis felt, I thought…but I knew. He was just four-teen. A kid. Probably couldn't help the instinctive reaction. I didn't want to embarrass him. And I was so in love with you. I didn't want to know that I'd turned him on. Didn't want to deal with it. I pretended it didn't happen…didn't even tell Maddie…"

She'd forgotten all about it. With Maddie's death. Blade being named as the only suspect. The end of life as she'd known it. She'd forgotten the moment by the river. Not the hug she'd initiated. But the boy's reaction. It had been a second in time.

"Oh my God, oh my God."

She was rambling. Blade wasn't stopping her.

He wasn't leaving her, either. She'd expected him to.

At least to turn his back on her drama.

She stared over at him, let herself drown in the intensity in his gaze in that so small space. "The profile he gave us… it fits completely," she told him. Naming everything Kelly had relayed. Seeing the pieces sliding concisely into place. And then, as more lucidity came to her, her mouth dropped open. Until she said, "Oh my God," as more facts dropped into place. More recent occurrences. "And the stressor," she started, looking up. "Blade, he lost a patient, about four months ago. A *sixteen*-year-old girl. Maddie's age. She died by suicide. His first patient loss. I knew he took it hard, but…"

Blade's gaze continued to bore into her. Didn't seem as focused.

"You think I'm losing it, don't you?" She didn't blame him. She was doubting herself. First thinking Blade had killed her sister. Then figuring Jasmine was helping the killer—and she still wasn't sure the agent wasn't doing so.

Except…if it was Remy…he knew where they were every single second, because he was getting all the reports.

Blade still didn't speak. But was all intent and deliberate action as he stood, started putting things back into the satchel. "We have to go," he said. And then, just as abruptly, stopped. Turned to her, dropped to his knees in front of her. "I've been trying to place a face," he said urgently. "Since last night. Studying those photos. I remembered a face looking at me that morning. Not so much the face, but the look of fear in someone's eyes. I was thinking it was me. I'd been sick. Was looking at my face in the mirror in the boys' bathroom… It wasn't me, Morgan. It was Remy. When he was guarding you. Everyone else avoided looking at me. And Remy…he was confident and oddly in control as he kept people away from you. But me…he looked over and he looked scared. Like, right then and there, scared out of his wits. Like I might do something to him in front of everyone, I thought. But now…he was scared because he somehow knew I didn't do it. He thought I knew something, and that it was going to come out. It was that kind of look."

The words hit her hard. She knew pieces were flying into place. Didn't want to see them get there. "And Shane was the first person he killed," she said slowly, watching it fall.

Blade was throwing things out of the tent. She carried out what she could. And when he joined her outside, said, "He knew Shane killed Maddie."

Blade's nod broke something inside Morgan. All those years…she'd been searching for the truth…the proof…that the man she'd thought she loved had killed her sister. Remy had been her strength. Her life preserver. Grieving with her, sharing his own grief of his completely changed life with his mother gone. And later, always telling her there was nothing wrong with her for having loved Blade. Telling her there'd been two sides to him, and there's no way she could have seen that other side.

He'd held her when she was sobbing, had listened to her on the phone so many times over the years, promising her that she'd find the proof she needed someday.

Letting her think that when she did, the man she'd loved would be in prison, where he belonged. Feeding her beliefs, her hatred for Blade Carmichael.

But for herself, as well. Because she'd fallen in love with a murderer.

He'd let her live in hell, let Blade live in hell, for seventeen years.

Telling her again and again that she'd find her proof.

When he'd had it all along.

Blade had thought, over the past few days, that knowing who they were after was going to make their quest easier. A manhunt would be underway. They'd get the guy. Instead, the nightmare got worse.

In part because the woman on the run with him had just become a permanent part of his soul. He never should have let it happen.

Not until they had all the answers to their pasts, the killer was behind bars and they had a chance to meet in more normal circumstances.

He knew his feelings weren't going to change. But Morgan's could. Did she even want a relationship? The family he wanted with her?

She traveled all over the country. While he worked with wood and concrete in the dirt in small-town Michigan.

None of which mattered in the moment, but distracted him from the shock of Remy Barton likely being responsible for his own seventeen years of hell. Distracted him long enough to get the tent rolled back up and into the satchel.

He and Morgan worked together, silently. There just weren't any words. They were after someone they'd both trusted. That Morgan cared about. A friend.

Until she stopped, staring up at him. "Kyle," she said. "He's been missing for a couple of days. Because no one has found his body yet?"

The rock in Blade's gut cemented over. "Remy may have killed him, but when he heard that Kyle was our main suspect, he hid his body, rather than framing me for the death," he said, aware of how much he'd begun to think like a killer over the years of trying to find one.

And went back to work when Morgan nodded.

They didn't know they were right. It was all just theory.

But it was the only one, ever, that filled in every single gap.

Before they left camp, they put a call from Blade's new prepaid phone into Hudson Warner's private line. A signal to not automatically be put on speakerphone.

Not that Remy would be there. But he could be on a call, even at four in the morning. A cabin cruiser had exploded on the lake. Blade and Morgan had no proof of that. Yet. But the conclusion was inevitable. And if the boat had exploded, there'd have been crews working it…people reporting in. Evidence flown to Sierra's Web by private jet. Morgan had told him how it all worked.

And if there was a chance no one knew he and Morgan were still alive, they needed to keep it that way. At least until they'd all talked. And he and Morgan had decided their next moves.

The call picked up in the middle of the first ring. "You're

okay." Warner's urgent tones sounded before they'd even identified themselves.

"Yes," they answered in unison. Blade staring out toward the lake. He had no idea where Morgan's attention lay.

"Thank God. I've been waiting for the area code to come up."

Blade left it for Morgan to explain the hours without contact. She said, "We thought it best to be presumed dead, just until we could get some rest."

"We just got word a few minutes ago that, so far, there's no evidence at all of human flesh, blood or remains…"

Blade had assumed as much, but still didn't like hearing the news. "Who knows?"

"So far, Jasmine Flaherty, Glen and I. Kelly got called to another case, a child's life in immediate jeopardy in Missouri. Silver is waiting to hear the preliminary results. Jasmine's orders were to have everything flown here. One chain of command. We got the first shipment, interior of the cabin, mostly, an hour ago. Half a dozen experts were in the lab waiting. Had everyone local on deck. Checked first for signs of life."

The longer they talked, the more Blade's blood was pumping. They had to get moving.

He had to do something. Anything that would bring them closer to ending the horror.

"We know who killed Shane, Morgan." Hudson's tone had changed. Almost hesitant, not in his findings, but in their delivery.

Blade held his breath, needing the truth, not wanting it to be Remy Barton.

"We tested his clothes for DNA," Glen's voice came over the line, sounding…tired. Really tired. Blade felt Morgan's hand slide into his and he curled his fingers around it. "There were tears." Glen took a discernible breath. "We matched them to Dr. Barton, Morgan. He and his wife had registered with a national database."

Her fingers clenched Blade's as her knees buckled. She recovered almost instantly, but for that second, as he'd held her weight, Blade grew stronger, being there for her. And knew he would stand by Morgan Davis, in whatever capacity she needed, for the rest of their lives.

Tears on the clothing worn by a dead body didn't make a man a murderer. But it definitely made him a suspect. Most particularly considering the short time frame in which Shane Wilmington's body had been deposited in the Carmichael Construction pit. And knowing what they were looking for, a Sierra's Web expert traveled to the morgue to test the other two corpses and found matching DNA there as well. Skin cells those times. No sign of remorse for the other two kills.

Jasmine had been notified around midnight and had immediately been issued an arrest warrant for the child psychiatrist. Only to find that the man wasn't at his home. And hadn't been for over a week. Prior to that, for the past couple of months, he'd been staying in the spare bedroom. Telling his wife that with the suicide of his patient, he wasn't sleeping well and didn't want to keep her up.

He hadn't been to a single one of his son's Little League baseball games that summer, when, in years past, he'd coached and never missed a game. He didn't eat dinner with the family anymore. Was always obsessed with work. His wife thought that he'd been afraid to take his thoughts out of his cases for fear of missing something that could ultimately save a life.

And…he'd been talking, constantly, about inviting Morgan to dinner. Had even mentioned that he was thinking about offering her a partnership in his private practice.

She'd keep a watch over kids for him, to make certain that he always had all the facts.

Morgan's heart squeezed, anguish seeping through her, as, moving away from Blade, she listened to Hudson and Glen fill her in on Jasmine's overnight report. She was a trained agent. Had a job to do. Gave the words her entire focus.

Tammy Phillips had been formally cleared of all three murders. With the help of surveillance tape, she had solid alibis. Wouldn't have had time to leave where she was seen to make a kill and dump a body where they'd been dumped.

And Kyle...was still missing.

A full-out manhunt was underway for both Kyle and Remy, with warnings that Remy Barton, while seemingly harmless, should be considered armed and extremely dangerous.

And, standing there on that small patch of beach, everything became clear to Morgan. Painfully, glisteningly clear. "I know where he is," she said, her tone deadpan, as emotion voided from her system.

Remy was at camp. At the river. She'd been his endgame all along.

The man was diabolically smart. Far more than she'd even realized. The fact that he'd been playing her—along with his wife, his kids, his patients, his community—for almost two decades was proof of that.

He'd manipulated them all. The FBI. Sierra's Web. Had managed to pull off perfect crimes one right after another.

To pull off a perfect life while others languished from the secrets he'd held.

And would continue to do so until he got what he wanted. Her.

"He told me over and over through the years that I'd find the truth. Get my proof," she said, as though in a daze.

In reality, she was finally on the path she'd been stumbling around looking for all those years.

"And the profile," she said, "he told us what we had to know. He was, in his own way, confessing. He knew I'd figure it out. He wants it over." And wasn't able to stop himself.

"That's why his last kill, the way he framed Blade, was easily put into doubt. He wants to be done."

Remy might also have known that the Sierra's Web forensics team had been closing in on him. He'd have heard detailed reports of the testing being done.

Just as he'd known that Blade and Morgan would leave the boat when he shot at it. He gave them time to get away before bombing the vessel.

Because he had to see Morgan.

Somehow, a grieving, pubescent adolescent had found something in Morgan that had eased his pain to the extent that he'd been convinced that she was, and always would be, his permanent panacea.

Until an innocent girl had killed herself. She'd bet Remy had been thinking about Morgan, instead of his patient, during his last session with the girl.

He'd reached out to Morgan after the girl died, but she'd been on a case and hadn't responded right away. And had been sent out on another immediately afterward. Had figured he would need time alone with his wife and kids.

Either way, didn't matter.

If Kyle wasn't dead yet, he would be. Others from camp would follow.

Morgan couldn't have that on her shoulders.

"He's waiting for me. I have to go to him."

"No." Blade's single harsh word came first. Followed immediately by Hudson and Glen in unison.

But in the end, none of the three had a say. She was a free woman. And she was going. They could help her or not, as they saw fit.

Blade had figured he'd already been living in hell, but he hadn't even scraped the surface. Watching Morgan, in full tactical gear, getting out of the vehicle, preparing to take on a serial killer single-handedly, he learned just how painfully hopeless life could feel.

Morgan was certain that Remy would be waiting for her by the river. Figured that he'd been staying somewhere at the deserted camp. That was where he'd been going every day, in between his kills, making calls from there, waiting for her to figure it all out.

Things he'd said to her over the years came back to her. Asking if she ever thought about visiting camp again…one time reminiscing about the river, and another suggesting that a cognitive interview on-site might help her think of something. She'd rejected that idea outright.

She'd said, on the drive to camp in the back seat of Jasmine's agency-issued vehicle, that it was as though those moments by the river with her, the day before Maddie was killed, were his last healthy memories.

The goal was to bring Barton in alive. There'd been no proof of a weapon in his hand. Nothing definitive enough to prove his absolute guilt. And authorities needed to question him about Kyle Brennan. To be able to locate his body if nothing else.

And when Jasmine heard that Morgan was going in regardless, the agent had agreed that Morgan had the training to make a live arrest. She'd have people ready to move in, but Morgan insisted that Remy not be spooked before she had a chance to approach him. Talk to him.

It was clear to everyone that the man had been asking to be caught.

Morgan believed she could bring him in peacefully.

And Blade? He got to be on the premises. A witness. Or so everyone, at his and Morgan's insistence, had determined. He had his own plan. He'd made a promise to himself—he would not let Morgan die avenging her sister's death—and it was a promise he had to keep.

So as agents gathered around Morgan, checking that her wire was emitting good sound, that her gear was all it could be, Blade quietly excused himself to the men's room.

And simply didn't return.

Chapter 21

Remy wasn't at the river when Morgan, hand on her gun, approached the log dam where she'd met up with him that long-ago summer. Keeping her back to a tree big enough to cover her, with the river in front of her, she sat on the same log she'd seen Remy on back then.

Just yards from where she'd been told her sister was murdered. The bend in the river behind them had had a big fallen tree across it, which had been used by campers and counselors, both boys and girls, to secretly access the other side.

She didn't look back. Hadn't been to the site since they'd told her her sister was dead. She wasn't there to reminisce. To relive. She was there to finish.

She listened for the sound of a killer's approach. Heard only the soothing sounds of the river's flow.

Being Remy's sitting duck, trying to be prepared for anything horrible that was coming her way, was excruciating. But no more so than her twin's death had been.

It had to be done.

Her mind didn't wander. Her focus was on Remy Barton. On remembering every conversation they'd ever had as much as was humanly possible. Asking for the impossible as well. She had to be ready for him. No matter what play he lobbed her way.

She had to know what he was alluding to, associate it as he did. Stay up with him.

She was hoping to walk with him out to meet Jasmine. To stand with him while he was taken into custody.

A cracking twig just to her right alerted her to his presence. While her heart jumped, her body remained completely still. The river's flow had prevented her from hearing his approach. And that, she was sure, had been part of the plan.

And then he was standing there on the bank. A step from her seat on the log. In his usual cotton pants and short-sleeved polo pullover, with expensive leather slip-on shoes, he sat down beside her. Close enough that their arms were touching. A test, she was sure.

She didn't scoot away.

Nor did he seem to move at all as he said, "It took you long enough."

"You know my weak point, Remy," she said, ready for him. "My heart sees what it sees."

She had to let him know he mattered to her. That he'd been an important part of her life. And as much as she hated to do it, she was going to have to promise to continue to be there for him. To testify on his behalf as to all the good he'd done in the world.

It was the only way to bring him in peacefully.

And because she was who she was, she'd do her best to keep those promises.

The sun hot on her forearms, her jean-clad legs, she tried not to let him see her sweating. And found the calm that she'd been seeking within herself.

The job would get done. One way or the other, it was ending.

She was getting what she most needed.

Remy, sitting on her left side, took her hand. Held it between both of his. Because she still had her gun hand free, she let him do so. "There are things you don't know," he told her.

"I know that you killed Shane." She'd talked to Kelly Chase on the way to the camp. Knew that it was better to get the worst out as quickly as she could. Get things on the table and let him see that she was still there for him. That she'd known, and she'd still come.

He nodded. Didn't commit one way or the other. Which meant still no confession for the wire she was wearing.

"We can plead temporary insanity, Remy. You were a kid when you saw him kill a sixteen-year-old girl. And having just lost another one…" She had no idea if such a plea would stick.

"I couldn't sleep that night. Had come down to the river. Saw him with her right back there." He nodded behind them. "Except, I didn't know it was him. Or her. I thought it was you and Blade. I'd seen Blade follow him back to camp and warn him not to leave again."

It took everything she had not to pull her hand away. To keep her features schooled into an expression of understanding.

Trying to fool one who was trained to figure out what people were thinking when they didn't even know themselves.

And one who'd been a close friend for almost two decades.

"She was holding the cross that I'd seen you wearing around your neck earlier," he said. "He'd just given it to her. I figured you'd given it to Blade, and he'd given it back to you."

Shane had had the cross she'd given Blade after dinner

that night? She had no idea how he'd come to be in possession of it, but they just had proof, on tape, that Blade hadn't been responsible for that piece of evidence against him, either. Was glad that she'd lived to know he'd heard that. His being permitted to listen to the wire feed as everything went down had been part of her bargain with Jasmine.

"So when he kissed her and left... I was thinking Blade just broke things off with you and I walked up to her." Turning, he put his face close to hers, forcing her to look him in the eye. Intimately. "You were my own personal angel that summer, Morgie. You were the only one who could ease the painful grief..."

She swallowed. Felt moisture in her eyes. Hoped he was far enough gone to think the tears were for him.

When all she could think about was her poor, sweet, outgoing sister.

And the rage sweeping through her. Because she knew what was coming. What he was about to tell her. Putting her free hand down near the butt of her gun, she nodded at the dangerous man. She could have the gun in hand in two seconds. Less than another to pull the trigger...

As she had the thought, Remy was the one who moved.

And suddenly, there was a barrel of a gun on his thigh. Pointed at the ground.

She'd expected him to come armed. They all had. But she was better trained. Was counting on her ability to aim and fire first.

"I wouldn't do that," he said to her.

And she nodded. "You're the boss, Remy. You've always been the boss. You've made that perfectly clear."

He'd killed Madison. There was no question now. And she had to sit there with him. Play his game. Or die.

"You want to know what happened or not?" he asked,

his tone resigned, either way. "You said you had to have the truth. I'm giving what you need more than anything else."

How many times had she told him, when he'd encouraged her to open her heart to the idea of a love interest, that she didn't have enough of a heart to give a man? That more than any relationship or family, she needed to find justice for her sister?

Maddie had been her heart and soul. Her other half. There was no love, no marriage, no family for her.

Or so she'd thought.

Blade had taught her differently. And she might sit there and die without him knowing that. What could she say, so he could hear over the wire, what he meant to her?

"And I'm here for you," she said, thinking of Blade. "You've been in my heart since that summer, Remy. You have to know that."

Blade. Not Remy.

"I went up to her, you…and put my arms around you, like you did with me earlier that day. But she pulled back, pushed me away. Told me that it was after curfew and if I didn't get back to my cabin, she was going to report me."

Oh… God. He was killing her without pulling the trigger. He'd known all along that the truth, his truth, would do so.

"And she…" Remy's tone of voice completely changed. It was like another man was sitting there as he tightened his grip on the gun, turning his fingers white, as he continued with, "And she…just turned away. I couldn't believe you, of all people, would do that, Morgie. That you'd *hurt* me like that. I was so…mad." His voice changed again, making him sound like a little kid. "And…and jealous. And…mad. And I picked up a fallen branch, swung it at her and ran."

She might die. She knew that. Played it out anyway. It

was her job to get it all on tape. She was finally bringing her sister justice.

Maddie. Who'd already conquered death. Because of Morgan.

"It was an accident, Morgie," the young voice said. "I didn't know until all the commotion before dawn that she was even hurt bad. I snuck outside, hiding, scared to death they'd know it was me, and that's when I saw Shane go into Blade's bunk and come back out again. He told me later that morning that he'd been happy to hear that Blade had done it, because he'd been afraid people would think it was him, because he'd been with her out there after the party."

And Remy had sat with her, hearing her scream at Blade, and hadn't said a word.

She had it all. Everything she'd said she was living for. Everything she'd had to have before she died.

Except…she'd been wrong about that, too.

She hadn't had a life with Blade, yet. Hadn't borne his child.

Remy lifted the gun off his leg, let it fall again, said, "And now, Morgie, it's all come full circle. We're going to get it right this time, me and you. We're going together. Here. Now. Right where it all really ended forever ago…"

Murder suicide.

He turned, and she caught a glimpse of the barrel of his gun pointing at her as she pulled her own.

She felt a blow even as she heard the shots.

And barely noticed the loud splash as body weight hit water.

He hadn't been in time.

The gun had gone off.

Blade had his man. Held Barton's arms so tightly behind the other man's back, he figured Remy's shoulder was out of the socket. And still the man thrashed in the water, fighting him.

He'd seen the gun go flying. Hadn't pulled his own. He had no authority to shoot.

He had to get to Morgan. Blade hadn't heard a second splash. Couldn't get a look at the log to see if she was splayed across it. Or how badly she was bleeding.

Please, God, and all fates that be, let her be alive.

Let her hold on.

The FBI agents would have heard the shot over the wire. They'd be there...

"Move again and you're dead." He heard hatred in the voice, saw the gun barrel pushing into Barton's head. And felt the man's muscles go limp.

"Don't loosen your grip, Blade," the most beautiful voice in the world said next to him. The same one that had just threatened to blow a man's head off. But in an entirely different tone.

"I have no intention of letting this bastard go," Blade said, his grip tight even as he weakened with relief. And a gratitude unlike anything he'd ever known.

Less than a minute later, a swarm of agents was upon them, and handcuffs were placed on the wrists dangling from the arms he held in a death grip. Morgan's gun disappeared from the man's head. And she told him, "You can let go now."

She might think so. He knew differently.

Dropping his hands from the dangerous man's body, he reached instantly for the one person he wanted to hold on to for the rest of his life.

Holding her by the arms, gently, as the river flowed

around their ankles, he searched her head, her face, her clothes, for signs of blood.

"He missed," she told him. "Because of you."

He noticed she wasn't pulling away from him. So he held her hand as they climbed up on the bank, and as they walked back to the caravan of cars. And as they both answered questions. He got in the car first, to head back to Rocky Springs, and when she slid in beside him, she didn't stop sliding until her shoulder and thigh were touching his.

They were two peas in a pod. Needing each other.

He could be misreading things.

He didn't think so.

And was glad when he heard Kelly Chase on the car's audio system, reminding Morgan that Madison's death was not on her.

"If I'd dealt with his attraction the moment I'd felt it..."

"No, Morgan," Kelly said again. "You sister made choices, as did Barton. I'd like you to call me tomorrow so we can talk more about this."

Morgan's okay was witnessed by Jasmine, her new partner, Kelly Valentine, and Walt, the agent in the back with him and Morgan. Blade was going to hold her to it.

There was no chance for the two of them to speak. No time when they were alone together. He had to give his statement separate from hers, but it was all formality. He'd been through it all so many times before, he recognized that law enforcement was just crossing every *t* and dotting every *i*. They had it all on tape. Just needed clarification of the end there, the part that they'd heard but couldn't see.

Remy lifting the gun, Blade lunging...

And suddenly, after a grueling morning...they were free. Jasmine offered to take Morgan back to Detroit with her. To drive her to get a rental vehicle until she could purchase a new one. Before Morgan could answer, Blade made his own offer. He'd left his truck at the precinct when they'd skipped town before dawn the day before.

"Come home with me."

Nothing else. No promises. Just that.

Her nod didn't promise anything either. They were simply two souls who'd been through trauma together. Leaving the precinct to debrief together. At his home on the beach.

Morgan was mostly silent on the drive to his place. They'd both been talking for the past hour. Had been over everything multiple times.

He didn't have a lot to say, either.

He offered her a glass of wine when they entered his house through the garage. She accepted and followed him out to the deck after he collected the bottle and glasses.

He sat in his normal chair. A rocker next to the side table. She took the other one. A match that had never had a mate.

He poured.

She held her glass for a toast.

He tipped his to it, still with no words. Was fine to keep it that way if it kept them together.

"To us," she said as he heard the clink.

He liked it. *To us.* So simple.

Yet said…everything.

"We know nothing about each other's daily lives." He tried to be reasonable, when his entire being was urging him to scoop her up, wine and all, and take her upstairs. For a few days at least. With breaks for food. And maybe playing on his private beach.

Time to sit at the water that had saved their lives and be thankful…

"If you're telling me you need time, just say so, Blade. I'm not going anywhere."

He glanced over at her.

"Not ever again," she said, staring him straight in the eye. "I know everything I need to know about you and about what I want and need. My heart, my soul, they know. The rest…it will come. And while it does… I'll be right here, welcoming it all in."

There was so much. Where would they live? Was she willing to move to Rocky Springs? Give up her life in Detroit? Her job was mobile. His was not. But he could start again. Did she still want kids? Was she…?

She was watching him. Sipping wine. Smiling. But when she saw him studying her, her expression grew serious. "Do you want a life with me in it?"

"More than anything on earth." Again, the answer was so simple.

"Then we'll figure out the rest."

"I want kids," he blurted, just too cautious to believe full-out.

"I'm ready."

"I'd like to live here."

"I was counting on that part. And thinking I'd limit my jobs to in state."

He smiled then and she asked, "What? You don't think I can? Or will?"

Shaking his head, Blade said, "I don't doubt you can do whatever you put your mind to, Morgan."

"Then what?"

"I've spent the past seventeen years of my life preparing for the worst. I'm finding that I'm not quite sure how to accept the best."

She left her chair then, but only to slide down onto his lap, wrapping her arms around his neck as she said, "Then that makes two of us, Blade. I'm still pinching myself. Saddened. And yet…feeling happier than I can remember feeling, too. Which feels…weird."

"Weird." He nodded, then tipped her chin with his finger. "I'm thinking maybe we spend the rest of our lives helping each other figure out how to live with daily happiness," he told her, feeling smarter than he had in a long while.

"Can we start by going upstairs and getting naked again? In a bed this time?" She sounded nothing at all like the Morgie he'd known.

And everything like the Morgan she'd grown up to be.

He was in love with both. Another truth. Just…there.

"You grab the wine," he told her, waiting for her to have both glasses in hand, and then, with her securely in his arms, stood.

Carried her into the house and up the stairs.

They'd fought their demons. Had kept their promises and found their truths.

Which had led them right back to the one place they'd both known, even as teenagers, that they'd needed most to be.

Together.

Forever.

* * * * *

Cameron Mountain Refuge
Beth Cornelison

MILLS & BOON

Dear Reader,

Welcome back to Cameron Glen! When I finished writing the last of the Cameron siblings' stories, I just wasn't ready to let this family go. There were more stories to be told, I knew, and first among those stories was Jessica Harkney's. Something told me Matt Harkney's ex-wife needed a new beginning, and her story quickly came together. I hope you enjoy the evolution of Gage and Jessica's relationship from friends to lovers as much as I did writing it.

This story is dedicated to Patience Bloom, who for many years and many books was my editor at Harlequin. I had just completed and turned in *Cameron Mountain Refuge* days before I got word from Patience that she was leaving Harlequin to pursue other projects. As much as I hated to see her go, I knew our friendship would remain. So, Patience, thank you for your years of guidance and faith in my writing, your friendship, and shared love of books, cats and chocolate! This one's for you.

Best always,

Beth Cornelison

Beth Cornelison began working in public relations before pursuing her love of writing romance. She has won numerous honours for her work, including a nomination for the RWA RITA® Award for *The Christmas Stranger*. She enjoys featuring her cats (or friends' pets) in her stories and always has another book in the pipeline! She currently lives in Louisiana with her husband, one son and three spoiled cats. Contact her via her website, bethcornelison.com.

DEDICATION

For Patience

Prologue

The water was rising, along with her panic. She was trapped, and soon she would drown. She banged on the window, desperately trying to get free. To save herself. To save her friends. But she couldn't get out. The water gurgled higher...to her chin, her mouth, her nose. Suffocating. Lungs burning. They would all die. And it was her fault.

Then a giant bee appeared at her window. With his face. Gloating. Sneering. Buzzing. Buzzing. Buzzing.

Jessica Harkney woke with a gasp, her heart racing. Gulping air. She cut a quick glance around her, disoriented. Confused. He'd been there. But where was he now? The buzzing continued...

Clarity slapped her. Nightmare. Again. How long would the same replay of that awful night haunt her dreams? And did she deserve to be free of the nocturnal torture?

The buzzing sounded again as her phone vibrated on her nightstand. Taking a calming breath, she answered the call—her boss—and glimpsed at the time.

Damn! She was late. She tossed back her bedcovers.

"Sorry!" she said immediately. "Horrid night. And I...overslept."

After spending most of the night staring wide-eyed at her ceiling, a parade of worries and regrets tumbling through her head, she'd drifted off around 4:00 a.m., turned off her alarm when it chimed at 6:00 a.m.—and remembered nothing else but the nightmare until now. Eight thirty.

"I was worried about you since…you're usually so punctual," her boss, Carolyn, replied.

And because your life has been such a traumatic mess lately. The words, while unspoken, hovered in her boss's tone.

Raking her raven hair out of her eyes, Jessica groaned. "I know. I—I'll be there in forty minutes."

"Can you make it thirty?" her boss said, firmly but without an edge. "We have a meeting with John Billings at ten, and we need to prep."

Grimacing, Jessica flew to the bathroom, took the world's fastest shower, threw on the clothes she'd laid out last night, whizzed through the kitchen to start her Keurig brewing a cup of coffee, dumped a messy pile of cat kibble in her cat's food bowl, grabbed a banana and a bagel, stuffed her phone in her purse and unplugged her laptop from the charger.

"See you tonight, Pluto! Be good!" she called to her buff-colored feline as she raced out to the garage, feeling like a juggler. She had her bagel in her mouth, her laptop under one arm, the banana under the other, her purse over her shoulder, her shoes in her left hand, her coffee in the right. Opening the door to her rental car with her pinky, she set the coffee in the drink holder and tossed everything but the bagel on the passenger-side seat. Sliding behind the steering wheel, she took a bite of the bagel, then set the rest on top of the dashboard. After she cranked the car engine, she slipped her high-heeled pumps on her feet and strapped on her seat belt.

Only when she reached up to the visor to push the garage remote did she realize her mistake. She hadn't replaced the door opener yet since the accident. With a shudder for the unpleasant reminder of her recent trauma and a grunt at the inconvenience, she unbuckled her seat belt again and climbed out. As she rounded the back end of the rental car, waving away the stink of exhaust, a figure stepped from behind the open storage room door.

She screamed and stumbled backward, away from the man who approached her. When she recognized him, her jaw hardened, and heat coursed through her veins. "How did you get in here? What do you want?" she snarled, then flapped a dismissive hand. "Never mind that. Just…get out!"

"Not until we talk. You owe me that much, Jessie. I saved your life." He took a decisive step, blocking her path back to the open car door. Her purse. Her phone.

She gritted her teeth in frustration. "How many times do I have to tell you, I don't want anything to do with you. Stay away from me!"

"Look, Jessie, stop being so stubborn. I love you! If you weren't so defensive, you'd see—"

When he took a step toward her, she slipped off a shoe and threw it at his head.

"I said stay away from me!" She backed up again, knowing she needed her phone. "I'm calling the police."

His eyes narrowed with menace. "No cops. Just talk to me. I will keep coming back until you see that you love me the way I love you."

With quick steps, she rushed to the passenger side of the rental car and jerked the door handle. Locked. Damn it! Another wave of panic swooped through her. She glanced around for something with which to defend herself. Her tennis racket was on the wall behind him, but she wanted something bigger, heavier. More lethal.

When she turned and darted toward her garden tools, propped against the far wall, he surged up behind her. She seized a shovel as he wrapped an arm around her waist. With a thrust, he threw her to the ground. The shovel clanged down beside her. As she scrambled to get up, he kicked her in the temple, and she saw stars. Blinking, trying to shake off the blow, Jessica rolled to her belly. As she rose to her hands and knees, she put her hand on the shovel's handle. She angled a woozy and wary glance up at him. "Get out."

He glared back, growling through gritted teeth. "You made me do that. If you hadn't—"

She swung the shovel at him, hitting him far too weakly in her injured state to do more than anger him.

He grabbed the shovel, yanked it from her grip and tossed it out of her reach. Then leaning over her, he grabbed a fistful of her hair and bent her head back. "Now you're going to be sorry."

She sucked in a breath, coughing on the collecting exhaust from the idling rental car, then spit in his face.

His face suffused with color, the veins on his forehead bulging. He swiped the spittle off with his free arm, then shoved her down again. His foot connected once, twice with her ribs. Pain juddered through her. With trembling arms, she tried to crawl away from his abuse, but he stomped on her hand. Yelping in pain, she balled herself in fetal position and wrapped her arms around the back of her head, her only thought now of protecting her most tender and vulnerable places.

He kicked her again in the side. The hip. An unprotected part of her head. He stepped back, coughing. Then, getting on his hands and knees, he stuck his face in hers. In a sibilant tone, he whispered, "A restraining order? You thought you could get rid of me? Not a chance. Learn this lesson. Don't piss me off, Jessie."

She heard him grunt as he got back on his feet, heard him stomp across the concrete floor, heard the side door to her garage open and close. And then the only sound was the rumbling purr of the rental car's engine as it filled her garage with poisonous gas.

Chapter 1

Two months earlier

"You kill me!" Jessica said, holding her sides as she laughed. "You did not say that to his face!"

"I did," her best friend, Tina Putnam, née Coleman, assured her. "The twerp deserved it. This is the third woman he's broken up with since January! He's forty-three years old, for crying out loud. What's he waiting for?" She sipped her margarita, then shaking her head, added, "God knows I love my brother, but he's hopeless when it comes to women. I've never seen a man so adverse to commitment. And other than his apparent allergy to responsibility and marriage, Gage really is a good guy."

Jessica smiled as she nodded her agreement. Gage was good folk, as the Southernism went.

Across the table of the Charlotte, North Carolina, Mexican restaurant, Holly Teale arched an eyebrow. "And he's sexy as hell, too."

Tina sputtered and coughed as she took another slurp of her margarita. She wiped her mouth with her napkin and chuckled. "I wouldn't know about that. He's my brother!"

"Well, he's not my brother, and if I weren't married—

I'd hit that." Sara Callen gave her shoulders a little waggle as she lifted her beer and drank.

"You're not involved with anyone at the moment, Jessica." Holly twirled a lock of her red curls around one finger and gave Jessica a meaningful glance. "What do you think? A little wham-bam-thank-you-ma'am with Tina's brother?"

Jessica pulled a face and shook her head. "Good grief, no! I've known Gage as long as I've known Tina."

"So?" Holly said.

"So…it would be too weird. He's practically *my* brother." Jessica shoved her last bites of enchilada around her plate and shook her head. "Besides, I've sworn off men. This one—" she hooked her thumb toward Tina "—convinced me to try another dating app." She rolled her eyes. "Let's just say, it didn't go well. Of the three men I did finally go out with, after playing text-tag with several, one proved to be married and looking for some extracurricular activity—"

Her friends gave the appropriate groans and wrinkled noses.

"One was, well, how to say this politely—"

"Boring as hell," Tina supplied for her.

Jessica pointed at her friend. "That. He spent the whole night talking about his coin collection and going metal detecting on Saturdays. I mean, I have nothing against coin collecting in principle, but by dessert, I wanted to hit him over the head with his metal detector and run screaming from the Dairy Queen where he'd taken me for our meal."

Holly and Sara chortled. "Dairy Queen for a first date? I love me some DQ, but my God, for a first date?"

"He never once asked what I do, or if I had children, or if I had hobbies…" Jessica shook her head. "Then most recently I went out with a guy that seemed okay at first, but the more we talked, the longer the date lasted, I just got this strange vibe off him."

"What kind of strange vibe?" Holly asked, fishing a tortilla chip out of the basket in the middle of the table and crunching down on it.

Jessica twisted her mouth as she thought. "Hard to say exactly. He seemed genuinely interested in me, and he wasn't bad-looking. Early forties, blond and had all his hair, good build, stylish glasses and pleasant enough face. We talked about the usual get-to-know-you stuff. Movies. Jobs. Books. Travels. And we had a lot in common." She paused. "Maybe too much. Everything I liked or I said interested me, he said he loved, too. All the same music and movies and podcasts. It was…" She paused, gazing out the restaurant window as she reflected on the odd date. "*Too* perfect."

"Trying too hard to find things in common?" Sara asked. "Needy…"

"Maybe. He acted confident and self-assured, but again, it was…too much."

"How so?" Holly asked.

"Hmm." Jessica, the designated driver for the evening, sipped her iced tea. "He was rather…annoying in his certainty that we were a good match, and that we would be having many more dates in the future. For instance, when I told him I enjoyed canoeing and kayaking, he said, 'Well, we'll be sure to go boating this summer. Nothing better than a day on the water.'"

"This summer? It's March, and he was already planning your dates for this summer?" Tina asked, giving Jessica an incredulous look.

"Right? So that was weird. But like I said, he was pretty nice, and we did, apparently, have a lot in common, so—"

"You saw him again," Holly guessed correctly.

"Twice more," Tina said, holding up two fingers for emphasis. "I told her she should listen to her instincts if he gave her a funny feeling, but…"

Jessica pulled a face as she glanced at Tina. "But Henry was so persistent, and since I couldn't give a good reason *not* to go out, I just…gave him a second chance. Then a third."

"And the other dates? How was—Henry, you say?— then?" Holly's eyes lit with intrigue, and she leaned forward, her expression eager.

"The same. No…even weirder, I think. Cloyingly agreeable. Arrogantly assured of our destiny. But also polite and good at conversation and a good tipper."

"Well, that's always a positive sign," Holly said. "My mama always said you can tell a lot about a person's character by the way they treat servers in a restaurant."

All four women bobbed their heads in agreement, and Jessica sighed.

"But…I couldn't shake the vibe that something was off with him," Jessica continued, the uneasy sense returning as she described the events of the last week. "So when he asked for a fourth date…well, he didn't as much ask as *assume*, saying he'd 'be by my house on Friday at seven to pick me up.'"

"That's nervy," Sara said, sounding affronted on Jessica's behalf.

"My thoughts exactly. I told him I would be busy and couldn't go out Friday, and he demanded to know what I had planned."

Her friends issued more grunts of disdain.

"I told him it wasn't his business, which clearly irritated him, and when he continued to insist I tell him why I wouldn't see him on Friday, I told him I no longer wanted to see him. He didn't give up, though. He continued to call and text every day. After a few days, I had to block him to make it stop."

"Good riddance. He sounds too controlling and overbearing," Tina said, patting Jessica's arm.

"Except…he still showed up that Friday at my house expecting to take me to dinner."

"What!" Holly gasped, her expression aghast.

"I, of course, refused to go out with him, which didn't go over well. He got loud and hostile." Jessica paused to sip her tea, remembering the confrontation. "It was…ugly. He called me names, got in my face, then—get this—he told me he *forgave me* for my rudeness, and that I should get my coat. We were still going to dinner."

Her friends exchanged incredulous looks.

"Are you serious?" Holly asked.

"What a jerk!" Sara said.

Jessica nodded. "I told him to leave, or I would call the police. That didn't go over well, either, but when I got my phone and started dialing, he took off."

"Like a roach running for cover when the lights are turned on," Tina added, one dark eyebrow arched in disgust.

"I hope you still reported him to the cops." Holly's eyes were dark with concern.

Jessica shrugged. "No. I think he got the message. But I deleted the dating app from my phone. Like I said, I'm done with men. I'm fine on my own. And I have my posse." She raised her tea glass to each of her friends, smiling at them one at a time.

"Hear! Hear!"

"That's right!"

"Darn tootin'!"

The four clinked glasses, and as Sara finished taking a sip of her drink, she sputtered a laugh. "Holly Teale, did you just say *darn tootin'*?"

Jessica chuckled. "She did."

Holly raised her hands, looking innocent. "What's wrong with that? My grandma used to say that."

"Exactly. Your *grandma*!" Sara lifted an eyebrow as another round of tipsy giggles erupted around the table.

Jessica sipped her tea, glancing around the restaurant, aware she and her friends were being rather loud.

And her gaze landed on a fair-haired man at the bar who was glaring boldly at her. Her stomach swooped, and she felt the cold drain of blood from her face. She set her glass down with a thump and muttered a bad word.

She stared down at their table, focused her energy on trying to calm her swirling gut. Lord, but she'd eaten too much, and this rush of anxiety was not mixing well with her spicy meal.

"Jessica?" Tina touched her arm and angled her head in concern. "Something wrong?"

"I always thought it was just an expression," Jessica muttered.

"Huh?"

"Speak of the devil, and he will appear," Jessica said. She lifted her gaze to the bar again to discover the devil had risen from his seat and was headed over to their table.

"What? Who?" Holly asked, then pivoted in her seat to see what Jessica was looking at.

"The guy I was just telling you about," Jessica said, panic rising. "Henry. He's here! He's coming ov—"

"Well, well, well. Imagine meeting you here," Henry said in a singsong tone, something cold behind his green eyes. He bent and gave Jessica a kiss on the check. "How are you doing, sweetheart?"

Scowling, Jessica swiped her cheek with her palm. "I'm not your sweetheart. What are you doing here?"

He raised both hands. "Getting dinner and a drink, of course." He grabbed a chair from the next table and pulled it up, saying, "Y'all seem to be having a great time. May I join you?"

"No," Jessica said firmly, her heart pounding in her ears. Locking her elbow, she placed a hand on his chest to discourage him pulling closer to the table. "You need to leave."

Her friends exchanged wary glances.

When Henry only pulled a lopsided and sardonic smile, a chill crept through her. He took the hand she'd braced on his chest and held it between his. "Jessie, honey, I know you're still mad about last week. I said some things I shouldn't have, but so did you. You provoked me. Let's let bygones be bygones and start over."

She yanked her hand from his and stood. "I mean it, Henry! You need to leave. Now."

He folded his arms over his chest and shook his head, grinning at her like she was a petulant child. "Not until we work this out."

Now Tina shoved her chair back and rose to her feet. "I'm getting the manager."

As Tina disappeared toward the front of the restaurant, Holly pulled out her phone. "Forget the manager, I'm calling the cops. He kissed you against your will. I believe that qualifies as battery."

While she appreciated her friends' defense of her, she motioned for Holly to stand down. She preferred to get rid of Henry without a scene, with minimal hullabaloo. If she could.

Holly frowned at Jessica, but she put her phone back on the table.

"Look," Henry said, his tone indicating he thought he was being reasonable and more than fair. "If your friends don't want me here, we can go somewhere and be alone. A movie? Bowling? Whatever you want."

"Hey, are you deaf? She said she wants you to leave!" Holly said, her back stiff and her hand still resting on her phone. "Get lost, pal!"

"Shut up, bitch!" Henry snapped, his eyes blazing. "This doesn't concern you."

Sara gasped. "Hey! You wanna take it down a notch? Jessica asked nicely for you to leave, and I think you—"

Henry shoved his face right in Sara's, snarling, "I don't much care what you think." He waited a beat, his grin malevolent before jabbing her with a finger in the chest and adding, "Bitch."

Jessica saw red. "Get away from her!"

Henry turned back to Jessica as if startled by the dark timbre of her voice. "Are you talking to me in that tone?"

"I am. You can't think I'd stand by mildly while you verbally assault my friends?"

He just snorted dismissively.

Jessica gritted her teeth. "Leave now, and I will let this go. But if you don't walk away right now—"

His shoulders squared. "Don't threaten me. You won't like what happens next, Jessie."

She didn't bother correcting him on his use of the nickname she'd despised since her mother's first loser boyfriend used it on her. She simply wanted Henry gone. Instead, she glanced back toward Holly and said, "Okay, call the cops."

But at that moment, Tina returned with the restaurant manager, and Henry raised both hands as he rose from the chair and took a step back from their table. "It's cool. I'm going." He hesitated, giving Jessica a direct look. "But I'll see you again, Jessie." He blew her a kiss as he strode across the restaurant floor and out the door.

Gage Coleman stood to the side of the locked window and smashed the panes with his axe. When no flames leaped out, he nodded to Cal Rodgers and turned on the headlamp on his headgear. He climbed through the broken window, into the bedroom saturated by dense smoke. Despite his protective turnout gear, he felt the intense heat of the flames devouring the other end of the burning house.

"Madeline? Honey, where are you?" he called, searching for the five-year-old girl still trapped in the house. "I know you're scared, but I'm here to help you." He felt blindly and moved slowly across the floor, his feet occasionally kicking an unseen toy or other obstacle. Using the beam of his headlamp, he made out a closet door, sitting partially open. He entered the closet, searching the floor, behind the stacked boxes, under the dirty clothes.

"Madeline?" Nothing. No answer.

Cal Rodgers wiggled through the open window, his

headlamp flashing in the small room, and he aimed his hand toward the door. "I'll check the bathroom."

Gage nodded and felt his way to the single bed. Getting on his hands and knees, he peered underneath. No Madeline.

But a pair of eyes reflected his headlamp.

His priority was the little girl, but he wouldn't walk away from a pet. Lying flatter to stretch an arm to the far corner where the eyes blinked back at him, he grabbed the scruff of the cat and dragged it out.

The feline was unmoving, either from shock or unconscious from smoke inhalation. He cuddled the cat to his chest and moved quickly to the window. "Smith!" he shouted to the first man he saw. "Come get this cat."

His coworker rushed over and took the limp animal. Gage didn't stay to see what Eddie Smith did with the feline. He had a child to find.

"Madeline!" he heard Rodgers calling as he searched the en suite bathroom, and Gage added his voice.

"Where are you, Madeline? Can you call to us?"

He completed his search of the girl's room with no results and headed out into the hallway. "Come on, Madeline. Don't be scared," he called, knowing children were often as frightened of the big men in turnout gear and face shields as of the fire. "I'll get you out and take you to your mommy and daddy." The smoke was thicker here, and so black he couldn't see even a foot in front of him. "Mad—"

His foot connected with something, and he crouched to determine what was in his path. A small, dark-haired girl in a white nightgown was crumpled on the floor. "Rodgers, I've got her!"

Gage scooped the child in his arms and heard her whimper. *Thank God, she was alive!*

Turning back toward the bedroom, he carried Madeline through her bedroom and handed her out to Rodgers, who'd already crawled back out the window.

As he turned to climb out the window, his headlamp flashed across the rumpled covers of the girl's bed, and he spotted a colorful lump. A gut impulse sent him back to the bed, where he grabbed the item. Without pausing further, he turned and hurried out the window. Only once he was standing in the yard did he lift his face shield and study what he'd brought out. A ragged and obviously well-loved stuffed unicorn stared up at him with unblinking black-thread eyes.

Gage's heart thumped wistfully, remembering his sister Tina's favorite stuffed animal, a frog with a wide mouth, that had gone to college with his sister and still held a spot of pride on her spare bedroom shelf.

He scanned the area until he found where EMTs were treating the little girl. Carrying the pink-and-yellow toy to the child, he knelt beside the girl's mother, who clutched Madeline's hand as she sobbed tears of relief.

Madeline's dark brown eyes were open—definitely a good sign—and she wore a clear plastic breathing cup over her mouth and nose that fed her lungs oxygen. The child's gaze turned to him, then dropped to the unicorn. Her eyes widened.

"Hey, Madeline." Gage held out the toy, thinking how much the girl with her long black hair and dark eyes reminded him of someone else—a woman he'd cherished most of his life. If he'd followed his heart instead of his head years ago, he might have a daughter who looked like Madeline, thanks to the woman's genes. "I thought you might miss your friend."

Nodding, the little girl reached for the doll and hugged it to her chest.

Madeline's mother turned to him with a teary smile and rasped, "Thank you! You've no idea how much Beanie means to her."

He grinned and tugged on the unicorn's yarn mane. "Is that her name? Beanie?"

The woman shook her head. "No. The unicorn is Crystal. She's also treasured. I mean our cat."

Gage followed the woman's gaze to the driveway, where her husband held a sooty white cat for another child to pet.

"You're the one who saved Madeline…and Beanie. Aren't you?" she asked, clutching his arm.

Gage was uneasy with the hero worship in the mother's eyes, but he bobbed a nod. "Yes, ma'am."

"How can I ever thank you?"

He stood and shook his head. "Just doing my job, ma'am. Knowing Madeline's all right is all the thanks I need."

As he hurried back toward the fire truck to lend a hand with the hose, he cast a last glance at Madeline hugging her unicorn and thought again of Tina and her frog. He was still close to his younger sister, who lived just a few miles from his apartment. They'd been close enough in age that they'd shared a lot of the same friends in high school. In fact, they still maintained many of those same friendships today, some twenty-odd years later.

Hanging with the girls tonight. TTYL! Tina had texted him earlier that night.

The girls. Which meant at that very moment, his sister was enjoying a fun night out with *her*. His ebony haired, brown-eyed missed opportunity. Jessica Harkney.

Chapter 2

Jessica's body shook in the wake of the adrenaline, anger and embarrassment the confrontation with Henry had caused. She could feel the eyes of the other restaurant patrons on her, heard the low murmur of Tina's and Holly's voices as they discussed the events with the manager.

"You okay, sweetie?" Sara rubbed a hand on her back, and Jessica jolted.

Nodding, she sent Sara a warm smile. She had to shake off the incident. She would not rent Henry Blythe space in her head. Nor would she let him and his brutish shenanigans ruin the night for her and her friends. Before he'd shown up, they'd been having fun, letting off steam, enjoying the sort of girlfriend bonding that healed the soul. Henry would not steal that from her.

With a deep inhale and a cleansing exhale, Jessica shook her hands out as if physically flicking the menace of the man from her fingers. "I say we've earned dessert." Jessica flagged a passing waitress. "Can we have an order of flan, some sopaipillas and one tres leches cake with four forks please?"

Holly blinked at her. "Who has room for dessert?"

Jessica shrugged. "Maybe no one, but I'm feeling rebellious. I usually want dessert but feel guilty ordering it, as if it's too indulgent, too expensive, breaking my never-ending diet. But to hell with guilt and restrictions! Life was meant to be lived!"

Tina laughed and raised her glass. "I'll drink to that! Bring on the carbs!"

With the continued good humor of her friends, the rich flavor of the desserts, and another half hour of distracting conversation and uplifting giggles, Jessica could almost put Henry's interruption of their night behind her.

But as the four of them walked out of the restaurant and piled into Jessica's small sedan, the spring night had a bite. A chill that had nothing to do with the weather crept through her as they crossed the dark parking lot. Maybe the eerie sensation was due to lingering echoes of Henry's confrontation. Or maybe the prickly nip on her neck was just her own heightened awareness of her surroundings, thanks to the personal safety training her ex-husband had insisted she take early in their marriage. She couldn't say what hovered in the humid North Carolina night, humming like cicadas in July, but Jessica paused before climbing in the driver's seat to take her friends home. She scanned the parking lot, the side street, the shadows behind the dumpster where a stray cat scuttled into the tall grass.

Seeing nothing to concern her, she shook her head and slipped behind the steering wheel.

"Home, please, Winston," Holly teased with a fake accent, collapsing in the back seat in a fit of drunken giggles with Sara. Jessica rolled her eyes and grinned. The four of them each had a different chauffeur name that was dusted off when they took their turn as the designated driver for girls' night. Sara was Geoffrey. Holly was Hubert. Tina was Lyle. Complete foolishness. Completely random, but the sort of silly private jokes that were the stuff of yearslong friendships.

Jessica pulled out of the parking lot, turning toward the state highway that would take Holly home first. Holly lived outside of town in the same farmhouse her grandparents had bought seventy years earlier, raised chickens as a hobby and kept the financial books for her parents' dairy farm in lieu of rent on the house.

"Can I get some eggs when we get to your house?" Tina asked, turning her head to look to the back seat at Holly. She raised a hand to shade her eyes and squinted. "Jeez, dude. Easy on the brights."

Jessica, too, raised a hand to block the glare as a truck with its high beams on pulled close to her back bumper, the headlights glowing brightly in her side and rearview mirrors.

"Sure. I'll trade you eggs for your brother's phone number," Holly replied.

"Wha— Seriously? That again?" Tina twisted back to face forward. "What is y'all's fascination with my big brother? There is a reason he's never married, ladies. He's a man-child."

Jessica winced and tapped her brakes to try to get the truck to back off. "That's harsh. He's not that bad."

Tina shrugged. "Well, he is a commitment-phobe. A confirmed bachelor with the housekeeping skills of a teenage boy. You know that's true, Jessica. You ladies deserve better in a spouse."

The truck behind her revved its engine and continued to hover close behind Jessica's car. Irritation at the tailgater spiked. Had the truck followed her out of the restaurant parking lot?

"Oh, you misunderstand," Holly said, leaning toward the front seat. "I don't want to marry him. I just want to play with him. Have any of his past girlfriends mentioned to you how he is in bed?"

Sara shrieked with laughter, making Jessica jolt. She shook off the start and, pressing a hand to her thumping heart, joined the chuckling.

Tina stuck her fingers in her ears. "La la la la la, not listening to this kind of talk about my brother. *My brother, y'all!* Just stop!"

"Come on, Tina, you have to admit—"

The truck behind them tapped Jessica's back bumper, jolting the car and cutting Holly's reply short. The four women gasped or muttered a curse in surprise and alarm. Against her better judgment, Jessica sped up a little, assuming the guy was simply bothered by her careful, not-quite-the-limit speed.

"What is it with jerks tonight? Is there a full moon?" Tina asked.

With a roar of his engine, the truck resumed its position tailgating Jessica.

"I'm calling the cops for real this time," Sara said, and the back seat lit with the glow of her cell phone. "Yes, my name is Sara Callen. My friends and I are driving home from a restaurant, and we're being harassed by an overly aggressive driver in a pickup truck." Sara gave their location on the highway and the direction they were traveling, sounding far more clear-minded and professional than Jessica figured she would have been after four potent margaritas.

The truck bumped them again, and Jessica heard Sara cuss. "I dropped my phone."

The snick of Sara unbuckling her seat belt filtered to Jessica from the back seat. A flicker of worry licked Jessica. "Stay buckled, everyone. I'm gonna pull over so this creep can pass, but...just in case—"

"Yeah, I'm back," Sara said to the emergency operator. "Right, a reckless driver. Can't tell what color it is. He has his brights on, blinding us. He's bumpin' us intentionally."

At the first wide spot on the edge of the road, Jessica pulled over, and the truck passed them and roared away. She exhaled her relief, glad to be rid of the menace.

"Okay, never mind. My friend let 'im pass, and he drove away," Sara reported to the operator. "No, sorry. No tag numbers, but the truck was some light shade. Gray or white maybe. Possibly tan. Hard to tell in the dark."

Jessica took a moment to wipe her damp palms on her jeans and glance over at Tina.

Her bestie gave her a crooked smile. "You okay?"

Jessica nodded. "Just wondering why some people have to be such jerks."

Tina blinked. "As you look at me?" She snorted as she laughed. "Are you trying to tell me something?"

Tina's teasing helped soothe Jessica's ruffled nerves. She was good about that—calming her, encouraging her, sympathizing with her, sharing a grumble when needed. She swatted playfully at her friend. "Of course not. You're not a jerk." Then with a wry grin, she added, "Not usually, anyway."

"Unh!" Tina grunted in mock affront.

"Yeah, thanks," Sara said, presumably to the emergency operator. "Bye." Then louder, "She said to call back if we see the truck again, and especially if we get any more identifying information. Tag numbers, make or model of the truck."

"I think it was a Chevy," Holly said.

Tina shook her head. "Naw, pretty sure it was a Ford."

As she pulled back onto the highway, Jessica turned on the air-conditioning. Despite the cool spring night, she'd broken out in a sweat. Adrenaline after the run-in with the aggressive truck? Perimenopause? Could be either or both.

Stupid hormones reminding her she was getting older. Her son was finishing his second year of college, for cripes' sake! Sure, she'd been barely twenty-two years old when Eric was born, barely more than a kid herself, but she couldn't believe how quickly Eric had turned from a cuddly toddler to a precocious grade-schooler to a legal driver and now a sophomore at the University of North Carolina.

The cool air did its job, and a couple of minutes later she turned the air conditioner off again. Tina gave her a knowing grin.

"Shut up," Jessica mumbled.

Tina raised both hands. "I didn't say anything. I'm sure my days of hot flashes are coming."

They reached a stretch of road that passed through a more rural landscape, leaving the shopping plazas and fast-food restaurants of town behind. The road narrowed and became darker thanks to the absence of streetlights and the neon glow of businesses' signs. Though night had fallen, Jessica knew the gently rolling hills were marked with woods and streams and dotted with occasional ponds where Eric and his friends had gone fishing throughout his youth.

Jessica angled a quick glance toward Tina. "Did you see the prom pictures Kathy posted on Facebook of—"

Her question was interrupted by the roar of a souped-up engine. Despite the highway's double-line, no-passing zone, the owner of the loud engine passed Jessica and cut in front of her, nearly clipping her front fender. She braked to avoid the truck, her heart beating triple time against her ribs. "Jeez, man! What the—?"

"That's the same truck from before!" Sara cried from the back seat.

"Seriously?" Jessica asked. "But—"

"It is." Tina pointed at the bumper of the light-colored truck. "I remember that bumper sticker." She pointed at a red, white and blue decal on the tailgate of the truck declaring support for a candidate from a past state election.

Jessica's gut swooped as she focused on the sticker. A flash of recognition curled through her, and bile rose in her throat. "That's Henry's truck!"

"Henry, the jerk from restaurant?" Tina asked, though her tone said she knew what the answer would be.

Jessica nodded, trying to find her voice amid her shock…and concern. "Pretty sure. He had a silver truck and a sticker like that. I remember thinking how we had different taste in political candidates. At the time, I wrote it off as no big deal."

"But the truck from before passed us, so how…" Holly sighed, then started again. "Good God. Did he circle around somehow to find us again or pull off to lie in wait until we passed him? That's…creepy!"

Jessica swallowed hard, trying not to get over-wrought. "Maybe it's just—"

The truck's driver slammed on the brakes, and Jessica reacted just in time to avoid rear-ending him. Accelerating again, the truck pulled away, and Jessica followed warily. "He toying with us. The SOB!"

Tina turned to the back seat. "Sara, call 911 again. Tell them to send the cops."

"Way ahead of you, girl," she said, then, "I called earlier about an aggressive driver. Well, he's back." She gave the highway number again and a mile marker.

"Should we pull over somewhere and wait for the cops?" Tina asked.

"And make ourselves an easier target for him to harass us?" Holly replied. "We'll be at my house in a couple more miles, then y'all can come inside until—"

"Look out!" Tina shouted.

As they came around a blind curve where the road crossed a bridge over a small river, the silver truck sat blocking the lane. Jessica had no time to stop. Instead, she cut the wheel hard to the right. An angled guardrail appeared in her headlights.

She tried to correct her path. Too late. Her friends screamed. The left side of car went up the guardrail like a ramp. Momentum, loss of traction, angle. Somehow, someway, the car careened up. Briefly airborne. Landed with a jolt, upright.

In the middle of the river.

Chapter 3

Gage and his fire company had only been back at the firehouse long enough to strip out of their bunker gear and start a conversation about dinner when the alarm sounded again. Suspected car accident. A 911 call that ended unexpectedly after reports of an unruly and harassing driver.

"Seriously?" Smith said. "But I'm starving!"

"Come on, rookie," Gage called, tossing the young firefighterΔ a protein bar from the box he'd been raiding when the alarm sounded. "Duty calls. This is what you signed up for."

The men hustled out to the truck bay to don their gear again and load the engine, moving faster than their tired bodies preferred. But haste was required. Every second counted and could be the difference between saving a life…or not.

Water was rising fast in the car's cabin, creeping closer to her mouth, her nose. Soon she'd not be able to breathe. To speak.

Other than the gurgle of water, the sawing of her frightened breaths, the car was chillingly silent.

"Tina?" Her friend slumped forward against her seat

belt, head lolling. She angled the rearview mirror to check on her friends in the back seat, but it was too dark to see anything. "Sara! Holly! We have to get out!"

Jessica turned her attention to escaping the car. She could only help her friends if she survived herself. When she tried to roll down the window, nothing happened. The waterlogged electrical system was useless. The thread of terror twisted tighter. She pounded the side window with her fist, trying to break the glass, to escape the death trap her car had become. The rising water had reached her neck.

Get out! Get out! *Get out!*

Drawing a shuddering breath, she battled to keep panic at bay. The only way she'd survive was to keep her wits. She unbuckled her seat belt, then Tina's. She tried to shake Tina awake. "Please, Tina! Wake up! We have to get out."

The clock was ticking. *Save yourself.*

The thought caused a sharp, guilty ache to slash through her.

She'd seen the YouTube videos about surviving various deadly scenarios. She'd just never imagined she'd have to use the information, had never purchased a rescue hammer for her map pocket. Now, glancing around her as the lake's muddy water burbled higher, she tried to come up with something, anything that would break the safety glass of her window. She needed something heavy with a sharp tip that would deliver a high impact, concentrated blow to break the safety glass.

Nothing. She thought of nothing heavier than the ballpoint pen she kept clipped to her visor. She tried her elbow. Pain juddered through her arm. Still the glass held.

Could she call 911? Her phone had been in her purse on the floor of the front seat when the car went in the water. Who knew where it was now. The thing was almost certainly nonfunctional after being submerged in the lake water. She prayed Sara's call had been enough to have help sent.

Contorting herself awkwardly as the river water reached her chin, she slipped off her shoe to whack at the glass with the high heel. But the resistance of the high water made it impossible to get a full, hard swing.

Images of her son, Eric, her beautiful boy, her pride and joy, flashed in her mind. A stinging grief squeezed her chest as she imagined the police contacting him at his college dorm to tell him she'd perished in a car crash. Had she fussed at him the last time they spoke? Told him she loved him more than anything?

She pushed with her feet, struggling now to keep her nose above the surface. A ragged sob tripped from her. She yanked the door handle and drove her shoulder into the driver's door. Even knowing that the weight and pressure of the lake's water against the door would make it humanly impossible to push it open, she had nothing to lose in trying.

But the door didn't budge and wouldn't until the water had filled the car completely and equalized the pressure on each side—at which point she'd have been under water holding her breath for how long? The notion terrified her.

She heard a whimper and jerked her gaze toward Tina. Her friend had raised her head, wide eyes taking in their situation. A dark trickle of blood seeped from a gash on her forehead.

"Try to stay calm," she called to Tina. "I'm trying to get us out."

"Jessica!" Tina cried, groping for her arm, her grip squeezing.

Could she kick the window out? Worth a shot, but maneuvering in the tight confines of her front seat as water pooled higher was not a simple task. As she twisted slightly on the driver's seat, wiggling her legs out from under the steering wheel, a movement outside her window startled her. She gasped, inhaling a mouth full of water that made her cough, sputter. The glow of her headlights illuminated the lake where a man had swum into the river. Her initial relief, her joy at being rescued, chilled when she recognized his face. *Henry.*

A flash of rage swept through her. The accident was his fault. His erratic, reckless driving was the reason she and her friends were trapped, about to drown.

He had something in his hand, and he banged it on her window once. Twice. Jessica took a large gulp of air, just before his third strike broke the glass. A gush of river water poured in and filled the interior of her sedan. Henry reached in and grabbed her arm, but she fought him. Turning to Tina, she tried to grasp her friend under her arms, tried to drag her from the seat. But Henry's grip on her was stronger, and he hauled her through the window. Jessica kicked, both fighting Henry and to propel herself to the surface.

The river's current was surprisingly swift, enough to tug her downstream. She gasped air and tried to swim back to the car, back to help Tina, Sara and Holly. Henry blocked her, grabbed her shirt and dragged her toward shore.

"Stop!" she choked out as her head bobbed above the water. "Let go!" She slapped at his hands, but she couldn't tread water, battle the current and free herself from him all at once.

"I'm saving your life, you ungrateful bitch!" He found purchase on the muddy riverbed, walked toward the bank, tugging her by her shirt until she, too, could stand. She twisted and pried at his hands, struggling to free her blouse from his grip. When he clung stubbornly, making her stumble as he hauled her closer toward shore, she ducked and shimmied until the blouse slipped off over her head.

He growled his frustration, then shouted, "What are you doing? Do you want to drown?"

Jessica faced the submerged car, heaving deep, ragged breaths as she calculated the best way to rescue her friends.

Moving well upstream of the car along the slippery mudbank, Jessica wasted no time diving back into the river. Though her arms trembled with fatigue, she swam out to her car and grabbed the car frame where her window had been. Jagged glass cut her hand, but she clung on. She tried to swim down into the car to find Tina, but the current was too strong. She almost lost her grip on the slick car.

Over the roar of adrenaline in her ears, the wail of a siren reached her. She spied the flash of red and blue lights on the surrounding trees. Help had come. She just prayed they were in time to save her friends.

As Gage's company arrived at the vehicle accident, he lit the headlamp he strapped on and grabbed an ad-

ditional spotlight. Jumping from the engine even before
it had come to a full stop, he shone his spotlight around
the area, assessing the scene alongside the other fire-
fighters. The glint of metal in his flashlight beam caught
his attention. Along with the panicked plea of a woman.

"Help!" she screamed. "My friends are still in the
car!"

The car in question was submerged in the river's
tricky eddies, and the woman clung precariously to the
roof of the car, barely visible above the muddy water line.

Gage raced to retrieve rope, a personal flotation vest
with carabineers and a lead line, as did his coworkers.
The station chief barked directions as they organized
themselves for the rescue. "Coleman, Rodgers, you're
going in. Barksdale, Smith, anchor the rescue line.
Someone ask dispatch how far out the ambulance is!"

Adrenaline pumping, Gage hooked the straps of his
safety vest at his sternum, then clipped his lead to the
main line in deft movements. Barksdale had crossed
the highway bridge with the heavy rope that would be
secured on the opposite shore, giving the men in the
water a steady line to hold, to tie off to as they worked
in the current.

"Ready?" Gage called to the men tying off the line.
He secured a headlamp, shoved on his gloves for better grip in the water and got the signal from his captain
when the throw line was anchored.

He hurried to the edge of the river, stopping only long
enough to clip onto the anchor line before he waded in.
Beside him, Cal Rodgers did likewise. When the water
level reached his waist and the water pulled at him, he
pushed off with his feet and swam. He fought the cur-

rent as he scissor-kicked and pulled with his arms, steering himself to the vehicle. The beam of his headlamp bobbed in the darkness as he half swam and half dragged himself to the vehicle. The car wasn't far from the bank of the river, and the water was not more than five feet deep. But if someone was trapped inside, that was more than enough to fill the interior and drown the trapped occupant in little time.

His first attention went to the woman clinging to the edge of the roof where the driver's window had been broken out. As he neared the car, she tried to duck under the water and go back inside the car. The current quickly caught her, and her grip faltered. Instead of wiggling into the car, she was swept back up and across the roof of the vehicle. She screamed as she scrabbled for a handhold, finding none and coughing on the water that filled her mouth.

"I got her!" Gage called to Cal. "Check the car!" He just reached her and hooked his arm around the woman's waist in the nick of time. The men on the bank immediately tightened the slack in his safety rope to keep them from drifting. He dropped another rope, tied in a lasso, over her head and settled it under her arms. "I got you, ma'am. Reel us in!"

The woman sputtered again as water splashed in her face, then rasped, "No! Have to…friends in car!"

"We'll get them next," he said, "I need you to be still. Don't fight me." His headlamp swept across her face, and recognition jolted through Gage. "Jessica?"

Her head tipped up, her terrified gaze finding his. "G—" Water splashed into her mouth, and she choked. Coughing and retching, she flailed an arm toward the car.

"Easy now, I have you. Hold on to me." Renewing his focus, Gage pulled at the anchor rope and, hand over hand, pulled them through the river back to shore.

When they reached the bank, Captain Remis helped him get Jessica up to high ground and wrap her in a blanket. Already she was shivering from the cold water, from adrenaline. Shock was a real possibility. When she swiped water from her eyes and pushed her dripping hair back from her eyes, she smeared blood on her face.

"You're bleeding somewhere. Let me check you for injuries." Gage tried not to think about the fact that he knew his patient, his sister's best friend. He'd spent numerous game nights with Jessica, shared holiday meals with her after her divorce—and had kept his attraction to her a closely held secret.

He took hold of Jessica's wrists to turn up her palms, which bore small, seeping cuts. She shook her head violently as she coughed and tried to drag air into her lungs.

"What's wrong?" he asked Jessica as he flagged Captain Remis with a raised hand. "I need the medical kit. How far out is the ambulance?"

"G-Gage," she rasped, between coughs. "T-Ti—" She rolled away from him abruptly, onto her hands and knees, and vomited in the grass. When she sat back on her heels, she raised a bleak look to him.

"Hey, it's okay. I see worse almost every day." He smiled, trying to comfort her.

"No." She shook her head again, then scooted a short distance away from the mess, her gaze on the river. She dragged in a sob and muttered, "I couldn't get— I tried to—"

"Jessica." He put an arm around her, pulling her into

a hug, knowing he needed to get back to work, but wanting only to hold her. Damn, she'd had a close call tonight. The idea was too unsettling to consider. "You're safe now. You're okay."

She wiggled loose from his embrace and clutched at his life vest. "Gage, listen!" Her expression was haggard, distraught.

Jessica. Car accident. His last text from Tina.

Hanging with the girls tonight. TTYL!

A chill of foreboding settled in his bones.

Tears filled Jessica's eyes, even as she confirmed his dread. "Tina, Holly and Sara are still in the car!"

Chapter 4

Horror punched Gage in the gut, stealing his breath. *Tina!*

His brain screamed, "Save her!" while his body sat frozen, numb for precious seconds, grappling with Jessica's revelation.

Clutching his vest, she shook him. "Gage! Did you hear me?" Her voice was still thin and strangled, but the urgency in her tone was clear. "You have to get them out!"

With a hard blink, he shook himself from his shock and shoved to his feet. He staggered toward the riverbank, his wet clothes and equipment slowing him, tripping him. He reached for the anchor line to clip himself back on, his hands shaking. *Tina!*

Take care of your little sister and your mom. You're the man of the house now. His father's request, spoken days before cancer claimed his life, rang like a dissonant bell in Gage's head.

"I'm going back out," he told Smith, who frowned at him.

"Not yet," Smith said. "Rodgers and Barksdale are still out there. Three passengers inside."

"I know!" Gage shouted, his voice louder than he

meant. "One is my sister! The others are her friends. I know them!"

Captain Remis approached. "What's going on, Coleman?"

Gage flung a finger toward the submerged car. "I have to go back out. My sister is trapped in there!"

"Your sister?" Remis scowled. "No. You're sitting this one out. We'll get her, but I need people I know won't take unnecessary risks—"

"Screw that!" Gage shoved past his boss. "Do *not* sideline me. That's my sister out there!"

A shout from the water reached them, and Cal Rodgers appeared with a limp woman in his arms. "Two more in the car! Coleman, get out here!"

Gage helped Smith pull Rodgers to shore, one arm around his rescue, the other clinging to the rope.

From behind Gage, a newly arrived team of rescuers rushed past. EMTs from one of two ambulances scuttled down the riverbank along with the second fire truck's crew. The second fire company deployed their swift water rescue equipment and more men into the water. Police officers brought blankets. In the buzz of activity, Gage wound his way through uniforms to reach Rodgers and the petite woman he recognized instantly as Tina. He fell on his knees beside his sister and slapped at her cheek.

"Tina!" He felt her neck for a pulse, but his own hand was shaking too hard to be helpful. "Tina, can you hear me? It's Gage. I'm here, Tina. Talk to me."

Rodgers gave him a sympathetic look before pushing him out of the way and rolling Tina to her side. Water poured from her mouth and nose. Again, Rodgers blocked him when Gage tried to get closer. "Move back, man. I've got this. Let me work."

Gage gritted his teeth, but gave way, knowing his partner was in a better mind space to help Tina. He rose on shaky legs, watching Cal administer first aid, check her pulse.

"She's alive. I've got a pulse," he told Gage. "Over here!" Rodgers called to the arriving EMTs, before bending to pinch his sister's nose and give Tina a breath.

Gage stumbled back a step, allowing the medical team to surround Tina, and glanced back up the hill to the spot where he'd left Jessica.

She stared back at him with wide, sad eyes, her hands holding the blanket closed at her throat. From the shadows of the woods beyond her, a man approached her, bending to talk to her. Jessica whipped a startled gaze to the man, then shrank back from him. "No! Get away from me!"

Prickles of alarm sluiced through Gage, and he fought free of the ropes still attached to Tina and Rodgers. As he jogged back toward Jessica, weighted down by his soaked uniform, he watched the man stick his face in hers. Jessica screamed and crab-crawled backward.

"Hey!" Gage yelled, his tone an angry warning.

The man stood, glanced back at Gage, then set off at a run down the highway. Gage itched to chase the guy, but his first concern was Jessica. Tina.

"Are you all right? Who was that guy?" He crouched beside Jessica, his headlamp casting her already pale face in a silver circle.

She squinted against the light and turned her head. She was breathing too shallowly, too fast. "He...he tried..."

Reaching up, he flicked off the power to his headlamp. He placed a hand on her knee and squeezed. "You're hyperventilating, Jess. Take slow breaths."

She lifted her eyes to him now that the blinding beam was doused. Her throat worked as she swallowed, and the blanket fell off her shoulder as she stuck her hand out to grab his. She cast a tense glance to the highway where emergency vehicles crowded the road and light bars strobed in a dizzying array of reds, golds and blues. "Is he gone?"

"The guy who was just talking to you? Yeah. He disappeared that way—" Gage pointed down the highway away from the fleet of rescue vehicles "—when I headed up here. You know him? Who is he?"

"The accident… He—" Jessica drew a shaky breath. "He caused the accident." She held his gaze, her dark brown eyes drilling him. "Gage, he did it on purpose."

Gage's brow furrowed. He blinked, the thick fringe of his eyelashes, spiked from the river water, framing his gray eyes. "What do you mean?"

Jessica opened her mouth to explain, but a knot of emotion choked her. She shook her head. There'd be a time and place to explain later. But at that moment, she could only think about her friends. She shook her head, then shifted her gaze to the rescue efforts behind him. "Is Tina…?"

His hand tightened on hers, and, still in a squat, he pivoted on his toe to check on the cluster of men surrounding his sister. "Alive." His voice was choked. "She had a pulse anyway."

Jessica let a whimper roll from her chest. "What about

Holly and S-Sara? Have they—" Her voice cracked and tears stung her eyes.

"I don't know," Gage said, his tone low and sympathetic, trembling slightly with his own pain. "Let me go see what I can find out. I...I need to get back to work."

When Gage tried to stand, tried to free his fingers from her grasp, she clutched tighter, reluctant to let him go. "Gage!"

He narrowed his eyes as he faced her again. Tiny laugh lines—could she call them that in such a horrid, stressful time as this?—formed at the corners of his eyes, his mouth. "Yeah?"

Stay with me. I'm scared. I don't want to be alone.

Another voice in her head, one she'd nurtured since she'd first recognized her mother's mistakes and weaknesses, silenced the fearful pleas that leaped to her tongue. She released him and balled her hands in her lap, inhaling deeply. Finally, sensing Gage's impatience to get back to his rescue duties, back to his sister, she settled on "I—I'm sorry."

The tilt of his head, the twitch of his mouth said he wasn't sure what she was apologizing for, but he must've decided against asking. "I'll be back in a minute."

As he trotted away, he shouted to the EMTs and pointed out where she sat in the night's shadows.

Jessica pulled the blanket closed at her neck again and shivered. She cast an uneasy glance around, looking for Henry, certain he was somewhere just out of sight, watching her. The hiss of his hot whisper in her ear moments earlier replayed in her mind. *You have only yourself to blame. I don't like being ignored or dissed! Don't disrespect me like that ever again, Jessie!*

She shook her head and waved a hand by her ear as if the memory could be batted away like a bothersome bee. The commotion of the rescue team in the river refocused her attention, and Jessica caught her breath. Only her car roof was visible as the men, attached to a spiderweb of ropes, worked to pull her friends from the car.

How long had they been underwater? Had they even survived the initial crash in the river? Had Sara still been unbuckled? Renewed grief and guilt scraped through her. Though Henry's reckless behavior had been the catalyst, she'd been behind the wheel. Her driving choices and reactions had sent the car into the river. If she'd turned the wheel left instead of right, if she'd pulled to the shoulder and stopped, if she'd stomped the brake or let her car rear end the truck—

If, if, if only...

The litany of doubts and unused alternatives spun in her head as she stared through the darkness at the spots of light from the teams' headlamps and flashlights. Then someone turn on a giant spotlight, and the horrific scene was lit in all its tragic glory.

A woman with a medical kit that looked like Eric's fishing tackle box arrived and squatted beside her. The EMT introduced herself as Tracy, and as the medic began checking Jessica's pulse and the reactiveness of her pupils to a penlight, she asked the expected questions. Did Jessica know her name and where she was? Was she in pain anywhere? Had she lost consciousness?

Jessica answered each query numbly, but her attention remained on the rescue effort. She leaned to the right to gaze over Tracy's shoulder to follow the activity at the river. Two men carried a litter to the waiting open bay of an ambulance. Another pair of rescuers huddled over another of her friends on the shoreline, administering CPR. More men were still in the water, fighting the current to pull her third friend from her car. *Please, God, please let them be okay!*

"Can you walk to the ambulance?" Tracy asked. "You should go to the hospital to get a more thorough exam by a doctor. I think you inhaled some water, and that gash on your head may mean you have a concussion."

"I—I think so."

Tracy put a shoulder under Jessica's arm and helped her stand. Knees wobbling, she staggered toward the road and the waiting ambulances. As she passed the stretcher where the rescuers had resettled a woman, she glimpsed red hair. Holly.

The man attending Holly squeezed what looked like a clear plastic football, manually pumping air into the mask over Holly's mouth and nose. Bag-valve-mask ventilation, she'd heard it called on the medical dramas she watched on TV.

Jessica shrugged away from Tracy's support and shoved her way to Holly's side, grabbing her friend's hand. "Holly! Holly, it's Jessica! Can you hear me?"

"Stand aside, please, ma'am," one of the men said. "We need room to work."

"Holly, fight! You can do it! Breathe, Hol!" Jessica called as Tracy tugged her away from the stretcher. She stumbled back and watched the EMTs load Holly's stretcher in the back of one of the ambulances.

Tracy steered her to the back of a different ambulance where, moments later, Tina was brought up on a stretcher, pale and unresponsive. Gage was at his sister's side, his expression stricken. Jessica was hustled inside as another EMT called out numbers and medical shorthand regarding Tina's status. The urgency in the medic's voice shook Jessica to the core.

"Will she be all right?" she asked, looking to the EMT. When she got no response from the medic, she glanced to Gage.

His eyes met hers, and he shrugged. "I'll see you at the hospital."

When Gage turned to jog toward his fire crew, Jessica shivered, a cold fear and sense of isolation rising in her, suffocating her. After Tracy and a medic with the name Jim Carroway stitched on his uniform shirt climbed in with Jessica and Tina, the bay doors closed from outside.

Jessica tried to slide closer to Tina, tried to take her hand, but again she was nudged aside. "Sit back, please," Tracy said, "Let's finish your assessment."

With the bounce of tires over ruts and a wail of sirens, the ambulance set out for the hospital, and Jessica closed her eyes to pray.

Gage paced the sterile waiting room outside the ICU where Tina lay in a coma. She'd been hooked up to a zillion monitors and IV tubes and put on a respirator. How was this happening? He'd just talked to Tina this morning, teasing her about the burned hot dogs she'd served at her cookout the past weekend.

In the future, leave the fire work to the experts, Tintin.

Now his younger sister was barely clinging to life.

At least she's alive. The voice in his head stopped him, stole his breath as he replayed what he'd learned moments ago from Sara Callen's family. Sara hadn't survived the wreck, couldn't be resuscitated at the river. The news of her friend's death would devastate Tina when she woke. *If she woke...*

Gage clenched a fist and slammed it into his opposite hand. *Stop that. Don't be defeatist. Tina needs all the positive mental energy and optimism she can get.*

"Gage?"

He spun around, hearing the hoarse female voice behind him. Jessica stood a few steps away, wearing baggy blue scrubs. She had one hand on a rolling IV pole and a bleak look in her dark, bloodshot eyes. Even with her olive complexion, the only thing she'd ever gotten from her father, he saw the red facial blotches that said she'd been crying. Without questioning the impulse, he stepped over to her and wrapped her in a firm hug. The top of her head fit neatly under his chin, and he leaned his cheek against her damp hair.

"Jess—" was all he managed before his throat tightened, strangling his voice.

"How is Tina?" she asked, the words muffled as her face pressed into his chest.

He took a breath to steel himself, then levered away, pinching the bridge of his nose to battle down the sting of tears. "Critical. The doctor says the next twenty-four hours are going to be touch and go, but if she makes it—"

Jessica sucked in a sharp gasp and squeezed her eyes shut. "I'm sorry. I'm so, so sorry. This is all...it's my fault."

Gage frowned. "What do you mean? I know you were driving, but at the accident scene you said there was a guy who caused the accident, the man who approached you."

Her chin snapped up, and as she stared at him, her face turned gray. She wobbled, and he quickly wrapped an arm around her waist and escorted her to a seat in the waiting room. "Maybe you should go back to your bed. Weren't you checked into a room earlier?"

She sank onto the formed plastic seat and shook her head. "I'm just getting a round of antibiotics and fluids." She gestured vaguely to the plastic bag of clear liquid hanging from the wheeled pole. "Because of the cut on my head and the dirty river water and…" She paused, seeming to lose her train of thought. "I'll be released from the ER after that."

"Good. I'm glad you weren't more seriously hurt." Gage took the seat next to her and squeezed her shoulder.

Jessica glanced away, her chin quivering and her forehead creased. "If I could, I'd trade places with Tina, with any of them. It's not right that I survived, and they're all—"

Breaking off abruptly, she shifted her gaze to scan the other faces in the waiting room.

He assumed she was looking for her family. She had a son in college, if he remembered right. And she was still friendly with her ex-husband, Tina had said. "I don't think your people are here yet."

Her gaze flicked to him, and she pressed her lips in a taut line, clearly trying to rein in her emotions. "I asked the nurse not to call them. I'll let them know what happened later. I'll be okay, and I didn't want Eric upset for nothing. He's got tests this week and doesn't need—" Again she dropped her sentence, and with a shuddering sigh, she asked, "What do you know about Holly and

Sara? I don't see the Callens or Teales here yet. Have you heard anything?"

He clenched his back teeth. Damn it, he didn't want to be the one to break the bad news to her. But she deserved to know the truth. He stared down at his feet. He'd deliver the blow to her, but how could he look in her sad brown eyes as he did it? Gage cleared his throat and blurted, "Holly's parents are in with her. I talked to them a little while ago. She's is critical, like Tina, but stable. Holly is breathing on her own, but not conscious. The doctors will be running several tests to see—" He stopped and tried again. "Her brain was without oxygen for an extended period and they want to assess—"

"She could have brain damage?" Jessica finished for him and released a half sigh, half whimper of despair. "And Sara?"

Gage swallowed hard. He'd do anything to spare her the pain of what he must tell her. But there was no way around it. "She didn't make it, Jess."

When he heard no reaction from Jessica for several seconds, he angled his gaze toward her. She stared at him with a bewildered expression, as if she hadn't understood. He placed a hand on her arm, feeling the shiver that raced through her. "Jess?"

Slowly, as if the truth had needed time to soak in, her face crumpled, and her shoulders jerked as a sob tripped from her. *"No."*

He drew her into his arms to hold her as more gut-wrenching sobs rolled through her. "Yeah. I'm sorry."

I'm sorry? What paltry comfort for a woman who'd been through a trauma and lost one of her best friends.

A wave of grief washed through Gage, knowing he could still lose Tina.

Touch and go, the doctor had said. *The next twenty-four hours are critical.*

He stroked Jessica's back, offering what solace he could—and finding his own in her. She'd apparently bathed and washed her hair at some point, because her hair smelled clean. Floral. He probably stank of fishy river water, even though he'd hastily changed into dry clothes at the fire station before racing to the hospital. He inhaled the scent of her, taking the fresh aroma deep into his lungs. Something stirred inside him. Something he'd struggled for years to suppress—an affection and attraction deeper than anyone in his life knew. How could he be dwelling on his secret feelings for Jess while she was in shock and emotionally hurting?

His head knew wanting Jess, especially in this moment, was wrong, but he'd never been able to convince his heart and his libido of that truth. For almost as long as Tina and Jessica had been friends, Gage had hidden his truest feelings for his sister's *bestie*. She'd always been off-limits. First because he told himself she was too young, then she'd dated Matt and gotten married. Then, by the time Jess got her divorce, the bonds of the women's friendship had been too strong, too precious for Gage to risk. If he pursued his feelings for Jessica, he'd throw a huge rock into the equilibrium of the women's friendship. Or so he told himself. Maybe he was just a coward. Afraid of blowing up the yearslong dynamic of friendship he had with Jessica.

Besides, Jessica had never given him any hint she returned his romantic feelings. So he'd shoved the feelings aside and continued living his bachelor life. He couldn't justify settling for another woman, had never formed the same depth of feeling for anyone else. Why would he commit to second best while he had genuine feelings for another woman?

He moved his hand from her back to cradle her nape. Bending, he gave the crown of her head a kiss. In response, she raised her chin, her wet eyes meeting his.

"Gage," she started, as her gaze drifted away, taking in the rest of the waiting room. "I—" She hesitated again and drew her bottom lip between her teeth.

The impulse to kiss that abused lip kicked him hard, and he clenched his back teeth, pushing the clawing hunger down.

As if she'd read his thoughts, seen something damning in his face, Jessica tensed in his arms. Her back straightened, and her breath hitched.

Hell.

But when her face froze in a mask of fear and her body trembled, concern washed through him. "Jess, what is—?"

She met his gaze, a wild look in her eyes, as she rasped, "He's here!"

Chapter 5

Jessica curled her fingers into Gage's shirt and held tight so she wouldn't topple as her head spun. *Henry was here.*

Gage cast a brief glance over his shoulder, then narrowed his eyes as he studied her. "Who's here? What's wrong?"

"H-Henry."

Heart thundering, she peeked past Gage again. Her frantic gaze scoured the spot in the hospital corridor where she'd seen her tormenter, the man who'd caused her accident and hung around long enough to taunt her over the tragedy, to blame her.

But he wasn't there now. Her pulse ramped higher as she continued scanning the hallway, the waiting room, searching for him, panicked that he would approach her. Had she imagined him? He'd looked real enough, had met her gaze with a dark glare.

"Jessica?"

"He…he's gone." Henry's rapid disappearance bothered her almost as much as his being there in the first place. "He's gone! Where'd he go?" She heard the panic in her voice and inching closer to Gage, she actively slowed her breathing.

"Are you sure?" Gage loosened his grip and turned in his seat. "Who is Henry? Why does he scare you?"

"Get a grip," she muttered under her breath. Gage did not need to see her fall apart. No matter how devastating this night had been, she had to stay strong.

"Jessica? Who did you think you saw? Do I need to get security?"

"I don't see him now. But—"

"Hey," he said, carefully pulling her into a hug while avoiding the IV lines. "Take a breath. I got you. Tell me who you thought you saw. What's going on?"

A measure of relief trickled through her. Gage wouldn't allow anything or anyone to hurt her while he was around. Tina's brother had always been so protective of his sister and her friends. He'd always had Tina's back. And, by extension, Jessica's.

She clung to Gage and mustered an answer for him. "Henry is…th-this guy I went out with a couple times…"

Beneath her hands, Gage tensed.

She raised her head to cast a glance around. Had the doctor come out? Was Henry back? But no. No doctor with a report on Tina. No Henry.

You have only yourself to blame. I don't like being ignored or dissed! Don't disrespect me like that ever again, Jessie!

She suppressed a shudder and inched closer to Gage, more in his chair now than her own.

"Go on," Gage said, using a finger to pull her chin around and angle her gaze back at his.

She exhaled and sagged against him. "Henry kept calling and texting after I told him I didn't want to see him anymore. He wouldn't take no for an answer, and—"

A shiver raced through her. "He showed up at the Mexican restaurant where we had our girls' night tonight. He confronted me. And—"

A combination of fear and grief strangled her, and she had to take a moment to choke the emotions down.

Gage's eyes, the shade of storm clouds, honed in on hers, his jaw rigid. "Is he the guy that frightened you at the accident scene?"

She bobbed her head. "He followed us from the restaurant." Jessica swallowed hard. "He was chasing us and driving erratically, braking hard in front of me all of a sudden. He's the reason I swerved. I was trying to avoid hitting him, but…I lost control of the car and—"

A sob rose, surprising her, escaping before she could squelch it.

Gage tucked her closer, his hold strong. Secure. Just what she needed in that moment. She'd be strong later. She'd have to forge ahead with her life and face the repercussions of this night soon enough. But right now, in this moment, she drew comfort from the kindness of her friend's brother. Gage was grieving, too, she realized, and sucked in a sharp breath. "Jeez, I haven't even asked how you're doing. Tina…"

His dark brow dipped, his face grim. "I'm…managing. Holding on to hope."

Gage twitched a cheek in a failed attempt to smile, and a pang arrowed through her heart. She'd caused him this pain, this worry. She…and Henry. She sat taller, pulling away from Gage as the heat of anger poured into her cheeks. "I…I need to talk to the police. Report what happened." A sense of urgency raised her pulse. She searched the waiting room for a policeman. Hadn't there been a uniformed officer here earlier? "I have to tell them about Henry and his harassment. There were witnesses at the restaurant and—"

She stood too quickly, and her head spun, her knees buckled.

Gage caught her by the arms. "Jess. Hey, sit down a sec."

"The police—"

"Will be back by here in a bit to talk to you. The officer in charge said they'd get a statement from you after you finished with the doctor." Gage sighed and glanced away a moment before returning a penetrating stare to her. "He said they wanted a blood alcohol test on you if you were the driver."

Jessica nodded, guilt tripping through her veins again. *You were the driver.*

"They told me that in the ER. Already took the sample. But…I wasn't drinking. You know we always assign a designated driver."

He nodded. "That's what I told them, but they have procedures to follow."

"Of course." Jessica pinched the bridge of her nose as a throb built in her head.

"Jess?"

She cut a side-glance to Gage. "Yeah?"

"I really think you should call Eric now."

A different sort of pain twisted through her now. *Eric.* Her sweet boy. How would all of this bad news affect him?

"I…I lost my phone in the river."

He pulled out his phone and offered it to her. She took his cell and stared at it, hesitating.

"I can't. I—"

Gage blinked and tipped his head. "Don't you think he'd want to know you're all right?"

"But ignorance is bliss, and I don't want him worrying about the rest of it when there's nothing he can do. I'll tell him…later."

Gage twisted his mouth, as if he disagreed with her choice. "And Matt? Are you going to tell him?"

Jessica sat in silence for a minute, wavering. Maybe Matt should know. And her ex-husband deserved to weigh in on how and when they broke the news of the accident to Eric. Finally, she nodded, tapped in Matt's phone number and drew a breath to calm the fresh surge of emotion flapping in her chest.

"H'lo?"

When Matt's voice answered her call, she reached for Gage's hand and gripped it as she said, "Matt, it's me. There's, uh…been an accident."

Jessica spent the rest of the night beside Gage in the ICU waiting room, anxiously awaiting news on either Holly or Tina. Through the long hours, she continued scanning the corridors, the concessions alcove and passing faces for Henry. She was certain she'd seen him, but as the weary minutes of the late night ticked by without finding him watching her, she began to wonder if seeing him in the hallway had been a trick of light or something her traumatized mind had conjured. And yet…every so often a tingle would nip the back of her neck and some primordial sense would tell her she was being watched. She'd snap her gaze up and not breathe easily again until satisfied Henry wasn't there.

At least she had Gage with her for company. His presence gave her a measure of security. Given how Henry had fled rather than face confrontation from another male—the rescue teams, the restaurant manager—she hoped having Gage next to her would keep Henry at bay. At least for tonight.

But every half hour or so, Gage got up to visit Tina and ask the nurse about any changes in her condition. Only family was admitted into the patient rooms, so for a few minutes each hour, Jessica was alone in the waiting room. She'd asked Gage if he wanted to stay with Tina full-time, the way Holly's parents were staying with her, but Gage refused to leave Jessica to sit alone. "I'm ten steps from her room. I've told her I'm here, that you're here. If anything happens, we'll see the nurses go in her room," he argued when she protested.

In the early hours of the morning, Holly's monitors blared and the nurses rushed into her room. The Teale family was forced to step out into the waiting room, their faces wan with fear and worry. Holly's father held a tearful Mrs. Teale close to his side as they huddled just outside their daughter's door.

Jessica's heart raced, and her stomach swooped with alarm. Unhooked from her IVs now, she rose on trembling legs and walked toward the couple. She'd not had the opportunity before then to express her sorrow and concern and was desperate to know what was happening with her friend. But even before she reached the older couple, Mrs. Teale spotted her, and a mask of anger suffused her face.

"Stay away from us!" she spat at Jessica.

Jessica pulled up short. "Mrs. Teale, I just wanted to tell you how sorry—"

"No! You did this to our baby, and I will never forgive you!" The older woman's tone and expression were hostile.

Jessica was so stunned by the woman's vitriol, she could only stare at her wide-eyed.

Gage rose and hurried to Jessica's side. "Mrs. Teale, please." He raised a conciliatory hand as if to quiet her shrieks. "This isn't Jessica's fault."

"Isn't it? We talked to the police. They told us *she* was at the wheel, that reckless driving was involved."

"But—" Gage started, but Mrs. Teale ranted over him.

"The doctor said Holly's blood alcohol was high. Very high."

"But not mine. I hadn't been drinking," Jessica said.

"Forgive me if I don't believe you," Mrs. Teale said with a sneer. "You *would* say that to stay out of jail, wouldn't you?"

Jail? Jessica's heart tripped. Were the police thinking of charging her with something? She hadn't even considered that nightmare. "I...I—"

"That's enough," Mr. Teale said, tugging on his wife's arm. "Don't say anything else to her that could taint our case." He gave Jessica a cold glare as they turned their backs. "You'll be hearing from our lawyer."

Jessica's legs wobbled beneath her. Only Gage's supporting arm catching her elbow kept her from crumpling on the floor. Holly's parents were suing her?

The room spun as Gage led her back to a chair. Though she accepted her share of blame for the accident, she was troubled to think Holly's family consid-

ered her reckless or criminally culpable. She'd gladly
trade places with Holly or Tina if she could. She was
heartbroken and guilt-ridden over their injuries. Over
Sara's death.

A fresh wave of grief flooded her, and she lurched
from the chair and barely made it to the ladies' room
before she heaved up the rest of her dinner. Tears spilled
from her eyes as she let the waves of horror and loss from
the night wash over her.

She was still slumped on the tile floor in one of the
stalls when she heard a knock, the squeak of hinges and
Gage's deep voice. "Jessica? You okay?"

"No."

Footsteps. The unlocked stall door opening. A hand
on her shoulder. "You going to be sick again or do you
want to get up?"

When she didn't answer, he stooped and, placing
hands under her elbows, lifted her to her feet. When
she wobbled, he caught her close, holding her against
his broad chest and rubbing her back. He stood still, silent, with her in his embrace, until she stopped shaking.
When decorum dictated she should have pushed away,
she continued hugging him. Tonight, in the wake of so
much turmoil, Gage had been the only thing solid and
real she'd had, and she didn't want to let go.

Over the next forty-eight hours, she and Gage leaned
on each other a lot as they waited for Tina to wake from
her coma and take her first breath on her own. But her
friend never did.

After two days of holding vigil, eating little other
than burned coffee and vending machine snacks, and
making do with paper towel baths from the bathroom

sink, Gage convinced Jessica to go home. He promised to call her if Tina's condition changed.

"Get a shower, sleep in your own bed, get on with your life," he told her. "It could be days, even weeks, before there's any change with Tina."

"But I...I don't want you to be alone up here," she said, knowing he was Tina's only family available to visit. Their father had died two years earlier, and their mother had early-stage dementia and resided in a nursing home.

"I won't be." He inhaled deeply, his nose flaring and his gray eyes stormy. "Because I'll be going back to work tonight myself. I'll visit her when I can, of course, but... Tina wouldn't want us to stop living because of her."

Jessica caught her breath, ready to counter his assertion, but stopped. Nodded. He was right. She needed to return to work, return to some semblance of her life. And she had to prepare for what was coming. Sara's funeral.

She'd offered Sara's husband to help with meals, child care, errands—anything she could do to assist with the difficult days ahead. He'd politely declined, saying they had family in from all over. But Jessica knew the newly widowed father would need her support in the weeks ahead, even if he didn't ask.

In the ensuing days, at random moments when she'd usually text or call one of her posse—lunch breaks when she had to vent, bedtime when she wanted to reflect, odd moments when something curious or outrageous happened—she found herself calling Gage instead.

To his credit, he always acted glad to hear from her, and, with the exception of once when he was on a call-out from the fire station, he talked with her for as long as she wanted an ear to listen. But while she appreciated his friendship and willingness to field her texts and sporadic calls, Gage didn't fill the hole left by the absence of her best friends. One dead. Two hospitalized and critical.

Holly's family continued to be hostile toward Jessica, blaming her for the accident despite her explanations about Henry's menacing behavior. They had stopped talking about a lawsuit at least, but the rejection of her friend's family stung. Their silence concerning Holly's condition felt like an abandonment, adding to her sense of isolation.

"Give them time. Everyone reacts to grief and stress differently," Gage said when she mentioned the family's coldness toward her. "But keep showing up. Let them know you aren't giving up on Holly or them."

She attended Sara's funeral the next weekend, held nine days after the car crash because the family needed time for a younger sister posted with the Marines in Okinawa to be granted leave and travel. Jessica sat with Gage during the graveside service, well aware of the stares other attendees sent her way. When the last words were spoken and the mourners began to disperse, Gage draped an arm loosely over her shoulders and patted her arm. The awkward comforting gesture was enough to bring fresh tears to her eyes.

Bless him for trying to bolster her, to show compassion and to lend strength as their relationship waded through foreign territory. She was as uncertain as he was about the parameters of this grief-born connection they were forging. She felt adrift, rudderless without the anchors of Holly, Tina and Sara in her life, and she appreciated Gage's attempts to buoy her more than he could know.

"Ready to go?" he asked.

Drying her eyes, she nodded.

Together, they started walking toward his truck. She tried to stem her tears, clear her throat and pretend she was doing better than she was. She could be strong. She *would be*. Falling apart simply wasn't an option. And most important, she couldn't let Gage believe she was crumbling. She knew he was kind enough to inconvenience himself to support her if he thought she was in trouble or struggling emotionally. She refused to be that woman—a needy and drifting woman like her mother. While he'd been a comfort in the earliest days of her grief, the time had come for her to show a braver face and give him permission to return to his old role. Just Gage. Tina's brother. Not the stalwart she leaned on or needed to stay sane.

Jessica covered his hand with hers, and when she angled a sad smile at him, prepared to give him an out from babysitting her that evening, she caught a glimpse of blond hair at the edge of the crowd that made her stumble to a stop.

Her heart jumped to her throat as she narrowed her eyes against the harsh spring sun, confirming what she saw. Henry.

Chapter 6

Across the cemetery driveway, Henry stood with his arms folded over his chest, staring at her…no, glaring. His presence at Sara's funeral, the woman he was responsible for killing, was an affront to Jessica. Her grief morphed into a fury and scorn that stiffened her body and churned her pulse. "That ass."

Gage studied her, then glanced over his shoulder, following her gaze. "Who do you mean?"

"The guy I went out with a couple times," she said, her voice strangled. "The one I thought I saw at the hospital. Henry."

I don't like being ignored! Her body shook as adrenaline coursed through her.

"Wait… The guy who caused the accident?" Gage's body language shifted, alerted like a hunter spying prey. His square jaw tensed, and his nostrils flared. "What does he look like? What's he wearing?"

"Um…nondescript blond hair. Wearing a blue jacket. Wire-rimmed glasses."

Henry turned abruptly and stalked away, into a stand of trees that bordered the cemetery and out of her field of view.

"Where did you see him? I don't see a blue jacket."

Gage took a step as if to go after Henry, and Jessica caught his arm. "Wait. He's leaving. Let him go."

"What?" he asked, his tone dark and incredulous. "After what he did? My sister almost died because of him. Sara is dead!"

Jessica noticed heads turning, people frowning as Gage's volume rose.

"Out of respect for Sara's family, please don't cause a scene. Not here. Not now."

Gage looked unconvinced, but he pressed his lips in a grim line and nodded once.

She continued to squint against the sun, searching the area she'd last seen him. "Do you see him? I want to know what sort of vehicle he's driving today. The cops told me to let them know if I saw him again." She pulled her replacement phone from her purse. She could at least alert the authorities that Henry had been there, give them a heads-up to his current location, should they have a squad car in the area. The funeral procession's police escort to the cemetery had left once the hearse had parked, but maybe that officer was still nearby?

Gage, who stood at least eight inches taller than her own five feet six, craned his neck, then scoffed. "No. Too many trees and people."

Jessica sighed her disappointment. "Man, he's as slippery as an eel. He snuck away that fast at the hospital, too." She shivered. "Tell me you at least saw him before he got away. That I didn't imagine him."

Gage's expression said he wanted to tell her that, but couldn't. "Sorry, I haven't seen him since he approached you at the accident scene." When she groaned, he quickly amended, "But that doesn't mean you imagined him. I believe you when you say he was there."

"Oh, good. So at least *you* don't think I'm going crazy. That makes one of us."

His head tipped to one side, and he put a hand at the small of her back as they resumed walking to his truck. "You think you're seeing things?"

"Ugh. No," she said, flapping a dismissive hand. "I'm being too dramatic. Ignore me. I just…" She continued to scan the crowd, searching for Henry. "If he was here, if he was at the hospital… I wish I knew what his game was."

"His game?"

"Is he following me? If so, why? Does he want to apologize for the accident? Is he morbidly curious about the repercussions of the accident? Is he feeling guilty or—?"

When she didn't finish, Gage put a hand on her arm and faced her. "Are you worried that he's dangerous? That he's stalking you? That he wants to hurt you?"

Despite the warm day, a chill slithered down her spine. "Maybe. He certainly gives me the creeps. And having him pop up here, the same way he showed up at the hospital, is unsettling. And his turning up at the Mexican restaurant the night of the accident is feeling less and less like coincidence."

Gage tucked both hands in his pockets and exhaled heavily as he moved his gaze over the departing mourners. "I don't like the sound of this. And I don't like the fact that you live alone, in case he does try to cause you more trouble."

She flashed a half-hearted grin. "I'm not alone. I have Pluto."

His frown deepened. "I'm serious. Someone should stay with you."

"Oh, really? And who would that be? Not Eric. He's at school, and he needs to stay there. I won't bother him with this. His class work is too important. Besides, it's not his job to take care of my problems."

He walked the last few feet to his truck's passenger door and opened it for her. "I don't mean Eric. I'll do it. On the nights I'm not at the fire station, I'll sleep on your couch."

She shook her head firmly. "No." Placing a hand on his arm, she amended, "Thank you, but no. I can't ask you to do that."

"Jess," he started, sounding disgruntled.

"I don't want you—or anyone—moving in with me. I don't think the situation is dire enough to require a room-mate, or a bodyguard, or whatever it is you think you'd be. My doors stay locked when I'm home, and I keep my cell phone close. I can call the police if necessary."

"All that is a good start, but I'd feel better if I knew—"

"No, Gage. I will not be a burden or responsibility for anyone else. I don't want anyone to have to move into my house, and—before you suggest it—I don't want to go to anyone else's house, either. I'd be in the way, and—just, no." She sighed, searching for the words to explain the pact she'd made with herself years earlier. "I promised myself after I divorced Matt that I would be completely self-sufficient and independent until I needed a nursing home."

Gage pulled a face and scratched his forehead. "Surely you can make exceptions."

She shrugged one shoulder. "If needed. But it's not needed in this case." To put an end to the discussion, she climbed into the truck and pulled the door closed.

Gage circled the truck to the driver's side and slid behind the steering wheel. He cranked the engine, adjusted the air temperature and fan settings, then gave her a long, odd look. After a beat, he asked, "Does that mean you don't plan to marry again?"

She shrank back a notch, startled by his question. "I— Why do you say that?"

"Trying to understand what *completely self-sufficient and independent*—" he used two fingers to make air quotes "—looks like."

Why did that question, coming from Gage, unsettle her so much? For a minute, as they drove slowly out of the cemetery, Jessica said nothing, her thoughts returning to her loss of Sara, to Sara's family and the overwhelming shift her life had taken because of the accident. Would Tina and Holly recover fully or be left with brain damage? Would Sara's family, like Holly's, hold a grudge against her and cut her from their lives? How could her little posse of friends—heart sisters—have been so horribly shattered like this? She wanted to be independent and self-reliant, but her life now was…lonely.

Anger swelled in her. Her situation, her friends' injuries, the ruined lives—was all the fault of that jerk, Henry. Her jaw clenched, furious with the man whose recklessness had caused this tragedy. Anger bubbled for herself, as well, for having caved to her loneliness and gone looking for male companionship on a dating app. She hadn't needed a man when she had her best friends, her son. The tears that pricked her eyes now rose from her disappointment in herself.

As Gage pulled out onto the main road, she shifted on the seat to face him. "I'll tell you part of what self-sufficient and independent looks like."

He cast a side-glance her way, dark eyebrow lifted. "Yeah?"

"I'm done with dating. No more apps or fix-ups by friends. No more awkward get-to-know-you conversations or pretending you're having a good time with a guy, when all I really want is to curl up with a bowl of ice cream, a good book and my cat on my lap. Or hang out drinking wine and laughing with my girls." Her voice cracked as she realized she might never have a night with her posse again. She swiped at her leaky eyes and blew her nose in a tissue. "Damn it. I hate this."

Gage shot her a sympathetic glance and reached toward her, his hand hovering near her leg before apparently thinking better of it and snatching his hand back. He squared his body with the steering wheel, hands anchored at ten and two, and set his jaw. Under his breath, he muttered, "Yeah. I hate this, too."

Henry snuck through the crowd of people, making his way to his mother's old beater. As much as he hated using the rusty sedan that stank of her cigarettes and hairspray, he couldn't use his truck until the heat was off following the incident at the river. He knew the cops would be looking for his truck, that Jessie would have reported it, and so he'd stashed it behind the garage at work for the time being. He knew his boss wouldn't question why or give him up to the cops, because Bill didn't want any attention anywhere near his operation. The boss had too many undocumented men working for him, too many off-the-books salaries being paid, and a critical sideline business to protect.

He'd left his mother's car far from the rest of the funeral traffic, near the back drive of the cemetery so he could get away quickly if needed. By hanging at the edges of the crowd, staying behind Jessie through the service, he'd managed to go unnoticed…until he was ready for her to see him. He'd let her spot him, just so she'd know he was keeping tabs on her.

He hadn't expected to see her draped all over another man. He recognized the guy as the same one who'd been at the hospital. He obviously had some connection to one of the women in ICU, so it wasn't unrealistic that he knew Jessie, that he'd be with her at the funeral. His handsy familiarity with Jessie was a problem, though. He'd have to dig a bit and find out who this man was.

When he reached his mother's sedan, he dropped onto the torn front seat and sat for a minute, deciding his next steps with Jessie. She was an aggravating combination of hot woman and cold bitch. He chewed the inside of his cheek, seething over the way she'd tried to humiliate him in front of her friends. Going forward, she'd have to learn her place. His daddy hadn't taught him much before he died, but he'd showed him how to handle a woman, how to teach a woman her place. Authority, control and, as needed to earn her respect, a hand across her cheek.

Thanks to Jessie driving her car into the river and killing her friend, things were too hot to try again to talk sense into her. Too many people still were hovering around her, getting in his way. He could be patient, wait until she was alone to bring her in line. Talking to her at the restaurant had been a bad move. Her accident had set them back, drawn too many people into her orbit. But soon enough the hubbub would die down, and he'd get another chance to bring her around. He and Jessie belonged together, and one day soon, she'd see that, too. He'd make sure of it.

* * *

You're an idiot, Gage. A sap. Deluded.

The chastisement played on a loop in his brain as Gage drove Jessica home after the post-funeral gathering at Sara's house. In the past several days, as they both struggled to cope with the tragedy and stress that had befallen them, he'd thought they'd found a new common ground, a new connection and—yes—intimacy.

When Jessica had started calling him at night and sharing her thoughts and fears, her regrets and longings, a spark of something he'd banked for years had flickered to life. He'd dared to hope that Jessica might come to see him the way he'd seen her for years—as more than a friend.

But her quick refusal to have him stay at her house to protect her, her assertion that she had no use for men or dating or new relationships, had doused those hopes. He scoffed and shook his head, disgusted with his quixotic delusions.

"What?" she asked, turning damp, red eyes toward him. Those dark brown windows to her grieving soul had cried copious tears even before the funeral this morning, a beacon calling him to hold her and comfort her.

He flipped a hand. "Nothing."

"Mmm," she hummed, before turning to stare silently out the side window, not pressing for any more explanation or showing any further interest in what had drawn the huff of frustration from him. He told himself he wasn't disappointed she'd dropped the matter so easily. *You* did *say "nothing."*

Apparently, he'd imagined the growing connection and deeper trust between them. Apparently, nothing had changed for her. He'd stupidly assigned her need for support and a friendly shoulder for her tears this week as some sort of awakening in her, an acknowledgment of feelings she'd denied for twenty-plus years. He'd let the scent of her shampoo, the silkiness of her hair tucked under his chin, the strength of her grip holding him go to his wishful head.

Gritting his back teeth and squeezing the steering wheel, he jammed the newly inflated feelings back into the tiny box where he'd stored them for so many years, waiting. But like any blowup mattress or beach toy, getting all of his confused feelings and hopes regarding Jessica to fit back into the safe box was going to be difficult. His raft of emotions knew how it felt to hold her, inhale her floral scent. The edges of his years-old yearnings wouldn't tuck neatly away now that he'd shared so many frank conversations and emotional exchanges with her. The shared confidences had seemed like a beginning to him, but were something entirely else for her.

"Oh, shoot," she mumbled, looking around her and in the back seat of his truck.

"Problem?"

"I left my lasagna pan at Sara's house. The last thing Cody and the kids need is another dirty dish to wash and find the owner for."

"I can turn around, go back to get it." Gage moved his hand to his turn signal, prepared to do just that.

She puckered her mouth for a moment, debating. "No. Cody and his mom were all going to lie down with the kids for a bit and try to get some rest. I don't want to disturb them. The kids haven't slept well in days and neither have the adults. For different reasons." She raked her hair back from her face. "I'm guessing that, with the funeral behind them, the adrenaline and stress they've been running on will crash, and they'll get their first sleep in days."

Gage nodded. He understood about running on adrenaline and stress. He'd done much the same since seeing Tina's limp body pulled from the river.

Jessica pinched the bridge of her nose. "I'll text Cody. Tell him to set it aside dirty, and I'll come by for it tomorrow after work." Suiting words to action, she reached in her purse for the new phone she'd bought a couple days after the accident.

Gage had driven her to the phone store, then later the same afternoon, they'd gone to pick up a rental car, since at that point, her insurance company hadn't gotten her claim processed. He'd offered to go with her to shop for her new vehicle, once her insurance settlement was finalized, and had been rebuffed.

"I can do it by myself," she'd said. "In fact, I want to. I need to."

He hadn't understood her insistence to buy her car without his help, but he'd respected it. But now she was deferring to that same go-it-alone mentality when her safety was at risk. He needed to change her mind. Or… was he just looking for excuses to spend time with her?

At Jessica's house, he escorted her inside and gave her cat a pat on the head as he walked to her front door. "You be a good guard cat, okay, Pluto? You're her only line of defense here in case of trouble." Though he'd been joking, the statement niggled. If this Henry dude was following her, he *really* didn't like the idea of Jessica being alone. "Jess, are you sure you don't want me to stay here tonight?"

She pulled a frustrated face. "I'm positive."

"I know you don't want to impose and that you have a bug up your butt about being self-sufficient, but with Henry showing up at the cemetery—"

She scoffed a laugh. "A bug up my butt?"

He dragged a hand down his face. "You know what I mean. You can be rather stubborn."

One thin eyebrow lifted, and she growled under her breath.

He gave her a measuring scrutiny. "I don't have to report to the station until tomorrow morning. I could sleep on your couch—"

She placed a hand on his forearm, her touch stirring something warm in his belly, and she shook her head harder. "Really, Gage. No need. Thank you, but no. I'm going to get a hot bath, climb in bed and read accountant reports on my laptop until I fall asleep. Nothing better for insomnia than a boring spreadsheet." She pulled open the front door, and as he moved past her he stopped to give her a hug.

"Call if you need anything. 'Kay?"

She rose on her tiptoes to drop a quick kiss on his cheek. "Thank you, but I'll be fine."

He didn't leave until he knew she had his cell number programmed for speed dial on her new phone and had secured all her doors.

Though the day had exhausted him emotionally, Gage stopped by the hospital to check on Tina before going home. Her condition was unchanged. The doctors had warned him it would be a long journey for Tina, but Gage desperately wanted some tiny sign of improvement, some glimmer of hope. Not just for Tina, but for Jessica. Despite her bravado, he could see how the fallout of the accident wore on her. While the Jessica he knew was strong, independent and courageous, everyone had their breaking point.

And he feared Jessica was nearing hers.

Chapter 7

The weeks following the accident passed in a numb haze. Jessica went through the motions of life—getting up in the morning, going to work, being told to stay away by Holly's bitter parents, then sitting in the ICU waiting room in Gage's company. She talked to Tina via Gage's phone, held to his sister's ear, as if her best friend could hear her, because the nurses said they believed she could. But the only response Tina gave to Jessica's chatter was the lonely beeps and drones of the machines her friend was hooked to.

The highlight of her day was the brief check-in she had with Eric most nights. She used text exchanges more often now, instead of Facetime, because she feared he'd hear something in her voice or see something in her expression that would tip him off that her life was not as rosy as she painted it. She didn't want him worried about her or distracted from his studies.

On nights that Gage was at the fire station, she would text him updates from the police about the investigation into the accident and locating Henry. The process was taking a frustratingly long time. She didn't understand why they couldn't simply go to Henry's residence and

arrest him for leaving the scene of an accident or reckless endangerment or involuntary manslaughter.

The only reply the police department seemed willing to offer was the investigation was still open and that
they'd let her know when there was news.

The nurses were likewise unwilling to share information with Jessica about Holly or Tina, due to privacy
laws, a source of ongoing frustration for her. But she'd
learned to glean hints from the nurses, if only from their
facial expressions as they left Tina's room.

Every time she texted Gage with these updates, he'd
reply with, Thanks. And how are you doing?

Fine.

His reply each time was, I'm here for you if you need
anything.

Jessica's chest would warm at the sentiment, but she
knew better than to believe that Gage's offer was anything
more than the polite, expected platitude it was. Gage had
his own life, job and responsibilities. She couldn't expect
him to be there for her in the long term, so she was better off getting her act together and moving on with her
new normal.

One morning, about five weeks after Sara's funeral,
Nadine, the receptionist for Jessica's employer, rang her
desk phone.

"There's a gentleman here to see you."

Jessica frowned and checked her desk calendar, worried she'd forgotten an appointment. She had no in-person
meetings planned until the next afternoon. "Who is it?"

She heard Nadine ask for a name, then a muffled male reply. "He says he's your boyfriend," Nadine said, her tone intrigued. Then in a singsong whisper, she added, "He brought you flowers."

Jessica's pulse hammered, dread filling her belly. "I don't have a boyfriend. What did he say his name was?" But even before Nadine pressed the visitor for the information, Jessica knew.

"Henry Blythe," Nadine confirmed. "Shall I send him back?"

"No!" Jessica blurted, even as she heard Nadine calling, "Sir, wait! You can't go back there without—"

Jessica slammed the phone down and shoved away from her desk. She rushed out to the corridor to intercept Henry, wondering what in the hell he wanted. More important, how had he found her office? Had she told Henry where she worked? She could only remember telling him she was a corporate marketing manager, so how—

"Hello, Jessie."

She stumbled to a stop as Henry rounded the corner from the reception area and grinned at her. Rather than friendly or affectionate, his grin seemed smug and satisfied, as if gloating over having bested her somehow.

"For you." He held out the bouquet of white daisies and pink carnations.

She didn't reach for them, didn't want them. "How did you know where I worked? What do you want?"

"I wanted to surprise you. Take you to lunch for your birthday."

Her breath snagged. "Today's not my birthday."

But the day after next was. And she *knew* she hadn't shared that detail of her life with him.

He shrugged. "I know. But close enough. I've got other plans for your actual birthday." Another crocodile grin that pooled dread in her core.

When he stepped closer, still trying to hand her the bouquet, she moved back a step. She raised a palm toward him and shook her head. "I don't want your flowers. And I'm not going to lunch or anywhere else with you."

Henry's mouth tightened, and he cut a glance over his shoulder where even without being able to see around the corner, Jessica knew Nadine was watching Henry with interest. He walked closer to Jessica, moving out of the receptionist's view, and she edged farther away. "You're making me look bad here, Jessie. Will you take the damn things—" he shook the flowers so hard a daisy blossom fell off "—and get your purse or whatever else so we can go to lunch?"

"You're not hearing me, Henry," she said, trying to keep her tone low and even. "We are not a couple. I do not want to see you again, and if you don't leave now and stop following me, I will file a restraining order and—"

"Following you? I just thought we'd go to lunch. How's that following you?"

"I saw you at the cemetery and at the hospital. Now you've showed up here out of the blue? I want it to stop!" When her voice rose along with her anger, she took a beat to calm herself. She didn't want to cause a spectacle in front of her coworkers. Which, come to think of it, was probably exactly what Henry was hoping for— that she'd comply rather than cause a scene.

"What's wrong with you?" he asked, his tone accusing. "On our first date, didn't you say you thought we had everything in common? We are a perfect match." He wagged a finger back and forth between them. He lowered his brow, and his eyes sparked behind his glasses. "You belong with me! Why are you fighting it?"

Jessica gritted her teeth. "Your reckless, hostile driving killed my friend! That alone is reason enough to never—" She stopped short, realizing the opportunity Henry had handed her. If she could stall him here while Nadine or someone else called the police...

She wet her lips and tried to calculate the best way to backpedal without raising suspicion. Her heart thundered against her ribs, and after swallowing hard to moisten her dry throat, she said, "Fine. We'll talk. But not at lunch. We'll talk in my office." She took the flowers from him. "Wait here. I'll just have Nadine put these in water for me."

She strode past him, through the lobby, to Nadine's desk. She felt Henry's eyes following her. As she handed the receptionist the flowers, she leaned in, saying, "Stay calm, but I need you to call the police. Send them to my office. This is the guy who caused my car accident."

Nadine's face blanched, and her eyes widened. She shot a nervous glance to Henry.

"Don't look at him," Jessica whispered. "I told him I was going to have you put these in water for me. So smile, maybe sniff them."

Nadine gave her a strained smile and ducked her face to the flowers. An actress the woman wasn't.

With a deep breath for composure, Jessica turned and crossed the lobby back to the spot where Henry waited. His eyes narrowed with suspicion.

"What did you tell her?"

"I asked her to find a vase for the bouquet and to hold my calls while we talked."

She took a few steps toward her office, but Henry grabbed her wrist and pulled her up short. "Don't lie to me. I saw how she looked at me. What did you say?"

Across from her, Chan Woo stuck his head out of his office, his brow furrowed, and asked, "Jessica, is everything all right out here?"

Henry released her arm and turned his back to Chan.

She pasted on a fake smile. "Sure. I'm fine."

Chan hesitated a moment before he moved back into his office and closed his door.

Henry tugged Jessica out of the sight of Chan's office window and growled in a hushed tone. "You're going to be sorry you treated me this way. I deserve better, Jessie."

With that, Henry paced down the hall to the employee staircase and stormed through the door.

She chased after him, seeing the chance for the police to catch him slipping away. From the top of the switchback staircase, she called, "Henry, wait! We can talk. Come back up and—" The clang of the ground floor fire exit door slamming echoed in the stairwell.

Jessica clenched her fists and growled under her breath. Turning, she returned to the office corridor and found Nadine hovering outside her office.

"The cops are on their way," the receptionist said, her expression still anxious.

Jessica sighed and shook her head. "Too late. He's gone."

That night Jessica told Gage about the incident at work as they sat in the ICU waiting room, eating the fried chicken he'd picked up on the way to the hospital. She raised her wrist to show him the new bruises Henry had left with his viselike grip. "He did this, and he probably scared five years off Nadine Holloway's life."

Gage wiped his greasy fingers on a napkin before lifting her arm to examine the bruises. His expression darkened. "Did you show these to the cops when they arrived?"

"Well, no. They hadn't really darkened then, and I was more concerned with them tracking him before he left the area."

He pursed his lips in thought. "Well… I'm not exactly sure how the law works, but I'd say you have grounds for a restraining order here." He dipped his head and gaze, indicating the fingerprint bruises.

Jessica considered that. "If he's going to keep popping up uninvited and bothering me, that might not be a bad idea. How do I get a restraining order?"

"Again, I'm not a lawyer. But… I can put you in touch with a friend of mine who might be able to help."

Jessica shrugged, knowing this was her battle, not Gage's. "Thanks, but I have a lawyer. Surely the woman who handled my divorce could put me on the right track for a restraining order. I'm betting that sort of thing comes up frequently in her practice."

"True. So you'll call her in the morning?" Gage's voice was quietly encouraging, urgent.

"I will." Jessica realized that Gage was still holding her arm, his thumb gently stroking the tender underside of her wrists where Henry had left his mark. His touch stirred a heady thrum in her core, and a sweet and languid hum flowed through her veins. Two things struck her at once—the contrast between Henry's damaging grip and Gage's soothing one, and how much she liked the soft caress of his thumb. The slow back-and-forth motion was hypnotic. Pleasant. Even...erotic.

As the word entered her mind, Jessica yanked her arm away, catching her breath so hard and fast that she choked, coughed.

"You okay?" he asked.

She forced a laugh. "Mmm-hmm. You know me. I can stumble over a painted line on the floor and, apparently, choke on air. Such a klutz." She rolled her eyes and gave him a wry grin.

Gage tipped his head. "Really? I've always thought of you as one of the most poised and graceful people I know. You know, thanks to all your gymnastics and cheerleading in high school?"

"Oh, well..." She shrugged, not wanting to dwell on her flimsy cover story. She wasn't about to tell him she'd found his touch arousing, or that she'd wondered for the briefest moment what it would be like to have him touch *other* places on her body. "So..." she continued, guiding the conversation safely away from the scandalous path that had tripped her up. "I'll call Olivia in the morning and get a restraining order in the works."

"Good. In the meantime, let me take a picture of the bruises as evidence the judge may want. And I'm repeating my offer to stay at your house for a little while. You might need a little added protection until the cops do something about Henry."

She was shaking her head even before he finished speaking. "I've been taking care of myself since I was eight years old. Maybe earlier. I've got this."

"I'm not doubting your competence, Jess. But sometimes having someone else around is an effective deterrent to a creep that is looking to bully or harass you. His track record proves he's likely to flee the scene rather than contend with someone who might challenge his presence." He spread his hands and gave her a disarming smile. "Someone at your service, ma'am."

She patted his chest and returned a grin. "I appreciate the offer. But I'll be fine."

"So you've taught Pluto to attack on command, then? Or dial 911 in a crisis?"

Just the thought of her derpy feline managing any level of training or defensive maneuvers made her laugh. "Not even close."

Sighing, Gage folded down the lid on his meal and stowed his trash in the carryout bag. "I just want to know you're safe, Jess. I've already got a sister fighting for her life. I can't stand the idea of something happening to you, too."

He looked so sad, so pained, Jessica couldn't help but put her arms around him, lean her head on his shoulder. "I know. And you're the best of friends for being so considerate and protective of me. Especially since I'm the one who—"

"No!" He returned the embrace. "Stop blaming yourself. One person is to blame, and he will be brought to justice, one way or another."

For a moment she just took comfort from his hug, something she'd had too few of since her divorce and Eric's leaving for college. Surely just her craving for human contact had spurred her carnal thoughts of Gage a few moments ago?

When she backed out of his arms, she added her dinner trash to his, musing, "I just don't understand why the police haven't found him and taken him into custody yet. How hard is it to find a person, if you know their name and have their vehicle description?"

"Good question." He pulled out his phone and motioned to her arm. She held it out for him to photograph. "I understand they get overwhelmed with cases and a shortage of manpower but…this delay is curious." He bent his head over his phone. "I'm texting you a copy of the photos now."

"Thanks." As Jessica found the small hand wipe that came with the greasy combo meal and tore open the packet, her thoughts strayed in another direction.

How did you know where I worked?

She stilled. Henry had never answered that important question. She hadn't shared more than superficial information about herself, as a matter of standard practice and safety. She hadn't even given him her cell phone number, choosing to communicate through messaging apps for their first dates. So if she hadn't told him the name of her employer, which she was 99.99 percent sure she hadn't, what sort of digging and prying had he done to locate the business she worked for? A chill wriggled through her, knowing how much personal information could be gleaned from the internet by someone willing to do the work. Knowing Henry had employed even a fraction of that kind of research to track her down was…unsettling.

A whistle cut into her thoughts, and she jerked her attention to Gage. "Huh?"

His hand was extended, and he chuckled. "I said, 'Do you want me to take that for you?'"

"Oh. Thanks." She handed him the used wet wipe to add to the rest of the trash.

"Where were you just then? You looked worried."

She exhaled and dropped her shoulders. "Just wondering how Henry found my office. He must have done some checking up on me or followed me from my house one morning or—" She gave a shudder. "It's creepy."

Gage's brow dipped. "It is."

His concerned look asked, *Are you sure you won't change your mind about having me stay on your couch tonight?*

Jessica shook off the uneasy feeling that crawled through her. "I refuse to let him cow me or make me change or restrict my life. That's how bullies win." She stood and dusted biscuit crumbs from her lap. "I'll be fine."

Despite her assurances to Gage, Jessica wished she could be half as confident as she pretended. She made a mental note to call her lawyer in the morning about the restraining order. If Henry was upping his game, she'd have to do the same.

Over the next couple of weeks, Jessica, with the help of her attorney, filed and won a restraining order against Henry. While she couldn't tell the judge where to find Henry to serve him with the legal documents surrounding the case, her attorney had posted a legal notice in the local paper. In court, the police report from the car accident and sworn statements from the manager of the Mexican restaurant, Gage, Chan Woo and Nadine Holloway were enough to convince the judge to issue an initial temporary order. But even with the legal measures in place, she found herself looking over her shoulder, startling at noises at night and checking her rearview mirror more often than usual. And every time she did, she chastised herself for renting Henry the space in her head.

She started visiting the hospital more often and staying later, using the excuse that she owed it to her friends to keep vigil. In truth, her house seemed emptier, lonelier than usual lately, and she enjoyed knowing Gage would be at the hospital to keep her company. His presence gave her more than companionship, she acknowledged privately. He anchored her with something familiar, someone kind when her world was topsy-turvy and uncertain.

Eric came home for a long weekend in early May, and she cherished the few days with her son before he left to visit his father, then return to campus for summer semester and the job he'd secured at a Chapel Hill restaurant.

When Memorial Day rolled around three weeks later, a day when she and her posse would have traditionally held a cookout and potluck in someone's backyard, she invited Gage and Sara's family to join her at her house for grilled hamburgers, hot dogs and all the fixings. Gage accepted readily, but Sara's widower, Cody, declined, saying he planned to take the kids to his parents' house for the weekend instead. And so just she and Gage ended up having dinner at her house, a pitiful semblance of the sort of gathering they used to have. More and more, she and Gage were going it alone, and Jessica became increasingly aware of the sacrifices he was making to keep her company, check on her and give her support. His attention was exactly the kind of pity and indebtedness to him she didn't want…but which she found herself craving more with every passing day.

Gage took the wet salad bowl Jessica handed him and dried it before stacking it with the other dishes after their Memorial Day dinner. Jessica had cooked an enormous meal, enough for twenty instead of the two that their party had been. Her abundant preparations gave him further evidence of how much she missed her friends and longed for the life that had been destroyed earlier that spring.

For nine weeks now, she'd put on a brave face, never complained, and continued to faithfully visit the hospital after work, even though Tina remained in ICU, her condition unchanged. But all the strained smiles meant to convince him she was fine and the ritual of her routine didn't change the sadness that shadowed her dark eyes or the worry that had etched tiny lines at the corners of her mouth.

"I think the rest of these will keep," he said, nodding his head toward the last few pans that soaked in the sink. "You've got to be tired after all the prep and cooking you put in today."

She rolled her shoulders and stretched her neck, even as she said, "Naw. It's no big deal."

He stepped over to her and gave her shoulders a firm squeeze. The groan that rumbled from her throat both called her a liar concerning her fatigue and lit a fire in his belly. He all too easily could imagine that purr-like expression of pleasure as her response to intimate acts between them. And he'd let himself imagine such acts with growing frequency over the past weeks, an indulgence he'd never dared except as a randy teenager when his lust for Jessica was new. His sultry daydreams were a risk, he knew. If she learned the kind of relationship he wanted from her, the dynamic between them could implode.

He had to be careful. He refused to risk the yearslong friendship they had or destabilize Jessica's last pillar of support, when so much of her life was falling apart. Still, as they'd grown closer, spent more time together, shared more of the sort of daily chatter and commiseration that spouses might, he'd found it easier to imagine their relationship eventually following the trajectory they seemed to be on. For all the awfulness of the last few months, he couldn't begrudge the excuse he'd been given to get closer to Jess. He yearned for their increasing intimacy to become physical, for her trust of him to grow, allowing him to share his true feelings.

He moved his massage to her neck, and she allowed her head to loll forward, her raven hair spilling over her shoulders and hiding her face. Having met Jessica's mother when they were in high school, he knew she had light brown hair and a fair complexion. He'd never asked Jessica about her father, only knowing what he'd overheard Tina tell their parents when they'd asked about Jessica's absent father.

"He was a one-night stand," Tina had said, "and her mother lost contact with him before Jessica's birth."

Did Jessica know anything more than that about the guy? What had it been like growing up with that blank regarding your heritage, a whole invisible branch of your family tree?

Curiosity poked him now as the ebony strands of her hair tickled his hands. Her dark coloring must have come from her father, and he wondered how she'd felt seeing that glimpse of him when she looked in the mirror.

"Can I ask you something?" he ventured.

"I think you just did."

"Ha ha. I'm wondering…about your father."

She didn't say anything, but her chin came up a notch and she pulled away from his touch.

"I'm sorry," he said. "If that's a touchy subject, you don't—"

"I never met him, but I saw a picture of him once."

Gage slid his hands in the back pockets of his jeans. "Oh? I was under the impression from Tina that he was—" he caught himself, wanting to be tactful "—not really a part of your mother's life."

Jessica chuckled and took her unfinished glass of wine from the counter. "Hmm. So Tina told you, huh?"

He wrinkled his nose. "Sort of."

After a dismissive lift of an eyebrow, she hitched her head, indicating he should follow her.

He took a beer out of her refrigerator and joined her in the living room. Pluto was curled up sound asleep on the chair he usually chose, so he took the spot next to Jessica on the sofa, angling his body to face her.

"My dad was a casual acquaintance my mom knew through a waitressing job she had at the time. He was one of several men she'd slept with in that time frame, and she didn't know which of the men was my dad until I was born with black hair and a dark complexion."

He nodded once at her confirmation of his suspicion but let her continue without interrupting.

"He was Native American. Cherokee. At the time, my mom lived near the reservation in the western part of the state, and he was a regular at the diner where she worked. Someone took a picture of her blowing out candles on a birthday cake, and he was in the group of people standing around her, singing."

"Cherokee, huh? I'd guessed he was from India or the Middle East. Do you know his name?"

"Mom wouldn't tell me. She didn't want me trying

to find him someday. She didn't even put his name on my birth certificate."

"Did she tell him about you?"

"I doubt it," she said and took a sip of her wine. "My mom was…selfish. Shortsighted. Impractical. She didn't care about anyone's rights or happiness but her own, right up to her death by overdose. And that includes her daughter's."

Hearing the despondency in her tone, Gage scooted closer to her and drew her into a one-armed hug. "I remember that—her death when we were in college. I'm sorry I didn't make it back for her funeral."

"Pfft, do *not* worry about that. It was not so much a funeral as me, Matt, Tina and my college roommate spreading her ashes in a wildflower field outside of town." She toed off her sandals and tucked her bare feet under her before leaning against his side.

Gage hummed an acknowledgment. With the arm around her shoulders, he reached up to give her head a finger massage before leaving his hand resting lightly on her hair. "Want to watch a movie? I bet we can find *Saving Private Ryan* on some channel this weekend."

She groaned. "Wonderful piece of cinema and touching tribute to our men in uniform, but I'm not sure I can handle the gore and tension of that movie tonight. I need something light and funny. Something feel-good."

Gage reached for the remote of her television and turned the screen on. "All right. Stop me if you see something that fills the feel-good prescription." He pulled up the programming guide screen and began scrolling.

Jessica made a few noncommittal noises now and then, showing half interest but no enthusiasm for anything. When he scrolled past an airing of *Saving Private Ryan*, he chuckled and said, "Told ya."

"Your psychic powers amaze me," she deadpanned, then took the remote from him and turned the TV off. "Gage, are we old now?"

"Depends on how you define old."

"Hundreds of channels available, but I'd rather just have silence and a glass of wine."

"Naw. Quiet is…self-care, not age. I'm older than you, but despite a few gray hairs, I'd like to think I still have a little gas in my tank."

She sat up and twisted to face him. "You have gray hairs?"

"Not a lot. And not all of them somewhere the public would see 'em…"

Jessica's eyebrows shot up. "Oh."

He sent her a devilish grin. "Wanna see?"

She sputtered a laugh. "Gage!"

"Oh, get your mind out of the gutter, Harkney. I meant my chest." But his teasing, challenging grin lingered.

She moved her feet back to the floor and, after holding his impish stare for a moment, she tugged up his T-shirt to expose his stomach. "Where?"

Sitting forward, he pulled the shirt higher and found a couple of said stray gray hairs on his chest. He pointed them out. "Satisfied?"

Jessica canted forward, lifting a finger to the grays. "Well, well, well." She grasped the hairs and plucked them.

"Agh! Hey!"

She tossed him a smug look. "Problem solved."

"That hurt!"

Flattening a hand against his chest, she pulled a pouty

face and gave the offended spot a rub. "Aw, did Gagey-poo get an owie?"

He should have knocked her hand away and yanked his shirt down. In their younger days, when they teased and engaged in horseplay, he'd have nudged her away with his shoulder and a tickle or scared her away with an armpit or spit string. Annoying brotherly stuff like what he waged on Tina. But...

Her soothing hand on his chest felt heavenly and sparked his libido. The unbrotherly feelings for Jess that he'd been fighting in recent weeks flashed hot. His breath caught and held. His gaze locked with hers. He swallowed hard.

Jessica's playful grin froze then shifted as he stared into her eyes. He couldn't say what his face revealed, but she'd read something there. Her pupils grew. Her lips parted. And a ragged breath whispered from her.

He covered the hand she still rested on his chest with his, then curled his fingers around hers. Her attention fell to their joined hands as he lifted hers to his lips and brushed a soft kiss on her knuckles.

Was this it? Was this the paradigm-shifting moment he'd waited for all these years? Gage waged a rapid-fire debate in his head. Act on his impulses or rein in his heart as he had for so long? Should he lean in and kiss her now, giving her the truth about his feelings in one simple act of affection?

Something warm and encouraging flickered in the espresso depths of her eyes. Desire? Curiosity? Consent? Adrenaline as potent and stirring as the day of his first house fire buzzed through his brain, his limbs, his blood. Her heated look, the beer he'd had at dinner, or some wishfulness he'd pressed down long enough prodded him. He leaned in, dropped his gaze to her lips, angled his head...

Jessica jerked back. Snatched her hand from his. Her breath as she exhaled quavered in the silent living room. She inched away from him on the couch, shaking her head, her brow creased with confusion. Maybe even consternation.

Gage's heart sank. His gut tightened. Had he destroyed everything he'd fought all these years to protect in a matter of seconds? In one foolish move?

He surged to his feet, fisting his hands at his sides, and strode across the floor. He stood with his back to her for a moment before he said quietly, "I'll see myself out."

He made it as far as her front door before her voice reached him.

"Gage?"

He paused, his hand on the doorknob. The quick patter of bare feet on carpet, then tile announced her approach. His heartbeat crashed against his ribs, and his dinner soured in his stomach. *Damn it, man! What have you done?*

Jessica placed a gentle hand on his back, and he flinched as if burned. "Gage?"

He turned to face her, trying not to look as guilty as he felt. "Yeah?"

Jeez, his voice sounded like he'd been chewing glass.

"Thanks for coming over tonight," she said in a quiet voice. "I...I had a good time."

Tenderness wrenched in his chest as he heard her attempts to normalize his exit. As if he hadn't just shattered the framework of their twenty-six-year friendship.

"Yeah." He could play along. "It was good. Dinner was great. Thanks."

He opened the door and stepped stiffly out onto her porch.

"Um...call me or...text me tomorrow? You know... if you go by the hospital."

Hating the formality, the awkwardness and uncertainty now between them—his doing—he nodded. "Mmm-hmm. Be sure to lock the door behind me. Huh?"

A shadow of something flickered over her face. "Always."

Gritting his back teeth, he closed her door and sighed.

What just happened?

Jessica leaned against her front door, her mind spinning. Had Gage really tried to kiss her? Had she imagined it, panicked for nothing? And what if he had kissed her? What would that have been like? Gage was a handsome man, no doubt about it. Charming, kind, intelligent.

And a serial dater. A commitment-phobe. Not the sort with whom she would ever consider a romantic relationship.

A snort ripped from her at the absurdity of her line of thought. Good grief! This was Gage Coleman, Tina's brother she was having these delusional thoughts about. Just because they'd grown closer over the past couple of tragic and stressful months, just because she felt isolated and alone without her posse, just because she'd failed miserably to find a match on the dating app, didn't mean she and Gage were suddenly somehow anything more than the friends they'd always been.

She returned to the living room, grabbed her wineglass and finished the dregs in a gulp. The merlot did little to calm her thoughts or settle her rattled nerves. She glanced over at her cat sleeping on the recliner. "Let's finish in the kitchen and go to bed. What do you say, Fuzzface?"

Pluto raised his head and yawned before hopping down from the chair where he'd been napping.

In the kitchen, Jessica fed the cat, put away the dried dishes and wiped the counter before heading upstairs. She would read until she fell asleep, she told herself as she performed her nightly ablutions. But her novel couldn't keep her mind from wandering—to Henry showing up at her office, to Tina and Holly still in the hospital, and to the strangely alluring pull she'd felt toward Gage tonight.

With a groan, she punched her pillow and rolled over. "Girl, you really are down the rabbit hole, aren't you?"

The next morning, after getting little sleep, she grumbled when the alarm on her phone told her it was time for work. She shut it off and flopped back, pulling the sheet to her chin and trying to muster the energy to rise and start a new week.

Sometime later, she was stirred from a bad dream about drowning by the incessant buzz of her phone. Squinting against the morning sun in her window, Jessica answered the call, noticing her bedside clock as she did. She was late for work.

"Sorry!" she told her boss as she threw back the covers and hurried toward the shower. "Horrid night. And I...overslept."

Chapter 8

As the sun rose higher and burned off the last bit of morning fog, Gage left the hospital with a bit of a bounce in his step. He'd been summoned to the hospital early that morning to find that, after more than two months, his sister had *finally* been taken off the respirator. She'd been awake, though still quite weak and not very communicative. But if she continued breathing on her own and meeting small benchmarks, she would be moved out of ICU to a regular room in the next few days. The doctors said she still had a long way to go and would have to have physical therapy to rebuild her strength, but...

But. Gage exhaled, releasing some of the tension that had twisted him in knots for the last sixty-two days. Tina was breathing on her own, making progress at last! He wanted to shout it, wanted to hug someone, wanted to share the news with...Jessica.

He didn't question why Jessica was his first thought, even before any of his colleagues or extended family. She'd been just as torn up over Tina's slow progress as he had, and he wanted to give her the good news. He wanted something, anything that could ease the guilt and grief and worry that had been plaguing Jessica since the accident. He took out his phone to call her, then hesitated. Last night's debacle replayed in his mind. She'd played it off, tried to gloss over it, but he'd not heard from her since. Not that it had been all that long. Twelve hours at the most.

He refused to let his bad judgment last night spoil what they'd had for twenty-six years. And he wouldn't let any awkwardness ruin his good news. He wanted to deliver the news of Tina's progress in person, wanted to see Jessica's face, her smile…hell, he wanted to see *her*.

Though he was still kicking himself for having nearly kissed her, he'd only make things worse if he let it change the dynamic between them. His phone said it was 9:12 a.m. He twisted his mouth, debating. She'd be at her office by now. Normally, he wouldn't bother someone at work, but this news was big. Important. He wanted her to have a report of Tina's progress to boost her day, give her hope.

Gage climbed into his pickup truck and headed toward the downtown office building where Jessica worked. Fifteen minutes later, he was at the receptionist's desk, asking to see her.

"Um, I don't think she's gotten in yet." The woman glanced to a coworker as if for confirmation. The other woman shook her head.

"She's still not in?" a third woman asked as she walked past. "I know she overslept. I called her earlier, but she promised she could be here by a little after nine." The well-dressed, gray-haired woman huffed her frustration and checked her smartwatch. "It's been almost an hour since she said she'd be here in forty."

A band of worry tightened in Gage's chest. "And that

was the last you talked to her? She hasn't called to explain her delay?"

Concern puckered the older woman's brow as she told the receptionist. "Nadine, try Jessica's cell again."

Gage held up a hand. "Let me. I need to talk to her anyway." He dialed Jessica's number, and it rang until it went to voice mail. "Jess, it's Gage. Call me when you get this. It's important."

The receptionist gave him a weak smile. "She's probably in the elevator on the way up here right now."

"Let's hope so," the gray-haired woman said, her tone nervous. "We have an important presentation to make at ten."

Gage tried again without luck to reach Jessica, both calling and texting, his apprehension rising. After pacing the reception area for ten minutes, he left a message with the receptionist for Jess, in case she arrived right after he left, and then headed for her house.

She could have had car trouble. She could have fallen in her shower and not be able to get to her phone. She could be—

The fear that had niggled since the first unanswered call roared through his brain, hastening his pace back to his truck. Her stalker could have come after her again.

Gage broke the speed limit every mile of the way to Jessica's house. As he parked in the drive, he assessed the property, not immediately seeing anything amiss. But when he climbed out from behind the wheel and headed toward her front door, the sound of an engine running and the faint smell of exhaust sidetracked him. He stepped over to peer in the window of the garage door.

Jessica lay sprawled on the concrete floor while her car's engine idled, filling the space with carbon monoxide. Adrenaline jolted through him, and he scrambled to raise the main garage door. The door wouldn't give. *Damn it!* Her automatic opener must be engaged.

Spying a side door, he raced around the corner of the house. The lock around this door had clearly been jimmied, the wood frame around the strike plate damaged. New waves of worry rushed through him as he yanked open the side door, did a quick scan for an intruder and raced to Jessica. He coughed, the built-up exhaust choking him.

"Jess!" he said, crouching, trying to rouse her. When she remained unresponsive, he scooped her into his arms and draped her over his shoulder in the classic firefighter's carry. Once outside, he set her gently on the grass of her front yard and patted her cheeks. "Jessica? Jess, come on, sweetheart. Wake up. Please, Jess, wake up."

His voice cracked, and he stopped long enough to shove down the emotion and pull his phone from his pocket. He dialed 911 and gave the operator the pertinent information. Yes, she had a pulse. Yes, she was breathing, barely. Yes, he'd moved her to get fresh air. Knowing he could do nothing else for Jess, he returned to the garage to turn off the car's engine and use the wall-mounted button to open the main garage door. Fresh air flowed in, and the poisonous gas flowed out of the garage. Next, he went inside the house to open her windows and front door and to shut Pluto, who seemed fine, safely in a bathroom with the exhaust fan on.

Finally, he returned to Jessica's side and cradled her head on his lap, wishing he had his station's oxygen mask for her. He stroked her bright pink cheeks and held her hand. "Don't leave me, Jess," he whispered, his voice a croak.

Closing his eyes, Gage said a prayer for her and didn't stop praying until the ambulance arrived.

Jessica drifted slowly out of a thick fog, her head throbbing, her ribs aching, nausea churning in her gut. She preferred the drowsy oblivion…let herself slide back toward darkness. Someone patted her face and gave her a shake. The motion made every pain gripping her more intense. She reached up to bat the pestering pat away, her arm weak, and encountered a plastic cup on her mouth and nose.

"Jessica, can you hear me?"

Her pulse kicked at the sound of the male voice. A thread of fear crawled through her though she couldn't say why. Her brain scrambled to sort out the reason for her sense of danger. Images flashed. Sensations. Scents.

Rising water. A hissed threat. Drowning. Can't breathe. Pain. A kick. Protect your head.

A scream rose in her throat, along with her panic. She sat up fast and blinked at her strange surroundings. Fresh anxiety swelled in her when she saw unfamiliar faces around her. A guy whose dark hair had frosted tips. A woman with glasses and a single blond braid. She heard the rumble of an engine, whine of a siren. Felt the bounce of tires over potholes.

A tangle of tubes and wires fettered her as she shrank away from the man next to her. Her sudden movement sent another paroxysm of agony through her chest, her head. Feeling her gorge rise, she gripped her stomach.

"Easy," the man said, covering her hands with his when she clawed at the plastic mask. "You're safe. Let's leave the mask on. You're getting the oxygen you need."

"Sick," she said, the mask muting her voice. But the man next to her understood. He pulled the mask off and grabbed a plastic bag to hold in front of her when she retched. She wiped her mouth on stack of gauze squares he handed her and added them to the bag of waste.

"Better?" Frosted Tips asked, and when she nodded, he nudged her shoulder, easing her back down, and replaced the oxygen mask. "We're about a minute out from the hospital and your husband is going to meet you there."

Husband? More confusion and panic spun through her. She furrowed her brow as she battled the thundering pain in her head to focus her thoughts. Husband? Matt?

"Who's coming?" she muttered.

"Gabe," the guy said.

The woman shook her head. "I think he said Gage."

Gage. She opened her mouth to deny he was her husband, but stopped. Despite the shrieking pain racking her body and head, a wash of something warm and calming flowed over her at the thought of Gage. There was a jostling bump, then the vehicle stopped, and doors opened at her feet.

And then Gage was there. The second she was unloaded from the back of the ambulance, his well-cut face and comforting strength was at her side. "Jess, you're awake! Thank God."

He grabbed her hand and strode quickly alongside her as she was hurried into the hospital. He only gave way once, so that the stretcher could be pushed through the narrow exam room door. Gage settled at the far side of her gurney, clutching her hand between his, as the medics passed her care off to the ER nurses.

She watched a nurse check monitors and get out supplies, still drifting in a sense of the surreal.

"Jeez, Jessica. You scared the hell outta me." She focused her attention on Gage when he spoke, his fingers cupping her cheek and his gray eyes as bright as silver with worry. "What happened? What do you remember?"

"I don't…know. I was going to…ask you the same thing."

His dark brows drew together. "I found you sprawled on your garage floor, the car running. You'd apparently been breathing the exhaust for quite a while. You were passed out, your cheeks red."

Jessica digested that information. She remembered a rushed morning. Juggling items to get in the car. "I was going to work," she said, but sounded more like a question.

"Did you fall? Get dizzy and faint?"

A sputter of anxiety ignited in her again. "I—I don't know."

"Sir, can the questions wait?" the attending nurse asked. "You seem to be upsetting her. Both her pulse and blood pressure just spiked. We want her calm and comfortable so we can be sure she's stabilized."

Gage pressed his mouth in a taut line as if chastened and nodded his understanding.

As much as she wanted answers about what happened, the stir of fear and panic that hovered like a mist around her told her the truth wasn't pleasant. The initial confusion and panic faded, and her muddled thoughts began to clear. But new questions rose.

She glanced at the nurse who was wrapping a cuff around her arm to check her blood pressure. "I hurt... here." She motioned to her rib cage, stomach, lower back. "A lot. And I threw up. In the ambulance."

The nurse nodded. "Nausea is common with carbon monoxide poisoning."

Jessica touched her aching ribs and gasped as she winced. The blurry image of a man hovering over her holding something...a bat? A stick? The man was angry. Yelling.

When she tensed as if to brace for a blow, her abdominal muscles objected with a throb.

"Ma'am, I need you to take slow, deep breaths, okay?" Her nurse squeezed the rubber bulb and the cuff inflated.

Jessica nodded, swallowed, and holding the nurse's friendly gaze, took several intentional breaths—slow, but not too deep. Deep breaths hurt. Each inhale, she flinched and backed off, remiss to hold the air in when her ribs throbbed.

The cuff deflated, and the nurse read the small electronic screen. "A bit high, but that's understandable. I'll check it again once you've had a few minutes to relax, enjoy some more of that good air." She tapped the mask. "At this point, this is your best medicine. So keep breathing deep and even. Okay, ma'am?"

She nodded. "Jessica."

Both Gage and the nurse leaned closer to hear her repeat the mask-garbled word. She lifted the mask and glanced at the nurse, digging down for her sense of humor, one of the tools that had helped her survive the ups and downs of her life to date. "My name is Jessica. *Ma'am* makes me look around for someone's mother."

The nurse chuckled and helped her replace the oxygen mask. "All right, *Jessica*. Your other numbers look pretty good all things considered. You're lucky this guy found you when he did."

She angled her head toward Gage and mustered a grin. "Yeah." Careful breath. Exhale. "He's one of the good ones." Careful breath. Exhale. One of the good ones...

She shivered as a voice hissed in her memory.

A restraining order? You thought you could get rid of me?

She gasped, startled by the flash of memory, then moaned when lightning pain streaked through her abdomen.

She clutched her middle, splaying her hands over her left ribs. But it was the shadowy images teasing her brain that made her tremble. *Don't piss me off, Jessie.*

"Jessica?"

She worked to bring the rest of the memory to the fore, but the effort wore her out, and each time an image flickered in her brain, she shied away from it, as if something inside was trying to shield her from something awful.

"Jess, what is it?" Gage brushed the hair from her forehead.

"H-he kicked me," she muttered.

The nurse's head came around sharply, and she sent Gage a wary look before focusing on Jessica. "Who kicked you?"

Gage leaned closer. "Jess, did Henry do this? Did he hurt you?"

She moaned and nodded. "Guess the restraining order didn't work."

Angling his gaze toward the nurse, Gage said, "We're going to need to file a police report."

Gage dragged a hand over his face, standing aside as the hospital staff settled Jessica in her room. He'd seen too much of this hospital in the last few weeks as he kept vigil over Tina. Now Jessica was here.

Without parents and with her son at college, he was all Jessica had, it seemed.

She had work associates, of course. Her ex, Matt, in Valley Haven. But her best friends...

He didn't finish the thought, because it led back to his own grief and the reason he knew which vending machines on which floors had the best snacks. Instead, he took a seat beside Jessica as the orderly withdrew and the nursing assistant double-checked the oxygen flow before retreating with a smile.

Jessica angled her head toward him, her eyes troubled, her brow lined. "You don't have to stay."

He shrugged one shoulder. "Where else am I going to go?"

"Home. Coffeehouse. Batting cage. I'm sure there are hundreds of things you'd rather be doing," she said, her voice slightly muffled and her breath fogging the oxygen mask as she spoke.

"Nothing that won't keep. Besides, I have all the comforts of home right here. A hard chair—" he slapped the arm of the uncomfortable visitor's seat "—and my choice

of at least six only slightly pixelated television stations."
He picked up the remote wired to her bedside and flicked
on the small screen on the opposite wall. "And since I
had planned to spend most of the day upstairs with Tina
anyhow—" He slapped his palm to his forehead. "Oh
man! In all the confusion and concern for you, I almost
forgot. I…have good news to tell you."

Her black eyebrows lifted, an invitation to continue.

"Tina was taken off the respirator last night. She's
breathing on her own this morning."

Tears filled Jessica's eyes, and she sniffled as she
gave him a wobbly grin. "That's fantastic. Oh my good-
ness!"

Her hand shaking, she swiped at the moisture leak-
ing from her eyes.

Gage leaned forward again and patted her arm. "I
figured you could use some good news, and I wanted
to give it to you in person."

"And you ended up saving my life instead." She exhaled heavily. The edges of her eyes crinkled, hinting
at her smile.

"Well…" He quirked up one cheek while he shoved
down the roil of unrest over the close call. "Glad to be
of service."

Her expression shifted, her gaze darkening and growing stormy. "There's something I don't understand." She
carefully rolled to her right side to face him, holding her
ribs as she moved.

"The doctor said confusion and brain fog, memory
gaps, were normal considering your condition."

She closed her eyes and shook her head slightly in

dismissal. "Not that. I— How did you know to come to my house?"

His hands fisted on the arms of the stiff-backed guest chair as his mind brought back images of her lying unconscious, curled in a ball on her cold concrete floor amid the clouds of exhaust.

"I started at your office, but when you weren't there I drove to your house to check on you."

She nodded again as if understanding. Then scrunched her nose. "So, if you hadn't had news about Tina to tell me…"

Gage sat back and frowned. He hated to think what would have happened to Jess if he hadn't found her when he did. "Yeah."

"In a way, Tina saved me today as much as you did." Her eyes sparkled with tears as she settled back in her pillows.

A knock on her door called their attention as a plain-clothes police officer stepped into her room, flashing his badge. "Ms. Harkney? I'm Detective Nick Macnally, Charlotte PD. I understand you need to file a police report? An assault?"

Gage stood and shook the officer's hand and introduced himself. Officer Macnally then took a statement from them each regarding Henry's violation of the restraining order, breaking and entering, and assault.

"Can he be charged with attempted murder? He left her there to die from the exhaust fumes," Gage said.

"That'll be up to the DA's office. I'm just here to take your statement." He flipped his notebook closed and clicked off the recording function of his phone. "And having done that, unless you have more to add to what you've told me, I'll get going and let you rest."

Jessica shook her head and offered a muffled "Thank you" through the oxygen mask.

Turning his focus back to Jessica's needs, Gage asked, "What can I do? Another pillow? Is the room warm enough? Should I call Eric or Matt for you?"

Her eyes widened, and she gave her head a vigorous shake. Tugging the mask down, she rasped, "Don't bother them. I'm going to be fine, and there's nothing they can do to change things for me, so…just let it ride. Would you call my office and tell them what happened, though?"

"Done. They send their best wishes."

She replaced the mask and took a deep breath, her eyelids drooping. "All I need now is a nap. That pain-killer they gave me is making me drowsy."

He ducked his chin in a nod of agreement. "I'll let you sleep, then. I should get back upstairs and look in on Tina anyway." He moved to the side of her bed, intending to kiss her forehead, but balked, echoes of last night, the alarm in her eyes when he'd almost kissed her, replaying in his head. Instead, he simply gave her shoulder a light squeeze and flashed a grin. "I'll be back to check on you later."

Jessica experienced a strange pang as Gage left the hospital room. Being alone and facing the creaks and shadows, the doubts and recriminations, had been easier at home. Being in the hospital, a victim of Henry's violence, shook her to the marrow.

You aren't alone. The hospital staff won't let Henry hurt you.

But what about after she was released from the hospital? Henry had shown he could find her, that no judge's order to stay away fazed him. What would happen to her if the police continued to stall out on finding him, arresting him? And even if Henry were caught, he could get bailed out, more vengeful than ever, free to harass and stalk her, before his case ever went to trial.

She shuddered and weighed her options. While she knew Gage would stay with her, lend his presence as a deterrent to Henry, how could she justify asking him to do that?

The oath she'd made on the last day she'd darkened her mother's door played in her mind like a video on rewind. When her mother learned of Jessica's plan to attend college, using money she'd squirreled away for years, one acorn at a time, she'd gone ballistic.

"You're not going anywhere! You can't just abandon me!" her mother had screamed. "After everything I've done for you, feeding you and putting a roof over your head, how dare you think of running out on me when I need you most?"

Eighteen-year-old Jessica had wavered for a moment, guilt tugging at her. What would become of her mother after she left?

But then her mother had narrowed a heated glare on her and screeched, "You always were an ungrateful bitch. You've taken everything I've done for you for granted!"

And Jessica had felt slapped out of her sympathy for her mother. Not only had her mother essentially ignored Jessica most of her childhood, Jessica was the one who'd taken the initiative to work weekend and summer jobs, earning just enough to keep them from getting evicted when her mother couldn't pay their rent. Jessica had worn a hand-me-down uniform for cheerleading, skipped meals, cut corners and kept them afloat. She'd managed all this while maintaining her grades, winning scholarships, and putting pennies in an account that, after five years, had barely been enough for her first semester's tuition.

Her mother, meanwhile, had drifted from one boyfriend to another, playing the victim and acting helpless, growing increasingly dependent on men and on Jessica. The thought that her mother would try to block her from pursuing her education and shame her out of following the dreams she'd sacrificed for, all while she cursed and blamed and guilted her daughter, had galled Jessica.

Anger had burrowed to her core, and she'd grated out a promise, an oath to herself and her mother as she stormed out of her mother's home for the last time. "You have a very warped and selfish view of history, mother. I will not stay and enable you any longer, and I will never be like you, surrendering power over my life, my survival or my self-worth to anyone, especially not a man."

She'd kept that promise to herself through the years, no matter the cost. How could she give in now? She refused to let her fear of Henry make her dependent on Gage.

Her resolve wavered, however, when Gage brought her home from the hospital the next day, and she found a message spray-painted in black on her garage door.

I'll be back.

* * *

On a rainy evening in June, Jessica had just finished her microwave dinner and was rinsing the tray for the recycling bin, when through the window over her kitchen sink, she spied a car pulling into her driveway. She didn't recognize the dark sedan, and her heart stilled. Anxiety squirmed in her gut as she dried her hands on a towel and hurried to her living room window for a better look. She'd spent the last several weeks since getting discharged from the hospital looking over her shoulder and jumping at her shadow. The arrival of a car she didn't recognize rang enough alarms to chill her to the core.

When a tall, raven-haired figure climbed from the back seat, Jessica caught her breath.

Eric!

Her son's unexpected arrival brought tears of joy and relief to her eyes—but also concern. She flew to the foyer, unlocked the door and snatched it open before Eric had even reached the porch steps.

"Hi, Mom." Eric flashed a lopsided smile that said he knew he'd surprised her and was proud of himself for keeping his arrival a secret.

"Oh, honey! What are you doing home? I'm thrilled to see you of course, but—"

"No reason. I had a free weekend and…" He flipped up a dismissive hand.

She opened her arms, and, dropping his bag of laundry and his suitcase, he stepped into her embrace. His hug was long and strong, and she cherished every second. "Oh, Eric, you give the best hugs."

Whether her compliment or the warble in her voice influenced him, she didn't know, but he gave her an extra squeeze before stepping back and retrieving his belongings. "We have no class Monday for Juneteenth, and since I worked double shifts earlier this week at the restaurant, the boss gave me a couple days off. So I thought I'd drop in as a surprise."

"I'm so glad you did!" She held the door for him as he bustled inside and dumped his bags in the foyer. The sight of her son, even after only a few weeks away, filled her with such joy she couldn't even bemoan the smelly sack of laundry stinking up her entry hall.

Eric rubbed his hands together and gave her a speculative look. "I haven't eaten yet, and I'm starving. Want to order a pizza?"

She cleared the lump from her throat so she could speak. "I would love nothing more."

Over dinner—she nibbled a slice of pizza without telling Eric she'd already eaten—Eric told her all about his summer classes, his coworkers at the restaurant and the plans he'd made to take a study semester abroad. "Dad said he's okay with it if you are."

"A semester abroad? Wow. That sound fantastic!" She tried to hide the sinking feeling that diminished her genuine excitement for her son's opportunities. Having Eric four hours away was bad enough without him being an ocean away—or farther. "Where are you planning to go?"

He shrugged a shoulder as he stuffed the last bite of crust in his mouth. "Not sure." He chewed a minute, then said, "There are great programs in Switzerland and Japan, but the program in Paris would count toward my premed work. So, does that sound okay to you? It's not too late to sign up for French in the fall. I have to show a proficiency in the language for the programs in Switzerland and Paris. I can swing it if I knock out my Poli Sci requirement second session this summer."

She nodded, unable to speak as unbidden emotion tightened her throat, and she realized she'd been counting on Eric's presence, his company, his protection later this summer from Henry's lingering menace. That expectation was wrong in so many ways, it was no wonder she hadn't allowed herself to examine her feelings as she anticipated Eric's homecoming. Sure, she was happy to see her son and thrilled to hear about his life at UNC, but putting anything else real or perceived on her son's shoulders was unfair, inappropriate and just…wrong.

"Hey, I saw a white Camry in the garage when I came in. Is that another rental or could they not fix whatever was wrong with your old car?" Eric asked and helped himself to another slice of the pepperoni pie.

When Eric had been home in May, she'd only told him she'd had a car accident that required the rental she'd been driving, and he'd mercifully asked few questions, once he'd been assured his mother was unharmed.

"Oh, right. That one's mine. The insurance company finally paid up after my accident, and I bought that one a couple weeks ago." She pressed a hand to her stomach to quell the quiver that memories of the accident still stirred, then forged ahead. Eric needed to know the truth…or *some* of it. And so, as succinctly and gently as she could, she caught her son up on the key events of the past months, carefully avoiding mention of her dates with Henry Blythe and his continued harassment. The full extent of the car accident and its fallout were tragic enough.

Eric's face grew still and pale as she explained about the night she and her friends had ended up in the river, trapped, drowning. She hated dumping the sad news on him, soiling this golden time in his life.

"Aunt Sara is dead?" Eric had called the members of the posse his aunts in a nod to the close relationship the women shared with his mother. *Like sisters.*

She answered his questions about the accident, about Holly's and Tina's conditions, and her own health. Tina, she told him, remained stable with small improvements to her blood pressure and amount of oxygen she needed, while all she knew of Holly were the bits and pieces she'd gleaned the night of the accident. She reassured him as best she could, keeping a stiff upper lip, not wanting to add her own fragile state to the worries she was unloading on her man-child. But her composure slipped when he asked, "And what happened with the guy who caused the accident? Did they catch him? Is he being charged with manslaughter or anything?"

Jessica fisted her hands on her lap. "He has not been taken into custody yet, but...the police are working on it." She forced a smile. "They'll get him."

Eric tossed down the crust he held and leaned back in his chair, his expression stunned. "Damn, Mom. I'm so sorry! Why didn't you tell me when it happened? I could have come home—"

"Which is why I didn't tell you. You didn't need the distraction from school, and there was nothing you could have done here to change anything. I was unhurt...essentially. Physically. You were where you needed to be, so I chose not to tell you."

He exhaled harshly and narrowed his gaze on her.

"I'm not a little kid anymore, Mom. I can handle bad news. And I want to be there for you." He sat forward and leaned on his arms as he drilled her with a dark gaze so like her own. "Don't shut me out again. I want to be in the loop on things like this. Okay?"

Her heart warmed with pride for her only child. So mature, so grown-up, so precious to her. "I hear you."

"Do you promise?"

Not a chance. She would never stop protecting her boy, trying to shield him from the brunt of life's pain, and sparing him from his desire to flip their roles and take care of her. She crossed her fingers under the table and lied, "I promise."

Eric returned to Chapel Hill two days later, and Jessica felt his departure deeply, as she did every time he left.

This empty nest business is...for the birds! She gave a wry chuckle at her lame joke as she watched his Uber take him away.

She had only been back inside her quiet house for a few minutes before she heard a knock at her front door. Assuming Eric had forgotten something and puzzled why he would knock instead of using his key, she hustled to answer the door.

But it wasn't Eric.

Chapter 9

When she answered the door, she found Detective Nick Macnally, the officer who'd taken her police report at the hospital, on her porch. His hands were jammed in his pants pockets. His expression grim. A heavy throb pulsed through her, and she could feel the tensing of her neck, her muscles bracing for bad news.

After a terse, perfunctory greeting, she showed the detective into her living room and motioned for him to sit.

Macnally perched on the edge of her couch and propped his arms on his thighs as he leaned forward. "I wish I had better news for you, but the truth is, our search for Henry Blythe has hit a dead end."

Jessica's stomach plummeted. "How so? Can't you just look him up in the DMV records or tax files or—"

"Of course, we could. And we did search all the usual records and databases." Macnally shook his head. "No Henry Blythe exists in Charlotte or any other part of the state. At least not anyone that fits the physical and demographic description you gave us. Not even close."

"That's…not possible!" Jessica gripped the arm of

her wingback chair, her head spinning. "What about the truck? The license plate—"

"The plate was stolen. The owner had reported it missing from their car three days earlier."

Jessica sat in stunned silence for a moment, staring at her lap, goggling at what she was learning. "So he… used some sort of alias or something? And changing license plates makes it sounds like he intended something nefarious and wanted to cover his tracks."

The detective ducked his chin slowly. "Appears so."

A new thought occurred to her, and she jerked her head up. "What about his profile on the dating app?"

Macnally spread his hands and twisted his mouth in a discouraging frown. "Deleted, apparently. We found no Henry Blythe, H. Blythe, or any variation of spelling on the app you mentioned—"

"What about—"

"Or any other dating or meetup app our techs could find."

Jessica furrowed her brow and plowed her fingers through her hair, wincing when her fingers met the tender spot where Henry had hit her. "This is crazy! So—" she exhaled harshly, her frustration and fear roiling in her chest "—how do we find him?"

"We'll try other resources, keep the case open." He cleared his throat. "I'm sorry I don't have more to offer." He paused and tipped his head as he regarded her. "Given the lengths this guy has gone to in order to avoid being found, it might be a good idea for you to have someone stay with you for a while. Or stay with family or a friend. This amount of preparation and planning doesn't say ordinary stalker to me. My gut is telling me he's planning something more drastic."

Jessica flopped back in her chair. Her head pounded, and the ragged edges of despair crowded in on her. "More drastic? Like what?"

He twisted his mouth. "I don't mean to alarm you, but he could escalate. Kidnapping is a possibility. More violence. Like I said, he's gone to a lot of trouble to avoid detection. That reeks to me."

"Well..." She lifted a trembling hand to her mouth. "You may not mean to alarm me, but...you have."

"I'd be remiss if I weren't honest with you. I really think you need to stay with someone. Being here alone, where he knows you live, is asking for trouble."

Jessica chuffed a harsh sigh. "But where? My three best friends are either dead or in the hospital still because of Henry—or whatever his name is. My son is at college. I don't know my father, and my mother is—" she sighed, choking down the lump in her throat "—dead."

Macnally gave her a look of regret. "Then...get out of town. Get a dog. Buy some pepper spray at a minimum. Men like this guy stalking you don't typically just go away, even with a restraining order."

"As he's proven."

"My best advice to you is to make a change of some kind for your own protection. We'll continue to do everything we can to find him, including added drive-bys to watch your house, but until we catch him, you need to take extra measures to stay safe."

Jessica nodded her understanding. She didn't like the truth bombs Macnally had dropped on her. In fact, she hated the idea of leaving town or hiding from Henry—

for lack of his real name. She'd never been one to run from her problems, even if it meant making difficult choices.

But was leaving the area avoiding her problem, or was it the hard choice she had to make to stay safe? If Detective Macnally was advising she lie low somewhere away from Charlotte, caution said she should heed his recommendation.

She walked with the detective to the front door, thanked him again, and locked up tight in his wake.

That night, she got no sleep. She jumped at ordinary sounds—the ice maker cycling, the wind rattling her loose shutter, Pluto jumping onto her bed. She couldn't live like this. Her blood pressure had to be through the roof.

But if she left, where would she go? She could hardly move into the men's dorm at UNC with Eric. The expense of a hotel room would add up quickly.

Gage? She weighed and discarded that idea for the same reasons she'd turned down his help in earlier weeks.

Cameron Glen. Just the name of the vacation retreat property owned by the family of her ex-husband's new wife filled her with a warmth and comfort that beckoned to her. The times she'd been invited to Cameron Glen for family functions, she'd reveled in the bucolic setting, soaked in the peacefulness and savored the beauty of the landscape. The Cameron family's hospitality and genuine affection toward her had been an unexpected and cherished bonus. Each trip, by the time she would return to Charlotte, she'd feel refreshed and empowered to take on the daily grind again.

But just as she wouldn't impose on Gage, she couldn't be a burden to her ex-husband and his new family, no matter how kind and welcoming they were. She'd also have to make arrangements with her boss to take a leave of absence or to work remotely. Henry had shown that her office was on his radar same as her house.

She was on her third cup of coffee when she finally convinced herself she had to follow Macnally's advice. Her first call was to her boss, who was understanding, if stressed by how they'd cover Jessica's workload while she was out.

"Look, that's my problem, not yours," Carolyn said. "You have enough on your plate. I'll get a temp to cover for you, and I promise your job will be here when you get back. Just…be careful and come back in one piece when you can."

After finishing the call with work, Jessica gathered her composure for her next call. She chose to ask her ex-husband's wife, since Cameron Glen belonged to Cait's family and it was more within her purview to grant or deny Jessica's request. She and Matt had parted amicably, both realizing several years earlier that their lives had diverged and neither was happy in their marriage anymore. But they'd made an effort to remain friendly for Eric's sake.

For several years, they'd navigated separate lives, sharing custody of their son without quarrel. And then, quite unexpectedly, Matt had found Cait and remarried. Jessica had been truly happy for her ex, and in a more serendipitous twist had found a friend in Matt's new wife. Cait Cameron had been both generous of spirit and warm toward Jessica, and her family genuinely welcoming of Jessica for Cameron family gatherings and special occasions like Eric's birthdays, his high school graduation, even Thanksgivings when Jessica would have otherwise been alone. Cait and her family made what could have been awkward and strained seem the most natural and happy of events.

Over the last three years, Jessica had bonded not only with Cait, but with all of the Camerons. In fact, last year, when a corrupt man tried to blackmail the family into selling the family's property at Cameron Glen, Jessica had been included in a scheme to protect the land from that and future hostile buyouts. Jessica had pulled together the funds to purchase a tiny share of Cameron Glen, the sizable retreat property in Valley Haven, near the Smoky Mountains, that had been in the Cameron family for generations. In addition to the vacation rental cabins, several members of the Cameron family had homes in Cameron Glen, including Matt and Cait and their young daughter, Erin.

"Hi, Jessica! How're you doing?" Cait's chipper voice greeted her and instantly a measure of relief and the sting of tears swelled, telling Jessica she had made the right choice in calling.

She squelched the automatic and polite response of "Fine," choosing to be honest. She could with Cait, which was one of the reasons she'd decided to call. "Not so great. Rather a mess, in fact."

"Oh, Jessica," Cait said, her tone full of sympathy. "What's going on?"

"I'm…being harassed by this guy I had a couple dates with."

"Harassed how?"

Jessica curled her free hand in her lap to stop the trembling. "He keeps…showing up. At my house. At my office. Following me and…trying to hurt me." Her voice did squeak then. "Remember my accident this spring? He caused that. He's responsible for killing my friend Sara and putting Tina and Holly in comas."

"How horrible! You've…told the police, I'm sure."

"Mmm-hmm," Jessica affirmed, her throat tight.

"So why is he not in jail?"

"I…I've tried a restraining order against him, except…he ignored it." She paused again when her voice threatened to crack. "And the name I gave the police, the name he used on our dates…doesn't exist. That is, when they ran his name, the men that came up through government records were all wrong. Wrong age. Wrong race. Wrong physical description." She sighed her frustration, the breath shuddering. "Cait, I'm scared. I don't feel safe here. He's gotten into my home, my garage and was lying in wait for me."

Cait gasped.

"He attacked me and…left me for dead."

"What!"

"He's threatened me. Cursed at me. Vandalized my home."

"Jessica! I— What are you going to do? How can I help?" The urgency and concern in Cait's voice heartened Jessica.

"I know it's a big ask, but…"

"Doesn't matter. Ask. You're family, Jessica. We'll do whatever we can for you. You know that."

Tears of gratitude leaked onto her cheeks. "I need to get out of town. Now. For the rest of the summer possibly. The detective working the case thinks I'm at risk, and he advised me to move out of my house for a while. I need to go somewhere safe until the cops can catch him, somewhere I can have some peace of mind and…find my way forward. So I was hoping…could I—"

"Yes. Come here. Come to Cameron Glen," Cait said before she could finish the question.

"Thank you. So much. But…where would I stay? I don't want to impose, and I hate to take up a cabin that could be rented and earn income for your family. I mean, I can pay rent—"

"You're a part owner. You came through for us when we needed help, and that grants you privileges. You won't pay rent."

"Are you sure the rest of the family will agree to that? I…" Jessica bit her bottom lip, already feeling significantly better about her situation. Still, guilt nagged at her. The Camerons weren't broke, but neither did they need to lose income during the height of vacation season.

"I'm sure they'll be fine with it when I explain the circumstances. Besides, I've been given the authority as the rental manager to make decisions regarding the cabins without constantly conferring with the family. They trust my judgment."

"If you're sure…"

"I am. In fact…" Cait's voice held a note of inspiration. "I may have an idea that benefits us both, if you're game."

Chapter 10

"So the Juniper cabin is undergoing renovations that had been put off in previous years, but became mandatory after a pipe burst and flooded the kitchen late this past winter," Jessica told Gage later that evening when she called him about her plan. "As long as the cabin was getting those repairs made, the family decided to do a complete upgrade and remodel, including adding a second bedroom/bathroom suite."

"Okay," Gage said, sounding wary. "Why do I feel like you're leading up to a big announcement of some sort?"

She took a steadying breath. "Because I worked out an arrangement where I will live in the cabin throughout the stages of repair in exchange for keeping tabs on the carpenters, electricians and plumbers that would need access to the cabin."

"What about work?" he asked, and she could hear a note of regret or disappointment in his tone that made her pause. As much as he'd been her support in the past few weeks since the accident, had she been his? He had buddies at the firehouse, friends from school still in the area, but…clearly he'd chosen to spend time with her over them. Was that by choice rather than a sense of obligation?

"Well, summer is the busiest time at Cameron Glen for cabin rentals and making reservations for autumn, so I offered to help out at the rental office part-time. With an almost-two-year-old underfoot, Cait welcomed the chance to pass off bookkeeping, cabin maintenance and daily guest requests to me."

"Uh-huh. I meant your job here."

"Oh, right." She picked at a loose thread on her bedspread. "I'm not resigning, if that's what you mean. I will work on a few things, finish up a couple current projects remotely. I can use Zoom to attend meetings. But Carolyn was understanding and promised my job would still be there when I got back."

"That's great. So…you do plan to come back?"

His hopeful tone triggered a pang in her chest. She'd miss seeing him regularly. She was surprised at how quickly he'd become a fixture in her life, an anchor but also a confidant.

"I do," she said. "I just…don't know when."

"Hmm." He was quiet for a moment. "When do you leave?"

"Tomorrow."

"That soon?"

"No point in stalling. Especially if Henry is, in fact, lurking and dangerous."

Gage gave a low whistle. "You always were a woman of action. What can I do to help?"

"I don't need help."

"Do you have a plan for how to get out of town without being followed? If this bastard is stalking you, he could have eyes on your house or be keeping tabs on you going to work, or—"

"Damn. I hadn't thought of that." A shiver crawled through her. "Do you have a suggestion?"

He grunted again, a sound that said he was thinking. "The key is to not let him know you're relocating, so he can't see suitcases leaving your house. And if we could somehow get you in my truck without him noticing, that'd be good, too. He's less likely to follow me out of town."

"Gage, you don't need to drive me—"

"If it will keep you safe, get you away undetected, I do. I'll be there early. Say, six, seven?"

"Good heavens, Gage. I have to pack still. Make it ten." She chuckled, then sobering, added, "And thank you. You're a good friend."

She heard another low hum, then a small sigh. "You're welcome."

Late the next day, Jessica and Gage arrived at Cameron Glen and were met by a large contingent of the Cameron family. They circled the truck as Gage parked at Jessica's home for the summer and greeted them both with smiles and hugs and expressions of concern for Jessica's recent traumas and the prolonged hospitalization of his sister.

Gage shook her ex-husband's hand. "It's been a while. How are you doing? I hear congratulations are in order. A wife and baby since we last talked."

"Yes. Thanks." Matt's answering smile was bright, though tinged with something awkward, as if he felt guilty for having so much happiness and good fortune while Gage remained single, childless and coping with his sister's illness. "I understand you're still with the fire department."

"I'm so glad you've come to stay here this summer," Cait's mother, Grace, said, pulling Jessica's attention away from the men's pleasantries. "Please make yourself at home, because, in a way, it *is* your home, too."

Jessica nodded and flashed a lopsided grin. The gracious welcome from the Camerons soothed the jagged emotions that had been seesawing in her for months. The beautiful landscape of Cameron Glen put her at ease, as well, and she knew she'd made the right choice in coming. "I do have one special request, which I hate to impose, but...I brought my cat, Pluto, with me. While he'll be fine with me at night, do you mind if I take him with me to the rental office during the day? All the construction work noise would be scary for him, and the nails and loose wires and things would be dangerous—"

"Of course," Cait said before Jessica could finish. "Or bring him to our house. Unless you think an overly enthusiastic toddler would terrify him."

Jessica shrugged. "I guess we won't know until we introduce them. He's generally laid-back, so I think he'd be fine." She opened the truck's back door and pulled the travel carrier out.

To camouflage her escape, Gage had pulled into Jessica's garage, and they'd closed the door to hide their activity as they loaded the few clothes and belongings she was taking to Cameron Glen. Jessica had hidden on the floor of his extended cab, until they'd driven several miles out of town.

"Speaking of introductions," Jessica said now, "Gage needs to meet everyone."

Grace nodded but said, "What if we save those for tonight. I've planned a family meal, and we want you both to join us."

Jessica smiled and heard her stomach growl as if in anticipation of good food. "Thank you. Let me see what Gage thinks. I'd hate to answer for him. Right now, I need to get Pluto out of his cage so he can explore his new digs."

Gage saw her holding the travel carrier and hurried over. "I'll get that for you."

Following Gage's cue, the men, including Matt's brothers-in-law, carried all her bags and miscellany from the truck inside the small cabin.

"So, what did you tell your boss in Charlotte? She just let you take leave for some unknown months?" Cait's sister Isla asked, her own toddler propped on her hip. CeCe, born the same day as Cait and Matt's daughter, held a fistful of Isla's long red-gold hair, and Isla winced when her daughter pulled too hard.

"Well," Jessica said, "my boss knew everything that happened recently, from the car accident and my grief over my friends and…other stuff. She was completely sympathetic to my situation, and while her hands were tied regarding corporate rules that limited paid personal time, she promised my job would still be waiting in the fall, even if I'm not getting a salary all summer."

Isla pivoted toward Cait. "Can't we pay her something for helping in the rental office?"

Jessica shook her head. "You're already giving me lodgings rent-free. I can't accept anything more."

"But—" Isla fumbled her daughter's fingers free from her hair again "—you helped us out financially when we were in a pinch. I just want to repay the favor."

"You have. You are." Jessica touched Isla's arm and gave her a grateful smile. "I'll be fine. I have some savings. It's just for a little while." *I hope.*

Detective Macnally had tried to be encouraging at first, but Henry's apparent use of an alias had thrown sand in the gears of the investigation. The detective couldn't honestly say when she'd be safe to move back to Charlotte.

Jessica balled her hands and battled down the swell of anxiety that thought stirred in her. Exhaling and jamming down the agitation, she straightened her shoulders with determination. She'd take things as they came, one bridge, one decision, one challenge at a time, as she had her whole life. She'd found the strength and courage to take care of herself when her mother couldn't. She'd handled being both mother and father to Eric while Matt was deployed overseas for months, and she'd adapted to the life of a divorcée, relying on herself alone to deal with the messes life threw at her.

Her current mess might be bigger, scarier, murkier, but she'd grope day by day to feel her way through, determined not to show any weakness or depend on anyone for her survival.

The men emerged from the cabin again, and Gage moved to her side. "So, do you want time to unpack or shall we go grab a bite to eat before I head back?"

"If I may," Grace interjected, "I'd like to have you both to join us for dinner. We're having our weekly family gathering tonight, and since Emma and her family are out of town, there's more than enough for you two to dine with us."

Jessica glanced at Gage, measuring his interest. His returned look clearly deferred to her choice.

"It sounds wonderful to me. Cameron family dinners are something to experience, according to Eric," she said.

"All right. Then we accept," Gage said. "Thank you."

Grace bobbed a nod. "Good. You take an hour or so to unpack and relax, and we'll see you at our place—" she turned and pointed to a large house up the hill from the Juniper cabin "—which is right there, at six thirty. Sound good?"

"Sounds great," Jessica said.

Cait gave Jessica a hug, and Matt shook Gage's hand again as the Camerons dispersed. Gage and Jessica entered the cabin and went in search of Pluto. She found the cat sniffing around the bedroom, exploring all the new smells. Reassured that her cat was okay and settling in, she returned to the front of the cabin. Gage stood in the kitchen, unloading a few items she'd brought over in a cooler into her refrigerator.

She did the same for the box of dry goods she didn't want to go stale before she returned at the end of the summer, filling the pantry shelves with crackers, instant oatmeal and granola bars.

Those small tasks done, she eyed her suitcases, but Gage caught her hand and led her to the den. "The rest can wait, can't it?"

She lifted a shoulder. "I guess. Why?"

He perched on a recliner and propped his arms on

his legs, raising a somber gaze as he addressed her. "I just wanted make sure you're going to be all right here."

She smiled and settled back in the recliner angled next to his, tucking one foot under her. "You'll meet most of the family tonight. But you've already seen how kind and gracious they are. That wasn't fake or for show. They've always been incredibly warm and welcoming toward me. I'll be fine."

He nodded, but his expression remained serious. "I'm sure they'll be accommodating and kind. But I mean… will you be *safe*? You're still alone in this cabin."

A thread of unease wound through her, and she rubbed her palms over the goose bumps that rose on her arms. "I suppose we'll see. The doors have locks. I believe the cabins have security cameras outside. And I'll have a number of protective Cameron men close by. While here, I'm out of Henry's sphere, in theory. That's the best I can do."

"Unless I stayed here with you."

A jolt of surprise—and unbidden longing—coursed through her. She leaned forward, dropping her foot back on the floor as she gaped at him. "What?"

"If you want me to, I—"

She held up a hand, cutting him off. "You can't just up and move over here for the summer. You have a job—"

"I'll ask for leave."

She blinked. "What about Tina? You can't leave her alone over there in the hospital."

He frowned. "Yeah. I don't like being away from her, but…" He clamped his mouth in a taut line for a moment. "I can commute to Charlotte a few times a week to check on her."

She gave him a dubious frown. "She needs you more than I do."

His brow creased. "Does she? She's not the one with a lunatic harassing her, potentially trying to kill her. I don't like leaving you here alone."

Jessica shook her head, and pushed down the tiny voice in her head screaming, *Yes! Please stay!* "Gage, no. I've told you so many times, I can't ask you to—"

"I'm volunteering. I can ask the station chief for a few weeks of time off for a family emergency."

She chuckled, a bittersweet pang tugging at her core. "I'm not family."

He took her hand in his and held her gaze, his own piercing, intense. "Aren't you? Family doesn't always mean blood relations."

A tingle rushed from where his fingers touched hers, crackling through her body like an electric charge. Her heart pattered a staccato rhythm as she studied the strong, masculine cut of his jaw, his straight nose, his magnetic gray eyes with a thick fringe of lashes.

Good grief! Holly and Sara were right. He is *a gorgeous man.* Maybe she'd always known it, but in that moment, she saw her best friend's brother in a new light—one that made her tremble to her core with a purely feminine desire. Catching her breath, she snatched her hand from him, confused and rattled by her unexpected lust. What was wrong with her? This was *Gage*, for crying out loud!

The same guy who'd had no fewer than ten different girlfriends since she'd become Tina's best friend in high school. The same guy who'd tossed her in the freezing swimming pool at Tina's New Year's Eve party last year. The same guy who'd been an usher at her and Matt's wedding.

She shoved to her feet, stepping away from him, and his expression fell. "Jess, what's wrong?"

He rose, too, moving toward her, even as she put more distance between them. She needed the physical distance in order to put the emotional space back in place. "I... I think I'll go check on Pluto."

She scurried from the room, fighting to calm the rapid-fire beat of her heart. Maybe this was some strange mental or emotional backlash because of Henry's attack in her garage and the car accident.

Since Memorial Day and what she'd interpreted as an almost kiss, she'd spent an inordinate amount of time thinking about the odd pull she'd felt for him that night. Had recent events so rattled her composure and shaken her world that she was imagining romantic feelings toward *Gage*? She scoffed an ironic laugh and shook her head. Ludicrous. All the more reason to spend the summer away from Charlotte, regaining her equilibrium and inner strength.

She found Pluto in the bedroom, sniffing the bedspread and her suitcases. The cat glanced up as she walked in and meowed. Jessica sat on the edge of the bed and stroked her cat's beige fur and soaked in the solace of Pluto's rumbling purr. "Everything will be fine, Pluto. We just needed a break from the turmoil, a little distance from the bad man."

She didn't know if Pluto bought her line, but Jessica had to believe it, because the alternative was unacceptable.

* * *

"Okay," Matt said with a grin, lacing his fingers, inverting his joined hands and stretching his arms in front of him as if preparing to do a major task, "are you ready?"

Gage wiggled the fingers of both hands in a "bring it on" gesture. "Do it."

Jessica's ex-husband moved to his wife and daughter, where he motioned with his hand. "You've already met my wife, Cait, and our daughter, Erin, who'll be two this summer."

Gage offered Cait a small smile and salute of recognition.

"This is Cait's younger sister, Isla, and her husband, Evan." He pointed to a strawberry blond and the dark-haired man holding a toddler with reddish blond hair next to her. "Their daughter, CeCe, shares a birthday with Erin."

"Isla, Evan, CeCe," Gage repeated. "Nice to meet you."

"Grace and Neil Cameron, the parents-slash-grandparents of this brood—no, *clan*—" Matt said with a nod to an older woman in a wheelchair, whose white hair showed hints of red. "And the matriarch of the family, Flora Cameron, who prefers everyone call her Nanna."

"A pleasure, Mrs. Cameron," Gage said with a little bow to the frail older woman.

"The pleasure is mine, lad. But you heard Matt. Call me Nanna. Please." The woman's voice held a Scottish burr. She reached a gnarled hand for his, and he grasped it. Her grip was remarkably firm. "We Camerons don't stand on ceremony. *Ceud mìle fàilte.*"

"Um, pardon?" Gage asked.

"Nanna grew up in Scotland," Cait said, "and has done her best to teach us all a bit of Scots Gaelic. She wants to keep Scottish traditions and foods alive in the family. She said, a hundred thousand welcomes."

"Thank you, Nanna," Gage said with a flirtatious grin. "I look forward to learning more."

"Yeah," said a light-skinned Black teenager leaning against the door frame. He pulled a wry grin. "We Camerons have the best Burns Night celebration in town."

The family chuckled, and Matt said, "The jokester over there is Daryl, the youngest of the Cameron siblings, who was recently accepted to Westpoint and will leave for basic training this fall."

Gage blinked. "Westpoint? Wow! Congratulations!"

Daryl lifted a hand in thanks and greeting as he grinned.

The front door opened and another couple with a baby hustled in. The man, whose bright blue eyes and chiseled cheeks marked him a Cameron, called, "Sorry we're late. Ravi slept late, and we hated to wake him. What'd we miss?"

"Just introductions," Matt said, waving the couple in. "This is Brody and his wife, Anya."

The petite South Asian woman smiled broadly over the baby's head. "Hello. You must be Gage. Welcome! This is our son, Ravi Neil, named for his two grandfathers." She pried the baby's clutching hands from her shirt and turned him to face the room. Ravi's dark eyes took in the crowd. His face crumpled, and he quickly buried his head in his mother's chest again with a whine.

Grace rushed over to Anya, arms outstretched. "Oh, Ravi. Will you come to Grammy?"

The baby shrank away from his grandmother, his whimpers increasing.

"Sorry," Anya said, patting her son's back. "He's going through some rather significant separation anxiety. Only mommy will do these days."

Matt clapped his hands together once. "Let's see. Who'd I miss?"

"Where are the all the Turners?" Jessica asked.

"Right," Isla offered, "our sister Emma, her husband and their daughters are out of town for a speaking engagement and mini vacation in Washington, DC."

Gage nodded. "The oldest daughter is Fenn? Eric's friend?" He cast a glance to Jessica for confirmation. "The one who was kidnapped a couple years ago?"

"Yeah," Jessica said. "She and her parents founded S.T.O.P., which teaches sex trafficking awareness and prevention in high schools."

Gage's eyes widened. "Impressive." He turned to the family. "I'm so glad she was returned to the family safely. Jess told us about it when it happened. My sister, Tina, and I were praying hard for all of you."

"Thank you. We appreciated every bit of support we got during that time. And we're so proud of our girl Fenn. She's been so brave and come back so much stronger these past couple years."

"So that's everyone," Matt said, his chipper tone dispelling the more serious turn the conversation had taken. "Shall we eat?"

Grace laughed and waved everyone toward the dining room. "You heard the man. Supper is served. Daryl, come help pour drinks. Neil, show Gage where he can wash up."

As Gage followed Neil to the front bathroom, he admitted to a tug of jealousy. The large, multigenerational Cameron family, all living so near each other, seemed an ideal situation in an idyllic setting. No wonder Jessica, an only child whose mother had never been supportive, loved this place so much. And how could he compete?

The light banter and friendly debates around the dinner table were a welcome distraction for Jessica. She was heartened to see how well Gage got along with the family, as well, though why that seemed so important to her she didn't want to examine.

I just want him to feel comfortable here tonight.

The justification was enough to appease her conscience, and the hearty meal, replete with fresh vegetables from Grace's garden and the fluffiest biscuits she'd ever eaten, proved a balm, as well. Maybe there really was something to that old *comfort food* expression.

"First thing Monday morning, after I get Erin her breakfast," Cait said, casting Jessica side-glances while cutting up small bites of cantaloupe for Erin. "We can meet to go over the current occupancy list and check in/check out schedule for the cabins. And the electrician should be at the Juniper cabin around eight a.m. to wire the new addition, so if you'd let him in to start working?"

Jessica nodded. "Sounds good. Will do."

The conversation turned to Daryl's to-do list before he left for Westpoint, which the teen took in stride. Young man, really, Jessica thought. Eighteen was old enough to vote and join the military, and his broad shoulders, cut jawline and stubble-dusted cheeks bore little resemblance to the kid she'd first met four years ago. Surreptitiously, she studied Daryl anew. He was handsome. Obviously a good student if he'd been accepted at Westpoint. Funny, in a dry wit sort of way. She could well imagine Daryl breaking hearts all over the place in the years to come—although, she amended, he also seemed the sort who'd be careful not to toy with a girl's emotions. Grace Cameron would have taught him that for sure.

"Well, dinner was delicious. Thank you again, Grace," Gage said, wiping his mouth with his napkin and pulling her attention away from the Camerons' adopted son.

"Not so fast. We have dessert. A family favorite. You don't want to miss it," Grace said.

"Tempting, but I should be getting on the road back to Charlotte." He angled his head toward Jessica, adding in a low voice, "Unless you've changed your mind about me staying on your couch."

Jessica's stomach swooped at the thought of Gage leaving, even if she was surrounded by friends as kind and welcoming as the Cameron family. Gage had been her rock for these past weeks. At the accident scene. During those difficult and emotional visits to see Tina in the hospital. In those late-night texts when she felt overwhelmed. And he'd saved her life when Henry had left her to die in her garage. His reassuring presence at her bedside as she recovered from the terrifying incident meant more to her than she could express, maybe more than she wanted to admit.

"You're driving home at this hour?" Nanna asked.

"Well, yeah. That was the plan."

"All right. You can stay on my couch tonight and drive home tomorrow," Jessica blurted before she'd considered the implications of what she was saying.

Neil faced her and lifted an eyebrow. "As I recall, your cabin currently only has one bedroom and no couch in the den."

"Oh," she said, her cheeks heating as the weight of the family's inquisitive and speculating stares fell on her. "Right. Of course."

Why had she asked him to stay? She'd shown her vulnerability, her fear like a child who couldn't let go of her parent's hand on the first day of school.

"Mom and Dad have an extra room you're welcome to use," Isla volunteered, sending her mother a meaningful look. "Don't you, Mom?"

Gage chuckled uncomfortably and lifted a hand. "I couldn't impose."

"No imposition," Grace assured him. "You're more than welcome. In fact, I insist."

Turning to Jessica as if to consult her, Gage lifted his eyebrows in query. Was he asking her advice or permission? Her pulse thumped, and in return she merely gave him a shrug.

"I think y'all are missing the point," Daryl said, lifting his glass for a sip. "She asked him to stay *with her*."

A few of the younger Camerons tittered and grinned, and Grace gasped, "Daryl, for Pete's sake! Mind your manners." Then to Jessica and Gage, she said, "I apologize for my son's cheek."

Daryl grinned unrepentantly. "Just saying…"

Jessica, face flaming, chuckled awkwardly. "You're not wrong. That had been my intent, though not for the reason you're thinking." She gave Gage a side-glance. "But the Camerons' offer works, too. Keeps you off the dark road and traveling late."

Gage placed a hand on her shoulder and squeezed. In a playful voice, he added, "Gosh, Jess. If I didn't know better, I'd think you cared."

A laugh rose around the table, easing the awkward truth of the situation. She did care about Gage. More than she wanted to admit. He'd been a better friend than she'd imagined he was prior to the accident. Before, he'd just been Tina's big brother, someone fun and safe to flirt with, because neither of them was actually looking for a relationship. He'd always been just…there. Just… Gage. Now the simple weight of his hand on her shoulder sent a crackling awareness through her veins. Her body hummed like a struck tuning fork. Why, as she considered the idea of him being hours away in Charlotte for the next several weeks, did she suddenly sense an odd attraction to him? Was it real or a strange manifestation of the unwise reliance she'd formed this spring?

As the conversation at the table moved on, she pitched her voice low, so that only Gage could hear over the guffaws and giggles around the table, and leaned toward him. "Stay."

His expression sobered a bit, and he nodded once. When Cait finished asking her mother to pass the basket of rolls, Gage said, "All right, Grace. I accept, on the condition that you allow me to treat you, your husband and Flora—er, Nanna—to breakfast at Ma's Mountain Diner. Jessica tells me their waffles are not to be missed."

Daryl spread his hands and cocked his head. "Ahem?"

Cait swatted at the teenager. "Like you'll even be out of bed for breakfast."

"You're welcome, too, of course," Gage said, then met Jessica's eyes and lowered his volume. "As are you."

A strange ripple of something sweet and intimate flowed through her, as if he were whispering endearments during sex instead of inviting her to breakfast at a country diner. Jessica took a moment to quell the odd thrum in her belly before smiling and saying, "Thank you. That sounds nice. But be forewarned. I'm known for my appetite at breakfast."

"True story," Matt said from across the table, "I've seen her eat as much at breakfast as Eric when he was a teenager. It was impressive."

Gage's gray eyes twinkled as he grinned at her. "Intriguing. I look forward to seeing this appetite in action."

Jessica felt a heat rise in her cheeks along with a surge of pure pleasure. Dipping her chin, she bit the inside of her cheeks to hide the sappy smile that tugged her mouth.

Why was she acting so giddy and ridiculous? Sheesh! She was reacting like a goofball over breakfast with Gage. No, not the breakfast invitation per se, but—she swallowed hard—Gage himself. His attentive and flirtatious gaze. The sexy timbre of his voice. His playful teasing. Nothing she hadn't shared with him in years past, and yet...

She gave her head a subtle shake. When she thought she had her smitten-schoolgirl reaction under wraps, she raised her head, and her gaze immediately clashed with her ex-husband's inquisitive and suspicious stare. Matt cut his eyes to Gage and back again before raising his eyebrows as if to ask, "What's the story? I know something's up."

Jessica frowned and gave Matt a subtle and dismissive shake of her head. But her heart thumped like a trapped rabbit. If her feelings had been so transparent to Matt, had Gage noticed the flush in her cheeks, heard the nervous quaver in her voice, seen the twitch of her giddy grin?

Through dessert, she studiously avoided Matt's knowing gaze and worked to tamp down the disconcerting flutter that accompanied each interaction with Gage, whether hers or a Cameron's.

Dessert—a raspberry, oat and whipped cream confection the family claimed was a traditional Scottish treat called cranachan—passed in a blur for Jessica. She got lost in her own thoughts as she tried to sort out her strange reaction to Gage and her growing despondency at the thought of his leaving tomorrow.

After dinner, the family invited her and Gage to stay for a few rowdy and competitive rounds of Trivial Pursuit and Pictionary. The laughter and games served as a welcome distraction, but when the play wound down and Gage offered to walk her back to her cabin, the strange buzz of attraction returned.

You're just grateful for all the companionship and support he's offered you since the accident, she rationalized as they strolled across a grassy lawn twinkling with fireflies and moonlight.

"This place is beautiful. I can see why you would want to buy a share of it." Gage's quiet baritone voice cut into her musing.

A smile bloomed on her face. "Isn't it, though? And

each season brings a new kind of beauty. You should see the azaleas and rhododendrons in the spring. And in autumn, the hardwood trees are a breathtaking counterpoint to the Christmas trees on the hills." She paused and sighed contentedly. "But the main reason I invested in Cameron Glen isn't because it's so heavenly here. The Camerons have always been so good to me, and they welcomed Eric into their family so warmly, even before Matt married Cait, that I was determined to repay their kindness. So when they needed to raise a bit of cash and divide the ownership to protect the property from poaching developers, I was all in." She slapped at a mosquito and laughed. "Ow. Stupid biters are the serpents in this paradise."

He gave a soft, humored grunt and fanned away a bug in his own face. "They are ubiquitous, huh?"

She elbowed him and chuckled. "Well, listen to you using a ten-dollar word."

"Excuse me," he returned, his tone playfully insulted, "which of us scored higher on the SAT in high school?"

"What! Good grief, who remembers that? I can't even remember what I made, much less you."

She crowded closer to him to avoid a rut in the ground, and he caught her elbow, steadying her as she stumbled a bit over the uneven ground. His touch fired fresh sparks inside her.

"I remember, because I was psyched to have done as well as I did, considering my grades didn't compete with yours or Tina's straight A's."

"So competitive!" Jessica shook her head. "But we established that well enough during Pictionary tonight, huh? Honestly, I thought you were going to burst a vein getting Cait and Matt to see a bird in the mess of squiggles you drew."

"Touché." His low chuckle rumbled from his throat and resounded like a pleasant thrum in her blood. "A guy doesn't play sports most of his life and not develop a competitive streak."

Dang it, what was wrong with her? Harboring any kind of ill-conceived attraction to Gage—Tina's brother, for crying out loud!—was a recipe for disappointment and future awkwardness. She needed Gage, the yearslong friend, the man sharing the same grief over Tina's injuries and slow recovery, her sounding board and support during this difficult time, far more than she needed a boyfriend or a lover.

Lover? Gadzooks! She really was down the rabbit hole.

She quivered deep in her core and freed her arm from his steadying grasp. Surely a few weeks' distance and calm here at Cameron Glen was all she needed to get herself in order and remind her libido that Gage was her friend and nothing more. That he couldn't be anything more without shaking the foundation she'd built her friendship to Tina on. That she had no desire for a man, especially a serial dater like Gage, in her life.

A gentle breeze stirred, carrying the scent of roses from the flower bed beside one of the cabins they were passing. Jessica inhaled deeply and held the sweet scent in her nose for a moment before letting it out. With each passing tranquil moment and lighthearted hour spent with the Camerons, she became more convinced that taking refuge at Cameron Glen had been the right move. Even if she would miss Gage.

The tag-on thought pierced her chest, and a despondent hum of resignation slipped from her, unbidden.

"Something wrong?" he asked.

Only that I've grown too attached to you.

She shook her head as the gravel of the driveway to her cabin crunched under her feet. "Just tired, I guess. So forgive me if I don't invite you in?"

"No problem. Sleep well, and I'll be around to get you for breakfast at—" He hesitated and ducked his head a little as he eyed her speculatively. "Seven a.m. too early for you?"

"Most days it's not. Though I'm not saying I *like* getting up before eight."

He chuckled as they reached the small porch where rocking chairs were positioned for the best views of the nearby ridge of the Smoky Mountains. "Then we'll make it eight…or even eight thirty."

She keyed open the cabin door and faced him. "No, I have a feeling Grace and Neil are early risers. Cait said her parents like to be up at dawn to work in their garden and walk the property before the day heats up. Seven is fine."

He bobbed his chin once in agreement, and in the dim porch light, she saw his gaze shift to something behind her. Before she could turn, his hand reached out, jutting past her ear as he closed his hand around…something. She gasped quietly, startled.

He brought his hand back in front of her chin and opened it slowly to reveal a blinking firefly. "Make a wish."

"You caught it. You make a wish."

His expression turned serious as if contemplating a

difficult math equation instead of a childhood super-stition. Then, as the small lightning bug flew away, he leaned close and kissed her lightly on her mouth.

She stilled, blinked at him, her body humming like the night frogs singing in the trees and water. "Was that your wish?"

She hoped her tone sounded light and amused rather than stunned. Or choked by an onslaught of desire…

The corner of his mouth twitched as he took a step back from her. "Maybe."

"Um." She curled her lips in, pressing her hand to her mouth and undecided whether she was savoring the tin-gle left by his kiss or trying to purge the lingering mem-ory of it. Furrowing her brow, she whispered, "Gage, I don't think…"

He cleared his throat, and his expression darkened. "Don't. I…apologize. I guess I got caught up in the al-lure of the setting, the moonlight. The romance of this place. It…" He exhaled harshly. "It won't happen again." He took another step back before turning and hurrying off the porch. "Good night, Jess."

She opened her mouth to call him back or, at least, return his parting wish, but no sound came out.

It won't happen again.

Was that what she wanted…or what she feared?

Chapter 11

Hellfire. Why had he kissed her like that?

Gage gritted his back teeth as he walked back up the hill to the elder Camerons' house, his gut churning. The startled look on Jessica's face had been a cold slap of reality. Whatever else had changed in the past three months since the accident, her feelings for him clearly had not.

"Idiot," he muttered, watching the unfamiliar road at his feet for ruts as he stewed.

"I hope you don't mean me."

Gage jerked his head up to see Matt and Cait walking toward him, their sleeping toddler on Matt's shoulder. "Oh, no. Of course not. I'm the idiot."

"Why is that? I thought you were pretty darn smart at Trivial Pursuit tonight," Cait replied, grinning.

Gage hesitated, and in the silence, Matt asked, "Because you kissed Jessica?"

"Uh—" Gage sputter-coughed.

Cait elbowed her husband and gave him a *"Really?"* look.

"So…you saw that?" Gage plowed fingers through his hair and frowned.

"We weren't spying," Cait said, "But the porch light was on, and, well…"

Gage sighed and nodded. "Yeah. That's why."

"Why is kissing her such a bad thing?" Cait asked. "You two clearly have chemistry. That was easy enough to see tonight."

Gage jolted. "It was? I—"

Cait tipped her head. "Am I wrong?"

Grunting, he shoved his hands in the pockets of his jeans. "I don't know. Apparently, I misread some signals. Jess looked at me like I had two heads just now when I kissed her. I may have just ruined twentysomething years of a perfectly good casual friendship."

"Well…" Cait wrinkled her nose sympathetically. "You don't know that. Maybe you just caught her off guard."

"Oh, I did that at a minimum." He dragged a hand down his face, knowing the memory of the surprise on Jessica's face would haunt him well beyond tonight. Guilt kicked him. "Me mucking up things with Jessica is the last thing she needs right now. Since the accident, she's been in turmoil. She's had so much to deal with, beyond Sara's death and Holly and Tina being in the hospital. I was, kind of by default, her main support."

He glanced up at Matt and Cait, adding quickly, "Not that you haven't been kind and a good sounding board for her, but…I was local. I was who she called at night when things felt overwhelming. I guess I was kinda a substitute for Tina."

"Yeah," Matt said. "She mentioned how much you've helped her out. That you went to Sara's funeral with her. She has appreciated everything you've done." Matt shifted his daughter slightly in his arms, angling a look at her when the little girl stirred. Once Erin quieted again, he asked, "When you say she's had so much to deal with beyond Sara's death and her other two friends in the hospital, you mean her stalker?"

Gage raised his chin, narrowing a startled look on Matt. "Yeah. I knew she'd told you about the guy, but I wasn't sure how she framed it. She's…a little bit in denial about how dangerous this guy might be, even after the incident in her garage. I keep offering to stay with her. You know, an added layer of protection, but she's so stubborn, so determined to go it alone."

Cait and Matt exchanged a quick look, and Matt asked, "How dangerous is this guy?"

Twisting his mouth, Gage debated how much he could share. Henry Blythe's behavior, the threats he'd made, was Jessica's story to tell. But if Jessica was going to be safe this summer, she needed the people around her to be aware of everything Detective Macnally had said.

When he continued debating, Matt's expression hardened, and he took a step closer. "Gage, tell me. This is my son's mother we're talking about."

Gage tipped his head back and stared up at the stars, the winking fireflies, the yellow moon that had slipped behind a thin cloud. What the hell? Jessica was already mad at him for kissing her. If she wanted to be ticked off about his sharing the truth of her situation, so be it. The bottom line was, whether she liked it or not, Jessica needed every bit of protection possible.

Returning his gaze to Matt, he said, "All right. And for the record, Eric doesn't know about the stalker. Jess only told him a fuller truth about the car accident a couple weeks ago. About Sara's death. Tina and Holly in the hospital. She didn't want him worried about her or distracted from his class work. She pretended she was fine while Eric was home before summer semester started."

"Yeah. She asked me not to tell him the whole truth, but Eric's no fool. He sensed something was up. He's told me his mom seemed tense. Had been unusually tight-lipped about her life. Not calling as often as she normally would. I think he deserves to know what's happening."

"What is happening with Jess, beyond the mess we already know?" Cait asked and grunted, "Which is bad enough."

Gage scuffed his shoe on the asphalt road, kicking at a pine cone. He capsulized the confrontation in her garage and how Henry had left her unconscious on the floor. "She breathed carbon monoxide for a good while before I found her."

Cait gasped.

Matt scowled. "How badly did he hurt her?"

"Cracked rib, goose egg on her head. I don't think killing her was his intent. But by the time I found her—and it was a miracle I had reason to go by her house looking for her—she'd already breathed a great deal of carbon monoxide. She spent a day and a half in the hospital, but the doctors don't think she has any long-term damage."

"Good Lord!" Cait pressed a hand to her mouth, clearly stunned. "Why wouldn't she have told us this? Doesn't she know how much we care about her?"

"That's probably why," Matt said, turning to his wife. "Jessica has never liked to accept help from anyone and hates to think she's inconvenienced or burdened anyone. During the times I was deployed overseas, she took on single parenting like a lone wolf. She refused help from neighbors and denied herself time off for self-care. It's honestly pretty amazing that she agreed to stay here this summer."

"If she didn't feel she was contributing by working in the office and assisting with contractors on the cabin renovations, I doubt she would have," Gage said. He tucked his hands in his pockets and puffed out his cheeks as he exhaled. "So…do me a favor and keep an eye on Jessica this summer."

"Of course. Definitely," Matt said.

"I plan to check in on her regularly. My twenty-four on, forty-eight off schedule at the fire station will allow me to pop over now and then. I offered to stay full-time, but she refused. Of course." He grimaced. "And now I've gone and thrown a monkey wrench in things by impulsively kissing her." He huffed. "What was I thinking?"

Cait angled her head and grinned. "Maybe that she's more than a friend to you?"

Gage grunted softly and glanced away. "Unfortunately, it's not mutual."

"I was watching her with you tonight, man," Matt said. "I know my ex-wife. And…I wouldn't be so sure it's not mutual."

Jessica settled easily into a new routine at Cameron Glen. The mountain air, the change of scenery, the ample company of loving friends all provided a balm to her tattered soul. Pluto, too, seemed thrilled about the change of venue, chattering through the window at the chipmunks, bunnies and ducks that passed the cabin windows at various times throughout the day. When her need for her own car became obvious, she and Gage schemed a way for him to get it to her. Jessica hired a wrecking company to haul her car from her garage, as if it were in poor repair, and meet her and Cait at a rest stop along the interstate, after which she drove it the rest of the way to Cameron Glen.

As the late June days passed and July arrived, she spent more time conversing with Cait and her sisters the way she used to with her posse. Through those discussions, she began to gain some clarity on some matters regarding Eric, Henry…and Gage.

Eric, they reminded her, was an adult who didn't need to be shielded from the ugliness of life. She'd raised a strong, resilient and intelligent son who would only resent being kept in the dark.

Henry, they warned, wasn't likely to give up and go away. The Cameron women all agreed with Detective Macnally that her stalker's obsession with Jessica could easily become more volatile. They kindly suggested that now was not the time to put her pride in front of her safety. She needed extra protection, even at Cameron Glen. And as long as he was volunteering…

Gage, the Cameron ladies agreed, was the perfect candidate to protect her. And, oh, by the way, why wasn't she doing something about that hot firefighter who clearly adored her?

At night in her bed, in quiet hours strolling the retreat property, and when she should have been reconciling financial books at the rental office, Jessica found herself thinking about Gage. She thought about what should have been an innocent, playful firefly kiss, about the strange new stir of feelings he evoked, about the comfort their friendship had given her through the years.

And about the risk of losing that friendship if the delicate balance between friends and lovers was disturbed.

The only thing she could say for sure was that she missed Gage. Phone calls, texts, even Facetime didn't take the place of seeing him in person, having his steadying presence beside her when she visited Tina, being close enough to smell the crisp combination of soap, pine and coffee that clung to him, having him take her hand or squeeze her shoulder at the end of a long day.

So when he asked if he could come stay with her over the weekend in mid-July, she eagerly accepted. She even found an unused single bed mattress that she dragged to the Juniper cabin for him to sleep on in the living room, rather than have him bunk with the senior Camerons again. She wanted him near, wanted their privacy, wanted…

With a subtle shake of her head, she dismissed the rest of that thought unfinished. It was enough that Gage was coming to visit, to bring news of Tina, to fill the lonely place inside her that only he could fill. She could examine the ramifications of that curious dynamic later.

Henry, wearing a new disguise today, lurked near the janitor's closet watching Gage Coleman talk to his sister's doctor in the hospital corridor. The usual conversation. The sister was making small improvements. Full recovery would take time. So grateful to the medical team for all they'd done. Yada yada.

Big deal. Who cared? What was more important to Henry was that he hadn't seen Jessie visit her convalescing friend since late June. Neither had he seen any activity at her house for the past three and a half weeks.

Whenever he'd called her office, he'd been put on hold before the receptionist asked to take a message. Clearly something was up. Not knowing what that something was infuriated Henry. The idea that Jessie had gone MIA made him restless. He'd been so careful to avoid detection before, but he needed a plan to find Jessie.

He was stewing over what action he needed to take when Coleman said something that caught Henry's attention.

"I'll be out of town this weekend visiting a friend. Please ask the nurses to call if anything at all changes with Tina's condition. They have my number."

Visiting a friend out of town? Was it possible Coleman knew where Jessie was? Could the friend he was seeing be Jessie, holed up somewhere hiding? He decided immediately that he couldn't let this opportunity to possibly track Jessie down pass. When Coleman strode toward the elevator, Henry hit the stairs and reached the ground floor before Coleman did. He kept the other man in sight as he hurried to his truck, then tailed Coleman out of the parking lot. He kept a good distance between them, not wanting to tip off Jessie's friend. When Coleman hit the interstate headed west, Henry followed. A tingling sense told him he'd caught Jessie's scent again.

The hunt was back on.

Chapter 12

When Gage arrived at the Juniper cabin that afternoon, Jessica rushed out to greet him and flung herself into his arms for a long, tight hug. Neither of them said anything for long moments. They only broke apart to go inside when the voices of a family staying in another cabin wafted to them from the road. Jessica stepped back from Gage and gave the strolling family an awkward wave and greeting.

Gage picked up the duffel bag he'd dropped at their feet for the embrace and cleared his throat. "I've missed you, Jess. More than I thought I would."

"Same here," she admitted, ducking her chin so he couldn't see the extent of that reality in her eyes. Pivoting on her toes, she hitched her head toward the cabin. "I hope you're hungry. I've got lasagna in the oven and all the fixings in progress. Salad, garlic bread, and your favorite pie for dessert."

"Wow. That sounds terrific. Is it my birthday?" He scrunched his nose as if trying to remember. "No…that's not for a couple months. So, what's the occasion?"

She held the screen door for him as he carried his bag inside. "Just because I had the time to cook. And I wanted to thank you for everything you've done for me these past months."

He shook his head. "Not necessary." He paused when he stepped inside to inhale deeply. "Dang. That smells divine, Jess."

She refused his offer of assistance in the kitchen, directing him to get comfortable and watch whatever ball game or movie rerun he wanted while she put the pie in the oven.

The last minutes of the lasagna's cook time were spent relaxing together, laughing, sharing a bottle of pinot noir and enjoying a moment to just *be*. Gage caught her up on Tina's condition and a morsel of surprise good news.

"I ran into Holly and her parents in the hall outside Tina's room a couple of days ago."

"Holly? She's awake? Walking?"

Gage nodded and grinned. "Walking slowly. Able to recognize me. She asked about you. Her mother shut that down pretty quick, and after we went our separate ways, her father stopped me to tell me Holly has no recollection of the accident. Remembers nothing after leaving the restaurant. They plan to leave it that way and want your word you won't say anything to her."

Jessica goggled at him. "That's a horrible idea! She's going to remember at some point. I won't lie to her!" She huffed and balled her fists. "What did they tell her happened?"

"Just that she was in a car accident. No details about who else was involved or how it happened."

"She must feel abandoned by her friends. They won't let me see her, Tina can't and Sara's..." Her sigh was ragged and frustrated. "I have to fix that. When I get home, I have to talk to her parents again, convince them to let me see Holly. I know what it's like to feel abandoned by someone you love."

Gage drew her into his arms and held her close. He kissed her forehead and stroked a hand on her arm. The cuddle was far more intimate than she'd have been comfortable with even a few weeks ago, but somehow, now it seemed...right. *Because we're better friends.*

Even as she justified the nearness, the touches, a nagging voice whispered that she wanted more. This wasn't the Gage she'd known since high school. Not the guy who'd crashed her sleepovers with Tina and made fart noises with his armpit to drive them nuts.

This was the courageous firefighter who entered burning houses, who'd saved her from the poisonous gas in her garage, who'd been her ride-or-die since the accident. Yeah, they had grown closer as they coped with trauma and grief. Nothing wrong with that. And she savored his affection, his nearness enough to silence the jangling in her mind that told her to back off. He'd be leaving for Charlotte again soon, and she wanted the comfort of his body beside her, his soft laugh tripping down her spine, his enticing caress on her skin.

Only when the jarring buzz of the oven timer sounded did she drag herself away from him. Her body hummed pleasantly as she returned to the kitchen and set the strawberry pie and lasagna on the counter to cool. She turned off the oven and put the garlic bread in to warm in the residual heat. As she carried the salad to the table, she called, "Will you pour the wine, Gage? Everything else is just about done."

He helped her set the table and serve plates, then

tuned the television to an all-music channel that played soft rock. Gage paused as he headed into the dining room, a strange look on his face.

"Gage? Is something wrong?" Jessica crossed the room to him, angling her head in query.

He chuckled wryly. "No. I just realized what song this is." He aimed a finger toward the TV.

She glanced at the screen and read, "She's All I Ever Had" by Ricky Martin. "Do you remember dancing to it at my senior prom?"

"Um." She tried to think back. His senior prom would have been her junior year, and she'd gone to prom with... Mark Shane. "I remember one dance with you, but not the song." She wrinkled her nose. "I'm surprised you remember. You're sure it was this song?"

He nodded and took her hand, tugged her into his arms and began to sway. "Positive."

She swayed absently with him as she tuned her ear to the poignant words and melody, letting the music pull at her emotions, soften her mood. It felt natural to melt against Gage and move slowly as he rocked her gently. While she was surprised Gage would remember something as trivial as the song they'd danced to so many years ago, she found it sweet. She'd rarely seen this sentimental side of Gage.

She canted back in his arms to tell him such, but the words stuck in her throat when she saw his expression. The desire in his eyes puddled inside Jessica, leaving her breathless and her heartbeat scampering. She thought back to the grazing kiss he'd given her the night she'd arrived at Cameron Glen, excusing it as a firefly wish.

The impulse to kiss Gage now, not just a quick brush

of lips but a true kiss, a deep and passionate kiss, blind-sided her. Before she could overanalyze the yearning, she stood on tiptoes and pressed her mouth to his.

In response, Gage tightened his hold on her with one arm and cradled the back of her head with his other as his lips drew greedily on hers. The cabin fell away, the changing song on the television faded and only that moment between them existed. Raw and real and earthshaking.

Relationship-altering.

Some zap of reality restarted her brain from whatever short circuit had temporarily overcome her. Tearing her mouth from his, she ducked her chin and mumbled, "Good grief. I'm sorry. I don't know what came over me."

A groan that sounded almost angry rumbled from Gage's chest, and she peered up at him, unsure what she'd find in his expression.

His jaw tightened, and his gray eyes pierced to her core. "Don't apologize. And please, Jess, don't retreat from me again."

She blinked. "Retreat?"

"Like you did on Memorial Day and the day I brought you here to Cameron Glen. I know you felt the pull between us both of those times, and I saw you shut it down and walk away from it."

She wiggled free of his embrace, putting distance between them so she could think. Facing him again, she shook her head. "I don't know what you mean," she lied.

Her pulse beat in her ears, a panicked whooshing, as she scrambled for a way to right the situation, to grab back the sure footing she'd had with Gage just five minutes earlier. If things changed, if she lost his friendship, where would she be? The notion terrified her.

He took a step forward, holding a hand out to her. "Can you honestly tell me that over these past few weeks you haven't thought about kissing me? What it would be like to make love to me?"

Jessica stilled, pinned by his bright, penetrating eyes, while inside her emotions were in turmoil, her thoughts scrambling, her pulse a living creature she could feel kicking in her veins. "Are you saying you have?"

He chuffed a soft laugh. "Damn right. I'd have thought that was obvious." His expression sobered as he took another step toward her. "Have I messed this up? Read things wrong? I was under the impression that you'd begun to feel the same way. Isn't that why you just kissed me?"

Her body hummed as he took one more step toward her, moving close enough for her to feel the heat of his body around her, like a blanket he'd drape over her shoulders. "I feel…something. I can't define it, but—" *Can't or won't?* a whisper in her head asked.

He brushed her hair off her cheek, his fingertips grazing her face and shattering her train of thought. With a tremulous exhale, she leaned into his hand, let him cup her chin, smooth his thumb along her jaw. His gentle caress lulled her, made tiny sparks crackle in her core. How easy it would be to give herself over to the primal call howling in her soul. Need clawed at her, battling reason and practicality and…fear.

"But?" he prompted, his voice low and intimate.

Firming her resolve, she rasped, "But it doesn't matter. I can't."

"Why can't you?" he asked, his tone patient.

"It wouldn't be smart. I can *want* any number of

things, but that doesn't mean I can have them. Following my impulses or whims would only give me a few moments of pleasure in the big picture."

"Is that such a terrible thing? Aren't you allowed to do what you want instead of what your brain says you should all the time? Isn't it possible that those nudges toward spontaneity are your subconscious or a higher power showing you the right path?"

She moaned her frustration. "My mother was spontaneous and flighty and undisciplined, and it ruined her. She had a string of bad, sometimes abusive relationships and died penniless and addicted to painkillers."

"I'm aware. But you are not your mother."

She swallowed hard, feeling the lump that rose in her throat. Taking a beat, she lifted her chin, hoping to manifest the confidence she needed to push her temptation away. "I will not go down the slippery slope of momentary pleasure."

"What if the pleasure wasn't momentary? What if that inner voice you're shouting down is trying to lead you to a lasting happiness?" Gage caught her closer, wrapping his arms around her waist.

She put her hands on his chest, meaning to push away, but somehow curling her fingers in the soft flannel of his shirt. She was having more and more difficulty sorting her reason from her yearning, finding the practical in the maelstrom of heady longing sucking at her, making her tremble.

"For once, let yourself have a moment that's yours. Follow your heart," he whispered, the pinot noir–scented tickle of his breath taunting her. "Give yourself a chance to savor, like you would a fine wine or decadent chocolate."

Just once…

A moment to treasure…

As he ducked his head to kiss her, she closed her eyes and let herself just…*feel*. No thinking. No analyzing. No second-guessing or projecting what might happen tomorrow or next week if she…just. Let. Go.

Henry emerged from the bramble-dense woods and crept along in the shadow line of the trees until he spotted Coleman's pickup truck. *Bingo.* He had Jessie.

Henry curled up a corner of his mouth in a gloating smile. *Thank you, Mr. Coleman, for your services. I'll take it from here.*

After Coleman had turned in at Cameron Glen, Henry had continued into the small town of Valley Haven to do a bit of research. He'd found a pamphlet about the vacation rentals at Cameron Glen and studied the map of the property. He asked questions about the rental cabins at the gas station as he filled his tank and learned a bit about the family, the property and the security measures in place.

After getting some food at a local diner, he'd headed back toward Cameron Glen and parked on the side of the road. He'd made his way onto the rental property on foot, then scanned the property around the cabins, making sure no one was around, taking a moonlit stroll. He hadn't come this far just to have some nosy bystander report his presence or interfere with his plans.

All clear.

Sprinting to the back wall of the cabin, he sidestepped

around a pile of scrap lumber and other construction debris and moved to the nearest window. Peering inside, he discovered what was apparently the bedroom Jessica was using, though the lights were out and he couldn't make out much detail. Light illuminated the hall outside the bedroom like a beacon leading him to the next room. Easing along the cabin's outer wall, careful not to kick any construction trash or step on anything sharp, Henry moved around the corner to the next window. The lit window gave him a golden view into the den where he found Jessie and Coleman—*kissing*.

Rage flashed through Henry like a windswept wildfire. The chick at the hospital had lied to him. Coleman wasn't just a family friend to Jessie, he was her *lover*. The shock of the revelation left him shaking, seething. A sense of betrayal and disgust pounded in his skull. And just that fast, his plan changed.

He patted his jacket pocket, glad now that he'd brought his Glock. Forget scaring Jessie. If he was going to convince Jessie they belonged together, job number one was eliminating the competition. Permanently.

But not here. Not now. Too public. He needed to get Gage Coleman somewhere remote where he could leave all evidence of Jessica's lover behind. He ground his back teeth together and weighed his choices. Could he disable the guy and drag him into the woods? No. Even if he thought he could move the probably almost-two-hundred-pound man, the woods were still too near the cabins. The rotting body would be found too soon.

Henry's gaze shifted to Jessica's car, parked next to Coleman's truck. And a plan took root.

Chapter 13

The warmth of Gage's lips was a siren call, luring Jessica deeper, nearer. And like a sailor ignoring the imminent danger of a rocky shore and caught in Gage's thrall, she canted forward and let her body go slack. She melted into him, circling his shoulders with her arms. His mouth tested hers, a tentative touch, then parted slightly as he drew on her more deeply.

A sweetness like thick honey flowed through her, making her head, her limbs feel languid, sated…impatient. Drawing a shaky breath, Jessica sealed her lips against his, capturing his mouth and opening to him.

Gage smoothed his hands up her back, burying his fingers into her hair, then trailing his fingers back down her spine to start again. Savoring the intoxicating taste of his kiss and the heady magic of his exploring hands, Jessica lost herself, letting the rush of pleasure blot out everything except this man, this place, this exquisite kiss.

His fingers cupped and squeezed the curve of her bottom, pushed her hips forward, a silent invitation. Hungry, untamed noises rumbled from him, and she felt the vibration from his chest against her own. She freed several buttons on his shirt and slipped her hands inside to feel his hot skin against her palms. He answered by un-tucking her blouse from her shorts and dipping his fin-gers under her waistband to massage the sensitive skin at the small of her back.

When she let her head fall backward, exposing the tender arch of her throat to him, he moved his kiss to the pulse point there. With a tiny nip of his teeth, he stirred a fresh surge of electricity from her core, charging her need, amplifying her pleasure. A small moan escaped her, and he answered with his own feral growl. With tiny backward steps, he walked them toward the new couch, the closest horizontal surface besides the hardwood floor.

Her hands continued roaming across his muscles, tug-ging at buttons, rumpling his hair as she baby-stepped with him. She caught his face between her hands, tak-ing his mouth again in a savage kiss, and tugging on his bottom lips with her teeth.

"Oh, Jessica…" he mumbled, his tone thick with de-sire, "finally. *Finally.*" He slanted his mouth to kiss her deeply, then paused long enough to yank his shirt over his head without unfastening the last several buttons. "I have wanted this, wanted *you* for so long. So many, *many* years…"

His words, like a shard of ice, sliced through the muzzy heat of her passion. A jolt of sobriety snatched her back from the edge of the dangerous cliff where she teetered. Every muscle inside her tensed as she flinched back from him, replaying his words in her head. Surely she misun-derstood. Perhaps in her rush to slake her hunger she'd imagined his confession.

"Jess?" Gage said, his brow beetling. "What's wrong?"

"Wh-what did you just say?"

Gage straightened his spine, and a smile split his face as he met her eyes. "I said, I've wanted you for a very long time. And I have. But now…" His smile brightened, and he reached to draw her close again.

But Jessica jerked away, stumbling back a step. Two.

Her pulse, thrumming with desire a moment ago, now thudded heavily in her skull—dissonant gongs reverberating and filling her head with a nerve-splitting cacophony.

Gage's smile fell. "That bothers you?"

She struggled for a breath, seeing the past decades she'd spent as Tina's best friend and in Gage's orbit in a whole new light. Their entire past relationship had been a lie? "How long? Since…when?"

"I don't know exactly. I've always thought you were beautiful." He reached for her again, and she knocked his hand away.

Her head spun. Her chest prickled, then her neck, as the heat of anger climbed higher and settled on her cheeks. "You've…been living a *lie* with me the whole time I've known you?"

"Not a lie. That's harsh. Look, don't overreact—"

She barked a hard laugh. "Whoa! Do *not* tell me how to feel about this!"

He held up a hand, wincing with apology. "Sorry. I didn't mean—"

"Does Tina know?"

"I…don't know." His frown said he knew he'd messed up and was looking for a way to backpedal. "I never—"

Jessica's temples throbbed as one new and humiliating thought tumbled after another. Hadn't she sworn, after seeing her mother live with the carnage of liars and their

lies, that she'd never accept dishonesty in her own relationships? How was it possible a man she'd thought dependable, had welcomed in her closest social circle, had been
hiding secrets from her? Was she that bad a judge of character? Could she not trust her own perceptions of men?

Gage exhaled heavily and spread his palms in appeal.
"Can we just…take a minute. Take a breath before we
say or do something that we'll regret."

"You mean like, 'Oh, by the way, I've spent the last
twenty-three years pretending to be someone I'm not'?"
she said sourly.

"I thought I was doing the right thing keeping it to
myself," he returned with just as much salt.

"Lying is never the right choice."

He blew out a frustrated breath and furrowed his brow.
"I never lied to you, Jess!"

"Oh, really? Isn't omission its own kind of lie?"

"I— Not in my book. Not when the truth would have
caused problems."

"Problems? Ya think?" She growled and curled her fingers in her hair. Her thoughts were too scrambled and poisoned with a brew of emotions to sort out what was what.

Spinning on her heel, she stomped to the cabin door
and snatched her keys from the side table.

"Jess, where are you going?" A note of concern sharpened his tone.

"I don't know. I need air. I need…space." Without
looking back, she rushed from the cabin and scurried to
her car. The driver's door was unlocked, and she climbed
behind the wheel. Her hand shook as she tried several
times to get the key in the ignition.

Movement and a loud knock on the side window sent

a jolt of adrenaline through her. She yelped and cut a startled look to Gage.

He opened the driver's door and frowned at her. "Jess, come back inside. Please. We'll talk and—"

"No. I clearly can't think straight around you. Just—" She put a hand in the center of his chest and pushed him back. Closed the door. Turned the key in the ignition. The engine rumbled to life.

When he tried to open the door again, she gripped the handle and dragged it back. "No, Gage. I need some time by myself. Please!"

Still unaccustomed to her new car, she squinted in the dark to find the door lock button on the armrest. Instead, she hit the window open button. The mirror adjustment.

The passenger door opened before she found the door lock, and Gage climbed in the front seat with her. "Look, I'm not sure what just happened or what upset you, but can we please just go inside and talk?"

Tears puddled in her eyes, and she shook her head. "I'm not sure I can explain it. I…I just…need to get away for a bit."

He sighed. "Jess, running away isn't the answer. Besides, you're not in a good state of mind to be driving."

She opened her mouth to argue when a strange clicking sound came from the behind her.

"Actually, driving is exactly what you should do now," a cold male voice said.

As she and Gage whipped their heads toward the back seat, Henry snaked his arm around Gage's throat. He drew his grip so tight across Gage's neck that her friend gasped for breath. Pinning a dark glare on Jessica, Henry shoved a gun to the base of Gage's skull. "Drive us away from here, now, or pretty boy lover gets a bullet in the head."

Chapter 14

Icy fear slithered through Jessica. For a fleeting moment, she thought of opening the car door and running. But doing so would mean abandoning Gage to a madman with a gun and an agenda. Meanwhile, in the back of her brain, the message of safety videos she'd seen at college scrolled through her mind. *Never let an attacker take you to a second location. If you get in a car with a kidnapper you are as good as dead.*

Bile rose from her gut, hot and bitter, as her brain scrambled for what to do.

Clawing at Henry's arm, fighting for air, Gage flung his head backward. But Henry anticipated the move and dodged the blow. "Nice try, Coleman, but I wasn't born yesterday." Angling the gun, he poked it at Jessica. "Why aren't we moving yet? Drive!"

Panic flooded her gut, and without a better idea, she put her car in gear and backed out of the short gravel driveway. Once on the narrow road leading out of Cameron Glen, they passed other vacation cabins where guests were cozied in for the night. Then they approached the small farmhouse that was Isla and Evan's home. Her gaze angled toward the yellow glow of their front porch light, and she calculated. If she pulled in their driveway, if she blasted the car horn, if she—

"Be smart here, Jessie," Henry growled. "If you rouse your friends out of their house, I'll shoot them the minute they step on their front porch."

Was he serious? Would Henry really shoot innocents because of his obsession with her? Could she really presume he was bluffing, and risk her friends' lives?

Gage was gasping louder, clearly desperate for air, and he finally got his head turned enough that he could duck his chin behind Henry's arm. As Jessica rolled slowly past Isla's and toward the property exit, Gage sank his teeth into Henry's arm.

With a roar of pain, Henry jerked his arm away.

Gage folded forward, coughing and sucking in deep breaths, but before he could right himself and make any defensive move, Henry retaliated.

Slamming the butt of the gun down on the back of Gage's head, he snarled. "You sonofabitch! I should kill you now and be done with it!"

"No!" Jessica screamed, stopping the car and reaching for Gage. He lay slumped against the passenger door, not moving. Horror slithered through her, and tears dripped onto her cheeks.

"Drive!" Henry roared. "Or there's more for him where that came from."

Anger and fear curled together in her belly, vying for top spot. She wrenched around to glare at Henry and shove a finger in his face. "Don't you touch him! Your beef, your perverted fascination is with me. Leave him out of it!"

"I wish I could, darlin'," he said, "but he became a

part of this the minute he put his hands on you. I saw you two kissing and groping each other like dogs in heat. So obviously I have to get rid of him if you and I are going to move forward."

The contents of her stomach curdled. She wanted to argue the fact that she'd never have anything to do with Henry, but riling him further while he held a gun didn't seem advisable.

Gage still hadn't moved. The idea that he could be dead sliced painfully through her chest. She lifted a hand toward him again, and Henry made a hissing noise through his teeth as he waved the black gun at her.

"Just…let me see if he's breathing. Please?"

Henry's jaw clenched, and he grabbed Gage by the hair and pulled his head back. Jessica gasped in dismay at the rough treatment, but held her hand under Gage's nose until she felt the soft tickle of his breath. She gripped his wrist, as much taking solace from the connection as looking for a pulse.

"That's enough." Henry jabbed the gun at her again. "Go!"

"Which way?"

"Which way is town?" he asked.

"Right."

"Then go left. Take us out into the boonies, the mountains. The farther from people the better."

Quaking inside, Jessica pulled the car onto the highway. She sent up a silent prayer that she could figure out an escape, some means to rescue herself and Gage. Before it was too late.

Henry grew silent as she drove, sitting behind her with the gun aimed at Gage's head. The clear message was if she tried anything that didn't align with his plans, Gage would pay the price. When a bluish glow filled the dark car, she looked in the rearview mirror to watch Henry. With one hand, Henry was flicking through screens and scrolling on his phone. What in the…? Did he really think the middle of a kidnapping was the best time to check his email?

Could she use this moment of his distraction to her advantage? Maybe. But how? Drive the car off the road into a tree or sign post? If they'd been closer to Valley Haven or another town, maybe. But not knowing how far they were from civilization, how soon another vehicle might come by, she decided stranding herself and Gage on the side of the road, miles from help, with an enraged Henry wasn't a good idea. How far had they come?

Time felt elastic, both stretching out, tense and fragile, and retracting as the miles between them and Cameron Glen rolled on. She hadn't paid attention to road signs at first, preoccupied with Gage's condition and Henry's gun. She was all too aware that it had been her fit of anger and confusion that had sent her bumbling outside to her car and into Henry's snare.

If she hadn't left the cabin, what would Henry have done? A moot point, she acknowledged. Better to focus on the reality of her plight instead of the what-ifs and self-recriminations.

They passed a sign indicating a junction with another rural highway, but being unfamiliar with the smaller roads in this part of the state, she learned nothing about their location.

"Take the next left," Henry said.

She met his gaze in the mirror. "What? Why?"

"Because I said so!" He aimed a finger, pointing out the road as they approached the reflective signs marking the turn. "Here."

She did as he said, scanning the roadside for any landmark that might help her if she was able to get away from Henry. A side-glance to Gage's limp form put a hole in that fantasy. She could not, *would not* abandon Gage.

"So you've…" Her voice was thick with anxiety, and she paused to clear her throat, wanting to sound calmer, more in control. "You've been following me? Watching my house?"

"What of it? You wouldn't talk to me, so I had no choice."

She noticed he'd turned the facts around, putting the blame on her, but she didn't argue with his screwy logic.

"And how…how did you know I was at Cameron Glen?"

Henry grunted. "I didn't for a long time. But I'd seen you so often this spring with *him*—" he motioned toward Gage with the muzzle of his gun "—so I started watching him when you disappeared. I knew he made frequent trips to the hospital to visit the vegetable."

A fresh wash of fiery anger flashed through her at his callous reference to Tina's earlier condition, but she clamped down on it.

"So today, I heard him tell one of the nurses he would be heading out of town to visit a friend for the weekend and asked her to call him immediately if anything changed. I figured the *friend*—" Henry said the word with so much sarcasm and loathing that Jessica felt a chill "—might be you, so I followed him." He paused.

"Tell me, Jessie. Do you think the vegetable knows her husband is cheating on her with you?"

Jessica sputtered a startled laugh. "What?"

Henry jabbed her with the gun. "What's so damn funny?"

"The woman in the hospital is Gage's *sister*. Not his wife. And I've told you, we're not a couple."

"Liar. You were kissing him. I saw you."

"That was—" What was it? Earthshaking. Divine. Intensely intriguing. Something that needed to be further explored?

She shook her head. That answer wasn't helpful in dealing with Henry. "It wasn't planned. It was nothing. He's a *friend*. Just a friend." If she could drive that point home, convince him Gage wasn't a rival, would it deescalate the danger for Gage?

She sent Tina's brother a side-glance. Why hadn't he woken up yet? How long did it take people who'd been knocked out to recover consciousness? Was something more seriously wrong with him?

She had her answer roughly ten minutes later when Gage stirred with a groan. She sucked in a sharp breath of relief and cut a glance toward him.

Gage caught Henry's attention, as well. He smacked the gun into Gage's temple, and Gage slumped again.

"Hey!" Jessica cried, irate. "I told you not to do that!"

Henry only snorted. "Yeah. You did. But I never agreed to those terms. *I'm* in charge here. *I* make the rules. And rule number one is, lover boy stays out until we get where we're going."

Maybe she should be thankful Henry hadn't shot Gage and dumped his body, but she couldn't work up any gratitude, considering he'd kidnapped them and brutally knocked Gage out twice.

"Where *are* we going?"

"Found us a place to stay for a few days through a rent-a-house app. Real private so nobody will bother us."

Private. As in remote. Her chest squeezed as she imagined why he would want to be far from civilization and other neighbors. Her mind dwelled on this detail when a deer bolted out from the edge of the road, right into their path. She gasped and cut the wheel hard, narrowly avoiding the animal, but causing the car to fishtail as she corrected.

Henry cursed at her, which did nothing to help the jolt of adrenaline charging through her. "Are you trying to kill us?"

"Did you want me to hit the deer? That wouldn't have ended well for anyone!" she shouted back.

Henry reached up from the back seat to smack her cheek. He hit her hard enough that she bit her tongue, tasted blood.

"Do not speak to me that way. Ever. Again," he grated. "Understood?"

"Or what?" She'd seen her mother cower to bullies too often to stand down, to submit without at least a show of defiance. While her head said it was foolish to argue with an armed and unpredictable man, neither did she want to go out with a whimper instead of rebellion.

Henry leaned forward, putting his mouth right beside her ear. "Or I can make your life miserable, make lover boy wish he was dead." His breath was hot on her skin and smelled like morning breath times ten.

More miserable than you've already made me? She

bit the inside of her cheek to hold the snipe back. Defiance was one thing. Unnecessarily poking the angry bear was another.

Forty minutes and several more turns onto increasingly more pothole-riddled roads, Henry directed her to turn in at a weed-choked dirt driveway. The twin beams of the headlights illuminated a double-wide trailer on cinder blocks that had seen better days…a long time ago.

"This?" Jessica asked, aghast. She hadn't expected a Holiday Inn, but she found it difficult to believe the owner of this hovel thought anyone would pay money to rent it. Except maybe for a meth lab. Or a serial killer's lair.

And yet Henry had. She hesitated before turning off the car's engine. Cutting the motor was resigning herself to going inside this dump. She didn't remove the keys from the ignition, though. Maybe if she stalled long enough…if Henry climbed out first…

"Give me the keys," Henry said, as if reading her mind. He held out his hand and waited until she complied. "Now get out. Leave the headlights on for now, then come around this side and help me get lover boy inside."

"He's *not* my lover." Her relationship with Gage was none of Henry's business, but clearly his misconceptions about their relationship fed Henry's choler toward Gage. If she could convince Henry she hadn't slept with Gage, maybe he'd feel less threatened by him. Maybe she could keep Gage a little safer. "We're just friends."

Henry slapped her again. "Stop lying!" A darkness filled Henry's tone, a fury. "Friends don't claw at each other's clothes like that and stick their tongues down each other's throats." He made a growling sound deep in his throat. "If I didn't need him alive to keep you in line, I'd whack him right now, just to be rid of him."

Keep her in line?

"Go on! Get out!"

Heart sinking, she shouldered the door open and climbed out into the humid night. Around her in the darkness, unseen cicadas, crickets and tree frogs filled the air with night song. A mosquito whined in her ear, and she slapped at it. The vegetation tickled and scraped her calves as she waded through the unkept grasses and burr-laden weeds. She prayed there were no worse booby traps or vile creatures lying in wait, hidden by the darkness.

By the time she'd circled the front fender and reached the passenger side, Henry had climbed out and was unceremoniously dragging Gage from the front seat, his arms hooked under Gage's. She hurried forward, wanting to protect Gage from Henry's rough treatment. Even as she caught Gage's feet, Henry allowed Gage's lolling head to bump hard on the ground as he dropped him in the dirt. She set Gage's legs down gently and scowled at Henry. Not that he saw it with only the headlights to illuminate the night.

Henry took a moment to tuck his gun in the waist of his jeans at the small of his back. A shiver chased through Jessica. That gun was the difference between their captivity and having the upper hand. If she could wrangle control of the weapon from Henry, the tables would be turned. But how could she get it from him?

"All right." Henry nodded his head to Gage's feet. "Let's go."

Bending, she lifted Gage's legs again and staggered

over the ruts and rocks of the yard to the concrete-block steps to the trailer door.

Henry jerked his chin, telling her to go first. "Owner said it was unlocked. Go on in."

Unlocked. What did that say about the property and the owner's disregard for the condition of the place?

She juggled Gage's right leg while she twisted the pollen-coated doorknob and shoved the door open. The scents of mildew, old cigarettes and something more rank and organic slammed into her immediately, and she gagged at the fetid smells. "Good grief! It's ripe in there."

Henry clearly caught a whiff, too, because his nose wrinkled. "Well, I wasn't expecting the Ritz. We'll open some windows and air it out. Now go on. Coleman's getting heavy."

Taking a last gulp of outside air, she edged inside, moving slowly, blindly, in the unlit room.

"Get the light," Henry said.

She set Gage's legs down and groped until she found a light switch. When she flipped the lever, a light fixture came on, and one of the two bulbs popped loudly and blew out. The one lit bulb was enough to see the disaster of their lodgings. Cockroaches skittered across the cracked and curled linoleum. What furnishings were available were soiled and water-stained. The couch cushion had a rip with the stuffing spilling out and had previous tears that had been repaired with silver duct tape. Animal droppings of all sizes were littered across the floor, and based on the chattering noises from the overhead, she'd guess either a squirrel or raccoon had nested in the ceiling. Black mold grew on the walls and human trash, beer cans, cigarette butts, old syringes and fast-food wrappers cluttered every surface. Darker stains soiled the shag carpet and countertop that might have been dried blood.

Jessica felt her gorge rise. If she had a week and ten gallons of bleach to clean this place, she doubted she'd feel it was sanitized and safe yet. And Henry expected them to sleep here tonight?

"This is disgusting!" she said, her tone reflecting her horror. "You can't be serious about staying here!"

Henry put Gage down on the filthy floor and braced his hands on his hips as he turned slowly, surveying the cesspool. "It is nasty." He grunted. "But functional. And cheap. It'll serve my purpose for now." He sniffed again and shook his head. "Once I get you two secured, I think I'll sleep in the car."

Before she could ask what he meant by secured, Henry unbuckled Gage's belt and slid it out of the loops of his khaki pants. He wrapped the belt around Gage's ankles and drew it tight. Pulling a folding Swiss Army knife from his jeans pocket, he set about making a new hole in the leather where he could buckle the belt and keep it tight and secure on Gage's legs.

Jessica hugged herself despite the summer heat, wanting to curl in a ball, shrinking inward as much as she could to protect herself from the filth around her. She tried to breathe shallowly through her mouth to avoid the worst of the stench. How did she get out of here? She had to set aside her shock at the condition of her surroundings and focus her brainpower on saving herself and Gage.

Despite the recurring impulse to run, to save herself even at the risk of being shot at, she always shied from that instinct when her conscience reminded her she couldn't leave Gage. Her heart bumped at the notion that Gage would be safe at home if not for her. He should never have been caught up in her predicament with her stalker. And yet...

She sighed. Selfishly, she was glad Gage was here on some level. That she wasn't going through this horror alone. Gut churning, she swore to herself that no matter what it took, she'd get them both out of this mess—literally and figuratively. She owed that much to Gage.

She eyed the black gun at Henry's waist. Could she snatch the weapon while he was bent over Gage's legs, cutting a new slit in the belt for the buckle? If she did get it, would she be able to use it? When they'd been married, Matt had taught her to use a military-issue pistol they'd kept in their house, but that didn't mean she'd be able to figure Henry's weapon out before he seized it back. Another idea formed as she watched Henry roll Gage to his stomach and pulled his arms behind him. If Henry could knock Gage out, she could return the favor. She glanced around, looking for something heavy enough to wield as a weapon. But she saw no lamps, no empty liquor bottles, no frying pan.

Henry pulled the laces out of Gage's boots next and used one of the thin cords to bind his wrists. Jessica's breath came quicker as she sensed the clock ticking. If she didn't act soon, Henry would tie her up, as well, and leave her defenseless. Her own shoes, pitifully lightweight canvas tennis shoes, may be comfortable for knocking around the house, but were useless for knocking someone out. As her frustration and fear grew, her hands jiggled at her sides and her gaze darted from one corner of the trailer to another. Nothing but filth and useless detritus. Damn!

Jessica fisted her hands so hard her fingernails bit into her palms. *Her fingernails...*

She might not be able to knock Henry unconscious, but she'd be damned if she'd stand by and do nothing. Taking a ragged breath for courage, she edged more directly behind her captor and mentally counted to three.

Lunging at Henry from behind, she jumped on his back. With a feral roar, she curled her fingers and gouged at his face, knocking his glasses aside and aiming for his eyes. Henry jerked upright, battling her clawing hands, cursing a blue streak. All too easily, he flung her off, knocking her to the floor.

He turned to her, his face suffused with red, brow line taut and jaw clenched. "You will be sorry you did that, Jessie. Very sorry."

She scrambled to get to her feet, but he caught her by her hair before she could get out of his reach. With a hard tug that shot needles of pain from her scalp and made her eyes water, he drew her close enough to glare at her, nose to nose. "I'd planned to leave you unrestrained as a courtesy. But seeing as how you're not being nice, looks like you'll be tied up like Coleman."

She fought to free his hand from her hair, grabbing at his wrist and trying to pry his fingers loose. "Let go, you animal!"

With his free hand, he seized her wrist and twisted it behind her before untangling his other to wrench her free arm behind her, as well. With one large hand, he was able to clamp her wrists together and pin her against the nearest wall, while with his now available hand, he scooped a discarded plastic grocery sack from the floor.

Jessica's cheek was flat against the mildewed drywall, her field of vision limited, but she heard him ripping the bag. Despite the biting grip of his hand holding her arms and the weight of his hip shoving her belly first into the wall, Jessica bucked and writhed and struggled. She wouldn't submit quietly to this cruelty. She almost twisted free once, but he slammed his free hand into the back of her head, making her skull crack hard against the wall. The crinkle of plastic gave her only warning before he looped the sack around her wrists several times and tugged a tight knot.

Discouragement and dread balled inside her. Henry grabbed her arms and turned her to face him. He wore a gloating grin that soured her mood further. "You're a heartless bastard. How can you think I'd ever want to be with you?"

His grin dimmed briefly, before he cocked his head to one side and adjusted his glasses. "And yet here you are. And here you'll stay until you see reason. We were meant to be together, and together we will be. One way or another."

Without warning, he grabbed her face between his hands and slammed his mouth on hers. She struggled and wrenched her head aside, tearing away from his assault. Ducking her head, she wiped the remnants of his kiss on her shoulder, trying not to gag. When he went in for another try, she stomped hard, aiming for his foot.

But her lightweight tennis shoes were worthless for inflicting the kind of pain that would help her cause. All her kicking and stomping accomplished was to tick him off again. Fisting his hand in the front of her shirt, he dragged her, stumbling, to the ripped and stained couch and shoved her down on it. Casting his gaze about, he zeroed in on an empty set of plastic six-pack rings and folded it three times crossways. Pulling off her shoes, he shoved the plastic rings over her feet until the rings circled her ankles.

"A rather ill-prepared kidnapper, aren't you?" she taunted.

He glared at her. "This was not my original plan. Finding him—" he thrust a finger toward Gage "—groping you changed things."

For a moment, Jessica's mind flashed back to the heated kisses she'd shared with Gage.

I have wanted this, wanted you for so long.

Yeah, that moment had changed things for her, too. She still hadn't had a chance to process Gage's confession. Jessica opened her mouth to deny an intimate relationship with Gage again, but Henry had seen what he had seen. They had been kissing. At this point, she couldn't predict what tact was best for ensuring Gage's safety. Disputing the truth of what Henry had witnessed would anger him. Confirming the truth would make Gage a more certain target of Henry's jealousy. So she said nothing, choosing instead to try to negotiate with Henry. Test number one...after more than an hour of driving, she needed to use the bathroom.

She took a slow breath through her mouth, still trying to block the worst of the trailer's stench. In as calm a voice as she could muster, she said, "Henry, would you please take the plastic off my hands and feet. I need to use the bathroom."

An involuntary shiver chased through her. She didn't want to think about how nasty the bathroom in this cesspit would be.

He snorted. "Nice try. The restraints stay on until *I* say they come off."

She worked to show him an earnest face rather than a frustrated or hostile one. "I honestly need the restroom. Please. Don't make me have to soil myself."

He lifted one eyebrow as if realizing how that might, in fact, play out. He'd have to be accommodating or…

Huffing his disgust, he removed the plastic at her ankles and walked her to the bathroom. After checking that there were no windows in the bathroom she might use to flee, he stood back and let her enter. "Hurry up."

"And my hands? How am I supposed to do this with my hands bound behind me?"

"That's your problem. The hands stay tied." He jerked his head toward the bathroom, where the fluorescent light flickered.

Jessica sighed and stepped in the small room, trying not to look too closely at the stains and debris in this room. With effort and some awkward contortions, she managed to take care of her business. When they returned from the bathroom, Gage was groaning and beginning to stir.

Relief surged in Jessica. She darted to Gage's side, dropping on her knees next to him, before Henry could stop her. "Gage, thank heavens! Can you hear me? It's Jessica."

She wanted to touch him, to soothe him, to hold him and tell him how sorry she was for involving him in this train wreck.

"Jess?" He angled his head toward her, his gaze reflecting a dullness and confusion. His arms twitched and his frown deepened as he realized his hands were tied. "What happened? Why—"

She saw Gage's attention shift, sensed Henry moving up behind her.

"Well, look who's back with us. Enjoy your nap, Coleman?" Henry chuckled, the tone smug and grating on Jessica's nerves.

Gage's jaw tightened, his glare darkening as he tested the bindings on his arms and legs with abbreviated tugs and twists. "You sonofabitch! If you've hurt Jessica—"

Henry scoffed as he crouched beside Jessica and leaned close to Gage's nose. "You should be far more worried about what I might do to you."

Chapter 15

Gage's head throbbed and his vision blurred, but his greater concern at the moment was what this cretin had in mind for Jessica. And his uselessness while trussed up like a Thanksgiving turkey.

"Jess, are you hurt?" He drank in Jessica's gaze, assessing her well-being and state of mind as best he could without a chance to hold her, talk privately with her.

"I—"

"Come on. That's enough." Henry grabbed her arm and yanked her to her feet. Her arms were bound behind her, as well, it seemed. Fury burned in Gage's core, the spike in his pulse making his temples pound, and a fresh rush of hatred for the guy pumped through him.

Henry rolled his shoulders and surveyed his captives. "Clearly, I'm gonna need something else to hold y'all. What have we got around here?" He strolled into the kitchen and dragged open drawers, checked cabinets.

Gage used the moment to meet Jessica's eyes and ask quietly, "Are you all right? Has he hurt you?"

She hesitated, then shook her head. "Nothing to worry about. How's your head? I'm so, so sorry about—"

"Bingo!" Henry called from the kitchen and returned,

twirling a mostly depleted roll of duct tape on his finger. "You first, Coleman." Henry crouched as he peeled a strip of tape from the roll with a nerve-splitting *strrrppp*. When Henry moved to wind the tape around Gage's ankles, Gage rocked backward. Lifting his legs, Gage landed a flat-footed kick from both of his heels in Henry's face.

Jessica gasped.

Henry howled in rage and pain, grabbing his bleeding nose and cursing. The returned kick, which landed in Gage's ribs, while not immediate, wasn't entirely unexpected. Worth it, Gage decided, to have given Henry at least a taste of his wrath.

"No!" Jessica cried. "Please, both of you stop this! Pummeling each other gets us nowhere!"

Henry shook off the blow and wiped the blood from his nose with his sleeve. Then, grabbing Gage's bound legs, he flipped Gage to his stomach and, with rough motions, reinforced the binding on his hands. Gage used all his strength to keep his hands as far apart as he could, hoping to keep even a smidgen of slack in the binding. When Henry stepped back, Gage rolled to his side to glare up at their captor. "If your intention is to win Jessica over, you can bet you're scoring big points with this cluster bomb. Nothing says 'I love you' like kidnapping and brutalizing a girl and her friend."

Henry took Jessica by the arm and dragged her to the filthy couch. He continued dabbing blood from his seeping nose as he faced Gage. "Either shut the hell up, or I'll shut your mouth for you."

Before Gage could reply, his cell phone, which was somehow still in his pocket, rang.

Henry tensed. Frowned. Stepped over to snatch the phone from Gage's pocket.

Gage's heart sank. If he'd had any chance of later using the phone to call for help or find their way back from wherever they were, that chance was now gone.

After checking the screen, Henry turned Gage's phone off and jammed it in his own pocket. "Oops, looks like you missed a call from the hospital," he said with an ugly sneer. "Hope your sister's okay."

Rage boiled in Gage's gut, competing with concern for why the hospital was calling. What *had* happened with Tina? "If she dies," he growled, "her blood is on your hands."

"On my hands?" Henry snorted and jabbed a finger toward Jessica. "She's the one who overcorrected and drove into the river. Any blood to be claimed is hers." He straightened and arched an eyebrow. "Which reminds me," he said, walking closer to Jessica, who glared from the couch. He peeled a fresh strip of tape from the roll. "I broke your car window and got you out before you drowned. You still haven't thanked me for saving your life."

Jessica looked ill. Her normally tanned complexion leeched of color, her expression a toxic mix of revulsion, guilt and pain. "I wouldn't have been in a flooding car if you hadn't forced me off the road! Your reckless driving, your intentional harassment of us on the road is what caused that accident. Sara's blood is already on you, and because of you, Tina and Holly will probably never be the same!"

Henry shrugged and knelt to wrap tape around her ankles. "You're wrong."

"You could have saved them when you pulled me out, and you didn't!" Tears choked her voice, and her dark eyes blazed with contempt.

"We'll just have to agree to disagree on that. Besides, you were the only one I cared about. Although, if I'd known how much trouble you were going to be, maybe I'd have let you stay in that car."

Jessica shook her head, her heavy breathing a sure sign of her upset and turmoil. "Why would you save me at the river, only to knock me out and leave me to die from carbon monoxide in my garage days later?"

Henry propped both hands on his hips and frowned at her. "Letting you die was never the plan. You made me mad in your garage when you wouldn't hear me out, wouldn't talk to me, wouldn't give me a chance. After I left, I realized you'd need help, and I went back to save you before anything bad happened." He cut a sharp look at Gage, his tone growing resentful. "But then he was already there. Had you on the front lawn with the ambulance workers."

Gage wanted to shout at the pissant, tell him something bad *had* happened to Jess. That she'd had enough carbon monoxide in her system to require a few days' treatment in the hospital. But Jessica spoke first, and her need to vent, to have her say took precedence over his.

"Henry," she said, her voice taut and low, "let me make this *perfectly* clear. I didn't want to talk with you then, because there is nothing to discuss. I want *nothing* to do with you. Ever. I have never felt anything for you and never will. The restraining order I got should have made that obvious."

Henry shifted his weight and narrowed his gaze on

Jessica. A prickle of alarm skittered through Gage. While Henry had to know the truth, Gage feared what her brutal assessment would do to his temper. Would he retaliate by hurting Jessica?

Henry sniffed and looked away for a moment before exhaling harshly. "Once again, you are wrong. You picked me out of all those men on the app, because you liked what you saw. We had *everything* in common. And when I asked for another dinner with you, you said *yes*." He leaned close to her and shouted in her face, "Because you liked what you saw and wanted me!"

Jessica shuddered but met his glare boldly. "You agreeing with everything I say and pretending to like everything I do is not a real connection. It was forced and fake, and I knew it from that first night. I could have said I like eating dog poop, and you'd have agreed with me. The truth is, even before you showed your evil, depraved and irrational side, I was certain there would *never* be anything between us. Your cloying, desperate need to make yourself seem so agreeable was a big red flag."

Henry's hands were shaking, and his face grew red. "Liar! We went out again. You kissed me good-night. You let me think you were in love with me."

"You showed up unexpectedly, and I gave you the benefit of the doubt. Those subsequent dates were as big a mistake and a failure as the first. Then *you* kissed *me,* and I told you *no.* If I was too polite in saying 'go to hell,' then let me correct that now. *Go to hell, Henry!* You are a hateful, sick man who has caused me nothing but grief and heartache. I don't want anything to do with you!"

Henry paced across the room and back, shaking his head. "Nope. Nope. That's wrong. That's all wrong."

"Henry, don't do this. Untie me. You have to let me and Gage go!"

Their captor continued to grouse and shake his head. "I can't. It's too late for that now." He fisted his hands as he glowered at Jessica. "You're either mine or you're no one's."

Gage's heart sank, realizing how truly deluded Henry was. If Jessica couldn't get through to him with the truth, he'd have to find another way to get himself and Jessica free. As he racked his brain, trying to tamp down the tumult inside him and find the calm to make a new plan, Henry snorted loudly.

"This place is a dump. I'm sleeping in the car." With that, he stomped across the floor, shut off the lights and slammed the trailer door behind him.

Once she heard the car door slam and knew they were alone, Jessica turned her full attention to Gage. "The truth, Gage. How bad is your head? You were unconscious for a long time."

"Actually, I roused a little before we arrived but played possum so I could listen and plan. Unfortunately, the bump to the head as he dragged me from the car put me out again, just as I was about to spring into action."

"Do you think you have a concussion?" she asked into the darkness. "Before he dragged me away I saw a bump on your head. That's a good sign, isn't it? That the wound is swelling out instead of pressing in on the brain?"

He chuckled without humor. "Listen to you. When did you go to medical school?"

"I raised an active little boy. You pick things up. All mothers are nurses by the time their kids move out. So how bad is your head? Any nausea? Blurry vision?"

He grunted. "I'll be all right. Did he hurt you? Did he…" He fell silent before exhaling loudly. "Did he *do* anything to you?"

"Nothing overly grievous." Then, realizing her answer wouldn't calm his worry, she added, "I'm fine, Gage. Really."

For several minutes after that neither of them said anything. Fatigue battled with her need to figure a way out of their situation. Given his silence, she figured Gage was working on that problem, as well, until he said, "I wish I could hold you right now."

A shiver chased through her despite the sticky heat inside the trailer. Being in Gage's arms sounded pretty wonderful, now that she thought about it. His solid presence, his comforting smile, his reassuring strength had gotten her through the past four terrible months. The need to be near him, even if their bound arms didn't allow them to embrace, roared through Jessica so powerfully her head spun.

"I think I can make it to you." She tested the theory by flopping onto the floor and wiggling like an inchworm to scoot across the floor. She breathed through her mouth, trying not to inhale the stench of the carpet or think about the filth she'd seen before Henry turned the lights off.

"Jess, did you fall? What was that thump?"

"Like I said, I'm coming to you. Keep talking so I can find you."

"What am I supposed to say?" He groaned. "Besides I'm sorry, that is."

"What do you have to apologize for?"

"Considering you hadn't seen or heard from Henry since moving to Cameron Glen, it's pretty obvious that I led him to you today." His heavy sigh voiced his frustration. "All I've wanted to do since I learned about this creep is keep you safe, and instead, I…brought danger to you."

She bumped into a warm, solid body and used her toes to inch higher, so that her body was aligned with his. "Let's not assign blame or start down the what-if path tonight. We have bigger issues to solve. Namely, how do we get back home?"

He placed a kiss on the top of her head, and she laid her cheek on his chest. His heart beat steady and strong beneath her ear, and it soothed her like a lullaby.

"I don't know," he murmured, "but I swear that I will get you out of this. One way or another."

Chapter 16

Jessica spent a restless and uncomfortable night on the floor beside Gage. Though they both dozed, she made sure to wake Gage every couple of hours and check on him, in case he had a concussion. Not that she could do anything for him if he did.

Fortunately, he roused easily, could answer her questions and said his head hurt less as the hours passed. "I think we dodged a bullet," he said sometime around dawn. Without her phone, her only sense of time was the weak light peeking through the blinds and the twitter and chirp of birds greeting the day. Despite her circumstances, Jessica took a moment to focus on the birdsong. The peeps and trills calmed her, and she imagined herself in a meadow, by a babbling brook—

She moaned. Maybe not the brook considering her full bladder.

"You okay?" Gage asked.

"Define okay."

He chortled. "Can I do anything to help?"

"Tell me you've come up with a foolproof plan to get us out of here." When he grunted, she continued, "Okay, not foolproof, just…possible."

"Well, obviously, step one is getting out of these constraints. I've spent most of the night trying to free my wrists, but all I did was tighten the knots."

Struggling to a seated position, she glanced around the trailer. Shifting to her side, she again wiggled her way back toward the sofa and an abandoned soda can. "We need something sharp. Maybe if I flatten this can, the sides will rip and I can—"

The trailer door opened, and Henry appeared, looking rumpled, half-asleep and grumpy. He switched on the overhead lights and moved into the living room, saying nothing. He stopped in front of Gage, glared at him and nudged his feet as if to check that they were still bound. Turning, he gave Jessica an up-and-down scrutiny. Apparently satisfied his prisoners were still secure, he headed to the kitchen. Through the cutout section of the wall over the breakfast bar, Jessica followed Henry's progress as he moved from one cabinet to another, opening and slamming doors closed. Each shelf Henry checked appeared to be empty, or at least not yielding anything that satisfied their jailer, because his huffs of irritation grew louder and each slam of a door more forceful.

Finally, Henry bit out a sour curse and jammed his hand through his hair, leaving it all the more mussed. "I'm starving, and there ain't diddly squat in this place to eat!"

"You were expecting a breakfast buffet?" Gage asked.

Returning to the living room, Henry glowered at Gage. "You can shut up!"

Finding the roll of tape he'd discarded last night, Henry tore off a strip—the end of the roll—and slapped it over Gage's mouth.

Henry tossed the now-empty roll aside and paced the

dirty shag carpet, his expression dark. "Damn, I'd give my left nut for a cup of coffee."

Yes, coffee! Jessica thought. Her stomach growled just at the thought of food. Last night, they'd never gotten to eat the dinner she'd made for Gage. Her mouth watered, picturing the lasagna and pie sitting on her cabin's kitchen counter. And then an idea struck her. "So… what's stopping you? You have my car, my keys. I'd love a coffee and breakfast biscuit myself."

Henry glanced at her, clearly suspicious.

Jessica snorted and wiggled her bound feet. "We're not going anywhere, but nothing is keeping you from driving back into that little town we came through last night. I remember a couple fast-food places and a diner there. Maybe a small grocery where you could stock up on snacks for all of us."

Suspicious of her motives or not, she'd clearly gotten Henry thinking, craving. He rubbed one hand on his chin, then pressed the same hand to his stomach as it audibly rumbled. With a nod of his head, he said, "I am gonna need supplies if we're going to stay here for a while."

Jessica sent Gage a quick look. His eyes met hers, and he ducked his chin in an almost imperceptible nod.

"Then you'll bring me back a coffee? And a sausage and egg biscuit? No, make it bacon." She saw Henry swallow hard as if salivating at the idea of bacon and eggs, and she piled on. "Lord, I love bacon. And hash browns if they're crispy. Chocolate chip cookies for snacks. And peanut butter filled pretzels. Maybe some fruit. And diet colas. Some pastrami and Swiss cheese for sandwiches. Taco-flavored chips."

Henry finally snapped, "That enough! You'll get what I give you." He dug out the keys from his front pocket and bent close to taunt Gage. "And as my mother used to say, you'll get nothing and like it." With a low chuckle, Henry crossed back to the trailer door. "Y'all stay here. I'll be right back. Maybe…" He laughed then, as if he'd told the best joke, closing the door behind him.

Jessica heard the snick of the door locking and met Gage's eyes again. Next came the car's engine, the crackle of the tires on gravel. Then silence. She exhaled heavily, and let a small laugh out herself. "Thank God."

Gage's eyebrows rose as if to say, *Now what?*

She rolled her shoulders, loosening the muscles there and said, "Okay. We're on the clock." She rolled the can closer and, lifting both bound feet, stomped the can. Instead of flattening, it slipped off her canvas tennis shoe and spun away. She growled her frustration. "This would be so much easier if I could just—" She paused as an idea came to her.

Gage grunted from behind the tape and lifted his eyebrows in query.

"Let's see if I'm still as flexible as I was as a cheerleader in high school, shall we?" She wiggled and scooted her cinched wrists as low as she could behind her. Hunching her shoulders and inching her hands under her bottom, she slowly scooted backward, an inch here, a centimeter there. Little by little, she scrunched her hands under her thighs, then brought her knees to her chest. With some more inching and wiggling, she stepped through her linked arms, bringing them out in front of her.

Relief spun through her, and she flashed a broad smile at Gage. "Ta-da!"

A muffled chuckle tumbled from his throat, and the dip of his chin said, *Impressive!*

Gage's approval burrowed deep inside her, warming her. After all the ways she'd cost him, burdened him, landed him in danger, she'd finally done something right. With a cleansing breath, she bent over and used her bound and numb hands to pick at the tape around her ankles. Because her hands were still bound, her progress was slow, but bit by bit, she loosened an end of the tape on her ankle. After what felt like hours, she finally had a large enough piece to unwind the strip.

Next came the plastic six-pack rings, which, over the next few minutes, she stretched and tugged off over her feet. With her ankles freed, she stood and stretched and shook the ache from her leg muscles. Turning her attention to Gage, she hurried over to him and grasped the edge of the tape covering his mouth. "Fast or slow?"

He cocked one eyebrow, and she rolled her eyes at her goof. "Nod for fast, shake for slow."

He nodded, and she ripped the tape from his mouth with one quick motion. He yowled in pain and squeezed his eyes shut for a moment. His jaw muscles flexed as he gritted his back teeth before exhaling and meeting her gaze. "That smarts. Especially since I haven't shaved in two days."

She winced in sympathy. "Sorry."

He lifted a corner of his mouth. "Necessary. Don't sweat it. What's next?"

She raised her arms. "I have to get this off somehow." She studied the plastic bags tied around her wrists. "With my teeth I guess."

He shrugged. "I guess."

She moved back to the sofa and nibbled at the grocery bag Henry had torn and knotted to bind her wrists. Again, the task was a practice in patience, in micro progress and backtracking when she tugged the wrong piece and tightened the knots again. She groaned her frustration.

"Hey." Gage hitched his head. "Bring it here. My turn."

She crossed to him, kneeling to be at his level on the floor.

He chomped his teeth and teased, "You know the saying—two mouths are better than one."

"Is that a saying?" she returned wryly, but held her wrists to his mouth where he squinted at the knots then began his own nibbling and tugging. When he worked a strip of the bag loose, she bit it from the other side and pulled it free. Her forehead grazed his as she worked a newly exposed knot on her side. She sensed more than saw his eyes lift to meet hers. A breath away. Nearer than she'd ever been to him…except when they'd kissed. That knowledge snagged the air in her lungs. She stared, her heart thudding so loudly she knew he could hear it.

His right eye had a small patch of green set against his gray iris. Why had she never noticed that before? And this close she saw the tiny creases that fanned from the corner of his eyelids. Laugh lines.

Jessica jerked her gaze away. She had no business noticing such details. Those were intimate observations lovers made, the kind of details one only saw up close.

Even as she worked to calm the flutter in her veins, Gage worked the last strip of plastic free from its knot. The grocery bag fell away. Her hands were free.

Jessica tossed the bag aside, then rubbed her sore

wrists and wiggled her fingers, stimulating the blood flow. Pinpricks of pain sparked in her hands as the numbness receded.

"Excellent," Gage said, smiling. "Now me. I have a small utility knife in my pocket. Can you fish it out?"

She gaped at him and scoffed. "You have a knife? Why didn't you say so before?"

"How would you have used it while your hands were bound?" He lifted his brow and gave her an even look.

She returned his look with one of her own. As she studied him, the morning sunlight peeked through the cracked blinds and lit his face with buttery rays. In his face, she saw the fatigue of a restless night. The lingering pain from Henry's blows to his temple. And the kindness and affection of a yearslong friendship that for him had been more. Deeper. Respectfully silenced. Unrequited.

I've wanted you for a very long time. His words, spoken after a kiss that had shaken her to her core and had been hot enough to melt her bones, whispered through her again. She'd answered his confession, his honesty, by running away. By landing him in the grips of a dangerous man. Gage had never been anything but kind and protective and thoughtful. Even when, through the years, he'd included her in his brotherly teasing and antics, he'd respected her and respected her marriage to Matt.

As she continued to stare at him, he arched a dark eyebrow. He thrust one hip toward her. "This pocket. Time's a'wasting."

Without stopping to second-guess the impulse, she framed his face with her hands and leaned in to kiss him.

Chapter 17

Beneath her palms she felt Gage jolt, heard his sharp intake of air. She'd surprised him, surprised herself. But he didn't pull away, and neither did she. She savored the heat of his mouth, the light scrape of his two-day-old beard, the silky caress of his tongue tangling with hers. The kiss was every bit as tantalizing as she'd remembered from last night. Jeez, had it just been last night? But this kiss held a hint of something new and fragile, something precious and poignant. When she finally canted away, her eyes searching his, she whispered, "Sorry."

He twitched a grin. "Don't be. That was nice."

Jessica cleared her throat, gave her head a small shake. "No… I mean, yes, it was. But…I got you into all this. I—" She swallowed hard. "I freaked out last night when you said you—"

"Uh, yeah," he interrupted. "About that. Can we… forget I said that?"

She blinked, stung. "You didn't mean it?"

"I meant it, but… I shouldn't have said it. I shouldn't have laid it on you when you're already dealing with—"

She silenced him with another deep, lingering kiss. Then, resting her forehead against his, she released a slow exhale and closed her eyes. "Let's save this con-versation for…later. Like you said, time's a'wasting."

Gage nodded. "Right."

Sitting back on her heels, she pointed to his hip. "This pocket, you say?"

He leaned back and angled his hip toward her. "All yours."

Evidence of what their kiss had done to him strained against his fly, and she gave him a wry grin. "A knife is not all you have in your pocket."

His smile turned sultry. "Your fault."

Holding his gaze, she slipped her hand in his front pocket until her fingers found the slim knife and curled around it. After extracting it, she flipped open the tools until she found a small blade. Crawling behind Gage, she sawed through the duct tape at his wrists. "Brace yourself. One, two—" She ripped the tape free, yank-ing several black hairs from his arms.

"Augh! Jack bless a milk cow!"

She chuckled at his nonsensical expression, one she'd heard Tina use, as well, and flung the sticky bindings aside. After freeing his ankles, she rose to her feet and offered him a hand up.

Gage worked through a series of stretches and shoul-der rolls, groaning as he relieved his muscle kinks and soreness. "Okay, so what's the plan? Are we lying in wait for Henry to ambush him when he gets back or hoofing it out of here, not knowing where we are or how far it is to someone with a working phone?"

Jessica smoothed her hands over her shorts, debating. "I'm not keen on the idea of trying to ambush an unstable man who still has a gun in his possession."

Gage hiked up an eyebrow. "It's not ideal."

She cast her gaze around the filthy trailer and chewed her bottom lip. "I just want to get out of here. Everything about this place disgusts me and creeps me out. It feels…evil."

"And then what? He has your car."

She nodded. "I'll get it back when the police catch up to him. What matters to me now is not being here when he gets back, even if that means we go on foot."

Gage's brow creased, and he twisted his mouth, clearly analyzing the situation for himself. Bobbing his head once, he said, "All right, then. We'll hike outta here. But we're kinda far from civilization. We should grab a thing or two from here before we bolt."

"Like what?"

"Like…" He strode across the room and collected one of the plastic grocery sacks from the floor, along with an empty soda bottle and the pop-top lid from an unknown can.

Jessica eyed him skeptically. "We need trash?"

He wagged the soda bottle. "For carrying water, after we rinse it out. This pop-top lid is metal and will reflect sun a bit like a mirror." He paused before adding, "In case we get really lost and have to signal for help."

"How lost can we get if we just follow the road we drove in on?" she asked.

"True enough, but do you really want to be on the same road Henry will be driving back up here on in a few minutes?"

"No."

"We can keep the road in sight, but until we are a

good ways from this trailer…" He shook his head. "Let's not make it too easy for him to find us again, huh?"

Next Gage collected both his shoestrings and hers, peeling them away from the tangle of duct tape they'd become enmeshed in.

"What are these for?" she asked, taking over the separation of tape and her laces.

He gave her an odd look. "To lace our shoes."

She slapped a hand to her forehead and burst out laughing. "Oh, my word. I can't believe I asked that. My only excuse is, I haven't slept. I was on a different thought path. I just—"

Gage's laughter joined hers, and he wrapped her in a hug. "Oh, Jess, I'm *so* not going to let you forget this."

She cringed. "Ugh. Rightfully so."

They were still chuckling over her brain fart a few minutes later as they re-laced their shoes, and she carried the soda bottle to the kitchen sink. The water that poured from the tap was rusty brown, and Jessica wrinkled her nose. "Gross."

"Let it run for a while," Gage said, glancing over her shoulder. He turned to start opening cabinets, much the way Henry had. And like Henry, he found nothing of use. "It could just be from disuse. I still think anything we get out of the pipes here is better than not having anything to drink in this heat."

The color of the water slowly cleared, and she rinsed and filled the soda bottle, trying not to think about who might have drunk from that bottle before. They weren't in a position to be picky. She handed the water to Gage, and he placed it in the grocery sack. He also added a can of roach spray he found in the cabinet and an empty beer can from the floor of the bedroom to their oddball collection.

She wrinkled her nose in confusion as he looped the bag handles together for easier carrying. "You'll explain the reason for those things later? Right now, we need to make tracks. Henry could be back any second."

"Agreed, and I will." He moved to the trailer door and opened it slowly, peering out to scan the yard before stepping through.

A dense fog hung in the air, making the morning humid and shrouding the woods around the trailer. The gray veil spiked Jessica's trepidation about their escape, as if Mother Nature was hiding potential threats.

Gage held a hand out for Jessica as she stepped down the wobbly cinder block stairs from the door to the ground. They'd only made it a couple of steps toward the line of trees when the whir of tires on damp pavement, the rumble of an approaching car engine sounded from the road.

Jessica turned an anxious look to Gage. "Do you hear that?"

Gage's mouth tightened, and he nodded as they both looked to the cover of the woods. "Run!"

Chapter 18

Matt stood on the porch of the Juniper cabin, waiting for Jessica to answer his knock. Her car was gone, but Gage's truck was in the drive, so he presumed they were together. Maybe gone to breakfast in town?

Except that Eric had texted him this morning asking if Matt knew why Jessica was not responding to her son's texts. He'd texted several times last night and again this morning. He'd even *called* her phone, which Eric let him know was tantamount to emergency measures for his generation. Jessica hadn't answered. The lack of reply from Jessica counted as an emergency in Matt's view. She might ignore a text from her ex-husband for a day or so, but she'd *never* ghost her son for even an hour.

Matt knocked a second time, and when no one answered again, he dialed Jessica's phone. The faint sounds of a familiar ring tone played from inside the cabin. Matt frowned. Wherever she'd gone, she'd not taken her phone with her? That was extremely out of character for his ex-wife.

He dragged a hand down his cheek, debating. While he wasn't one to worry under normal circumstances, recent circumstances weren't normal. Jessica had a man stalking her. Matt took a seat in one of the rocking chairs on the cabin's porch and thumbed through his contacts. When he found Gage's number, he hit the dial icon. The line rang several times, then went to voice mail.

"Gage, it's Matt. I'm looking for Jess, and she doesn't have her phone with her. I was hoping she was with you and that you could tell me she was okay. Call me when you get this. Thanks."

He disconnected and clenched his back teeth, not happy with this turn of events. For Gage to not be answering his phone either hiked Matt's concern up a notch. Shoving back to his feet, Matt tested the front doorknob. Unlocked. After Jess had promised to keep her doors locked always, whether she was home or not. Whether she had company or construction workers present. Breaking that promise was also not like Jessica.

"Jess?" he called into the cabin as he let himself in. No answer. Matt moved deeper into the quiet cabin, checking the rooms with a sweeping gaze. He edged from the living room through the kitchen, where dirty pans were stacked in the sink, past an uncut pie that waited on the stove. He smelled something like burned toast and opened the oven. Though the oven was cool, overtoasted garlic bread slices sat on a cookie sheet, forgotten. He remembered Jessica's trick of heating bread for a meal in the residual heat of an oven she'd turned off. Scowling, he moved into the dining area. On the table was an uneaten meal, a lasagna by the looks of it. An open bottle of wine. Half-full glasses. Jessica's phone lay next to one plate. Jessica would not have left food out to spoil, dishes unwashed. His ex-wife hated loose ends, was compulsive about order and housekeeping. She'd never been spontaneous or rash.

A chill of dread filled Matt's gut, because wherever Jessica was, she'd left the cabin abruptly, unprepared. And that boded all kinds of ill.

Spinning toward the woods, Jessica sprinted across the weedy yard. Gage, ever protective, stayed even with her, though she knew he could easily have outpaced her. Over her ragged breathing and thudding steps, she could hear the car getting closer. The rumble louder. She pumped her arms and pushed herself to run faster. Faster…

She reached the woods and plunged into the morass of fallen leaves, underbrush and low branches. Gage darted past her, leaping over a rotting tree trunk, and leading the way into the shadowy forest. Jessica shot a glance over her shoulder as the grumbling engine noise crested.

An old pickup truck sped past on the highway, spewing exhaust. Relief spun through her. Not Henry. They were—

Jessica stepped in a leaf-camouflaged hole. When her foot stuck, she sprawled on the ground. Her ankle wrenched to an unnatural angle. Pain came, quick and intense. A cry of agony ripped from her throat. One look at her crooked ankle told her the damage was significant. Critical. Disastrous.

Gage was at her side in an instant. "Jess! Are you o—" His question dropped off as his gaze landed on her ankle. He plowed a hand through his hair and muttered a bad word.

Tears of pain and frustration filled her eyes. "No, no, nooo!"

"Hey," Gage said, his arms circling her, "it's going to be okay. I'm going to take care of you."

His words, meant to comfort and calm, stirred a different ache in her chest. A devastating reality sliced through the haze of pain and the pulse of adrenaline. With an injured ankle immobilizing her, she was dependent on Gage for the foreseeable future. Her injury ruined their plan of escape. She had to rely on Gage, to whom she was already so indebted, to rescue her from a situation she'd just made a hundred times worse.

Her anger, frustration and loathing turned inward, roiling and climbing her throat. Tipping her head back, Jessica loosed a feral howl from the depth of her soul. Balling her hands in fists, she pounded the ground and shouted a guttural "Aaagh!"

Gage stroked her hair and cradled her face in a cupped hand. "Hey, hey…easy. You're gonna be okay. I know it hurts, but I'm going to help you."

She gritted her teeth, swallowing hard as the sharp throbbing of her ankle and deep disappointment in herself churned nausea in her stomach. Raising damp eyes to his, she snarled, "That's exactly what is wrong."

"Um, what?"

She squeezed her eyes shut, determine to hold back the rising tears. "Oh, man, could I be any more of a cliché?"

Gage gave her a puzzled look as he scuttled closer to her foot and gently gripped her heel. "This may hurt. Hang on." He eased her foot free from the hole, and the movement shot new waves of pain up her leg.

Jessica hissed, clenching her teeth, but choking down the wail of pain that swelled. She took a few deep breaths, trying to ride out the incredible ache blazing from her ankle. The foot and joint were already swelling, and she knew she'd be hiking nowhere today. She was stuck here, with Henry due back any moment. "You should go on without me."

Gage, still gently probing her ankle in full first responder mode, cut an incredulous look over his shoulder. "What? Not a chance."

"Gage, I can't walk on *that*!" She thrust a finger toward her injured foot with a glare of disdain. "But you can still save yourself."

A sternness she'd never seen in Gage before firmed his face, and he pivoted to grasp her shoulders. "There is no way in hell I'm abandoning you, so drop that narrative right now. We're getting out of this together. I promise. Trust me to take care of you, Jess. Okay?"

"But I can't—"

"I'll carry you." The resolve that blazed in his eyes burrowed into her, and she could easily believe that he would move mountains and swim oceans for her. The assurance should have comforted her. Instead, it rankled. Knowing how dependent she was on him sat uneasily, like a rock in her shoe. She didn't want to cost him so much. Cost him more than she already had.

One traitorous tear escaped her eyelashes and tickled her cheek. When she lifted a hand to dash it away, her fingers bumped his as Gage wiped her cheek with the pad of his thumb.

"I'll be right back," he said, then rose to run back toward the trailer.

Jessica watched the road anxiously as she waited for Gage to return. The first vehicle they'd heard hadn't been Henry, but the next one easily could be. She grimaced. If only they'd known that truck wasn't Henry. They could have flagged down the driver and been on their way to town, a phone or the police for help right now.

But what about another car? How long would it be if

they waited for someone else to drive by? She chewed her bottom lip, trying not to think of how much her foot hurt, trying to reason out their options. While hoping to catch a ride with a passing car seemed a good choice, hitchhiking along on the side of the highway made them sitting targets for Henry. And yet *she* would be hiking nowhere fast. She would slow Gage down.

The trailer door squeaked, and Gage emerged, holding something blue balled up in his hands and casting a wary glance toward the road before running back across the yard to her. When he reached her, he handed her what proved to be a bed sheet. "I can tear this in strips to bind your ankle in a minute, but right now I want to get us out of view before Butthead gets back. You're too visible here." He gathered the plastic sack they'd filled earlier and handed her that, as well. "You're going to have to hold all this. Okay?"

"I… Yeah. But what—" She swallowed the rest of her sentence as he stooped and placed an arm behind her knees and another under her arm and across her back.

Jessica gasped as he scooped her up. She clutched the items in her lap with one hand while throwing her other around Gage's neck. Cradled against his chest, she clung to him as he set out, striding quickly into the misty woods.

"Gage, you can't carry me all the way to…wherever," she said, although at the moment, held in his arms was exactly where she wanted to be. The position was as close to a hug as they had time for at the moment, and if she were honest, she really needed a hug right then. She was scared. She hurt. She hated how much of this disaster fell squarely on her shoulders.

"I won't be carrying you this way…the whole way," he said, sounding winded already. "Just a bit. Just 'til I think…we'll be safe enough…to stop for a minute… while I wrap your ankle."

Her bad ankle bumped a low hanging branch, and she yelped softly as pain juddered through her.

He cursed. "Sorry. I'm trying not to jostle you more than I have to."

"No. Don't apologize. I'm—" she gritted her teeth, forcing down another gasp as her injured ankle knocked her good one "—fine," she finished on a wheeze.

"Know what I wish?" he asked.

"That a Boy Scout troop with cell phones and a pre-made travois would magically appear out of the woods right about now?"

He huffed a short laugh. "Boy Scouts and working phones…would be helpful. Not what I was thinking, though."

"What do you wish?" she asked, overwhelmed by a desire to give him anything he wanted, to make up for everything she'd put him through, in any way possible.

"You remember that dinner…we had with Tina…and my friend Robby…last New Year's Eve?"

She did remember. The food had been divine. They'd all stuffed themselves and sworn they'd be frequent customers at that restaurant in the future. "The nice steakhouse in Concord?"

"Yeah."

Her stomach growled. She definitely could go for a meal like that right now. "Yeah."

"Remember how I talked you into splitting the cheesecake with me?" he asked.

Her mouth watered. "Mmm."

"Yeah, I'm kinda wishing now I hadn't done that."

She furrowed her brow. Angled a look up at him. "Are you saying...?"

He flashed a devilish, lopsided smile.

"Hey!" She poked him with her elbow, and he chuckled between heaving breaths. "Fine!" She sputtered a half laugh, secretly pleased to have him baiting her this way. "Put me down then, if I'm so all-fired heavy!"

This teasing-Gage was the Gage she knew. The Gage she understood. The Gage she'd pushed from her mind when she kissed him this morning.

She'd *kissed* him this morning. And it had been such a good kiss. *Oh man!* She couldn't think about that now.

"Watch your head," he said, and she bent her chin to her chest to avoid a frond of something with thorns. A few steps further into the cover of the trees, she heard another car. This time the whoosh of tires on pavement slowed.

Gravel crunched. The engine cut off. A door slammed.

Jessica locked eyes with Gage, her breath frozen in her lungs. "Henry!" she mouthed.

He nodded, then kept moving with a quicker step, less mindful of the slapping branches and clawing vines. She tucked her face into his shoulder to avoid the worst of the battering foliage and whispered a prayer for help, for protection, for success in their escape. At this point, with her ankle likely sprained at best and possibly broken, praying was the best she could do for them.

Her thudding heart and Gage's pounding steps counted the seconds until she heard the distant slap of the trailer door, then Henry's furious scream. "You're a *dead man*, Coleman!"

Chapter 19

Matt headed back to his cabin, already working through contingencies. He knew through research for his suspense books and the recent misfortunes of the Cameron family that the police didn't consider an adult "missing" until they'd been gone for a much longer time than in the case of a child. An adult had the free will to go off alone and not communicate with family or friends if they chose. Unless specific suspicious circumstances were established—witnesses to violence against the individual, physical evidence of a serious crime—the police weren't going to do much in the next few hours. But Matt had an ace up his sleeve. He had a phalanx of Camerons who could search and make phone calls to jump-start the process of finding Jessica and Gage.

As he neared his cabin, his head lost in thoughts of next steps, a familiar car pulled up beside him and stopped. He scowled as he stepped to the driver's window of his son's Honda. "Eric, what are you doing here?"

In that moment, with the morning sun highlighting his chiseled face and dark features, his son looked so much like Jessica it made Matt's chest squeeze. "I was worried about Mom. This business with the guy harassing her, then not being able to reach her has me kinda freaked. When she didn't answer my calls this morning, I got in the car and started driving. I called you from the road."

"Why didn't you tell me you were on your way?"

"Because you'd have told me not to come, not to worry."

Matt nodded. "You're right about that."

"And you should know me better than to think I can write off this kind of anomaly with Mom. What kind of asshole knows his mother could be in danger and does nothing about it?" Eric gave him a level look.

"Not my boy," Matt said, reaching through the open car window to ruffle Eric's hair. "All right. Let's go to the house and talk."

Once Eric had parked, and Cait had greeted her stepson with enthusiastic hugs, Matt and Eric gathered in the living room of their family's cabin. Matt explained what he'd found at the Juniper cabin and his reasons for holding off on calling the police. "In and of itself, an uneaten meal and forgotten phone are not evidence of foul play. They're out of character for your mom and suspicious to us, but I don't think the police would see it the same way. I didn't see any blood or signs of a struggle to indicate they'd been taken by force."

"That's good. Right?" Cait said, clearly trying to buoy Eric's spirits. "Maybe there's a perfectly innocent explanation for all this. Huh?"

"I guess," Eric returned, his tone and expression glum. "But Mom knows better than to worry us. Especially when we all know this guy she met through the dating app has been making trouble."

Eric's watered-down description of the problems

Henry had caused let Matt know Jessica had likely not given Eric the whole picture. That fit. Jessica would have wanted to shield Eric as much as possible. He exchanged a look with Cait when she shifted in her seat and wrinkled her brow. Cait, too, sensed that Eric's understanding was limited, he could tell. Matt gave his wife a subtle headshake that said, *Leave it for now.*

In the silence of their mutual brooding, the soft pad of bare feet signaled the arrival of the resident two-year-old. Erin's face lit when she saw her older brother and she squealed, "Ewic!"

Eric grinned and rose from the couch to sweep his sister up into his arms. "Hey, Pipsqueak!" He blew a loud raspberry on her cheek, winning peals of laughter, before pretending to drop her, then immediately caught her again. Erin's happy squeals grew louder as her big brother repeated their favorite game.

"Mowr!" the toddler demanded, but Cait got up and took Erin into her own arms.

"Maybe later, Butterbean. Let Eric talk to Daddy right now while you get dressed," Cait said, escorting Erin back to her bedroom.

"Okay." Eric returned to the couch and pinned a hard look on his father. "I'm not going anywhere until I know Mom is safe. So…what are we going to do to find her?"

Gage didn't slow his pace for several minutes. Goal number one was to be not found by Henry, so he pushed on, deeper and deeper into the woods. He followed no particular vector other than getting Jessica away from Blythe. His head still ached from the blows Henry had delivered last night, but he ignored the pain. His plodding steps became automatic, allowing his mind far too much time to think. About their next move. About Jess's injury. About her kiss.

She'd stunned him with that lip-lock this morning. But what had brought it on? Gratitude to be escaping? Apology? Or…just maybe…a change of heart? They hadn't really talked about his confession to her since it happened. Or her freak-out over it. In hindsight, he could see why it had been so shocking to her, so paradigm-shifting. She'd seen him as one thing for more than twenty years, and suddenly, at a moment in time when her world was already crooked on its axis, he'd dropped his little truth bomb on her.

Great timing, man. He gritted his teeth and grunted his frustration with himself.

"If you need to rest, I think we're far enough from the trailer now that you can stop to catch your breath," Jessica said.

"I'm fine. I'm just…" He shook his head and immediately regretted it. "Never mind. But we are overdue to wrap that ankle." He glanced around for the best place to stop. He found a fallen tree where she could sit, and he set her down beside it. She let the bundle of supplies fall into a nest of leaves and eased herself onto the log. Her ankle had swollen to twice its normal size and was an angry red. Gathering the bedsheet he'd taken from the trailer, he used his pocketknife to start a few slits spaced evenly. He tore the sheet down the middle and handed half back to Jessica, then ripped a few strips. When she started to tear the other half, he stopped her. "Let's not rip that part up yet. We don't know what we might need it for."

She shrugged. "You're the boss."

Did he hear a note of frustration behind her reply? Brushing the question aside, he knelt in the leafy detritus of the forest floor and carefully grasped the heel of her injured foot.

She hissed in pain, and he glanced up at her. "Sorry. There's no way to do this that won't hurt."

She nodded and flapped a hand at him. "It's okay. Do what you must. I'll…bite a stick or something if I have to." She flashed a lopsided grin, which he returned.

All things considered, she was still in pretty good spirits, so…there was that. He found the end of the first strip of sheet and started winding it around her foot, tugging it tight and moving upward with each circle. Eyes shut and teeth bared in a grimace, Jessica endured his manipulation and the squeezing pressure of the wrap on her injury nobly. When he finished, tying off two ends in a simple knot, he noticed her complexion was a bit wan.

"You okay?"

She gave him a tight, jerky nod.

He brushed the hair back from her face. "I wish I had some Advil or something for you."

"It's okay. I'll live." She swallowed hard. "Hey, I survived thirty hours of back labor without painkillers when Eric was born. I can do this."

"Attagirl."

She took a deep breath and blew it out slowly through her pursed lips. Gage's attention snagged on her puckered mouth, and heat skittered through him. Jamming his palms against his eyes, he battled down the bump of lust and rose to his feet. Rolling his shoulders and flexing his back, he worked the fatigue from his muscles, preparing to carry Jessica again. He found the bottle of water and drank before passing it to her. She sipped then recapped the bottle.

"Want me to ride piggyback now? You know, the way Eric used to do when he was a kid?" she asked, while loading their supplies and the rest of the sheet into the plastic bag.

"You'd probably prefer that to the firefighter's carry, huh?"

"The one where you drape a person over your shoulder so that their head is dangling down your back?" She arched an eyebrow. "Uh…*yeah*. Nice as your ass is, I'd rather ogle it from right side up than upside down, all the blood rushing to my head."

"You think I have a nice ass?" He shot her a cocky grin.

She snorted. "Not the point, Coleman." She wiggled her fingers at him. "Hand up?"

He grasped her palm to help her get to her feet…or rather to her *foot*. She hung the sack from her arm and held her injured foot at an angle as he crouched for her to clamber onto his back. He hooked his arms under her legs, and she clasped her arms around his neck, riding on his back. He'd always thought "turtleback" would have been a better name for the hold than "piggyback" since the passenger clung to you like a tortoise shell.

In this position, Jessica's chin was right by his ear. As he walked, jostling her, her breath hissed and caught, whispered and exhaled, hot and tickling the fine hairs of his neck. He tried not to think about the way she was squished up against him, the way the ragged pants in his ear reminded him of the sounds of making love.

Instead, he concentrated on problem-solving. They needed to find their way to a phone, to someone who could drive them to the police and get Jessica to the hospital.

"Since I was unconscious for most of the drive to the trailer, I have no clue where we are. What can you tell me about the closest town and direction we need to head?"

Jessica sighed. "Not too much. I don't know this part of the state well, and the mountain roads were so dark and twisty I lost my sense of direction." She paused a beat then added, "Sorry."

"Stop apologizing. None of this is your fault."

"All of this is my fault." Her tone dripped dejection.

"Bull. It's Henry's fault."

"But if—"

"I mean it, Jess. I won't have you shouldering any blame." He stepped over a rill of runoff from the surrounding slopes and surveyed the way ahead, looking for the clearest path. "It is not your fault this maniac latched on to you and started harassing you, and I refuse to let you beat yourself up over the way things have transpired."

She said nothing for a moment, then murmured, "I'm responsible for the way I reacted—or overreacted—after our kiss at the cabin. If I hadn't bolted out there and climbed in the car where Henry was hiding—"

"Or if I hadn't blurted a rather huge admission without preparing you. I climbed in that car blindly, too. If I had done a better job protecting you, if I hadn't led Henry to your refuge—"

"Stop," she said, slapping his chest lightly with her palm. "I get it. There's blame enough to go around."

"Right. So now let's move past the blame game and put our heads together to get us home and put Henry behind bars."

"Okay. So I know the highway is a risky move. Henry could be patrolling it, searching for us. But if we hid out of sight of the road and waited for another driver—"

"Uh… Jess, would you stop to pick up a guy who bursts out of the woods at the last second, running out to flag you down?"

She rested her chin on his shoulder and groaned. "No. That reeks of crazy person."

"I'm okay with walking, carrying you. Our fitness program with the fire department requires us to stay in shape and be able to carry heavy equipment or an unconscious fire victim. But…" He slowed his pace and turned a full three-sixty, assessing their progress and their options. "I don't want to wander aimlessly."

Jessica lifted a hand to point. "It looks like there's an outcrop over there. Maybe we'll be able to get a sort of bird's-eye view of the terrain? Or see a house in the distance we can target?"

"Works for me." Gage trudged through the brambles and cleared a path with his foot through the slippery fallen leaves. He trekked over roots, rocks and ridges to the large granite rock that jutted out over a dense green valley. He set Jessica down carefully, and she clasped his arm as she stood on one foot to appraise the vale of yellow birch, rhododendron and hemlock.

"I don't see any houses or signs of a town."

"Me, either." He placed his hand over the one she'd wrapped around his arm and nodded toward a flat spot on the rock. "Let's rest a moment, huh?"

Jessica hobbled with his help to sit down and dug the water bottle out of the bag.

He motioned to her. "Ladies first."

Jess angled her head. "I'm not the one doing all the work." She thrust the bottle toward him. "Drink. 'Cause if you go down, we're sunk." She followed the observation with a frown and a mumble.

"What's that?" he asked, wiping his mouth with his arm after taking a swig of water.

"Nothing. You…wouldn't understand." Her gaze dropped to her hands, which she'd balled in her lap.

"You sure about that?" He offered her the water again, and she took a small sip.

"It's…complicated."

He took a seat beside her and nudged her with his shoulder. "Well, I may not have been a straight-A student like you, but I'm pretty good at figuring stuff out. Why not try me?" When she stayed silent, glaring at her hands, he added, "Jess, I just want to help."

Her head pivoted toward him then, and she heaved a dramatic sigh. "That's the thing, though. You're already doing everything! Thanks to my stupid ankle, you're having to carry me like a child. Do you have *any* idea how much I hate feeling useless and dependent and at the mercy of other people?"

He gave her a wry glance. "Sure I do."

"Really?"

Her dubious tone irritated him. "Really."

She scoffed. "Did *your* mother spend your childhood putting one loser boyfriend after another ahead of your welfare? Did you miss meals because your mom couldn't get her act together, or did you get left stranded at school because your mom was drunk and passed out with her latest bad choice?"

"I—"

"Did you have to raise yourself because your mother couldn't even take care of her own crappy life? That's feeling helpless. And that's when I learned not to depend on other people."

Gage had heard bits of Jessica's backstory before, but the pain behind her rant stung him anew.

"No, I didn't have that experience. You know what kind of parents Tina and I had."

"Mike and Carol Brady."

"Well, maybe not that saccharine, but...yeah. We had a good childhood." He paused, twisting his mouth. "And while we knew some of what you were dealing with at home, I guess I never knew all of it. I'm sorry."

She waved off his regret. "I kept a lot to myself."

"Still...what we knew...that's why we wanted to include you in our family stuff. Dinners, vacations, game nights. We knew you needed family, and we wanted to be your support. But—"

Her shoulders drooped. "And I appreciated it more than you could know."

"But..." He shifted to face her and drilled her with an unflinching stare. "Here's what I know about feeling helpless. I know how it feels to wake up after being knocked out to discover that you're in the middle of nowhere."

Her brow creased, and her dark eyes grew sad. Or maybe guilty?

He touched her knee. "Then you realize your hands and feet are tied, that you're being held by an unpredictable man, and that you are unable to protect or defend the woman you lov—" He cut himself off, swallowing the words he knew she didn't want to hear right now. Maybe ever. He shoved down the sting he'd known last night when she recoiled from his admission.

Retraining his focus on what he'd been expressing, he exhaled and started again. "Knowing that you're useless to help a good friend who is at the mercy of an obsessed and dangerous man." His gut clenched as he remembered the frustration and disgust he'd experienced last night and again this morning.

"I've watched a family's home burn to the ground because the fire had spread too far before our crew could get there. I've seen an accident victim die because I couldn't stop their femoral bleed fast enough. And as bad as it's been sitting by my sister's hospital bed, knowing how easily I could lose her and knowing I couldn't save her, last night was worse. You were at Henry's mercy, and I could do nothing to save you. So yes, I know how powerlessness feels, and it's not a feeling I'll soon forget."

"Oh, Gage…" A heart-wrenching sympathy passed over her face, leaving her eyes damp. Her nose flared as if she were fighting tears.

"It sucks to feel helpless, Jess. I get that." He framed her face with his hands. "But I know this, too. You are *not* helpless in this situation. You're strong, and smart, and capable. And if your ankle keeps you from walking, there is nothing wrong with accepting help from someone who cares about you until you're back on your feet. Literally and figuratively." His mouth twitched in a half grin for the unintended pun.

Her gaze dropped, and he nudged her chin back up.

"Receiving help doesn't make you weak or vulnerable. It makes sense. It's the smart choice."

She rolled her eyes and gave a small nod. "Maybe. I can't say I agree, but I won't argue the point with you."

"Jess, I—"

A rustling in the woods behind them yanked his attention from any further discussion. Had Blythe tracked them? The trail of disturbed leaves would have been easy enough to follow. He pressed a finger to his lips, telling Jessica to stay silent as he rolled to a crouch and peered deep into the shadowy trees. He squinted against the early rays of the sun as they cut through the lifting fog. Movement drew his gaze. A dark figure moved through the woods.

Chapter 20

"I'm riding with you," Matt said as he climbed in the passenger seat of his son's car.

"We'll cover more ground if we split up, take more cars," Eric countered.

"True." Matt buckled his seat belt. "But you've been known to be a bit rash when you get emotional. I want to make sure you don't end up in jail today if things don't go our way."

Eric glared at him. "Rash? What are you talking about?"

Matt scoffed. "Well, besides the numerous incidents in high school of underage drinking, truancy and general acting out, I remember a time when you ran away from home in sixth grade, once when you encouraged my wife's niece to climb out her bedroom window in the middle of the night to share ill-gotten booze, and once when you broke into an unoccupied cabin—"

Eric snorted as he backed his sedan onto the private lane. "I was a kid then and still dealing with a lot of stuff I have a better handle on now."

"Yeah. You've come a long way, and I'm proud of you. But your dad knows you have a hot head, so I'm riding shotgun, just in case."

Eric sighed and headed out of Cameron Glen. He pulled onto the highway headed toward the business area of Valley Haven.

"Besides, now that you're in college, I don't get as much time with you. Maybe I just want—" Matt fell silent as they passed a silver truck parked just off the side of the road. The Ford F-150 was tucked largely out of sight in the woods that bordered Cameron Glen. "Stop the car!"

"Huh?" Eric sent him a dubious frown but complied.

"That truck back there. Did you see it? The silver one." Matt unfastened his seat belt as Eric slowed to a stop on the shoulder of the road.

"What about it? Did you recognize it?"

"Not specifically. It shouldn't be there, for starters. That's Cameron Glen property. But…" He frowned as he racked his brain for the details Jessica had told him about the night of her car accident. "I think the truck her stalker drove was silver."

Eric's eyes widened. "Stalker? How bad has this guy been bothering Mom?" His expression grew darker. "How much danger is she in? Do you think this guy has her?"

Matt shouldered open the passenger door and swiped a hand down his face. "I've said too much. We didn't want you worried."

Eric scoffed and raised a hand as if to say, *What the hell?*

Matt jerked his chin as he climbed out of the car. "Keep a cool head, and let's go have a look at that truck."

Eric followed Matt, and they peered in the windows of the truck. An open box of pistol cartridges sat on the front seat along with a Cameron Glen brochure.

"Dad," Eric said. "Isn't this enough to amplify Mom's missing status?" He waved a hand toward the truck, his eyes wild with fear. "Doesn't this qualify as reason to believe Mom is in danger?"

Matt took out his phone. "It does for me. I'm calling the police."

Jessica froze, hearing the same crunch of leaves and snap of twigs Gage had clearly heard. She twisted at the waist as far as she could. Having any sort of threat at her back sent chills through her blood. When she tried to shift her injured leg, pain snaked up her calf and throbbed in her foot. Although she bit back the yelp, the catch in her breath and scuff of her pivot on the rock might as well have been a shout.

Gage held up a hand, telling her to be still. He slipped his pocketknife out of his pocket and unfolded the tiny blade. Not much of a weapon, but all they had.

Moving to his feet, he crept closer to the trees, his eyes narrowed and one hand shielding on his brow to block the sun. He sidled toward the nearest tree trunk of any size and stood behind it. An instant later the rustling became a crashing. Gage's body tensed along with her gut. But in the next instant, his shoulders dropped, and he exhaled loudly. "A deer. A nice-looking buck, in fact. Guess he finally smelled us and bolted."

He snapped the knife blade back into the handle and crossed to her.

"Can we get moving again? It was just a deer this time, but the longer we delay…"

"Sure. But first…" He gathered a few small stones and took the empty soda can from the bundle of supplies. "It was a deer this time, but…next time it could be a bear. This—" he rattled the can so that the rocks clattered and clanked "—will let bears know we're coming, and hopefully, scare them from our path. They don't want to tangle with us any more than we want to tangle with them."

He extended a hand to help her up, putting his shoulder under her arm as soon as her good foot was under her. Once she was steady, he squatted, allowing her to climb on his back again. She did, both savoring the feel of her arms around his wide shoulders and regretting the burden she was for him. He grunted as he hoisted himself up, and she tucked her face in the curve of his neck. "I swear I will pay for your PT or chiropractor to get your back in shape again after this."

"I'm fine," he said. "I am."

Though his tone was earnest, her continued helplessness and dependency on Gage sawed in her gut. She'd spent her life not wanting to need anyone, learning the hard way how to be self-sufficient…

Fate really had an ironic sense of humor.

Trust me to take care of you, Jess.

Scary as it still was for her, Gage had certainly proven himself in recent months and especially in the past several hours. As she rested her cheek against his ear, a wave of calm washed through her, knowing she could rely on Gage to get them through this crisis.

A tickle in her gut asked, *And what about beyond this debacle? What about that kiss?*

Gage was infamously commitment-phobic. He changed girlfriends like Mother Nature changed seasons. He claimed he'd had feelings for her for years, yet he'd never acted on them. How did he explain that? And why was she so reluctant to bring that subject up again? Maybe because it seemed too soon to lay his admission open and study it. Everything about their new dynamic felt so new, so hopeful and so fragile. He'd kept a bombshell secret from her for years, and she feared what other land mines she might encounter if she ventured down the path of the past with him.

The can of bear-deterrent pebbles rattled and clanked against his hip as Gage put one foot in front of the other. He tried not to think too hard about anything except the next step. And yet he knew his paced had slowed. They weren't making nearly the progress they had earlier in the day. But then, he *had* been trekking through the woods for several hours now. His back hurt, and his arms were tired from carrying Jessica.

He quickly shoved the complaint from his mind. He didn't care about tired arms or feet. He'd happily endure far worse discomfort, if it meant saving Jessica. He doggedly trained his thoughts on something other than his own plodding steps and aching muscles. But the notion that popped into his head was equally upsetting.

The hospital had tried to call him. Did that mean Tina had taken a turn for the worse? Man, he prayed not. He gritted his teeth, determined he wouldn't dwell on that, either. *Stay positive. Jessica needs your optimism.*

He knew the topic that gave Jessica the most joy and promise, the most determination to fight and survive. The beacon that had carried her through Matt's long deployments, her divorce and years of solitude. Her son. "So when will Eric have another chance to come home?

He will have a week or two off before the fall term starts, right?"

"Yeah." He heard the brightness in her tone, just as he'd hoped he would. "His exams are at the very end of July, then he gets two weeks off before fall classes start…hmm, around the middle of August. Don't remember the exact date."

"He is planning to come home then, right? Not go to the beach with buddies or anything?"

"Last I heard he'll come over to Cameron Glen. Especially since both Matt and I are there. Assuming I'm still there and not back in Charlotte or—"

"Hey. Listen," he cut in, coming to a stop and raising his gaze from the overgrown path. A low rumble rolled through the woods, confirming what he'd suspected. "Did you hear that?"

Jessica's grip tightened on his shirt. "Sounds like a car engine."

"Sorta. But deeper. More like a diesel truck."

Gage perked his ears and held his breath, listening, turning slowly to decipher from which direction the sound had come. The rumble they'd heard was joined by a familiar, piercing beep. The warning signal of a large vehicle in Reverse. "Well, unless Henry has stolen a fire engine or concrete mixer to search for us, that's not him. I'm following that noise."

He altered his path slightly, headed toward the grumbling engine. The noise didn't fade like a passing vehicle on the highway, but grew louder as he walked nearer to the spot where the sound originated. Encouraged by the first signs of civilization and help in hours, Gage picked up his pace, adrenaline and hope fueling him.

"There!" Jessica released her grip briefly to point through the trees to the flash of a bright orange construction vehicle in the midst of a clearing.

A tension he hadn't realized he'd been holding in released in his chest like the opening of a hydrant. Relief flowed out, and he marched the final yards through the forest with a grin spread across his face.

The first thing Jessica noticed as they emerged from the trees and waved down the workers at the construction site was the logo on the side of the bulldozer and backhoe.

Turner Construction.

A giddy laugh escaped her. "Gage, look! It's Jake's company!"

"Well, I'll be damned."

Their appearance had roused the attention of a man in a hard hat who stood with his head bowed over a blueprint. He conversed with a second man in terse shouts in order to be heard over the grumble of the diesel equipment. Having spotted them, the man in the hard hat strode across the uneven, upturned earth, frowning.

Gage met the man halfway, stopping by a pickup truck bearing the Turner Construction logo.

"Can I help you?" Hard Hat asked, his gruff tone at odds with the friendly question.

"You can if you have a working phone we can borrow or someone who can drive us to the nearest emergency room," Gage said, helping Jessica slide off his back. "We're stranded, and my friend has an injured ankle."

She stood on one leg beside him, bracing her hip and one arm against the truck's tailgate. Hard Hat dropped his gaze to Jessica's wrapped foot and rubbed the scruff on his cheeks. "We can spare someone for a while to drive you to the hospital up the road, I suppose."

"Is Jake Turner here, by any chance?" Jessica asked.

Hard Hat raised his eyebrows, clearly surprised she knew his boss's name.

Jessica smiled. "He's a friend of ours. Sorta family. Finding one of his work crews out here when we need rescue feels like providence."

"Naw. Mr. Turner's not here."

She shrugged. "It was worth a shot, huh?"

Hard Hat gave a grudging smile.

Gage pointed to the cell phone clipped to the man's hip. "Any chance that thing's got a signal out here? We'd like to call Jake or someone in the family to let them know where we are and that we're safe. They're bound to be worried."

Hard Hat unclipped the phone and passed it to Gage, who handed it to Jessica, saying, "After you call Matt, I want to call the hospital in Charlotte and check on Tina."

She squinted in the sunlight to see the screen of the cell and tapped in Matt's phone number. The call was answered with a dubious, "Hello?"

Jessica almost sobbed in relief. "Matt, it's me. Long story, but…we're safe, and we need a ride home."

She heard her ex-husband speak to someone else followed by a voice she'd know anywhere. "Mom? What the hell? Where are you?"

Tears filled her eyes. "Eric? What are you— Why—"

Then Matt came back on the line. "We're on our way, Jess. Where are you?"

She gave a small, hiccupping laugh. "I honestly don't know."

* * *

Two hours later, after the construction foreman had dropped them off at a small-town hospital, the local police had been summoned and an initial interview given, Jessica was reunited with her ex and her son. She and Gage were still in the waiting room doing paperwork when the two burst through the doors of the tiny ER like avenging angels, and Jessica fell happily into her son's embrace.

"Damn, Mom. We were so worried! What happened?" When she hesitated, deciding how much to tell her son, Eric held her by her shoulders and frowned at her. "Don't sugarcoat it for me. I'm not a child. I don't need protection from the bad stuff in this world. I want the whole truth."

Jessica looked at the young man scowling at her and goggled, realizing how much her boy *had* grown up. At nineteen, Eric was the age Matt had been when they got engaged. She nodded reluctantly and launched into the whole story, from the beginning. When she was finally taken to a curtained-off space in the exam area, Eric went with her to hear the rest of the disturbing tale. She described for the attending doctor and Eric how she'd stepped in the hidden hole and wrenched her ankle.

"I'm pretty sure it's broken," the doctor said, "but I'm going to send you for an X-ray before we decide what sort of cast you'll need. I'll go write up those orders, and someone from Radiology will come get you in a moment."

No sooner had the attending stepped out than a deputy from the sheriff's department peeked behind the curtain of the exam room. "I know you gave the city department a general rundown of what happened, but I have some more questions, if this is a good time."

She learned Gage had already given his account of events, and the deputy updated her on developments he'd already learned from the city police.

"A car matching the description of your sedan was found abandoned on the side of the highway, and a resident that lives about a quarter mile from the abandoned car reported their minivan stolen. So we're looking for the missing van and have put out a rough description of the man you say kidnapped you and Mr. Coleman." The deputy consulted his notes. "Henry Blythe."

Jessica sighed. "Except that's not his real name. That's just how I know him. The police department in Charlotte already ran that name and came up with nothing. Henry Blythe is an alias."

The deputy scratched his ear and grunted. "That's what Mr. Coleman said, as well. I've made a note of it. Can you come to the station when you finish here to help our artist create a rendering?"

"Happy to," she said. "The sooner that man is off the streets the better."

"Can't that wait?" Eric protested. "You've been through enough today. You need to rest, prop that foot up."

"I'll rest when Henry is off the streets." Turning back to the deputy, she said, "Tell your artist I'll be there as soon as the hospital discharges me."

Henry prowled the cheap motel room like a caged lion, seething at his miscalculations and the latest turn of events. He'd been sure Jessie and Coleman had been secure, and he hadn't been gone *that* long. His first mistake had been not building a better plan before taking Jessie, but when she'd climbed in the car where he'd been hiding, it had seemed like fate.

Now she was gone, in the wind—with Coleman. He clenched his teeth harder. Knowing he'd had his chance to kill that bastard to get rid of the competition and hadn't caused his gut to burn. But he'd thought he could use the firefighter to bend Jessie to his will.

He growled under his breath and dropped heavily on the edge of the sagging mattress. If he were Jessie, where would he go? She might be hiding in a hotel somewhere, or believing herself protected by Coleman, she might have gone back to Charlotte. Coleman's truck was still at the cabin in Valley Haven, at the vacation place… Cameron Valley or Colton Hills or some such.

Before he drove all the way back to Charlotte, it made sense to look for Jessie in Valley Haven first. Mind made up, Henry shoved to his feet and stalked to the motel room door. He peered out cautiously, checking for cops before heading to the van he'd snagged. Frowning at the behemoth, he decided he'd make a quick pit stop to trade for a less conspicuous vehicle. Then he'd find Jessie and make her pay for humiliating him. He no longer wanted anything from the troublesome bitch except revenge.

Chapter 21

Unfamiliar with using crutches, Jessica hobbled into the cabin that evening and dropped more than sat on the couch once in the living room. Her X-ray had confirmed a hairline break at her ankle, and she'd been given a walking cast along with crutches for extra support for the first few days of healing.

Noticing a citrus scent in the air, she gave Cait a puzzled look. "Do I smell lemons?"

"Oh, that's the cleaner I used to freshen the place up before you got here. I cleared up the food from the table and dishes from the sink and gave the place a general wipe-down. The last thing you needed was to come back to a day-old mess."

Jessica pressed a hand to her chest. "You're so thoughtful. How can I ever thank you? Not just for the cleaning help, but for everything this summer."

Cait shrugged. "It's what friends do."

Friends. Jessica's heart gave a bittersweet tug. While she was grateful for Cait's friendship, she missed her posse. The reminder of losing Sara fisted in her stomach. And what about Tina and Holly? Would she ever be able to share dinner and laughter with her best friends again?

"Special delivery!" Isla called as she bustled in with two large sacks from Ma's Mountain Diner. "I got a variety of vegetables since I wasn't sure of your favorites and plenty of fried chicken for that hungry man of yours."

Jessica opened her mouth to tell Matt's sister-in-law that Gage wasn't her man, but the words stuck in her throat. An instant later the moment was gone, as Gage, Matt and Eric trundled in after giving the area around the cabin a thorough search.

"No sign of the boogeyman," Matt announced, and little Erin, playing on the floor with her cousin, giggled, repeating, "Boogie!"

"Boogie, boogie, boogie!" Eric said and swept his laughing sister up for a playful tussle before tucking her under one arm and Isla's toddler under his other. "I'll take the pipsqueaks back to our place so y'all can talk."

Jessica shook her head. "I'm talked out. That sheriff's deputy and artist were nothing if not thorough."

"And I'm famished," Gage said, peeking in the bags Isla had set on the kitchen counter.

"Message received," Cait said, tugging at the sleeve of her husband's shirt. "We'll get out of your hair." She embraced Jessica and whispered, "I'm so thankful you're all right."

Jessica chuckled and swallowed the lump in her throat. "That makes two of us."

Once Matt, Eric and the Camerons had said their good-nights, Jessica helped Gage explore the varied offering of homestyle goodies Isla had supplied. For several minutes, neither said anything as they tucked hungrily into the spread of fried chicken, mashed potatoes and four different vegetables.

Only after he'd finished one plateful and was helping himself to seconds did Gage say, "You know, being back here at the cabin, having dinner with you, reminds me…"

His lead-in was enough to tell her where his thoughts were, and her pulse jumped. "Gage—"

He set his plate down and raised his gaze to hers. "It's kinda where we left off before—"

Jessica put her fork down and nodded. "I know."

"And since then, we haven't really addressed the elephant in the room."

"I suppose not." Feeling suddenly fidgety, she clasped her hands together in her lap to keep them still. "Listen… I'm sorry I freaked out. I don't want you to think—" She hesitated, sighed. "It's not that I don't care about you. Of course I do. But you flipped more than twenty years of friendship on its head, and it was…a lot to digest."

"I get that. I realize I shouldn't have blurted it out like that." Gage pushed his plate away and angled his chair to face hers more directly. "However…what I said was the truth."

"But how…? Why didn't you say anything for so long?"

Gage dragged a hand over his face and gave her a sad half smile. "Because I couldn't. At first, I struggled with the fact that you were so close to our family, Tina's best friend. It felt…*wrong* somehow. You'd been like a sister. I tried to convince myself I didn't feel what I felt. Then you met Matt and…man, was I jealous of that relationship." He gave a wry chuckle as he glanced away. "I *had* to keep quiet then. I wasn't going to spoil your happiness. And I thought, maybe this is for the best. I couldn't tell you I loved you when you were married to another man. I told myself your being with Matt would force me to move on and put my fascination with you behind me." He returned his gaze to her, his eyes full of an ancient pain that speared her soul. "But I didn't move on."

She ruminated on his confession for a moment, then asked, "I don't understand. You've dated a lot of women through the years."

He chuckled without humor. "Dated, yes. Fallen in love with? Nah. I couldn't commit to another woman when I was still in love with you."

Her heart thrashed in her chest like a wild rabbit fighting to get free. "I always thought you didn't get married because you didn't want to settle down or have kids. That you liked being a bachelor and playing the field."

He blew out a sigh and rubbed his cheek. "Of course I wanted to settle down and have a family. With you. And when that was not possible, I chose not to settle for second best. That's no way to start a marriage."

Jessica's lungs felt leaden, and a deep sadness dragged at her. Gage would have been a terrific husband and father. "So *I'm* the reason you never had kids? Never had a long-term relationship with a woman?" Her voice cracked as she saw the past twenty-plus years through a new lens.

He must have seen something in her expression of how that knowledge weighed on her, because he reached for her hand and pressed it between his own. "I'm not saying it's your fault. Don't take that on yourself, Jess. I made that decision, and I can live with it."

"But, Gage, I— If I'd known…" She let her words trail. What *would* she have done if she'd known his feelings? Certainly it would have been awkward at best. And how would it have changed her relationship with Tina if she hadn't been comfortable around Gage at the family events? *Tina...*

"You said earlier you aren't sure if Tina was aware of how you felt."

Gage's eyes grew round. "Well, I sure didn't tell her. I knew she wouldn't have kept it a secret from you, and I wouldn't have asked her to try. If she ever suspected, she never said as much to me." His brow dipped, and his silver gaze sharpened. "There was just too much at stake for me to toss a stink bomb into the mix. Your friendship to Tina. Your marriage to Matt. Our friendship." He paused and narrowed his eyes on her in a heartbreaking way. "We are friends, aren't we, Jess? Have I spoiled that by telling you my truth?"

Tears pricked her sinuses, and emotion clogged her throat. "Of course. But..."

His chest swelled as he drew a breath, as if bracing to hear what followed. "But?"

"I'm not sure what else we are. I know I've come to see you differently over the past several weeks. And the past few days, I—" She squeezed his hand and swallowed hard to clear her throat, choose her words. A breathy half laugh escaped. "You're definitely a good kisser."

He tugged up one cheek. "Just good?"

She cocked her head slightly to the side. "Fine. A great kisser. A mind-blowingly amazing kisser. Which only makes it harder for me to figure out what's happening. What I want."

His frown said that wasn't the answer he was hoping for. He sat back, releasing her hands and flattening his palms on the table in front of him. "I see."

"Gage, it's still new to me, this seismic shift between us. I…have questions."

"So ask. I want a clean slate with you."

"Well, what about after I divorced Matt? Why didn't you say anything then? I've been single for eight years now."

He lifted one eyebrow and nodded. "True. But do you remember what you told people after you divorced Matt?"

She paused and rewound her memories to the days after she split from Matt. "I probably said a lot of things I shouldn't have. What is it you remember?"

"That you were done with men, done with relationships, and only wanted to be a mother and have your independence from then on."

"Hmm. Right. That *was* how I felt. Even friendly divorces are hard."

Though her split from Matt had been amicable, it stung to see the relationship dissolve. Her reasons for going solo, her disappointment in what she perceived as Matt's unavailability and growing distance had only reopened the scars her mother left. Matt's months of deployment meant she'd essentially been a single mother for long stretches. And when Matt had been wounded in action and medically discharged from the military, he'd had demons of his own to fight.

They'd struggled to reconnect, each having grown in a different direction. Though intellectually she knew Matt hadn't truly deserted her, the ghosts of her childhood whispered to her that Matt hadn't been there for her when she needed him, just like her mother and absent father.

"So," he said, turning up a palm. "In the wake of

a declaration like that, what chance did I have in the months after your divorce?" He fisted his hand then and bumped it lightly on the table. "And then… I kept waiting for the right time to tell you how I felt. And kept pushing the conversation down the road because—" he lifted a shoulder and waved one finger between them "—of this. I didn't want to wreck our friendship or yours with Tina."

Jessica wrapped her arms around herself, nodding. "I get that. I do."

"You're important to me, Jessica. More important than I've let on through the years, because I didn't want to scare you away. But I decided, at some point, that having a little of you in my life was better than blowing everything up and losing what I did have." He drew his brow into a deep V. "I'm sorry if my silence feels like a deception. That was never my intent."

She sighed and gave him a gentle smile. "I know you well enough to know that's true. I shouldn't have accused you of that. I was in shock. Confused. Reeling."

He became still, and his eyes more intense. "And now? Where are we? What do you want?"

She pushed away from the table and stood. Rubbing her arms, she clomped in her boot cast to the window to look out at the long shadows as the sun sank behind the mountains. "I don't know. I have a lot to think about and things have been so nuts…"

"No pressure. I don't want to rush you." He gave a humored chuff. "Lord knows I've been patient long enough. A few more days or weeks isn't going to change things for me."

She faced him and lifted a cheek in a soft smile.

"Thank you." With another glance out the window, she said, "I think I'm going to go out for a bit. It's a pretty evening, and I have a lot to consider."

He arched an eyebrow. "In your cast? Aren't you supposed to keep your foot elevated?"

She chuckled. "I didn't say I was going for a run. I'll use the crutches and stay close to the cabin. But the outdoors helps clear my mind and center me. I need that right now."

"Let me come with you," Gage said, "You can lean on me when you're navigating the rough or uneven spots."

She shook her head. "Please, don't. I need…time to think. Some time alone to wrap my head around what's happening between us."

Gage pressed his mouth in a taut line and folded his arms over his chest. "It'll be getting dark soon."

Jessica chuckled wryly. "You sound like me when Eric was a kid and wanted to ride his bike after dinner. He used to say in his too-smart-for-his-own-good style, 'That's what streetlights are for.'"

Gage lifted a corner of his mouth. "I suppose. Still…"

"I'll just be at the fishing dock. You can see it from the front window." She tucked her crutches under her armpits and crossed to the front door. She flashed a wry grin. "If you get bored waiting for me, you could do the dishes."

He exhaled as if in concession. "Just…be careful. Remember the boards on the dock are uneven and—" He stopped himself and swiped a hand over his mouth. "Just…be careful."

She nodded. "Of course."

Setting out across the grassy lawn, which was easier to traverse than the gravel drive, Jessica took a deep breath of the fresh evening air. She walked slowly, even after making it to the paved road that wound through the glen. The last thing she needed was another tumble, and the hill down to the dock was steeper than she remembered.

Through a lit window, she saw the family renting the Pine cabin sitting down to dinner, and she heard the giggle of female voices coming from the direction of the Turners' house. She smiled, imagining the Turner girls, Fenn and Lexi, playing on the tire swing she'd seen earlier that summer.

The crutches thumped loudly as she hobbled to the far end of the wooden dock that extended well into the lake, affording fishermen better access to the deepest part of the stocked pond.

After some awkward gyrations, she was glad Gage hadn't witnessed, Jessica sat down on the end of the dock. She wished she could dangle her feet in the cool water, especially her already hot and itchy casted leg. Instead, she simply watched the dragonflies skim over the surface of the small lake and the first hints of the sunset cast a pink glow around the black silhouette of trees. A soft breeze sent ripples across the water, but soothed her soul.

Turning her head slowly to take in the whole setting—the fishing lake, the hillside striped with the crop of fragrant Christmas trees, the yellow glow of lights in cabin windows, the flower beds offering their splashes of color—she sensed a sweet peace that had been all too rare recently.

If she were honest, she couldn't credit the idyllic retreat setting for the whole of her calm and contentment. Her talk with Gage had been productive, given her insights and answers that settled the stormy seas inside her. Sure, she saw Gage in a new light, but she no longer felt the same shock that had initially rocked her equilibrium. What did it mean for their relationship going forward?

"That *is* the question," she muttered to herself as she leaned back on braced arms. Staring across the small lake, she watched one of the ducks that lived on the property nibbling plants in the shallows and allowed her mind to start sorting, analyzing, shuffling.

Initially, Gage's confession had terrified her. But why? She didn't shy away from telling the people who meant the most to her she loved them, and she treasured expressions of love from Eric, her friends, even Matt— though the words meant something different now. She'd probably even told Gage she'd loved him before—in the same breath she told Tina the same. So why had this felt different? Why had it scared her?

Was it Henry's obsession and twisted use of the word *love* that haunted her, tainting the words? She shuddered just remembering her stalker's misuse of the expression. No, Henry wasn't anywhere near the same category as Gage. She saw no cross contamination there.

Hadn't she already sensed her own feelings undergoing a shift toward Gage? She'd turned to him following the accident, texting him, confiding in him, sharing reciprocal support, understanding and grief over Tina's condition. She—

With a shake of her head, she stopped that line of thought. Her hesitation, her fear wasn't about how she felt toward him. That realization startled her. She exhaled, turning this discovery over in her head. She trusted her own feelings, but could she trust Gage's? She'd been viewing Gage as a womanizer, unwilling to commit. She'd used the same wary standard to judge him that she'd learned watching her mother's poor choices. But hadn't Gage proven himself reliable, loyal, genuine?

He'd rallied to defend and protect her when Henry's behavior became more threatening. He'd never backed down or walked away in the face of her continued push-back, her stubborn independence.

And he'd gone above and beyond to get her to safety, to literally carry her on his back to save her when she'd hurt her ankle. He'd patiently waited in the wings for decades, loving her, respecting her needs, her marriage, her independence. Gage had been one of the pillars of her life since high school. Like the petals of a flower sequentially unfolding or dominoes falling, each realization led to another, illuminating her life, her fears, her feelings. Gage's steady faithfulness. His unselfish dependability. His—

The dock vibrated, and the thud of heavy footfalls told her she had company.

His insistence that he needed to protect her, she added semi-peevishly to her growing "Gage list."

"I told you I wanted some time alone." She huffed with frustration as she twisted at the waist and looked behind her.

And froze.

"And I've told you, I'm tired of your games," Henry groused as he stalked down the dock, the wooden planks shuddering with each stomping step toward her. "This ends now, Jessie."

Chapter 22

"Either you're coming with me, or you're never going anywhere again." Henry's tone and expression were hard, cold. "I warned you not to humiliate me. I've given you chance after chance. But I'm done. This is your last chance."

Limbs weak with fear, Jessica fumbled for her crutches, burdened by her cast as she tried to stand. "Stay away from me! Why can't you leave me alone?"

He spread his hands, his voice cracking. "I can't stay away. I love you, Jessie."

"No!" she shouted, finally pushing unsteadily to her feet. She edged back a step, mindful she was at the end of the dock with nowhere to retreat. "You don't know what real love is. Love doesn't hurt and harass and torture. You have to stop this!"

Realizing she couldn't defeat Henry alone and injured, that she had to rouse back up, she screamed, "Someone help me! Gage, hurry!"

Henry's pleading face soured quickly. He surged forward and, knocking the crutches from her grip, grabbed her by the arms. "*Gage?* Seriously? What is it with you and that bastard?" He shook her so hard her teeth clicked and her head whipped violently. "If I shake you hard enough, maybe I'll rattle him loose from your head."

His hostile shaking rocked her already precarious balance. Without her crutches for support, she stumbled, teetered. Her walking cast slipped off the wooden planks, the sinking weight of it further destroying her equilibrium. Jessica gasped and clutched at Henry to break her fall.

But the heavy cast and laws of gravity won.

Jessica splashed into the lake, and her panicked grip on Henry pulled him in, as well. In a tangle of his limbs and hers, Jessica sank beneath the surface. Her heavy cast, quickly sodden, pulled her down like an anchor. The murky pond rushed into her sinuses, spiking her panic. She struggled to surface, but Henry's floundering on top of her and the deadweight of her injured leg hindered her.

With her lungs burning for air, Jessica kicked her good leg and spread her arms, trying to right herself, battling to break the surface. The muddy water and fading sunlight made it hard to see, to orient herself. Memories from that spring, of her car entering the river, of being trapped as the water rose around her, flashed in her mind. The helplessness, the agony of being unable to save her dear friends.

Finally untangling herself from Henry, she pushed off from the muddy bottom of the lake. She broke the surface long enough to gasp a mouthful of air before Henry's grasping hands dragged her back under.

For long minutes after Jessica left the cabin, Gage had stood at the cabin window and watched her on the dock.

The sinking sun cast her in a rich golden light, and he wanted to burn the image in his brain, wanted to drink in the beautiful picture she made. The peaceful setting, the evening glow, her serenity had mesmerized him.

But Jessica had asked to be alone, and in respect for her privacy, he'd forced himself to walk away, to turn his attention to cleaning up the kitchen. He could at least do something useful while he waited for her return. His pulse thumped, and anxiety spun through him as if he were waiting for a jury to come back with a verdict on his future. Would Jessica be a part of his life? Had he done irreparable harm to their relationship after all these years of biding his time and waiting for her?

He cracked open the window over the sink, letting the evening breeze refresh the kitchen. From his position at the sink, he had a tranquil view of the distant mountains and, directly behind the cabin, a hillside lined with two-foot-tall Douglas and Fraser firs, destined to be Christmas trees in a few more years. A wild rabbit hopped between the rows of firs, pausing to nibble the long grass. Gage studied the rabbit, deep in thought, until something startled the bunny, and it scampered away.

He craned his head, looking for what had spooked the shy creature, but saw nothing.

But then a scream sounded outside.

Jessica.

Like the rabbit, Gage ran. Out of the kitchen. Through the front door. Across the yard toward the lake.

At first he didn't see her. She wasn't on the fishing dock anymore. But sunlight glinted on a disturbance in the water. He saw two people struggling, flailing, splashing. And icy horror filled his veins.

"Jessica!" He sprinted down the grassy hill toward the lake. His speed didn't slow as he leaped onto the dock, and his feet pounded down the wooden walkway. He spotted Jessica's crutches, discarded at end of the dock, and his anxiety ratcheted up. As he toed off his shoes preparing to dive in the lake after Jess, he recognized who was grappling in the lake with her.

Anger twisted in his gut. *Enough* of this jerk coming after Jess! If the cops didn't do something about this guy, he would. He was a microsecond from jumping into the lake to help Jessica when he heard a shout. "Gage!"

He shot a glance over his shoulder to Matt and Eric. The father and son were across the lake on the Harkneys' back deck. "It's Blythe! Call the cops!"

Without waiting to see if they complied, he estimated the best place to land and jumped in the lake.

Jessica shoved against Henry's grasping hands. Between his grip and the sinking heft of her cast, her energy and her air were quickly draining. She wasn't sure if Henry was pulling at her trying to save himself or if he was intentionally holding under the surface.

Until his hands closed around her throat and squeezed. A new level of panic flooded her limbs, her heart, her lungs. Fueled by fear and adrenaline, she clawed at his grip around her neck.

His fingers were unyielding. Henry was too strong. She couldn't pry his hands away. But her hands were free to attack him. She tried to bash his nose with an upward strike of her palm. Resistance of the water drastically cut the power of her punch, virtually nullifying the effect.

Fast, powerful strikes weren't possible. So she curled her fingers and clawed at his eyes.

She heard his lake-muted growl as she dug her fingernails into flesh and raked his face. He thrashed his head to the side, but she kept swiping, digging at any vulnerable place she could reach.

Her lungs screamed for air, and darkness was creeping in from the edges of her vision. She was losing the battle. Slipping away.

Profound sadness washed through her. Regrets. She'd never see Eric get married. Never see the sunrise again. *Never get to tell Gage she loved him.*

The last thought sent a sharp pain through her.

At the end of her held oxygen supply, she gasped. And choked as pond water filled her mouth.

She had only an instant to realize Henry had released his hold on her before strong hands seized her arms and propelled her to the surface. She coughed, sputtered, then vomited dirty water. Blinking, she tried to clear her vision. Water and hair blinded her to all but a blur of activity beside her. Grunts. Splashing. Too soon, she was sinking again. She gasped a ragged breath just before her head went under.

Gage grappled in the water with Henry. The struggle was more of a wrestling match than a fistfight in the water. His attack had startled Blythe briefly, shifting his opponent's attention from Jessica long enough for Gage to grab her up, out of the water for a breath.

But Henry latched on to him from behind, an arm around his throat. Gage wrenched his head aside and chomped down on Blythe's arm. Hard. Drew blood.

Henry released him, shoving him away as his dark, angry growl rumbled in the splashing waves. Gage had only a moment to scissor-kick, suck in air and pivot to face his foe before Henry came at him again. As he braced for Blythe's attack, he saw Jessica sinking again, her arms flailing weakly.

He deflected the assault of Henry's grabbing hands as best he could while reaching for Jessica. He stuck his hand toward her, praying she saw it, could grasp it before she hit bottom. Their fingers brushed—and slipped apart.

Henry climbed Gage like a ladder, propelling himself out of the lake to get a new lungful of air, even as he pushed Gage deeper below the surface. Gage took the opportunity to wrap his arms around his opponent's legs, trapping them, hindering Henry's ability to kick or to stay upright. Gage savored having the upper hand, if only briefly, before realizing how much trouble Jessica was in. No matter how it pained him to forfeit his advantage, Jessica was his priority. Now and always.

He twisted and thrust out, buying some distance from Blythe. With a kick, he turned. Circling his arms, he propelled himself toward the bottom of the lake, toward the dark blur of Jessica's hair.

Her groping hand touched his foot, clutched weakly. But it was enough for him to reach her, grab her wrist, tug her upward. When he could wrap an arm around her back, under her arms, he flutter-kicked and brought her to the surface once more. He inhaled a restorative breath, but Jess only gagged and wheezed.

"Here!"

The voice called his attention to the dock, where Eric

lay on his stomach, arms outstretched. Gage lifted Jessica's arm within her son's reach. Eric seized hold of her and dragged her onto the fishing dock, rolling her onto her side.

Before he could register more than that, Henry had attacked him again, taking a fistful of Gage's hair and bending his head backward. A thousand pinpricks of fire blazed on his scalp. Fresh fury fired and fueled his fight. Gage dunked and performed a backward roll like the ones he'd perfected at summer camp years before. His feet flipped over his head, and he jammed his heel in Blythe's nose.

The fist yanking Gage's hair released, and Gage righted himself in the water, already preparing his next move—a move he never got the chance to deliver.

Chapter 23

Jessica lay on her side, coughing and gasping like a fish on land. Despite the tremble of fatigue and fear in her limbs, she struggled to sit up. When hands reached for her, she flinched away, until she swiped sodden hair from her face and blinked Eric and Matt into clarity.

"Where's Henry?" she rasped, her anxious gaze darting from side to side to find the source of her terror.

"Gage is handling him," Eric said, a note of hero worship in his tone.

"Yeah, I need immediate police and ambulance presence at Cameron Glen. The fishing lake pier…" Matt said, a cell phone to his ear.

As Eric shoved to his feet, his eyes rounded. "Dad, look out!"

Jessica twisted in time to see Henry levering himself up on the edge of the pier, arms braced, a malevolent glare on Matt.

Eric snatched up one of her crutches and swung it like a baseball bat. The crutch caught Henry across the temple, and her stalker's eyes rolled back. Jessica sagged as Henry toppled into the lake again. They had a moment's reprieve, but—

"Where's Gage?" Pulse thrumming, Jessica scrambled

on her hands and knees toward the end of the pier. As she spotted him in the water, unmoving, a cry ripped from her throat. "Gage! No!"

Eric spun to find Gage, and quickly tore off his shoes. "I'll get him." He pulled his cell phone from his back pocket and shoved the device into Matt's hands. When Eric jumped in the lake, fresh waves of horror crashed through Jessica. If anything happened to her son—

No! The mere thought strangled her. Not her baby, her only child! She squeezed the edge of the wood planks, searching for Henry to gauge the threat he posed. He, too, floated in the lake, his body still. A tremor crawled through her. How hard had Eric hit her stalker? Was he…dead?

A splash and grunt called her attention back to her son. To Gage.

Still panting for restorative oxygen, she watched Eric grab Gage's unmoving body under the arms. Her son hoisted Gage enough to keep his head above water as he scissor-kicked and pulled Gage closer to the dock. Setting his phone, line to the emergency operator still open, onto the dock, Matt sank awkwardly onto his good knee. He braced himself, trying to lift Gage out of the water. Jessica hurried to help, taking one arm, grabbing the waist of Gage's jeans.

While Eric pushed, Jessica and Matt pulled. The effort wasn't pretty, but they dragged him onto the dock.

"Gage? Say something! Wake up, please!" Jessica stroked his cheek with her palm, then gave his face sobering pats.

Soon, Gage groaned and raised a hand to wipe his eyes as Matt and Jessica rolled him on his side. Spitting out a mouthful of water, Gage slowly turned onto his stomach and pushed up to his hands and knees.

Seeing Gage rally, Jessica turned back toward the lake. She heard a swish of water but didn't see Eric. Her heart climbed into her throat. "Eric!"

"Easy, Jess. He's right here," Matt said, once again reaching toward the water.

Jessica left Gage's side to assist in extracting Eric from the lake. But it was Henry's lolling head that rose above the edge of the pier. Her heart tripped, and she physically recoiled as her ex and her son maneuvered Henry's limp body onto the dock.

Eric hoisted himself up and climbed out of the lake with the skill of the young athlete he was. But for all his newly acquired maturity and manly physique, her son's eyes were those of a frightened child's as he gawked at Henry. He lifted his stricken gaze to Matt, then turned to Jessica. "Did I...kill him?"

Jessica rushed to embrace her son, cradle his head against her shoulder. "Oh, Eric. My brave boy. You saved me, you saved Gage."

"But I—" Eric levered away from her hug to shift his attention to Henry.

His face tense, Matt pounded Henry on the back, and Gage, still sucking in air between coughs, crawled over to the other men. "Get him...on his back."

Jessica kept her arm around Eric, needing him for support as much as she guessed he needed hers. She watched Matt and Gage begin CPR on Henry—flipping him on his back, checking for breathing, for a pulse, then starting chest compressions.

She bit her bottom lip, choking back the sounds of distress that bid to rise. As much as she'd prefer for Henry to die, a fit consequence of his terror campaign on her and just karma for his part in Sara's death, she also couldn't wish the man dead when Eric had dealt the blow that knocked him unconscious, caused him to slip under the water.

Eric didn't need a front-row view of the lifesaving procedure. Nor did she. With a nudge, she tried to coax Eric to leave the scene. "Walk with me? Please?"

Probably only because she appealed to his protective and caring instincts where she was concerned, Eric moved stiffly down the dock toward shore. He cast repeated glances over his shoulder to the other men, his expression troubled.

When they reached the end of the pier, she veered away from the stairs and found a spot on the grassy hill to stand and keep vigil. She put an arm around her son's waist in a side hug, and he reciprocated with his arm across her back at her shoulders. The chirp of crickets and nocturnal frogs surrounded them as they stared back at the activity on the end of the pier.

Sensing a new presence beside her, Jessica cut a glance toward the new arrival and met Cait's worried eyes. Cait draped a blanket around Jessica and Eric, then rubbed a comforting hand on Jessica's back, no words necessary. Another stir of movement in her peripheral vision drew her attention to the crowd forming at the top of the hill by the head of the steps that led to the dock. Guests to the retreat had clearly heard the ruckus and were drawn out to see what had happened. Camerons, young and old, also assembled, ready to offer help. Cait sent a hand signal to her sister Emma, who turned and ran, as if silently dispatched on a mission.

The distant wail of a siren signaled the approach of the emergency assistance Matt had called for. She spotted Matt's daughter, Erin, in Grace's arms, Cait's mother ever ready to quietly assist and provide backup to her family during good times or crises.

The whole Cameron family was steadfast. Loving. Reliable in a way Jessica's mother never had been. A tug of jealousy besieged her until she realized the Camerons' loving loyalty extended to Eric.

The envy morphed to gratitude. Eric had been embraced by this inspiring family. And…so had she. The Camerons' compassion and generosity were not limited to blood ties. Their hospitality toward Jessica throughout the summer gave evidence of that. Cait's warmth and friendship had been a surprising serendipity when Matt remarried. And like concentric waves, the acceptance and devotion rippled out. Cait's siblings, parents, brothers- and sister-in-law—Jessica had been welcomed into the family, wrapped in the same familial love and support, adopted by their clan.

Tears sprang to her eyes as the truth penetrated the layers of protection she'd erected around her heart. Because of this family, she was not and would never be truly alone. Just as she'd never truly been alone for years, thanks to the constant and encouraging presence of her posse—Holly, Sara, Tina…and Gage.

Her focus returned to Gage, hunkered over the man who'd tried to kill her, the man who'd savagely knocked Gage out and bound them both, the man whose reckless disregard for life had cost Sara hers. Gage compressed Henry's chest over and over, unrelenting. A rescue professional in action. When Matt placed a hand on Gage's shoulder and shook his head, Gage shook it off. Continued working to revive his patient.

He was wholly committed to his calling as a first responder. Honorable to a fault. And had proven time and again his devotion and loyalty to her. The truth warmed her from the inside, filling her with light and hope like the sun brightening a new day. She stared at Gage, studying him with her new perspective. He'd said he'd never married anyone else because he'd been in love with her. He'd never forced his feelings on her, waiting patiently through her marriage to Matt, through her post-divorce healing.

Her attention only shifted again when an ambulance arrived and a stretcher was carried down the stairs and out the long dock. And only when the EMTs pushed him aside and took up the compressions did Gage stop rendering CPR.

"Mom," Eric said softly, a quaver in his voice, "if the guy dies—"

Jessica turned to her son, her stomach dropping when she saw how pale and frightened he looked. She knew where his mind had gone. "Oh, Eric, don't—"

"It will be my fault. I hit him with the crutch."

She grabbed her child into a bear hug and squeezed him as if she could crush the guilt and worry from him. "Don't go down that path, baby. You've done nothing wrong."

"But...I killed him."

"No. Maybe. It's not... Oh, Eric." She swallowed hard. "Even if Henry dies, you did the right thing. It was self-defense. You were protecting me and helping Gage. You did nothing wrong."

But even knowing the truth of the circumstances did little to quell the trip of fear down her own spine. What if the police didn't believe their account of the facts? And even if no charges were filed against Eric, how did he grapple with the trauma of what had happened today? With his part in Henry's death? Because she had a horrible suspicion the EMT wouldn't have any better luck reviving her stalker than Gage had had.

Chapter 24

By the time the police finished questioning everyone and Jessica had a new cast put on to replace her water-logged one, a new morning was dawning. Jessica was beyond exhausted, but she wouldn't sleep until she'd assured herself Eric was all right.

"Will you drop me off at Matt's house?" she asked Cait's brother-in-law. "I need to check on my son."

Gage gave her a skeptical look across the back seat of Emma and Jake Turner's minivan. Cait's older sister and her husband had won the debate over who would stay at the hospital to drive Jessica and Gage home. Cait, Isla and Brody had young children to put to bed. Matt needed to stay with Eric, whose interview with the police had taken longer than the others. And Neil and Grace were chosen to calm the retreat guests and reassure everyone Cameron Glen was safe.

"I will," Jake said. "But Matt texted to say they're fine. Daryl went over to sit with Eric and give him moral support."

Jessica smiled tiredly, happy to hear Eric had some-one near his own age to lean on. Her son's friendship with the Camerons' adopted son had strengthened in recent months. Just one more blessing the Camerons had been to her family.

"Just the same," she said, "I need to see him. Hug him."

Emma turned to smile at her. "I understand *completely*."

When they entered Matt's cabin a few minutes later, Eric surged from the couch where he was talking to Daryl and rushed over to give Jessica one of his wonderful bear hugs. She held her boy for long moments before finally rasping the question she'd been fretting over for hours. "What did the police say? Are they charging you with anything?"

He shook his head. "Based on our description of events and Henry's history of stalking and kidnapping you at gunpoint, they believed it was self-defense. And because they found no evidence I meant to kill him, they said I was free to go."

"Oh, thank heavens!" She captured Eric's face between her palms and kissed his forehead.

"Do you want to tell them what *you* learned from the police a little while ago?" Gage prompted.

Eric pulled back to eye her curiously. "Mom?"

Jessica took a deep breath and nodded. "We already knew Henry was using an alias, so the police ran his fingerprints and submitted a DNA sample searching for hits. And while it's too early for DNA confirmation, they got a hit with his fingerprints in the FBI's national system, called AI—" Her weary brain faltered.

"IAFIS?" Matt supplied.

"Yes, that." She exhaled and reorganized her thoughts. "Henry's real name it seems is Henry Cavendal. He was wanted in Ohio for killing his mother and another woman that he'd been dating."

"The dude killed his own mother?" Daryl asked from the couch. "Cold. Ice-cold."

"He'd been on the run, evading Ohio authorities for three years," Gage added.

"Eric, man," Daryl said. "You're a hero. You rid the world of one bad apple."

But Eric didn't look relieved. His brow still furrowed with guilt.

"Eric?" Jessica said, tipping her head, trying to make eye contact with her son.

He took a step back and forced a smile. "I'm okay. I just…need time to come to terms with everything."

When he returned to the couch, she tried to follow, wanting to do something, *anything* to relieve her son from the turmoil she knew he was suffering. Gage caught her arm, though, and murmured, "You heard him. He needs time. And you need sleep."

Even as she pivoted to argue the point, she wobbled on her crutches and her head spun. Gage caught her around the waist and nudged her toward the door. "You've seen him. He's not going to face charges. Either come willingly, or I will carry you out of here." His cheek twitched with humor. "You know I can…and I will."

With a final glance toward Eric, Jessica nodded and let Gage take her home.

Hours later, sunlight peeked through the curtains of the Juniper cabin's bedroom, nudging Jessica reluctantly from sleep. An arm draped over her from behind, its owner snoring softly at her back.

She remembered little of last night from the time she left Eric at Matt's cabin and hobbled on her crutches to fall into bed. Except…

"Stay with me. Hold me. I don't want to be alone tonight."

Too tired to fight or question what her heart craved, Jessica had only to whisper the request as she drifted to sleep, and Gage had cuddled behind her, his arms wrapping her in a secure embrace.

Now, feeling more rested but with muscles aching in places she'd never imagined existed, Jessica turned to face Gage, a process that involved untwisting the sheet from her cast and using a hand to help move the extra weight around her foot. The stir of activity woke Gage, of course, and she wrinkled her nose as she muttered groggily, "Sorry. I'm not too graceful or stealthy at the moment."

"Everything all right?" he asked, rubbing his eyes with the heels of his hands.

She opened her mouth to answer, then hesitated.

He sat up, frowning when she didn't answer. "Jess? What is it?"

"A pat response didn't feel right, and I realized I hadn't really processed everything that happened yesterday." Raking the hair from her face with her fingers and lying on her back, she stared up at the ceiling. "Henry is dead. He can't threaten me anymore."

Gage placed a warm hand on her thigh. "Yeah. You're safe, sweetheart."

Her gaze darted to meet his when he used the endearment, but before either of them could comment, his cell phone rang, and he turned to check the screen. His face sobered, and he held up a finger signaling, *Just a minute*. "The hospital in Charlotte."

He swung his legs out of the bed as he answered the call and listened carefully. "This is he. Yes?"

Gage carried the phone with him as he left the bedroom, and Jessica used the moment alone to send up a quick prayer that Tina was all right, was improving. She struggled to sit up and retrieve the crutches from beside the bed, then glanced down at the oversize T-shirt she wore like a nightgown. She found her bathrobe, used the bathroom and followed the scent of coffee and the low rumble of Gage's voice to the kitchen.

He handed her a steaming mug of coffee, fixed just the way she liked it, as he finished up his phone call. "Thank you for calling. I'll be there in a few hours to sign the paperwork."

He disconnected the call and stared at the blank screen for a moment, his brow furrowed.

Jessica's pulse kicked up. She was *so* tired of bad news and grief. "Just...tell me."

He exhaled long and hard as he met her gaze. "Tina's doctor is discharging her from the hospital today."

Jessica set her mug on the counter with a thunk that sloshed her hot drink. "What?"

A stunned smile grew on his face. "Her vitals have continued to hold steady, and he says she's ready for the rehab center. He's optimistic that with hard work and time, she can make a full recovery."

Jessica clapped a hand over her mouth to catch the sob of relief.

"I have to go back to Charlotte today and sign papers regarding the transfer, but..." He stopped and narrowed his focus more sharply on Jessica. "I hate to leave you in the lurch, so soon after—"

She waved him off. "Go! Go! This is great news. Tina needs you. Not me."

His eyebrow shot up, and she realized how harsh the words sounded. "All I mean is, Tina is the priority now."

He nodded once slowly, his eyes still locked with hers. "You're sure?"

She hitched her head toward the back porch where they could drink their coffee from the rocking chairs that boasted a view of the rising sun. Once she'd taken her seat and propped her crutches against the cabin wall, she inhaled the fresh air deeply and gathered her thoughts.

"Before you leave for Charlotte, I owe you some answers."

Gage's hand visibly tightened around his cup, and a spark of curiosity and wariness lit his gray eyes.

"Before Henry showed up last night, I had enough time to decide some things about us."

Gage stilled, seeming to hold his breath.

"I thought a lot about what you told me about how you feel, how you've felt for years without me knowing. Knowing that truth and considering everything that has happened in the past few weeks..." Her hands started trembling, and she set her coffee on the wobbly wooden table between their chairs. "I don't think we can be *friends* anymore."

He jerked his chin up, his eyes wild with confusion and hurt. He sprang up from his seat and paced to the edge of the porch, his hands clenched. "Jess, I don't—"

Pushing with her arms, she hoisted herself from the rocker to clomp the two steps to him.

Framing his face with her hands, she stroked his cheeks with her thumbs and took a breath for courage. No, not courage. She didn't have anything to fear. Not where Gage was concerned.

"Because," she said and crooked a grin, "I'd rather be your lover. Your life partner. Your *wife*."

He stared at her without responding for a moment as if replaying her words in his head, double-checking his hearing. "Um…"

"I've always been so scared of being vulnerable, of letting myself become that scared little girl whose mother wasn't there for her again. I told myself I had to be self-reliant at all costs. And…it has cost me. My marriage to Matt, my ability to trust most people…" She grasped his chin and blinked back the tears that filled her eyes. "But I don't want it to cost me *you*. I was so scared when I felt my feelings for you changing. But you have proven in so many ways that you have my back. That you are loyal and dependable and patient and…more important to me than my next breath. I want you in my life, in my bed, in my heart for the next twenty-five years and beyond!"

His eyes widened, and he swallowed hard. "So what are you— Um…"

She laughed and smacked a kiss on his mouth. "Gage Coleman, I'm asking you to marry me! And you'd better have something better to say than 'Um!'"

A tremor rolled through him, and a bright grin lit his face. "How about lover, life partner, wife *and best friend*? I don't see why we have to lose the friendship."

She slipped her arms around his neck and leaned into him, reveling in the sexy warmth of his smile and the strength of his embrace. "I'm good with that, but…

who's going to break the news to Tina that she's got to share her *bestie* title with you?"

"Ooh," Gage said, grimacing. "I'd take a bullet for you, love. But I'm remembering a time when I asked Tina to share the last piece of pumpkin pie at Thanksgiving. It got ugly. Mom ended up telling us neither of us got it. And you're an even better prize than pumpkin pie."

Jessica threw her head back as she laughed. "Are you saying you're scared of your little sister?"

Gage raised his eyebrows. "A little. But for you, I'd pick up the gauntlet."

Jessica smiled broadly and pressed a kiss to his lips. "Yes, love, I believe you would."

Epilogue

Six months later

Jessica chose an ivory silk suit for her second wedding. Her attendants, Cait, Tina and Holly, were resplendent in jade green dresses that captured the spirit of the Christmas season and set off the red poinsettia blossoms in their bouquets.

Tina still suffered headaches on occasion, but through physical and occupational therapy, had made an almost full recovery over the past six months. Holly was still working to regain mobility, and though she might never recover her full dexterity and muscle coordination, she was alive. Holly retained her sharp wit and kind heart, and she had stood up to her parents when they tried to keep Jessica away.

"She is not just a friend," Holly had told her family with a steady voice when Jessica visited her at the rehab center. "She is my heart sister. A member of my posse. Do *not* get in the way of that."

Jessica had never felt more loved, more grateful, or more blessed…until that moment as she walked down the aisle toward Gage and met his bright, loving gaze.

He'd asked Eric to be his best man, an honor that had

humbled her son and cemented the men's bond. And so, her two favorite guys in the world stood side by side, smiling their dashing smiles and mirroring the deep love she had for each of them.

The first two rows at the Valley Haven church were lined with four generations of Camerons, from Nanna to Cait's nephew Ravi. The family had declared Gage and Jessica part of their clan at the rehearsal dinner the night before, when Cait presented the couple with a Scottish wool scarf in the color pattern of the Cameron tartan.

Jessica wore the scarf now, draped across one shoulder and pinned at her opposite hip, the red and green tones the prefect complement of Christmas colors.

Taking her place at the altar, Jessica felt a happy tear drip on her cheek as she faced Gage. Never had anything felt more right in her life. She was marrying a man who'd proven to be her most ardent supporter, a smokin' hot lover, and—with Tina's willing and joyful acceptance of second place—her best friend.

Gage took her hands in his and returned a broad grin through the vows and exchange of rings, and even before the minister pronounced them man and wife, Gage tugged her close and placed a long, deep kiss on her lips. As he broke the kiss to the cheers of their assembled family and friends, he whispered, "I've been waiting a long time for this."

She stroked his cheek and answered, "Turns out, so was I. And I couldn't be happier."

* * * * *

A NOTE TO ALL READERS

From October releases Mills & Boon will be making some changes to the series formats and pricing.

What will be different about the series books?

In response to recent reader feedback, we are increasing the size of our paperbacks to bigger books with better quality paper, making for a better reading experience.

What will be the new price of Mills & Boon?

Over the past four years we have seen significant increases in the cost of producing our books. As a result, in order to continue to provide customers with a quality reading experience, the price of our books will increase to RRP $10.99 for Modern singles and RRP $19.99 for 2-in-1s from Medical, Intrigue, Romantic Suspense, Historical and Western.

For futher information regarding format changes and pricing, please visit our website millsandboon.com.au.

Romantic Suspense

Danger. Passion. Drama.

Available Next Month

Colton Undercover Jennifer D. Bokal
Second-Chance Bodyguard Patricia Sargeant

Cold Case Kidnapping Kimberly Van Meter
Escape To The Bayou Amber Leigh Williams

LOVE INSPIRED

Search And Detect Terri Reed
Sniffing Out Justice Carol J. Post

Larger Print

LOVE INSPIRED

Undercover Escape Valerie Hansen
Hunted For The Holidays Deena Alexander

Larger Print

LOVE INSPIRED

Witness Protection Ambush Jenna Night
A Lethal Truth Alexis Morgan

Larger Print

Keep reading for an excerpt of a new title
from the Intrigue series,
CONARD COUNTY: COVERT AVENGER
by Rachel Lee

Chapter One

Conard County Deputy Elaine Paltier drove along a dusty
gravel road on her nightly round of Wyoming's isolated
ranch country. Out here, excitement was rare, unless there
was an accident or injury, or the weather created a problem. The mountains to the west caught the bright moonlight on their snow-capped peaks, adding beauty to gently
rolling foothills and the early spring growth in the fields.

The routine, however, gave Elaine plenty of opportunity to ramble around inside her own head, allowing
her to think about her life, her job and mostly her young
daughter. Being a single parent had its difficulties, even
with help from her mother.

She didn't mind this part of her official duties, though.
Each assignment was only for two weeks before she'd be
relieved by another deputy. Hardly enough time to find
these patrols by herself to be boring.

That night, however, matters got exciting, although in-
directly at first. She saw two glowing red spots near the
Bixby ranch and wondered if they were tower markers.
But who would have erected them since her last two-week
tour? And if someone had, she'd have certainly heard
about it.

As she got closer, the glowing areas became more orange and bigger.

"Oh, God," she muttered, her heart accelerating. A range fire? But in two different spots? She grabbed her radio to call for backup from the fire squad, but the device hissed and refused to connect. The satellite phone was no better. Dead zones in these distant areas were not uncommon, providing unreliable service that could be maddening and dangerous at times.

Uncommon or not, she had to find a way to summon help. She pressed her accelerator, driving as fast as she dared on the gravel. Range fires could explode with incredible speed, and the green spring growth would offer no protection once a fire started and dried out everything around it.

Seeing the driveway for Beggan Bixby's ranch house, she pulled a sharp right and drove even faster to warn the old rancher—maybe get a better radio signal or use his landline, too.

Were those red blobs growing larger? Elaine couldn't tell, so she turned most of her focus to the looming ranch house. She flipped on her roof lights but no siren, to warn the rancher that she was approaching. All the while, tension increasingly tightened her muscles. A serious range fire could blow up in no time at all.

Then, scaring her half to death, a man appeared in the driveway right in front of her, turning blue and white in the flash of her light bar. He held a shotgun cradled across his breast almost like a baby. Much to her relief, it was clearly cracked open. Not yet a threat.

She jammed her Suburban into Park with a spray of gravel and opened her door, leaning out. "Mr. Bixby?"

Yeah, it was Bixby, in old jeans and a work shirt, with a stained, ancient cowboy hat jammed on his head. He was stomping his feet in anger. "You finally come to get rid of 'em?"

The question put her off-balance. Not at all what she'd expected to hear. *Finally?* "You mean the fire up north of here?" She pointed at the reddish-orange balls of light as she climbed out of her vehicle.

"Hell no. I ain't talking about them."

Elaine looked from him to the glowing light, more orange now. "How can you ignore them? I don't have to tell you about range fires. I need your phone."

"'Tain't no fire."

"How can you be sure unless we go look?" As if it could be anything else. The idea of a range fire made the skin on the back of her neck crawl. A disaster that could reach hundreds of square miles in no time at all. But now she was dealing with a man who'd lost his mind somehow? She had to get to his phone.

But Bixby had a ready answer. "I see them lights a lot. Now, you just do your job and get rid of them SOBs."

She nearly gaped at him. "You want me to get rid of those lights?" How the hell was she supposed to do that without help if it was a fire? And why did he keep dismissing them, then demanding she get rid of them? "I can get a fire truck out here to put them out. But I need your landline. Radio's not working."

Bixby stomped his feet some more and raised his scratchy voice. "You damn useless cop. *Not* the red lights. They ain't no trouble. So when are you going to get rid of them?"

Elaine began to feel some serious irritation, along with a sense of having slipped out of reality. "How am I supposed to get rid of the lights if you won't let me call the fire department?"

"I been calling you guys for more 'n' a month about

this. Y'all ain't done nothing about it. I don't give a rat's patootie about the lights. I keep tellin' ya, they ain't no problem—never have been. You ever listen?"

"Then why do you want me to get rid of them?"

Bixby was clearly reaching the end of his rope. He started to shout. "I ain't talking about them lights. I keep tellin' ya! Get rid of the cussed fools crossin' my fence. I don't want no gawkers cuz of them dang lights. This ain't a ranch like the one on the TV."

Elaine sought to make the connection, then did. In an instant, she *knew* she had fallen down the rabbit hole. She spoke carefully, needing to be sure she understood before Bixby escalated beyond his current anger and frustration. "I saw that show once."

"Well, I ain't that place, and I'm getting sick of freakin' trespassers climbing my fence and bothering my herd. Damn it, I got cattle to raise."

Elaine looked to the north, saw the lights were still there but didn't seem to have grown. They didn't resemble a range fire, which by now would have been a whole lot larger. Just lights, like Bixby had said. Her tension eased as she gave her full attention back to the old man. "Bet you got gawkers tonight." The idea of people chasing balls of light amused her. Clearly Bixby didn't share that feeling.

"Hell yeah." Bixby spat on the ground. Chewing tobacco. "Swear I'm gonna shoot one or two of them soon as I get a chance. Hell, I can't afford no security guys to protect my fence and my herd. I'm it."

Elaine's stomach tightened with apprehension. "Mr. Bixby, you don't want to kill somebody and put yourself in jail."

"I got a right to shoot anybody who comes on my land."

That was debatable, and would require a judge and

maybe a jury. She realized she wasn't going to be able to talk or scare him out of murderous intent—not right now. Her hands tightened with a sense of urgency, seeking a way to calm the situation.

She glanced north again at the lights, more curious now than anything. "What are they?"

"Damned if I know. Been showin' up from time to time all my life, but they ain't hurt no one and nothing. Seems like they ain't no problem, and I'm happy to leave them alone. But things might not be so simple if them jackasses keep crossing my fence and taking pictures and all that other stuff they do. Bunch of lunatics."

Elaine sighed, now having a clear picture of the *real* problem here, and it wasn't just a couple of lights or orbs or whatever they might be called. No, it was people who wanted to climb his fence—maybe even cut it—and wreak havoc on a rancher's land and herd.

Bixby spat again and resettled his shotgun in his arms. "Used to call 'em UFOs," he said. "Now they got a new name—UAPs. Don't make no difference. No little gray or green men ever been seen. Nothin' ever seen but them balls. Bet you can't even take a good picture of one."

Elaine studied Bixby, thinking he was a little more informed than a man who simply wanted to keep trespassers out. *UAPs?*

A recent term not yet in common vernacular as far as she knew. Maybe he'd been talking to some of these trespassers. Arguing with them. Given this man, it wouldn't surprise her. Maybe the only surprise was that he hadn't killed one of them yet.

Bixby glared at her in the lights from her vehicle. "What the hell you gonna do about them, Deputy? Them trespassers. I complained before, but you never even sent anyone out here. So what are you going to do?"

Since it was unlikely that half the Conard County Sheriff's Department could come out here to guard Bixby's land from trespassers, Elaine had no answer.

Which apparently didn't surprise Bixby. "Ha," he said. "What good are all you folks? Ya think I don't pay taxes like everyone else around here?"

"It's more about manpower," Elaine said finding a reasonable response, although minute by minute, Bixby was looking closer to a frazzled edge.

"Wouldn't take many of you to convince them jerks to stay away."

Well, he had a point there. A few deputies talking to these invaders might scare them off. Briefly.

"They'll just come back eventually," Elaine said honestly.

Bixby went off into a cussing fit that would have amused Elaine a whole lot more if he hadn't been holding a shotgun.

When he ran out of words and rage and fell briefly silent, Elaine spoke heresy. "You know, Mr. Bixby, those balls of light are hardly harmless to you and this ranch if they're causing these trespassers to overrun you."

Bixby glared at her again as if she were a fool. "They didn't bring them jerks. Like I said, the lights been there on and off my whole life. Even my cattle ain't bothered by them."

Bixby spat again, and this time he cocked the shotgun and waved it. "You get yourself out of here. Useless. Just useless."

Elaine started to turn, her back prickling with awareness of that shotgun. Leaving was the only choice to avoid a possibly dangerous confrontation. She'd only taken two steps toward her Suburban when Bixby spoke again.

"I know you," he said. "Elaine Paltier, George Henley's girl. Dang, wouldn't your daddy be ashamed of you right now."

Elaine stiffened but kept walking to her vehicle, then climbed in and switched off all her flashers. Bixby could go to hell.

Yet as she swung her vehicle around to continue her patrol, she saw the red lights again. Then she saw them wink out.

She braked and waited for five minutes or so, but they never reappeared.

A mystery that would always remain a mystery, she supposed. But she had a real life to deal with, and she resumed her patrol at an easy pace. Eventually her radio and satellite phone returned to normal function.

After a few more minutes, she returned to normal as well, smiling into the night. Red lights, trespassers and Mr. Bixby.

What a story!

Subscribe and fall in love with a Mills & Boon series today!

You'll be among the first to read stories delivered to your door monthly and enjoy great savings.

'WE SIMPLY LOVE ROMANCE